W9-DEW-991

DH.

CITY OF DARKNESS AND LIGHT

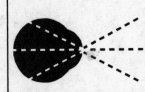

A MOLLY MURPHY MYSTERY

CITY OF DARKNESS AND LIGHT

RHYS BOWEN

WHEELER PUBLISHING
A part of Gale, Cengage Learning

GALE
CENGAGE Learning·

Farmington Hills, Mich • San Francisco • New York • Waterville, Maine
Meriden, Conn • Mason, Ohio • Chicago

GALE
CENGAGE Learning·

LIBRARY OF CONGRESS CATALOGING-IN-PUBLICATION DATA

Bowen, Rhys.
   City of darkness and light / by Rhys Bowen. — Large print edition.
    pages ; cm. — (A Molly Murphy mystery) (Wheeler publishing large print hardcover)
   ISBN-13: 978-1-4104-6890-1 (hardcover)
   ISBN-10: 1-4104-6890-9 (hardcover)
   1. Murphy, Molly (Fictitious character)—Fiction. 2. Women private investigators—New York (State)—New York—Fiction. 3. Large type books.
I. Title.
PR6052.O848C58 2014b
823'.914—dc23   2014004309

Published in 2014 by arrangement with St. Martin's Press, LLC

Printed in the United States of America
1 2 3 4 5 6 7 18 17 16 15 14

This book is dedicated to the memory of Sally Fellows. Sally was one of the first champions of the Molly Murphy series, a terrific friend and mentor to the mystery community, and an aficionada of all things historical. She loved good wine, good friends, good books, her dog. The only thing she hated was bad puns. At every convention we will go on looking at the empty chair where we expect to find her and sigh a little.

ONE

New York City, May 1905

Like many Irish people I have always been a strong believer in a sixth sense. In fact I had prided myself on mine. I credited it with alerting me to danger more than once during my career as an investigator. So I can't explain why it let me down on such a critical occasion, when an advance warning might have spared us all such grief. Maybe the perpetrator of this evil had not planned it in advance. Maybe it had been a last-minute order from above, so I had not been able to sense his intention or his presence . . . or their presence. I'm sure there must have been more than one of them. That was how they worked.

Anyway, there were certainly no uneasy thoughts in my head that bright May morning as I fed my little one his breakfast. He was eight months old now, a strapping boy with a shock of dark curls like his father and an impish smile. Now I think back on it I wonder if Aggie hadn't been the one with the sixth sense, although she had no Celtic connections that I knew of. She came into the kitchen while I was feeding Liam, bearing two letters in her hand.

"Mail just arrived, Mrs. Sullivan," she said. "Two letters for you. One with a foreign stamp."

"That will be from my friends in Paris, I expect," I said, taking them from her. "How nice."

I took in Sid's bold black script on the foreign envelope and noted that the other was my mother-in-law's weekly missive. The former would wait until I had the proper time to savor Sid's latest account of their adventures in Paris. The latter could simply wait.

"Aren't you going to read them?" Aggie hovered at my shoulder, still fascinated by the foreign look of the envelope.

"Later, when I have time."

"If anyone ever wrote to me, I'd want to read it right away," she said wistfully. Then she shivered and wrapped her arms around her scrawny body. "It's awful cold in here today, isn't it?" she said. "Cold for May."

"Is it? I hadn't noticed." I looked out of the window where early roses were climbing up a trellis. "It's a nice bright day. You can come with me when I take Liam for his walk and you'll feel warmer in the sun."

"I need to be getting on with the laundry," she said, eyeing Liam, who now had a generous amount of cream of wheat over his front. "That child gets through more clothes than a little prince and I expect I'll warm myself up scrubbing away at the washboard."

She stood there, still hugging her arms to her skinny body. Although she had been with me since Liam was born, and had an appetite like a horse, there wasn't an ounce of flesh on her and she still looked like a pathetic little waif. I had taken her in out of pity, after she had been forced to give up the child she had had out of wedlock, but she had surprised me by being a hard worker and wonderful with the baby. She'd been the oldest of ten and had grown up taking care of the younger ones — a valuable asset to her family, but that hadn't stopped her parents from throwing her out the moment they learned she was pregnant. She was pathetically grateful to come to us and I in turn was grateful for her knowledge in those first difficult weeks with the new baby.

"The laundry will wait," I said, smiling at

her. "Come on, get Liam changed out of those messy clothes and we'll go out."

She shook her head. "No, Mrs. Sullivan. I think I'd better stay and get those diapers out on the line, if you don't mind. A morning like this is too bright to last. There will be rain by the end of the day, you mark my words."

She had grown up on a farm in the Adirondacks so I believed her. "All the more reason for me to give Liam his daily dose of fresh air," I said. "It's been a gloomy spring so far, hasn't it? I was beginning to think summer would never come."

"It's been gloomy enough around here," Aggie said, "with Captain Sullivan going around with a face that would curdle milk and hardly a civil word in his head."

"It's not for you to criticize your employer," I said sharply and watched her flinch as if I'd slapped her. Then I relented, of course. "Captain Sullivan is under a great deal of worry at the moment. A policeman's job is never the easiest and right now I think he's battling a major problem. Not that he ever confides in me, but if his current bad temper is anything to go on, then I'd say he had a particularly difficult case on his hands. It's our job to make sure his life is as pleasant as possible when he comes home."

She nodded silently as she lifted Liam out of his high chair and bore him away up the stairs. I cleaned away the aftermath of Liam's breakfast and considered my little speech. I realized it had been a pep talk for me as well as Aggie, because I had found Daniel's current black mood hard to take. More than once I'd wondered why I ever thought that it had been a good idea to leave my life of freedom and independence as a private investigator to get married. I think I'd expected to be able to share in his work, mulling over complicated cases with him and giving him the benefit of my own experience as a detective. But that hadn't happened. Daniel remained tight-lipped about his work. He was gone from morning till night most days and only popped in for a hasty meal. A quick peck on the cheek as he ran out of the door again was the best I could hope for. *For better or worse* rang through my head. That was what I'd promised at the altar. I sighed and put the dishes in the sink for Aggie. Then I went up to my room to change my clothes. A walk in the sunshine would soon do wonders for my current mood.

Aggie was waiting for me at the bottom of the stairs with Liam already strapped in his buggy. "You could take those letters with

11

you to read," she said, handing them to me.

I laughed. "I believe you're more interested in my mail than I am."

"I love hearing about foreign parts," she said. "It's like a fairy tale."

"I'll read Miss Goldfarb's letter to you later if you like," I said. Aggie hadn't yet managed to learn to read, in spite of my efforts to teach her. I put on my hat, adjusting it in front of the hall mirror, then Aggie helped me maneuver the buggy down the front steps.

"I hope you have a nice walk, Mrs. Sullivan," she called after me as I set off.

I almost asked her again to come with us, but I reminded myself that she was the servant and the laundry was her job. I'd bring her a cake for tea, I decided. She loved the cakes I brought from the French bakery around the corner. As Liam and I bumped over the cobbles of Patchin Place I couldn't help glancing across at the doorway of number 9. It had been two months now since my friends Elena Goldfarb and Augusta Walcott, more familiarly known as Sid and Gus, had taken it into their heads to go to Paris, so that Gus could study art with the best painters of the day. I had never thought that Gus's talent for painting was as great as she believed it to be, but her cousin Willie Walcott had gone to study in Paris and was now apparently making a name for himself as a painter of the Impressionist school. He had promised introductions for Sid and Gus.

From their letters they seemed to be having a roaring good time, while I missed them terribly. I had come to count on their comforting presence across the street, their extravagant parties, and their bohemian lifestyle that Daniel only just tolerated for my sake. With Sid and Gus, life was never boring. You never knew when you'd open their front door and find the front parlor turned into a Mongolian yurt or a Turkish harem. They never had to worry about the day-to-day trivialities of normal life. They had enough money to live as they wanted, according to their rules. This is not to say that they were always frivolous. They were keen supporters of the suffrage movement and I missed attending those meetings at their house as well.

I sighed as I came out onto Greenwich Avenue and steered Liam's buggy around a pile of steaming horse droppings. Ah, well. They'd grow tired of Paris and come home eventually, wouldn't they? And in the meantime I had a husband to look after and a son to raise. Things could be worse. Liam leaned forward in the buggy, urging me to go faster, and babbled in delight when an automobile drove past us, its driver's long scarf streaming out in the breeze behind him as he steered the contraption around a slow moving dray. *Just like his father,* I thought, smiling at his excitement. We were seeing more and more automobiles these days. I know Daniel secretly hankered after one. He was allowed to drive the police vehicle when there was a special need, but that didn't include giving his family a ride.

I waited for a gap in the traffic before I pushed the buggy across into Washington Square, passing beneath the great arch and into the relative tranquility of the gardens beyond. Here activity was confined to mothers pushing buggies while toddlers clung to their skirts, bigger boys bowling iron hoops that rattled over the gravel paths, and even bigger boys playing a game of kick the can. I wondered why the latter weren't in school as it certainly wasn't a holiday. I suppose they could have been newsboys, taking a break from long hours standing on street corners.

I found a bench in the sun and turned the buggy so that Liam could watch the bigger children at play. He seemed more fascinated with the fountain in the center of the square and a flock of small birds that perched on the lip, daring each other to take a bath in the spray that flew out in the breeze.

With my son content for the moment I opened my letters. I dutifully read Daniel's mother's letter first, as he'd no doubt want a report on her doings and she'd no doubt want a reply from me. Usually her weekly letters were a recital of what she had done around the house, what her young charge Bridie was doing, interspersed with slivers of local gossip. But today I was surprised to read, *By the time you read this I shall be gone.*

My heart lurched in my chest. I have to confess that I wasn't overly fond of Daniel's mother, but this was so sudden. Then I read on.

I am writing this in haste to let you know that I am about to embark on a journey. I decided not to mention this plan to you in advance as I rather think that Daniel might have tried to dissuade me. And I don't think it would have taken that much to dissuade me since it was such a huge undertaking for me.

You remember my friend Letitia Blackstone? Her daughter Imogen married a young engineer who is now designing a bridge across the Mississippi River. Letitia wanted to visit her daughter who has just had a baby, but was reluctant to travel alone to such wild and barbaric parts. So she asked me if I would accompany her if she paid my way. Of course I agreed. What an adventure at my time of life to see a little more of our beautiful country before I die. And Letitia insists on doing everything first class so I don't expect it will be too uncomfortable or dangerous. It will also be a perfect opportunity for young Bridie. I'm taking her along as my companion as she's been worried recently about her papa and this will take her mind off things.

I stopped reading and stared out across the square. Poor little Bridie, whose father and brother had gone down to Panama to work on the building of the canal. None of the news that came from that hellhole had been good. Men had been dropping like flies, so it was said, from yellow fever and terrible working conditions. And there had been no news from Bridie's father for months so we had to assume the worst.

I read on. Martha the maid was to visit her ailing mother. The house was to be shut up and Mrs. Sullivan didn't know how long they would be away. She sent her warmest regards and a fond kiss to her grandchild. I folded the letter and put it back in its envelope. Well, that would be a surprise for Daniel. His mother was not the kind one would expect to make rash, last-minute decisions to go out into the wild west.

I glanced across at Liam and saw that he had fallen asleep. I adjusted his pillows, covered him properly and then turned to my other letter. It was as I expected, full of exciting tidbits of news of life in Paris. Sid wrote:

Willie has obtained an introduction for Gus to none other than Reynold Bryce. You know who he is, don't you, Molly? He made a name for himself as part of the Boston School back in the eighties — particularly with his paintings of the young girl he called Angela. Then at the height of his fame he took off for Paris and has remained here, becoming one of the leading lights among Impressionist painters. Anyway, he is THE patron and lodestone for American artists in Paris. His salon is where one needs to be seen. He holds an exhibition every spring and if he includes your work, you are IN! Gus is hoping he'll include her, naturally.

She's been painting some really interesting canvasses recently, although I think she may be a little avant-garde for traditionalists like Reynold Bryce. Gus says she's not sure whether she's a Fauvist, a Cubist, or simply a modernist, but she's thrilled to be among artists who dare to paint with her boldness. We met a rather dashing young Spaniard in a bar. His name is Pablo Picasso and he said that Gus's work shows promise. I'm not sure I can say the same about his daubings — most odd.

Speaking of young painters, we have just made an astounding discovery. Remember it was Gus's cousin who lured us to Paris in the first place. Well, it turns out that I have a relative here as well — a distant cousin. When we were about to leave for Paris my mother told me that we had family members who had settled there when the family left the turmoils in Eastern Europe. My grandfather came to America and my great-uncle's family went to Paris. Mama had no current address for them but their last name would have been Goldfarb like ours. I asked at several synagogues but to no avail — in fact the Parisian Jews did not exactly extend the

18

welcome mat. Well, I admit that I do not look like the good traditional Jewish woman, nor do I practice my religion, but it turned out that the cause of their caution had more to do with the current wave of anti-Semitism that has swept this city, culminating in the dreadful treatment of Captain Dreyfus — falsely imprisoned and shipped to Devil's Island mainly because of his race.

Having heard this, we're not sure how long we'll stay, though of course among the more bohemian community of artists and writers, race, gender, or even appearance don't matter a fig. Talent is all that counts. You'll be amazed to learn that I was the first of us to have a talent acknowledged here. We went to a soiree and were each instructed to write a poem. I read mine with great trepidation but it was pronounced good. At this gathering I was instantly drawn to a young man with an interesting face and such soulful dark eyes — clearly also Jewish. We started to share information about our ancestry and lo and behold he turned out to be my long-lost distant cousin, Maxim Noah. Apparently his mother was a Goldfarb. His parents are dead, and he lives in a studio with artist friends up on the hill called Montmartre. And the poets I met have invited me to join their group. It seems that in this city poetry is as important as painting. Did you ever imagine that such a place could exist on earth? If it weren't for the anti-Semitic sentiment and for missing our delightful godson Liam, we might never want to come home!

But I digress. As I mentioned, Maxim lives with some other young artists up in the rural part of Montmartre and invited us to visit him. "Primitive" is hardly the word to describe it, my dear. No heat, no running water, just a group of young men painting, creating, discussing. Maxim suggested that Gus and I take a place nearby, but I pointed out that we were no longer eighteen and that civilized New Yorkers needed heat and a daily bath.

But having finally made artistic connections in the city we wanted to move closer to the hub of the current art world. We have finally found a place of our own in that general area that suits our needs. Our previous lodging was in a more genteel area near the Seine — preferable in some ways but too far from the exciting world of the arts. What's more the landlady was a fussy old bird who objected to the smell of paint and our late hours. So we have found what we consider a wonderful compromise . . . a top floor atelier on a street close to Pigalle. Not as primitive as the streets further up the hill and mercifully close to a station of the Métropolitain railway — yes, dear Molly, they have a perfectly fine working subway here, making travel across the city quick and easy. There are already three lines with more under construction.

As you can see from the address at the top of this letter, our new home is on Rue des Martyrs. I must confess we picked it for its name. Gus was tickled pink to be part of the martyrs — she said she always knew that she'd have to suffer for her art! The street itself is a good mixture of commerce and residence, lively yet not too raucous. We can take advantage of the little cafés around Pigalle and yet escape from the hubbub by climbing the five flights to our little nest whose balcony gives us a glimpse of the new church that is being built at the top of Montmartre (if we lean out far enough). I wish you could see it, Molly. You'd love it here. Do policemen ever get time off for good behavior? Would Daniel ever consider traveling to Europe? If not, please persuade him to do without you for a while. You know we'd pay for your ticket if that was a problem. We yearn to see our adorable Liam. He must have grown so much since we parted from you. Think of the cultural opportunities of Liam being exposed to Paris at an early age. Gus says we are to keep pestering you until you agree to come. It's too lovely and breathtaking and exciting not to want to share.

Gus sends her warmest regards, as do I, and a big kiss to dear Liam.

Your friend Elena (Sid)

I shut my eyes, enjoying the feel of warm spring sunshine on my face and tried to picture Paris. Then suddenly I was back in Ireland, sitting in the schoolroom at the big house with Miss Vanessa and Miss Henrietta. When I was ten I had rather impressed their mother, Mrs. Hartley, with my eloquence and cheek and she had invited me to join her own daughters for lessons. They clearly didn't think much of this idea and never made me feel welcome but their governess was delighted to have a pupil who was so keen to learn. On this day she was telling us about a trip she had taken to Paris. I was plying her with questions about the Louvre and Notre-Dame when Miss Vanessa cut into our discussion.

"I don't see why we're wasting time like this. It's not as if you're ever likely to go to Paris, Molly," she said scathingly and her sister had tittered as if this was a great joke.

A sudden cold breeze swept across the square, almost snatching the paper from my hands. I looked up and saw that Aggie's prediction was right. Dark clouds were racing in over the Hudson. It would rain before the day was out. I folded the letter, replaced it in its envelope, and then stood up. I should get a move on and do my shopping for tonight's meal now, rather than later in the day. Liam slept on blissfully as I set the buggy moving in the direction of home. Another gust of wind sent spray from the fountain in our direction. And then it was almost as if I was having a vision: before they left for Paris, Sid and Gus had taken me to an exhibit of Impressionist painting at a gallery in New York. I had found the paintings delightfully light and fresh and free, although others viewing them had pronounced them as shocking daubs with no substance to them. Now, as I glanced back across the square it was as if I was seeing one of those Impressionist paintings of a park in Paris — a young girl holding onto a white straw hat with red ribbons flying out in the breeze, while her small brother ran to retrieve a red ball, pigeons pecking hopefully, and sycamore trees coming into leaf, casting dappled shade on the gravel walkways. I smiled wistfully as I moved on. Such a scene in Washington Square was the closest to Paris I was likely to get.

TWO

Clouds had almost swallowed up the sun by the time we returned to Patchin Place. The bumpy ride over cobbles woke Liam and his loud cries let me know that he expected to be fed again soon. I felt my breasts react in response. None of this newfangled bottle feeding for me, in spite of my mother-in-law telling me it was more hygienic and that ladies of quality never nursed their infants. I had not regretted my decision for an instant but the arrival of sharp little new teeth made me wonder whether weaning might be a good idea.

"I'm home, Aggie," I called, pausing in the front hallway to remove my hat and coat.

Her pinched little face appeared from the kitchen. "Laundry's all done and out, Mrs. Sullivan, but for how long, who can say?"

"You were right about the weather as usual," I said. "The rainclouds are already gathering."

"Maybe that's why I've felt so cold all morning," she said. "Could be a big storm coming." Liam interrupted this conversation with another wail. Aggie went to lift him out of his pram, but I stopped her.

"It's all right. He wants feeding. I'll take him up to the nursery."

Liam reached out to me to be picked up. I noticed how heavy he was getting as I swung him onto my hip. "I'm going to cut down your rations, my lad," I said. "You're getting too big."

"Don't say that, Mrs. Sullivan," Aggie said. "We never got enough to eat at my house. You don't know what that's like."

"No, I don't," I said, looking at her with pity. "It's almost lunchtime. Go and warm us up some of that stew. I've got a nice chop for Captain Sullivan's dinner, if he comes home in time to eat tonight."

"Oh, that reminds me," Aggie said. I paused halfway up the stairs and turned back to her. "A man was here this morning asking for Captain Sullivan."

"What kind of man? A policeman?"

"Oh, I don't think so." She chewed on her lip. "A swarthy type. Foreign."

"What did he want?"

"He just asked when Captain Sullivan was likely to be home. I told him I couldn't say, and that Captain Sullivan didn't keep regular hours. We'd hardly seen him at all lately. He then asked about you, and I said you'd be back shortly."

"Did you ask if you could take a message?" I asked.

"I did. And he said he had to deliver the message to you and the captain in person, so he'd be back when you were both home."

"How strange," I said. "Foreign? I can't think who that might be."

"I didn't like the look of him," Aggie said. "He had shifty eyes."

I smiled. "You think all foreigners have shifty eyes. Perhaps Daniel will know."

And I went on up the stairs. Liam was fed and put down for his afternoon nap. The rain started about three and we rushed to get in the line full of laundry. The rest of the day passed without incident. I reread Sid's letter over an afternoon cup of tea, sharing the interesting bits with Aggie. She was duly impressed. "Imagine traveling halfway around the world and then bumping into a long-lost cousin," she said. "And a handsome one at that. Maybe they'll fall in love and marry."

"I hardly think that's likely to happen," I said, smiling at her naïveté. Sid and Gus lived as a couple right across the street from us, but then I hadn't taken in the truth about their relationship when I first met them either. Such things had been outside of my sphere of experience too.

Darkness fell early with wind moaning through the chimney. I prepared our evening meal and put Daniel's chop out, ready to grill, in the hope that he might be home for dinner, just this once. Then about six thirty my wishes were answered. The front door opened, sending a blast of cold air right down the hall to us, and Daniel came in, his cheeks red from the wind, clapping his hands together.

"It's like winter out there again," he said. "Luckily the rain has eased off. I thought I'd get drenched on the way home." He looked around the kitchen. "Where's my favorite son?"

"Aggie's just putting him to bed," I said.

"Good. I hoped I'd catch him awake for once." He unwound his scarf, dropped it on a chair, and then bounded up the stairs. I heard his big voice and a baby's squeal of delight and smiled to myself as I put his chop on the stove. By the time he reappeared his dinner was ready.

"What a splendid sight," he said as I placed the plate in front of him. "It feels like the first decent meal I've had in weeks."

"You've never been home to eat," I said.

He nodded, his mouth full. "It's been a rough time," he said at last.

"Difficult case?"

"More like a war than a case," he said. "The commissioner decided the time had come to take a stand against the Italian gang that is terrorizing the Lower East Side."

"The Cosa Nostra, you mean?"

"That's what they call themselves, yes. And we thought the Eastmans were bad news. The Eastmans are child's play compared to these new boys. Protection rackets, extortion — all the usual stuff — but done with such incredible violence and ruthlessness. Anyone who betrays them is found with his throat slit from ear to ear. And they don't hesitate to take revenge on anyone who stands in their way."

"How do you plan to stop them?"

He shrugged. "I don't know that we can. We can slow them down, but new Italian immigrants keep pouring into the city, so they'll have keen new members all the time. But the commissioner says we must shut them down before they become too powerful, so try we must. We've got their big cheese behind bars now and I think we've enough on him to make a conviction stick, in spite of the dearth of witnesses willing to testify against him. We'll see if he manages to wriggle out of it."

And he went back to his eating.

"I had two letters today," I said, trying to change the subject to more cheerful matters. "One from your mother — you'll never guess what she's up to?"

"She's found a new way to make jam or she's hosted another coffee morning?" He looked up, grinning.

"No, she's off on a trip out West with her friend Letitia Blackstone. They're going to visit Letitia's daughter — the one whose husband is building a bridge across the Mississippi River."

"Good God," Daniel said. "Mother on a trip out West? I thought a journey from Westchester to the city counted as a long journey for her. I hope her health is up to it."

"She's as strong as an ox, Daniel. And it will be good for her. She's taking Bridie along for company."

"Amazing." Daniel went back to eating. "I suppose it's too late to dissuade her?"

"Why stop her? Travel broadens the mind. One needs adventures."

"I suppose you're right."

"And my other letter was from Sid." I held it up to him. "They're having a lovely time

in Paris. Sid's discovered a long-lost cousin and started writing poetry. Gus has an introduction to Reynold Bryce —"

Daniel grinned. "I shouldn't have thought Gus painted in a style he'd approve of. Didn't he do all those portraits of the angelic child, copies of which now grace half the nurseries in America?"

"He moved on and became an Impressionist, so I'm told."

"But Gus is certainly not an Impressionist." Daniel chuckled. "I'm not sure how you'd define her painting. Bad, I'd say, but I suppose you'd leap to defend her."

"It's not my cup of tea," I said, loyalty struggling with honesty, "but I'm not a qualified critic of the arts. I don't think we fully appreciate modern art, such as the pictures Gus paints."

Daniel snorted as he picked up his glass and took a long swig of beer. "Well, good for them. At least they're enjoying themselves and staying out of mischief with that damned suffrage movement."

"Sid wanted to know if policemen ever got time off to travel," I said. "She and Gus want us to join them."

"Travel to Paris? On a policeman's salary?" Daniel laughed. "Those women have

no idea what it's like to live in the real world."

I chose not to add that Gus had offered to pay my way if necessary. That would only insult Daniel's pride.

"I'm rather glad they're away for a while, to tell the truth," he said. "It gives you a chance to concentrate on your husband and son, and not get any more silly ideas in your head."

"Daniel Sullivan, don't you dare talk to me like that," I said angrily. "I think it's just grand to be a wife and mother, but I'll get all the silly ideas I want, thank you very much."

He laughed again. "I love it when you're angry. Actually I was afraid you were becoming too docile of late. Not the wild Molly from Ireland I first fell in love with."

"If you say any more patronizing things to me, you'll still find me wild enough, I'll warrant," I said, giving him a challenging stare that made him laugh all the more. I came around the table to him and he grabbed my wrist, drawing me down toward him. "And I wouldn't mind a good wrestle either," he said, his face now inches from mine. "I've been so damned preoccupied that we've hardly had a good. . . ."

Suddenly there was the sound of breaking

glass somewhere at the front of the house. Daniel and I broke apart and were on our feet instantly. "What the hell —" Daniel started to say as he made for the hallway. He had just reached the kitchen door, with me hot on his heels, when there was a tremendous boom. A great blast flung me off my feet, sucking all the air out of my lungs. As I was hurled backward I got an impression of a wall of flame, hurtling toward me before I crashed into the wall, hitting my head. Stars flashed before my eyes as a wave of pain came over me and I think I might have passed out. When I came to my senses I was lying with debris on top of me. My ears were ringing, my head swimming, and I was still fighting to breathe. I pushed a chair and what felt like big chunks of plaster from me and staggered to my feet. The air was so thick with smoke and dust that I found it hard to make out where I was.

I felt the edge of the kitchen table, solid pine and still standing, and moved around it. In the darkness I could hear the crackle of flame but no other sound. Somewhere in that black and smoking hell were my husband and son.

"Daniel!" I tried to shout but my voice came out rasping, like a bird's caw. I pushed

my way forward. "Daniel!" I tried again. The light from the fire, or maybe from the streetlamp outside, cast an unreal glow through the thick smoke. Where the hallway had been was now a pile of smoking rubble, and beneath it I spotted Daniel's foot. With utter desperation I threw off one chunk of plaster after another, pieces of glass, pieces of what had once been the hallstand, a hook with my new hat still attached to it.

"Daniel." I dropped to my knees beside him and turned him over. His face was blackened, like a chimney sweep's, with a nasty gash across his forehead. His jacket had been torn away and his shirt ripped. I lifted him gently and cradled his head in my hands. "Daniel, wake up, please."

I took his wrist and was relieved to feel a pulse. *Still alive then. Must get him free of all this. Out of here.* I dragged him back into the kitchen and opened the back door, letting in cold fresh air. I couldn't wait a second longer to see if he was going to wake up. All I could think about was Liam. He'd been upstairs in his crib, in his nursery at the front of the house. As I tried to pick my way over the rubble in the hall I heard coughing behind me, a curse and a groan. Daniel was sitting up, his hand to his chest, trying to breathe.

"Daniel." I rushed back to him. "Get up. Help me. Liam's upstairs. It's all on fire."

He staggered to his feet. "Liam," he gasped and came after me. We made our way down the hall, staggering like two drunks on a Saturday night. When we reached the place where the stairs should have been there was just a gaping hole with the upper steps hanging crazily over nothing.

"My son's up there!" I screamed, my voice coming back to me now. "And Aggie. Aggie!" I shouted her name. The only reply was the crackle of flames and the shifting of some beam.

"Get help," I tugged at his arm. "Get the fire brigade. A ladder."

Like an automaton Daniel made for the hole where the front door had been. I followed him, feeling the welcome cold rain on me. A crowd was gathering outside. I could see faces lit with the eerie red glow of the fire.

"My baby!" I screamed, rushing up to the nearest figure in the darkness. "My baby is trapped upstairs. Get the fire brigade."

"I'll get a ladder," a man's voice volunteered.

"No time for that." Daniel was already hauling himself onto a window ledge. "Give me a leg up, boys."

"You don't want to go up there. It's all on fire," someone shouted.

"My son is up there," Daniel said grimly. "Help me."

"Daniel, no!" I shouted. "Be careful."

Two burly men helped Daniel haul himself to the top of the window frame and I watched him reach for the upper window. The glass had shattered and flames were licking out of it. Someone had started a bucket chain in a pathetically futile attempt to put out the fire. Each time a bucket of water was thrown through a broken window there was a sizzling noise and steam rose, but the fire didn't subside. I watched Daniel haul himself inside, wanting him to go and not go at the same time. My heart was hammering. I found that I was holding my breath. In the distance I heard the bells of a fire engine, coming from the Jefferson Market station nearby. Then horses' hoofs drumming on the cobbles and shouts of: "Out of the way! Stand clear!"

And a fire engine appeared at the entrance to our alleyway. A hose was unwound. It all seemed to happen in slow motion as the firemen ran toward us.

"What happened?"

"There was an explosion," someone in the

crowd said.

"Gas main blew up? Someone turned on the gas and forgot to light it?"

Water was now being aimed at the front of our house, sending up a curtain of steam and smoke that hid the window into which Daniel had disappeared.

I grabbed a fireman. "My husband is up there," I said. "And my baby, and the nursemaid."

A ladder was placed against the wall. One of the firemen went up it and I heard him say, "Over here, sir. Come on. I'll get you out."

And a blackened, singed Daniel appeared at the window, clutching a bundle wrapped in a blanket in his arms. He handed it to the fireman then lowered himself onto the ladder and came down. I pushed past the firemen and ran to grab the bundle.

"My baby." I could hear myself sobbing as I snatched him from the fireman's arms. "Give me my baby."

"Just a minute, missus. Let's take a look, shall we?" I could hear from the tone of his voice that he wanted to spare me the sight of my child, burned and dead. I opened the blanket. A pair of terrified eyes looked up at me and he held out his little arms, letting out a huge wail. I grabbed him and held him tightly to me while he cried against my cheek. Daniel joined us, wrapping the two of us in a fierce embrace.

"Aggie," I said, suddenly remembering. "Our servant girl is still up there."

Daniel touched my shoulder gently. "She's dead, Molly," he said quietly.

"Are you sure? She might just be unconscious." I could hear my voice, bordering on hysterical. "Somebody should rescue her."

Daniel's arm came around me. "She died protecting Liam. I found her huddled over him. She was clearly trying to get him to safety when a rafter fell on her. He was lying wrapped in his blanket and quite unharmed under her body."

Only then did I allow myself to cry.

THREE

One of the firemen put a hand on my shoulder. "Someone get this woman some brandy. She's clearly in shock," he said. "Is there somewhere she can sit down?"

I shook my head. "No, I'm all right. We have to get poor Aggie's body out of there."

As I said the words there was a horrible creaking, grinding sound and part of the house collapsed, sending sparks up into the night sky. I noticed the firemen were now working feverishly to save the houses next to ours. An image of Aggie's poor, skinny little body, now charred in that inferno, kept hovering in front of my eyes. I felt sick and powerless and very angry. Liam had stopped crying, held safe against me, and was sucking his thumb.

A constable had now arrived on the scene. Daniel spotted him and called out, "Constable Byrne."

"Captain Sullivan, sir. Is that you? Don't

tell me it's your house."

"I'm afraid it is, Byrne."

"Was the fire an accident?"

"Quite deliberate, I'd say. Round up the other men in the area and find out if anyone was seen running away from here a few minutes ago. Get a description if you can. Is Lieutenant McCay on duty tonight?"

"Yes, sir. I believe he is."

"Then have someone send for him immediately. The commissioner will want to hear about this right away. Tell them I'll report in as soon as I've got my wife and child settled."

The constable hurried off. The fire captain came over to Daniel. "Excuse me, sir, but are we right in thinking this wasn't a simple gas explosion then?"

"I think you'll find that it was a bomb, meant for me and my family," Daniel said grimly. "Someone threw a brick to smash the window then hurled the bomb inside."

"Someone with a grudge against you?" The young man's face looked shocked.

"Someone trying to teach us all a lesson, I suspect."

The rain had picked up now, helping to put out the fire but drenching us as we stood there. Liam was crying again. Daniel turned his attention back to us. "We must get you out of this rain."

"Where can we go?" I said. "We've nothing, Daniel. No clothes, nothing."

"It will be all right, I promise," he said, his voice cracking with emotion. "I'll take you to the Hotel Lafayette for the night. That's not far, is it?"

I almost laughed at the absurdity of this. The Hotel Lafayette was where my good friend Ryan O'Hare, the flamboyant and roguish Irish playwright lived. I associated it with good conversation, wicked jokes, wild laughter. I allowed myself to be led away, looking wistfully across the street at Sid and Gus's house. If only they'd been home I'd have been taken in to warmth and security. They'd be wrapping us in blankets, giving us hot drinks, telling us that everything was going to be fine — when of course it wasn't. How could it be fine when Aggie was dead and we had lost everything, including our home?

We were soon installed in a room at the Lafayette, and Daniel ordered a tray with sandwiches and hot rum toddy to be sent up to our room. Liam was still sobbing softly, his little body trembling against me. I did what any other mother would have done, undid my shirt and put him to the breast. He suckled greedily as if desperately trying to calm himself.

"It's a good thing I'm still breastfeeding Liam," I said, "or I don't know what I'd do."

Daniel stood looking down at us, an expression of unbelievable tenderness on his face. "When I think how close I came to losing you," he said. "But you'll be safe enough here for the night. I'll come back as soon as I can."

"You're leaving us?"

"I have to report to headquarters," Daniel said. "This is what we feared might happen. I told you we had brought the Italian gang boss into custody. I'm afraid we suspected they might try to teach us a lesson, but I never dreamed they would take it out on our families."

"Then it really was a bomb and it was the Cosa Nostra?"

"I'm afraid so," he said. "I told you that they were particularly ruthless and violent and would stop at nothing."

"What are we going to do? Won't they try again?" I was shivering now, my wet clothes sticking to me, my hair plastered to my forehead. The back of my head was beginning to throb too, where I had struck the wall.

"We'll have to decide what to do in the

morning," Daniel said, "but I'm afraid I really must go now. I've warned the night staff not to give out any information about us to anyone so we should be quite safe. Maybe they'll be satisfied now that they've blown up our house and they won't try again." He bent to kiss me then rubbed Liam's curls. "Get some food inside you then try to sleep."

"As if I can sleep knowing that you're out there and there are people who want you dead."

"I can take care of myself," he said. "Don't worry."

Then he was gone. I perched on the edge of the bed, hugging Liam so tightly to me that he squirmed in my arms and broke away from my breast. How could I sleep not knowing if those men were waiting for my husband at this moment, or were looking for my baby and me? How could I ever sleep again? A few minutes later there was a tap at the door. I froze. I knew that someone would be delivering sandwiches and drinks but what if it was a member of the Cosa Nostra, who had found out where we were staying and wanted to deliver the fatal blow while Daniel was away? Hastily I put Liam down on the bed, buttoned my blouse then looked around the room for a possible weapon to defend us. It was Spartan and lacking in ornaments. There was a large jug on the washstand in the corner that looked sturdy enough. Hardly the ideal weapon but better than nothing. Slowly I inched the door open, the jug in my hand and ready. "Yes?" I said.

"Molly, my darling, aren't you going to let me in?" said a peeved voice that I recognized, and there stood Ryan O'Hare, dressed in a frilly white shirt and a black velvet jacket that was topped with a crimson opera cape. "Holy Mother of God," he said, reverting to Irishness as he did when upset. "Just look at you."

"Ryan." I felt tears welling into my eyes again. "I'm so glad to see you. Do come in. Excuse the way I look. Our house . . ."

"I know. I just met your husband on his way out. What a shock. I hardly recognized him. I took him for a chimney sweep. I gather someone lobbed a bomb in your direction and the house went up in flames. Thank God you're all alive."

"Not all." I gulped back a sob. "Our little servant girl, Aggie. She was trying to save Liam and she was killed. I feel terrible."

"My dear darling, Molly, you need a strong drink," he said. "You're shaking. And some dry clothes."

44

"I don't have any dry clothes," I said. "I don't have any clothes at all. It's all gone. Everything."

"Then we must remedy that. Stay there. Don't move." He undid his cape and draped it around my shoulders. "That should hold you until I come back." He went out and soon returned. "Here we are. These should be sufficient for tonight," he said. He held out emerald green silk pajamas, a black silk robe, slippers. "Give me time and I'll see what you can wear tomorrow. I've always thought you'd look stunning in breeches." He glanced down at Liam who had now, miraculously, fallen asleep. "I'm afraid I don't keep a handy supply of infant's clothes, never having had the need, thank God, but I think I have a traveling rug somewhere that you could use as swaddling clothes, or whatever they do to infants."

I laughed in spite of myself. "Ryan, you're too kind. Thank you."

"Well, go ahead. Put them on. You'll get pneumonia if you wait any longer."

"I can't change my clothes with you here."

He laughed, that delightfully wicked laugh that was so infectious. "My darling, as if you're in any danger from *moi*. Besides, I'm a theater person. I've seen it all. So go ahead and strip off, woman. There. If it makes you feel better, I'll look the other way." He turned his back and stared out of the window.

Gratefully I peeled off the damp and blackened garments. I was horrified at the ripped and singed fabric and now was aware of burns and scrapes on my body. I'd have liked to sponge myself down with hot water, but I certainly wasn't going to do that with Ryan watching me. Instead I slipped into the heavenly softness of those pajamas and then put on the robe. Ryan turned back so swiftly that I realized he must have been watching me in the dressing table mirror.

"You look divine, my darling," he said. "It's one of those moments when I wish I was the other way inclined so that I could ravish you before your husband returned."

I laughed again. He smiled too. "That's better. Now you look more like the Molly I know and love, the Molly who isn't afraid of anything."

"It's easy not to be afraid when you don't have a husband and child to fear for," I said. "When Daniel was lying unconscious and I knew my baby was up in that inferno I thought I'd die of fright."

"All's well that ends well," Ryan said. "You have all three come through unharmed. Houses can be mended. New

46

clothes and furnishing can be bought. . . ."

"On a policeman's salary?" I said, already lamenting all of those precious little items I had acquired as wedding presents that would now never be replaced. "And where will we live until they can fix the house? If they can fix the house?"

There was a tap at the door and a voice said, "Room service, madame." Ryan went to the door and a young man came in, carrying a tray. If he thought it questionable that another man was in my room and I was now wearing green silk pajamas, he didn't let his face show it. He merely put the tray on the bedside table, gave a little bow, and left. I realized I should have tipped him but of course I had no money. No purse, no comb . . . before despair could overwhelm me, Ryan had already picked up a steaming mug of hot rum. "Here, drink this. You'll feel better."

I took a sip, feeling the warmth spreading through my chilled limbs.

"There you are. Now you're looking almost human again. Almost human but horribly dirty. Wait a second." He bustled across the room and returned with a wet washcloth with which he proceeded to dab gently at my face. "And your hair is singed too," he said. "What a mess. My poor darling. Who could have done such a dastardly deed? Foreign anarchists? But who would want to assassinate Daniel?"

"It's foreigners all right," I said, "but Daniel thinks it's the new Italian gang, the Cosa Nostra."

"My dear, I've heard about them. Utterly ruthless. What has Daniel done to upset them?"

"Arrested their leader, I gather. He's had orders to shut them down. He feared they would retaliate and now they have." I felt tears close to the surface again and looked away, not wanting him to see me cry.

Ryan, more sensitive than most men, picked up a ham sandwich and waved it in front of my face. "Eat," he said. "You'll feel better. And finish that toddy too."

I did as he commanded, mechanically chewing at the bread, although it was hard to swallow.

"That's my girl," he said, stroking my cheek. "Now, you remember my former friend Fritz Birnbaum, the German doctor, don't you?"

"Of course I do," I said.

"Much as I find it repugnant, having not separated on the best of terms, I will swallow my pride and see if he's in his rooms. I think a doctor should take a look at you and maybe give you a sedative or a shot of morphine or something."

"I don't want a sedative," I said. "I want to be awake when Daniel returns. How could I sleep knowing that he's out there and in danger?"

"And your injuries? Don't they need treating?"

"I don't think there's much wrong with me," I said. "A nasty bump on the back of my head and a few cuts and bruises, otherwise I'm fine."

"I think you should let a doctor examine you, just in case. And what about your baby there? Is he definitely all right?"

Until now it hadn't crossed my mind that anything could be wrong with Liam. Daniel had said he'd been found quite unharmed. He seemed to be sleeping peacefully enough. I turned him over and opened his blanket to examine his chubby little limbs. He awoke, looked at me, and gave a sleepy smile. As I bent to kiss him his eyelids fluttered closed again. I heaved a sigh of relief.

"He looks perfect. Thank you, Ryan. You've been very kind."

"Then you should try to sleep."

"I can't see myself falling asleep tonight."

"I have some divine cocaine in my room. One little sniff of that and you'll feel marvelous. I always take it when I'm tense. Or opium? I'm sure I know someone who can find you some opium. They say it gives lovely dreams."

I had to laugh again and put my hand on his. "Ryan, stop, please. No, thank you. I don't think my husband would want to come home and find his wife drugged. Besides I want to stay awake to protect Liam."

"I'll stay with you, if you like, and keep guard."

I nodded. "Would you? I'd like that."

I changed Liam's wet diaper, substituting one of the hand towels from the room, then tucked us both under the covers. Ryan sat on the bed beside me and began to hum softly. The comforting warmth of the blankets and eiderdown began to work. In spite of myself I felt my limbs becoming heavy.

FOUR

"What the devil is going on here?" A deep voice cut through my slumber. I opened my eyes to an unfamiliar room, wondering for a moment where I was. Daniel stood over me, cleaned up considerably since I saw him last, with a plaster over the cut on his head, and now wearing his police uniform.

"Daniel, you're back," I said as memory returned. "Thank the good Lord."

"And come back to find a strange man in my bed?" he demanded.

I shifted my gaze to see Ryan's dark hair peeking from under the counterpane, on the other side of Liam's remarkably similar dark curls.

"Darling, that's not a strange man. It's Ryan."

At the commotion Ryan woke up and raised bleary eyes to us.

"Captain Sullivan. You've returned. Thank God for that. Molly was so worried. She was afraid to be alone so I said I'd keep watch for her."

"A fine job you were doing at keeping watch," Daniel said, his expression softening a little.

"I was only snoozing. If danger had arisen, trust me I'd have been on my feet and ready to defend her in an instant," Ryan said, getting out of bed and looking somewhat sheepish. "Well, now that you're back safe and sound, I'll just toddle off to my own abode and leave you to it. And get some decent shut-eye. That child of yours kicks like a mule."

"Ryan," I called after him as he made for the door. "Thank you so much, for everything. I don't think I could have made it through the evening without you."

He turned back and blew me a kiss. "Call upon me anytime. I'm always at your service, you know that."

"You might have been a little more gracious," I said as the door closed behind Ryan. "He was so kind, Daniel. He brought me down his own pajamas and robe. He forced me to eat and drink something, then he sat on the bed beside me until I fell asleep. He also made me laugh. I was in a terrible state when you left. I'd never have slept a wink otherwise."

"I'm sorry," Daniel said gruffly. "But how do you think I felt coming here after being out all night and the first thing I see is another man's head next to my wife."

"Daniel Sullivan, sometimes you are absurd," I snapped. "Let me give you a little hint — if I was ever going to go looking for a little excitement, it wouldn't be the night after my family was nearly killed by a bomb. And I wouldn't invite him to share a bed with my young son either."

"Oh, Molly." Daniel sank onto the bed beside me. He wrapped his arms around me in a fierce embrace. "I've had a hell of a night. And I don't think there's one part of me that doesn't hurt."

"I'm sorry, my darling," I said, stroking back his unruly mop of curls. "Have you had your injuries seen to by a doctor?"

"No time. Not necessary," he said shortly.

"And did you find the culprit?"

"What do you think? It wasn't late. There were plenty of people still around on Greenwich Avenue, along with all the students in Washington Square. The fellow would only have had to have hightailed it from a completely deserted Patchin Place and then he'd have blended in with the crowd." He sighed. "No. Nobody saw anything. We've nothing to go on. But we did find a paving stone

53

that had been thrown through our front parlor window, thus confirming my suspicions. Someone broke the glass then hurled some kind of primitive bomb inside."

"And Aggie?" I asked. "Did they find her body?"

"Yes. Badly charred, I'm afraid. Do you know of any next of kin who should be notified?"

"Next of kin? They turned her out when they knew she was pregnant, Daniel. They told her never to come back, that she was no longer their daughter."

"All the same, officially . . ." he began.

I shook my head. "I know the family had a small farm somewhere in the Hudson Valley. More than that I can't tell you." Then I cleared my throat, hardly daring to ask the next question that was going through my mind. "And our house? Is it completely destroyed? Everything gone?"

He nodded. "Pretty much. It's still smoldering in there so I didn't get a chance to look too closely, but I'd be surprised if there was anything —" He'd started the sentence sounding so matter-of-fact but then his voice cracked and I realized how deeply he too felt about what had happened to us.

"What will we do?" I asked, the bleak

despair coming to the surface. "Where will we go?"

"We'll be all right." Daniel stroked back my singed hair from my cheek. "I promise we'll be all right. The commissioner has said that there would be money coming and the department would take care of us. Whether that means they'll rebuild our house for us, or just give us enough to get by for the present, I can't say. I didn't like to press too much. But for now my main concern is to make sure that you are safe. I want you out of the city, far away from here." He paused, then frowned. "You can go up to my mother to start with. I don't want to put her in danger in the long run but . . ."

"Daniel," I interrupted. "She's gone, remember. On her trip out West."

"She's already left?"

I nodded. "Her letter said, 'By the time you read this I shall be gone.' She said she didn't tell us before because she was sure you'd try to dissuade her and she was determined to take her chance to have one big adventure in her life."

"She can't have got too far. We'll locate her and bring her back."

"No, Daniel. Let's not spoil her one big adventure."

Daniel gave a testy sigh. "No matter. You

can go to the house. Martha will take care of you."

"No, that won't work either. Martha has closed up the house and gone to her ailing mother. There's nobody there."

"Then you can stay in the house alone, surely. The hired man will have a key . . ."

"I suppose so," I said, thinking of being in that remote house alone with Liam, wondering and worrying about Daniel every moment. "But you won't be with me, will you? I'll be all alone."

"You'll be safe enough there, at least for the present. The hired man lives on the property, doesn't he? He'll keep an eye on you."

"That's not the point," I retorted. "I want to be with you, Daniel. I'll worry myself sick about you if we're apart."

"I have to stay on the job. I can't leave right now, you must see that. I'm sure Sergeant O'Halloran will let me stay at his place. But if you really will be too worried up in Westchester all alone, I'll find somewhere for you to go for the time being — somewhere far enough away where those bully boys of the Italian gang can't track us down immediately."

I put my hand over his. "Then I'll stay at Sergeant O'Halloran's with you. I don't want to leave you, Daniel, especially not at a time like this."

He took my face in his hands. "Don't you understand? I want you well away from the city, just in case these people try again. I can't take the risk that something will happen to you. I'd much rather track down my mother and ask her to come home, but you may be right. It is remote and I'm not even sure that Westchester is sufficiently removed . . ." he broke off, frowning. Then he said, "Of course. Why didn't we think of it before?"

"Think of what?" I asked.

He wagged a finger at me in an animated fashion. "Your friends in Paris. They've invited you enough times. You can go to them."

"To Paris, Daniel? Don't be absurd. I only mentioned it to you as a joke."

"But it's perfect, don't you see. You'll be safely out of harm's way."

"But the fare to Paris . . ."

". . . will be paid from police coffers, I've no doubt."

The desire to go to Paris and see Gus and Sid wrestled with my worry over Daniel. "I couldn't leave you," I said. "You need your wife and son with you at a horrible time like this."

His hand was still resting on my cheek. "I don't want to be without you either, but you must see this is the best course of action. The only course of action, Molly. If you remain in New York City you'll be on my mind all the time. I'll be constantly worrying that something terrible will happen to you and Liam. If you're safely with friends halfway across the world then I can do my job properly."

"I suppose so," I said reluctantly.

He got to his feet. "Then it's settled. We'll send a cable to your friends. First thing tomorrow morning we'll try and book passage on the next boat that's sailing for France. In the meantime I'll find a place for you to stay."

"And I'll need to find some clothes and toiletries for Liam and me. We have nothing, but exactly how I'm supposed to pay for it . . ." I broke off, tears welling up again at the hopelessness of our situation.

"We can certainly dip into our small savings," Daniel said. "But I'm pretty sure I can make the commissioner take care of us, given that this whole fiasco with the Cosa Nostra was his idea when everyone in the police force warned him against proceeding with it. Now, let me get a few minutes of sleep and I'm sure we'll sort everything out in the morning."

He took off his uniform and I gasped. His undershirt was scorched and torn beneath his jacket and his body liberally decorated with cuts, bruises, and burns. A lump came into my throat.

"Daniel, you poor thing. No wonder you're hurting so much. And I've no salve to put on your wounds."

"I'll survive, I expect," he said, flopping down on the bed next to Liam. "A little sleep will be a great restorative."

"At least let me clean you up a little." I took the washcloth from the washingstand, dipped it in water, and began to sponge grime from his various wounds. He winced and grunted as I inadvertently touched a burn or a bad cut. "You must go to a doctor with these. They could turn septic."

"I've had worse." Daniel grinned.

"Would you like Ryan's pajamas to sleep in? They're wonderfully soft."

Daniel snorted. "It would take more of an accident than this before I slept in emerald green silk pajamas, especially belonging to a creature like Ryan O'Hare," he said.

"He can't help what he is, Daniel," I replied gently. "And he is wonderfully kind. I'd never have made it through the night without him."

59

"All right, enough said. I'll give him his due," Daniel muttered. "Now for God's sake, woman, just let me sleep." He pulled up the covers, snuggling down next to a still-sleeping Liam.

"Would you like anything to eat or drink first?" I asked, but he was already asleep.

"Well, Miss Vanessa, it seems that you were wrong," I said as I slid back into my side of the bed without waking my sleeping men. "It looks as if Molly Murphy is going to Paris after all."

FIVE

Daniel departed again at first light. By the time he returned I had had some breakfast and fed Liam who was playing quite happily crawling around a strange room, hauling himself upright to peer out through the window at carriages passing below.

Daniel looked quite pleased with himself when he announced that a place had been found for me. One of his lieutenants had a sister who had married well and now lived comfortably in a brownstone in the East Fifties. She had a small child of her own and would be happy to take me in until passage could be arranged for me.

"I've inquired at a shipping agency," Daniel said "and there is a Cunard ship sailing in a couple of days, bound for Cherbourg by way of Southampton. I've asked them to see if there are any cabins available."

"No, not an English line," I said so vehemently that he recoiled in surprise.

"What do you have against them? Was it a Cunard ship on which you sailed to America in uncomfortable circumstances? You'll not be traveling steerage I promise you."

"No, it's not that. It's an English ship, Daniel. You must realize that my brothers were both known terrorists in the eyes of the English, although we Irish would call them fighters for freedom."

I realized as I spoke that I had probably never told him the full details of my time in Dublin. Our relationship wasn't on the firmest of ground at that point and Daniel had just been released from prison. I didn't want to tell him too much, even now, knowing that he might well agree with the English authorities.

"Come, Molly. Nobody is going to blame you for the reckless acts of your brothers," he said gently, but I shook my head. "You don't know it all, Daniel. I was involved in that failed prison break attempt that cost my brother Joseph his life. I had to flee from Ireland. I'm probably still a wanted person in the eyes of the English. I can't risk being on an English ship and one that would call at Southampton. You're worried for my life here. I'd be equally worried on that boat."

"You'd be traveling as Mrs. Daniel Sullivan," he said. "I don't see why they would ever put two and two together, but I take your point. I'm sure there will be a ship of the French Line departing soon enough and until then you can lie low in an area where we hope the gang will never think of looking for you."

"How can I even leave this room?" I demanded, looking down at my current attire. "I can hardly go through the city dressed in silk pajamas."

"All being taken care of even as we speak." Daniel lifted Liam into his arms, swinging him into the air and making him squeal with delight. "I met your friend Mrs. Goodwin just as she was going off duty after a night shift. She heard about what happened and offered to help. She'll be coming around later with clothes for you and she's going to escort you to the house where you'll be staying."

"How kind of her," I said. "Especially since she's been working all night and must be exhausted." Mrs. Goodwin was one of two female detectives on the New York police force. She had started out as a matron, supervising inmates, but had been so successful in undercover assignments that she was now a full-fledged detective. I had met her when Daniel was wrongly imprisoned and she had been helpful to me on several occasions since. "But did you mention Liam to her? He doesn't even have a clean nappy."

"She's a woman, Molly. I expect she's thought of that too," Daniel said, putting his son down hastily as he detected the wet towel now on Liam's nether regions. He went over to the tray that was still on the dresser. "I could do with some fresh coffee," he said, picking up the last remaining piece of cold toast and eating it greedily. "I haven't eaten a thing all night."

"Let me send down for some for you." I went over to the bellpull. He shook his head. "Too much to do. I'll have one of the constables bring me in a sandwich. I have to go back immediately. I've a vehicle waiting. I only came to see if you were all right and to let you know what's happening. You will be careful, won't you? I think you'll be quite safe here. You're registered under a false name and the desk clerk knows, but just in case don't open your door to anyone you don't know."

At that moment there was a noise outside and the door handle began to move. Daniel leaped across the room and wrenched it open. "Holy Mother of God," said a shocked voice outside. "You gave me quite a fright, Captain Sullivan."

"Oh, it's you again, O'Hare," Daniel said in a clipped voice. "What do you want now?"

"Such a warm greeting, it brings tears to my Irish eyes," Ryan said, coming into the room past Daniel. "As to what I want — first I wanted to see how Molly was this morning and if there was anything I could do to keep her happy. And second I've rummaged through my things and brought over some clothes she might wear until she has some of her own. I told her she'd look stunning in britches."

"My wife will not be wearing britches," Daniel said curtly. "And thank you for your offer. It was most kind, but I have a woman police officer coming over shortly with some suitable new clothing."

"Then 'all's well that ends well,' as we say in theater," Ryan said, giving me a breezy smile. "If you need company, Molly, you only have to summon me. I'm dying to read you a scene from my new play. So funny I have to chuckle every time I read it. Adam and Eve in the garden of Eden. Of course we'll have problems with the fig leaves and the censors . . ."

"I must be leaving," Daniel interrupted. "And Mrs. Sullivan will be leaving soon as well."

"Where are you going, Molly, my love?" Ryan asked.

"I'm afraid that has to stay a secret," Daniel said before I could answer. "One attempt has been made on my wife's life. I can't risk a second. The object is to get her away from the city as quickly as possible. And the fewer people who know of her whereabouts the better." He tried to usher Ryan from the room with him, but Ryan refused to be ushered and dodged nimbly to my side.

"I think I'll stay and watch over you until you are transported away," Ryan said.

Daniel sighed. "I'll come to check on you later today, when you are settled in," he said. "Take care of yourself."

"More to the point you take care of yourself, Daniel Sullivan," I went over to give him a kiss. "You're the one in danger, not me."

"I'll be careful, I promise," he said, managed a grim smile, and left.

Ryan stayed with me, keeping Liam so entertained with his antics and silliness that I managed to forget my own fears and laugh with him. Then the stunt would be over and the fear would creep back. If a gang wanted to finish off Daniel it would be so easy. They could be waiting for him around any corner in the city; they could be leaning from an

66

upstairs window as he walked past and throw another bomb at him. . . . How could I possibly bear to be parted from him? Then I told myself that I would bear it because it had to be borne. If Liam and I were safe then that was one less thing for Daniel to worry about and therefore he could pay full attention to taking care of himself.

After a while Ryan's exaggerated cheerfulness began to wear thin on both of us and we were both relieved when Mrs. Goodwin arrived. There was no sign of tiredness on her unlined, plain face made even plainer by the severe bun she wore. Ryan took one look at the high-collared navy blue uniform she wore and beat a hasty retreat. He only liked to surround himself with objects of beauty and couldn't abide plain women.

"Call upon me anytime, Molly dearest," he said as he blew me a kiss.

Mrs. Goodwin looked after him with interest. "What an extraordinary man," she said and I realized that normal people were startled by Ryan's flamboyant attire — today he was wearing his Lord Byron lace shirt and velvet trousers.

"Ryan O'Hare, the Irish playwright," I said. "An old friend who has been so kind to me and taken good care of us."

"Oh, yes," she said. "The one who writes

those controversial plays. Thrown out of England, wasn't he?"

I laughed. "Yes, he was. But it's so good of you to come here, especially after working all night."

She smiled, the smile softening the severe face. "Actually I didn't have too bad a time of it. I was in a hotel, waiting for a meeting of crooks that never happened. So I spent the night in a soft armchair with a drink at my side." She came over to me. "But you, my poor dear girl. I couldn't believe it when I heard the news. Shocking. Unforgivable. You'd have thought that these Italians at least thought the family sacred. Well, you all survived. That's the main thing."

"My poor little servant girl wasn't so lucky," I said. "She died trying to save my boy." And I heard my voice crack as I said it. "I feel so awful."

"Nothing you could have done," she said. "Our job is now to make sure you and your child are safely far away. Here you are." She put a parcel on the bed. "I popped into Stewart's department store on my way here and bought you necessities. I wasn't quite sure of your size but I think they'll do well enough for the moment."

I opened the string around the package and found a plain white shirtwaist and dark blue cotton skirt as well as undergarments, petticoat, hose. They were almost as unattractive as the uniform Mrs. Goodwin was wearing, but I knew she meant well and they were certainly an improvement on the blackened, tattered remnants of my own clothing. And, mercy of mercies, she had added some strips of toweling, saying as I saw them, "I wasn't quite sure how big your baby was, or even what babies wear, but I do know they get through a lot of diapers, so I thought these might keep you going."

I thanked her profusely, went to the bathroom down the hall to wash and change and gave Liam a bath at the same time. His clothes were soiled but they would have to do until . . . I broke off that sentence. Until what? It was frightening to realize, for the first time since I fled from Ireland and arrived, penniless and a fugitive in this country, that I couldn't envision a future. But when I emerged — washed, dressed in clean clothes, and with a relatively clean baby in my arms — I was determined not to let Mrs. Goodwin see my worry. My family had been though hell and survived. It would work out one way or another.

Six

"You stay here," Mrs. Goodwin said as we prepared to leave. "I'll go and hail a hansom cab for us. I don't want you to be seen loitering on the street. We might be followed."

I did as she said, waiting in the shadows of the foyer beside a large potted palm until she returned and swept us rapidly into a waiting cab. As we crossed Washington Square I called out suddenly, "Wait. I must see my house first."

"My dear, do you think that's wise?" Mrs. Goodwin put a warning hand on my arm.

I nodded. "I have to see for myself. I have to know."

"Very well. Driver," she leaned up to him, "take us first to Patchin Place."

"I can't get a cab up there. Too narrow for the horse and he don't like backin' up," the driver said testily.

"Then go as far as you can," she said. He

looked at her police uniform and didn't argue. There was a police constable standing guard at the entrance to Patchin Place. He was about to stop us but recognized either me or Mrs. Goodwin. The rest of the backwater was deserted except for another constable standing guard over what must have once been my home.

"I have to see for myself. I won't be a moment," I said. "Nobody's around."

Mrs. Goodwin sighed. "Then be quick. Your husband wouldn't want you risking your life again, you know that."

I handed Liam to Mrs. Goodwin. He promptly squalled and reached for me. Hardly an unobtrusive visit then. I swung myself down quickly and hurried toward my house. The brick façade still stood but there were black gaping holes where windows had been. The front door was burned and blistered and hung open and beyond it nothing that I could recognize as mine — just a pile of blackened rubble, still smoking in places. I tried not to picture Aggie's charred body.

The constable put out a hand. "You can't go in there, Mrs. Sullivan. It's not safe."

"What if there are some of my things that can be salvaged?" I asked. "My jewelry? Crockery? Anything?"

"You're not the one to do that," he said. "You'd better ask your husband. All I know are my orders are to let nobody in."

I turned away and climbed back into the cab. We said nothing as we left Greenwich Village and went up Fifth Avenue. Liam had stopped crying and now clearly enjoyed the new sights and sounds. For me it felt as if I was passing through a dream world where ladies in elegant dresses and parasols strolled as if they hadn't a care in the world. Why should they? They all had homes to return to. At last we turned east along Fifty-seventh Street and came to a halt outside an imposing brick house, with a flight of steps leading up to its front door and bay trees growing in pots on either side. Mrs. Goodwin descended first, took Liam from me as I climbed down. I went up those steps with great reluctance. This arrangement had been made in such a hurry and I wondered whether the occupants of the house, the lieutenant's sister and her husband, had really had time to think their kind gesture through.

How would I react if Daniel had said to me, "I'm bringing a strange woman and her child to stay with us. An Italian gang has already tried to kill them once by bombing their house. They may well try again if they find out she is here"?

The knock on the front door reverberated and soon it was opened not by a maid but by a pretty young woman in an exquisite gown. She held out her arms to me.

"My dear Mrs. Sullivan," she said. "Come in, do. What an ordeal you've been through." She half dragged me into the house. Mrs. Goodwin hesitated on the doorstep.

"And this is Mrs. Goodwin, a fellow detective in the police force, who was kind enough to accompany me here," I said.

"Of course. I've heard all about you from my brother," the young woman said. "The men are secretly impressed by you, although they would never say so to your face."

Mrs. Goodwin actually smiled. "Kind of you to say so."

"Come in, do," our hostess insisted. "Take some tea with us."

Mrs. Goodwin shook her head. "I've already been up all night on duty, so if you don't mind, I'll bid you both farewell and head for my bed."

I took her hand. "Thank you so much. You've been very kind."

"Not at all. Glad to help," she said gruffly as if trying to hold back any display of emotion. "Good luck to you, Molly, my dear." She went down the steps, waved, then got back into the cab, leaving me in the front hall with the lieutenant's sister.

"This is so good of you, Mrs. . . ." I began, realizing that I still didn't know her name.

She laughed. "I am Dorothy, but I'm usually known as Dodo. And when my brother telephoned me with your terrible news I told my husband that you had to come to us without delay."

"I hope he didn't object," I said warily.

"My husband adores me, Mrs. Sullivan. And do let me call you by your first name — I try to dispense with too much formality under my own roof, although my husband, whose upbringing in lofty circles was rather more formal than mine, sometimes frowns upon the liberties I take."

I smiled at her. "You may certainly call me Molly," I said. "I have a group of friends who abhor formality so the use of first names isn't at all strange to me."

"Splendid." She beamed at me. "But don't let's stand here a second longer. We should get the little one settled in his nursery and then we can have a cup of coffee in peace." She patted Liam's cheek. "What an adorable child. I know he's going to be great friends with my little Cuddles."

"My husband said you had a baby. Boy or girl?"

"A little boy. Almost a year old now. Officially he's named Alfred Homer Walton Phillips after his father, but who can call a baby those awful names? So he's Cuddles to me, although Alfred disapproves of baby talk. Come upstairs and I'll introduce you."

She led me up a broad stair, to a luxuriously appointed landing and then up a second, less grand stair, chatting all the way, and then opened a door at the front of the house. "Here we are, Nanny," she called. "Here's your new charge."

A plump elderly nurse appeared from a back room.

"Nanny used to look after Alfred when he was a baby," Dodo said. "And now she's come out of retirement to take care of little Cuddles. Alfred wouldn't hear of another nursemaid raising his son."

"Master Alfred is currently taking his morning nap," Nanny said, putting a warning finger to her lips that we were talking too loudly. "And it looks to me as if this young man is ready for sleep as well."

She took Liam from me and he didn't protest, looking back at me wide-eyed.

"I will come up to nurse him about noon," I said.

"Good heavens," Dodo exclaimed. "He is not on a bottle? Don't you find that terribly inconvenient?"

I felt them both staring at me as if I was some creature straight from the jungle, and blushed. "I don't think I keep to your kind of social schedule," I said. I turned back to the nursemaid. "I'm sorry about the state of his clothing. We were both left with nothing after the fire. So if he could possibly borrow some items from little Alfred, until I can shop for new ones, I'd much appreciate it."

"Madam apprised me of what happened. I've already looked some things out for him," Nanny said. "Don't you worry. All taken care of."

Dodo took my arm. "And my poor, poor darling. You've obviously lost all your clothes too. Never mind. You and I will have lots of fun going through my wardrobe."

"Oh, no, really," I said, now feeling overwhelmed with embarrassment and emotion. "I couldn't possibly borrow your clothes. How and when could I return them to you?"

She laughed gaily. "But I want to give them to you, silly. I'm tired of so many of my dresses, and one can't be seen in public in them more than a couple of times or people start to talk, don't they? Besides Alfred loves to show me off in new dresses. He's such an angel. He caters to my every whim."

She led me back down the stairs to an elegant sitting room where coffee and cakes were waiting for us. To have gone from bleak despair to this in a matter of hours was almost too much to bear. Dodo was the soul of kindness, trying to press so many items of clothing on me that I was mortified with embarrassment, feeling rather like the beggar at the gates.

"Really all I need is enough to tide me over," I said. "I didn't have this many dresses to begin with. My husband is only a policeman, you know."

"But I want to give them to you," she said. "Humor me, Molly dearest. Don't you see — then I'll have a splendid excuse to tell Alfred I have absolutely nothing to wear and he'll have to increase my dress allowance."

She had a maid carry armfuls to my room, adding shoes, hats, even a fur stole to the pile.

"I'm sure I'll be able to go shopping soon," I said, "so I'll only need clothes for a day or two."

"Don't be silly. Of course you can't go shopping," Dodo said. "My brother says you must remain in complete seclusion so that nobody knows where you are. A matter of life and death, Molly."

Privately I thought that the way Dodo

chatted incessantly meant that she would probably divulge my presence to her friends. I could just hear her telling the thrilling tale of how she rescued the poor woman whose house was destroyed by a bomb. But I also decided that none of her friends was likely to have connections to an Italian East Side gang. However I did see her point about going shopping. The department stores that stocked the kind of clothes I could afford were on busy streets and there was always a chance I'd be noticed.

Later that day I was outfitted, fed Liam, then watched him and little Alfred crawling around on the nursery rug, eyeing each other with interest. As I stood there my gaze was drawn to a picture on the nursery wall. It was a beautiful girl of around eight or nine, sitting on a rock beside the ocean with a shell on her lap. She was looking out to sea with wide blue eyes and her light blonde hair blew out in the breeze. She looked so ethereal that it was almost like seeing a supernatural being. And somewhere in the back of my mind, I recalled Sid's mention of the painter Reynold Bryce. And Daniel's remark, "Didn't he do all those portraits of the angelic child, copies of which now grace half the nurseries in America?"

"Is that one of Reynold Bryce's paintings?"

Dodo looked pleased. "Why, yes. It is. Only a copy of course. The real ones are all in famous museums, but it's so lovely, isn't it? Cuddles's godmother gave it to him as a christening present."

As the dinner hour approached Dodo insisted in coming up with me to select a dress to wear for dinner and chose something grander than I'd ever have considered for myself — also with a lot more frou-frou. She even insisted on lending me her pearls as they completed the outfit so well. I half expected the master of the house to query why I was wearing his wife's dress and his wife's pearls when I was introduced to him that evening, but he showed no indication that anything was amiss. He greeted me civilly enough and expressed condolences about my unfortunate current state, but I wondered if he had actually been consulted about my stay and would have approved of it. I definitely got the impression that he would not have been as generous with his wife's possessions as she had been. As we sat at dinner the first question he asked was how long I thought I might be staying.

"Only until alternative arrangements can be made, Mr. Phillips," I said.

"Where do you think you will go?" he asked.

I decided not to mention France. "My husband wants me far away from the city."

"Very wise." He looked relieved. "You can't be too careful. Who would ever have thought that these ruffians would dare to strike in the middle of New York City? Too many immigrants these days, I'm afraid. And it was a mistake to admit these wilder types from Southern Europe. They don't respect the law as we do. Brigands and cutthroats the lot of them."

"Don't be so gloomy, Alfred," Dodo complained, reaching across to slap his hand as if he was a naughty child. "We're supposed to be cheering up poor Molly, not worrying her even more. We're going to make her very welcome and give her a lovely time with us. You should see how happy Little Cuddles is to have found a playmate. They absolutely adore each other."

Actually they had been crawling over each other, taking toys away at will, but I thought it wise not to say this.

"I'm sure he'll have a brother or sister soon enough," Alfred said.

"I'm not sure that I want to give up my figure again so soon," Dodo said. "And it really was most uncomfortable going through childbirth, wasn't it, Molly."

Alfred coughed. One did not mention pregnancy in mixed company.

We had just had coffee served to us when there was a thunderous knock at the front door. Dodo gave a little gasp. "It's them. They've found you, Molly."

Alfred stood up, ready for action, but then we heard a maid's voice, calm and efficient, saying, "I'll tell the master that you're here, sir, if you'd care to wait." Then she appeared and dropped a curtsey. "If you please, sir, ma'am, but Captain Sullivan has come to see his wife."

"Show him in, Ethel. Don't keep him waiting," Dodo said before Alfred could answer. "And bring another cup and brandy glass."

The maid gave a perfunctory bob again and almost immediately Daniel came into the room. He was still wearing his police uniform and he looked hollow-eyed and exhausted.

"Daniel Sullivan." He held out his hand to Alfred. "I can't tell you how grateful I am for you taking my wife in on such short notice."

"Not at all. Glad to be of help," Alfred said gruffly and shook his hand.

"I'm sorry to trouble you at this hour,"

Daniel said, and I could see him staring at my new attire with interest, "but I wonder if I might have a word with my wife about arrangements that are being made for her."

"By all means," Alfred said. "Ethel, show Captain and Mrs. Sullivan into my study. Can I pour you a brandy first?"

"I won't take a drink, thank you. I've hardly slept in the last day or so and I'd probably fall asleep during the cab ride downtown."

"A cup of coffee then?" Dodo asked. "Some dessert? Some fruit?"

"I wouldn't say no to coffee," Daniel said. "Thank you."

"I'll have a tray sent through to the study." Dodo motioned to the servant, who led us down the hall and into a room lined with bookshelves. There were two leather armchairs on either side of a fireplace. Being May the fire was unlit and the room felt decidedly chilly, but I sat in one of the chairs. Daniel took the other.

"You appear to have settled in remarkably well," he said. "You look as if you're about to attend a ball."

"That was Dodo — Mrs. Phillips's doing," I said. "She insisted on plying me with her clothing — a little more fancy than I'm used to."

"It suits you well," Daniel said. "And Liam is all right?"

"Never been happier. He has a nurse to watch over him and a small playmate."

"That's good." He still looked worried and distracted, running a hand through unruly hair, some of which had been singed by the fire. "I came to tell you that I've secured a passage for you on a French ship. She's called *La Lorraine* and she sails for Le Havre in a week's time. I'm afraid the commissioner's allowance didn't run to first class, but at least it won't be steerage and, being French, I'm sure the food will be good. If you'd like to compose a telegram I'll have a cable sent to your friends in the morning, letting them know when the ship arrives and when you are likely to reach Paris."

I was on my way over to the desk when a terrible thought struck me. "I don't know their address, Daniel. The letter burned with everything else."

He gave a half grin, half grimace. "Actually it didn't. I went through the house today to see if anything could be saved and there was this letter, a trifle blackened around the edges but lying by the back door." He rummaged into a pocket and produced a folded piece of paper. It was scorched but still legible.

"How miraculous." I took it from him, looking at the dear, familiar signature and the address in Paris, written in Sid's bold black script. I looked up. "So clearly I am meant to go there."

"I don't know about miraculous. Fire does strange things. Some of my books are almost untouched while metal candlesticks have melted to a blob."

"You've managed to save some of your books. I'm so glad."

"I didn't manage to salvage much else," he said. "Your teapot. A few items from the kitchen. Some china."

"My jewelry case?" I didn't have much jewelry but the few items I had were precious to me.

He shook his head. "Not so far. I'm putting a couple of my men onto a more thorough search when I can spare them. I'm sorry, my darling. I'm really sorry that my actions put you in this danger. That we almost lost —" He broke off and cleared his throat. "Never mind. In a few days you'll be safely far away."

"And poor little Aggie? I don't want her buried in the potter's field, Daniel. I want her to have a proper funeral."

"I have someone trying to locate her family," he said. "If they don't come to claim the body, I'll make sure she gets a decent burial."

"I want to go to her funeral," I said.

He shook his head. "Out of the question."

"I want to, Daniel," I insisted. "It's important to me. She was important to me. I feel terrible that we let her down."

"We didn't let her down, Molly. We didn't ask anyone to come and bomb our house. You did your best for her. You gave her a home when nobody else would. You gave her a life again."

"But I have to say good-bye to her."

"The answer is no, Molly," he said firmly. "You cannot be seen anywhere near the city. If they find out where you are they could try again. I'm not risking your life for the sake of a dead servant. Now please don't mention this again."

This attitude fired my fighting Irish spirit. I opened my mouth to tell him that he couldn't order me around like this, but then I realized that he could. He was the husband and he had the final say, however unjust that seemed. Also I realized that he was probably right. I couldn't do anything to risk Liam's life.

"Now let's compose that cable, shall we," Daniel went on in a calm, reasonable voice.

"I'm in great need of a bed and sleep."

We wrote the cable together, asking if I might take up their kind invitation to stay, then composed a second one giving the time and date of the arrival of *La Lorraine.* A tray of coffee, a cheese board, crackers, and assorted pastries was delivered, and Daniel ate hungrily. Then he stood up. "I really must go. Please thank the Phillipses for me."

"Have you made any progress in finding out who did this?" I followed him to the door, not wanting him to go. "Are there any suspects?"

He turned back to me. "We've rounded up anyone who might have connections to the Cosa Nostra and locked them up in the Tombs. We'll see if a few nights in a cold cell might persuade one of them to talk, but I doubt it. They fear their gang bosses more than they fear us."

"I hate to think of someone getting away with this," I said. "It's not fair."

He reached out to me and stroked my cheek. "Life isn't fair, my darling. Surely you know that by now. But if we can finally pin a conviction on their leader and have him shut away in Sing Sing, then it might have been worth it." At the front door he took me in his arms and kissed me, hard and demandingly on the mouth. "And in the meantime," he said, "you'll be living it up in 'Gay Paree.' "

SEVEN

On May 21, 1905, Daniel, Liam, and I traveled to the Hudson Piers in a closed carriage. I carried with me one trunk of clothing, containing the most suitable items donated by Dodo Phillips. She was horrified that I planned to travel with only one trunk and so few items of clothing. I assured her that I would have no need of her more extravagant gowns, however lovely they were. Of course I couldn't tell her I was off to Paris and made her think I was heading for a remote location in the country. She had also given Liam enough gowns, capes, caps, and blankets to keep him well-dressed until he progressed to wearing pants. I was extremely grateful to her, of course. She had tried hard to keep me amused and entertained, giving up some of her own social engagements to stay with me and teaching me how to play mah-jongg. But her bubbly chatting was hard to take when I was trying to come to terms with my own reduced circumstances, not knowing whether my house could be rebuilt or where we'd go when I returned from Paris. And God knew when that would be.

The one remarkable thing that had happened during the week was that Aggie's relatives had been located and had come to claim her body. It turned out that her mother had never wanted to turn her out, but had been overruled by a stern and strict husband. It was pitiful to witness her grief now, Daniel had said. I hoped that her father would have his share of suffering eventually.

A cable had also come from Sid and Gus, more long-winded than mine had been, saying how excited they were and that I must send a telegram when I knew which boat train I was catching so that they could meet me at the station. I pictured seeing their familiar faces, beaming at me as the train pulled in, and I felt a bubble of hope for the first time in days.

"Here we are," Daniel said as the carriage turned in at the Twenty-fourth Street pier. "Wait here while I find a porter to take your belongings on board."

I looked out to see a sleek liner with two big red funnels and two tall masts. She wasn't as big as the *Majestic* had been, on which I had traveled from Liverpool in steerage, but she looked elegant enough and large enough to brave the Atlantic waves. Daniel carried Liam and swept us quickly up the gangplank.

"Surely you don't think that I'll be in danger traveling to Europe?" I said.

"I don't believe so," Daniel answered, "but these men do still have connections with other ruffians in the south of Italy." He sighed. "I don't know. Maybe we are making too much of their skills and their reach. Maybe the bomb was a lucky accident for them and they only intended to give me a warning, not burn down our house. It's hard to tell. They may just be a gang of local thugs after all. Still, I'm not prepared to run any risks with my wife and child. Don't forget to send me a cable the moment you arrive."

"Of course I will," I said. I looked at his face with longing. How could I bear to be parted from him for so long?

His eyes met mine. "How can I bear to be parted from you both?" he said, echoing my thoughts. "But we'll get through it, because we're both brave and strong and we want what's best for our son."

I nodded, biting my lip and not trusting

myself to speak. A steward came up to us and asked for my cabin number. Then he led us along narrow passageways to my cabin. He was very French-looking with slicked black hair and a jaunty black mustache.

"I 'ope madame will 'ave 'appy voyage wiz us," he said.

I noticed that other passengers who passed us were also speaking French. I wished that I had brushed up on my French during that week with Dodo rather than learning mahjongg and studying dress patterns for Dodo's future soirees. When I had taken my lessons with the Hartley girls at the big house my French had been quite good. The governess insisted that young ladies of good family should be fluent in French and we had conversation practice every day. I seemed to have a natural facility for language and was better at it than Miss Henrietta and Miss Vanessa. A lot had happened since I sat in the schoolroom at the Hartleys' mansion. I wondered how much French I would remember. I'd have to get in some practice during the crossing.

The steward let us in to my cabin. It was not the luxury I had experienced the last time I crossed the Atlantic from New York, but then that cabin had been first class. This one had a bunk bed on one wall, a built-in closet on the other with a small crib crammed in beside it. My trunk had been delivered and was taking up much of the remaining floor space.

"Zee bathrooms are to your right," the steward said. "I leave you now and bid you bon voyage."

Daniel shot me a worried glance. "It's not exactly the Ritz, is it? Will you be all right?"

"It's only for a few days, isn't it?" I tried to put on a brave face because there really was no alternative.

Liam was wiggling to get down. I realized that I'd have my hands full watching over him on a ship in the ocean, with no Aggie to help me.

"I really should be getting back," Daniel said. I knew that he hated emotional scenes and a long drawn-out good-bye was to be avoided at all costs.

I nodded. "Yes, I'd better unpack. Liam will want nursing soon."

"Don't come and see me off," he said. "Better that way."

I nodded again, not trusting myself to speak now. He took Liam from me, kissed him then held him out, looking at him. "Good-bye, son," he said and put him into the crib. Then he took me into his arms.

"Good-bye, my darling," he whispered. "Take care of yourself."

"And you too," I whispered back and kissed him. The kiss conveyed all the passion and longing we couldn't express in words. Then Liam started to cry and we broke apart.

"Watch out for those Frenchmen," Daniel said, attempting to be jaunty now. "They can be very fresh, I hear."

"I'll look forward to the challenge. And what you don't know can't hurt you," I teased back.

"I have to go," he said again. As he opened the door I called after him. "Daniel. Take care. Don't take any risks, please. I love you."

He blew me a kiss and hurried off down the hall and out of sight. Liam was bawling lustily now, holding out his arms to be picked up. I wanted to be on deck and watch as we sailed out of New York harbor, but I had to put my child's needs first. I picked him up, sat on the bottom bunk, opened my blouse front and put him to the breast. I felt the tension leave his body, and some of the tension left my own.

Suddenly the cabin door was flung open. I tried to jump up, bumping my head against the upper bunk, then tried to cover myself as an elderly woman came in. She stopped and stared when she saw me.

"What in God's name?" she demanded. "What are you doing in my cabin?"

"I'm sorry but you've made a mistake. This is my cabin," I said. "Cabin thirty-four, C deck. I have my ticket here."

"There must be some mistake," she said in a haughty voice. "This is definitely the cabin I was given because my friends are just across the hall. We asked for rooms together, you see. We're traveling as a group, but there are five of us and I was the odd man out."

"Maybe we're supposed to be sharing," I suggested, the thought not having occurred to me before. There were two bunks.

She stared down at me and my still-nursing baby, only partially covered by his robes that I had hastily pulled over me with distaste. "But they promised me," she said. "I know it was supposed to be a two-berth cabin, but they told me the other berth would be unoccupied."

"I'm afraid my decision to sail on this ship was made at the very last minute. The cabin would have been unoccupied when you booked it."

"But I can't possibly share with . . ." She frowned at us again and left the rest of the sentence hanging.

"Perhaps the purser will be able to find you alternative accommodation with somebody more suitable," I said.

"I heard someone saying that the ship was completely full. Really this is too tiresome." She gave an annoyed little sigh. Liam, now satisfied and curious to know with whom his mother was speaking lifted aside the layers of cotton and lace I had draped over him and peeked out at her. Her expression softened. "I'm sorry. That was most rude of me. If I am only paying for a berth in a double cabin, then I have to take my chances, don't I? One must make the best of it, I suppose. And it's really only to change clothing and sleep."

"He's normally a very good baby," I said, hastily fastening my blouse buttons. "He sleeps through the night well."

"I don't doubt it. So it's a little boy, is it? One can never tell."

I looked down at his curls and white lace robes and smiled. "Impossible to tell. I don't usually favor this amount of lace and ribbons but these garments were given to us. His name's William but we call him Liam."

"I'm sure we'll manage just fine," she said. "I'm Edith Pinkerton. Miss Edith Pinkerton. I'm traveling with a group of friends on a cultural tour of Europe. We are two widows and three spinsters — the other spinsters are retired schoolteachers, like myself. My bosom pal, Miss Hetherington, is a real aficionada of European art. She was formerly the art teacher at a ladies' seminary in Boston where they educated girls from the finest families. So it was she who set up our itinerary. We'll be visiting Venice, Florence, Rome, Munich, Vienna, and finishing up in Paris . . ."

"How lovely for you," I said when she paused to take a breath. "I'm Mrs. Sullivan. Molly Sullivan."

We shook hands formally. Then she looked around the narrow space. "The only question will now be who takes the top bunk. I consider myself quite agile for my advanced age, but . . ."

"I really don't mind taking the top bunk," I said, "but I may have to attend to my child if he cries and perhaps take him into bed with me."

"Take him into bed with you? My dear, isn't that most unhealthy? One should not give in to them or spoil them in that manner. And I'm surprised to find you nursing him yourself. I thought all modern mothers made use of the bottle. So much more hygienic."

"It's lucky I am nursing him," I said. "I don't know how one would heat up bottles at all hours on a ship like this."

"Oh, Miss Hetherington says that the stewards and stewardesses on these ships are wonderful," she said. "They will do anything for you, so I've heard. Of course last time she traveled on an English line. Whether the French will be as accommodating, we shall have to see, won't we?"

There was a tap at the cabin door and a steward's face came around it. "Your baggage has arrived, madame," he said to Miss Pinkerton. Then he looked at the cabin with the cot on one wall and my trunk on the floor. *"Mon dieu,"* he said.

"Is there perhaps another cabin that might be available for Mademoiselle Pinkerton?" I asked. "It seems unfair that she should have to share with a small child who might disturb her sleep."

He shrugged in that very Gallic way. "All is occupied, Madame. It seems that ze whole world wishes to spend springtime in Paris zis year."

"We'll manage," Miss Pinkerton said. "Leave the trunk in the hall outside the door. I'll go and find my friends and leave you to unpack, Mrs. Sullivan. Then your trunk can be taken away and I'll have room to unpack my small valise. Miss Hetherington warned us to travel light, since we have to take so many trains and she said sometimes one is required to jump on or off when the train is in motion."

She waved the steward away and shut the door behind her, leaving Liam and me alone in the cabin. I took out only the clothing Liam and I would need on the voyage, making sure she had half the closet space, then dragged the trunk outside, telling the steward he could put it into storage for me until we arrived. He put my mind at rest by assuring me that laundry would be taken care of during the voyage and a pail would be provided in the bathroom for dirty diapers. I had been worrying about how I would manage with a small child, but it really seemed as Miss Pinkerton had said, that the stewards would take care of everything. Feeling more content I went back to gather Liam from the cot and carried him up on deck. As I came out into the fresh air I got a shock. We were already underway. The tall buildings of New York were now behind us and there on our left we were drawing level with the Statue of Liberty, her green robes glowing in the late afternoon sunlight and her torch flashing.

"Look, darling," I said, pointing at her as many other travelers were doing. "Look at the lady." Liam grabbed at the railing, much more interested in the ocean below us. I held onto him tightly. "No, you are not going to get down," I said firmly. And I laughed. I felt a little of the tension slipping away as the New York skyline receded in the distance. In spite of everything — the loss of my house, my possessions, my sweet little servant girl — I could smile again. I was going to Paris, to my dearest friends. Maybe, just maybe, everything was going to be all right.

EIGHT

We stayed up on deck until *La Lorraine* passed the last spit of land and I felt the swell of open ocean. America was now irrevocably behind me and France lay ahead. Liam had fallen asleep against my shoulder. I toured the portions of the ship reserved for second-class passengers, including a pleasant dining room with white-clothed tables and a piano lounge with comfortable armchairs, sofas, and potted palms. I inquired about food for my baby and was told that the kitchen would prepare pureed vegetables and custards with pleasure and that the steward would keep an eye on my child if I wanted to dine unencumbered. Thus relieved on that point I went down to my cabin to change for dinner.

Miss Pinkerton was there, finishing her own toilet by sticking a large number of hairpins into her bun. She spun around with a guilty expression on her face as I entered, making me think that she had probably been through my things. Good luck to her. There was nothing to discover.

"I was admiring your gowns, Mrs. Sullivan," she said. "Such a fine quality of fabric. You clearly have a good dressmaker, or are they made in France?"

"Oh, no," I said. "These gowns were actually given to me by a friend who had grown tired of them. Her husband spoils her."

"Most certainly," she replied with a sniff. "I wondered where you were. I do hope you weren't staying away out of sensibility toward me. I do want you to feel that this cabin is yours as much as mine."

"I was up on deck, watching the ship sail past the Statue of Liberty," I said, "and after that I did a tour of our part of the ship."

"So did my friends and I," she said. "All quite satisfactory, don't you think? The lounge looks most inviting. I shall look forward to reading and writing at one of those small tables in the window. Or perhaps it will be warm enough to sit outside in a deck chair, at least until we sail into northern climes. I gather we sail quite far north up the American coast and there is always a danger of icebergs. Quite exciting, don't you think? I have always wanted to see one."

"From a distance, I hope," I said and she

101

laughed. "A good sense of humor. I like that, Mrs. Sullivan. Tell me, are you going to France or continuing your journey to another destination?"

"I'm going to stay with friends in Paris," I said. "One of them is a painter and they have been in Paris for the past few months."

"A painter. How exciting. Might one have heard of his work? Perhaps my friend Miss Hetherington is familiar with him."

"This painter is a woman," I said, "and her work is not yet well-known. She is hoping to learn from the great artists in Paris. In fact she has had an introduction to Reynold Bryce. Have you heard of him?"

"Reynold Bryce? Naturally I know of him." She stuck a final hairpin into the bun and closed the closet door. "In fact I attended a reception at an art gallery in Boston once, when he still resided and painted in our country. I must say I far preferred his earlier work. This modern style with lots of daubs and blobs leaves me cold. But Miss Hetherington says we must be open-minded and find the beauty in every piece of art. She is a good Christian woman, Miss Hetherington, and quite a fine painter herself."

I put the sleeping Liam into the crib and sat patiently on my bunk because there was not enough room for two of us to access the closet at the same time.

"Shall you be staying long in Paris?" Miss Pinkerton asked.

"I'm not sure how long I'll be staying," I said.

"Your husband must be a most understanding and generous man to allow you to travel without him. Or is he to join you in Paris?"

"I'm afraid not. He has to work."

"What is his profession?"

I decided that Miss Pinkerton was the type of nosy spinster who would spread any information around the whole ship. "He is employed by the city," I said cautiously.

"In what kind of capacity?"

"Just a glorified clerk in city government," I said.

"Hardly a mere clerk if he can afford to send his wife and child to Paris." She gave me a knowing stare. "Not a cheap undertaking. I was horrified when I found out how much a transatlantic passage would cost. I recently inherited a little money from my mother, but it has to last me for the rest of my life. Still, I could not resist when Miss Hetherington invited me to travel with them on this cultural tour."

"Of course not," I said. "Who could turn

down a chance to see the sights of Europe? Now might I be allowed to find something to wear for dinner?"

She tittered. "Oh, how silly of me. It is a trifle — snug — shall we say. And how fortunate that we are both slender. I shall go and see how my friends are faring and leave you to get ready. And of course you are welcome to join my friends and me at dinner, unless you have already sought out other dinner companions?"

"Thank you. You're most kind," I said, not being able to come up with a good way to refuse. And after all, I reasoned, any companions were better than none at all and she was trying hard to be accommodating when it must have been a shock to find herself sharing a cabin with Liam and myself.

Before I changed into my dinner gown I rang for the steward and asked if he could fetch the pureed vegetables promised for Liam. I wasn't exactly sure what concoction was in the bowl the steward produced but it smelled and tasted quite edible and Liam smacked his little lips as he ate. Having fed him, nursed him, and then put him down for the night, I was finally able to change, powder my nose, put up my hair, and make my way to dinner. The helpful steward had promised he would listen for Liam's cries and fetch me if necessary. But I have to confess I glanced back nervously as I made my way up the stairs. I was seated as promised at a table for six with Miss Pinkerton and her friends — all chatty older ladies who tried to make me feel welcome but plied me with constant questions. I had to fend off inquiries about in which branch of city government my husband worked and what exactly he did. When I gave a suitably vague response one of the widows warned me that a good wife should feign interest in her husband's business affairs, even if she found the whole thing boring or beyond her.

They wanted to know where I lived in New York and I said, quite truthfully, that my last place of residence had been in the East Fifties. They were impressed by this and then peppered me with questions about people they knew, or knew of, in New York. My answers were so vague or so unexciting to them that they finally shifted the conversation to people they had spotted in first class and snippets of gossip they had overheard. The menu was a hearty beef stew followed by an apple tart. Not elegant but tasty, confirming that the French know how to cook. After dinner we lingered over coffee and I was relieved to find Liam still sleeping.

"I have decided that I shall take the top bunk after all," Miss Pinkerton said as we made our way back to our cabin. "I have trained myself not to use the facilities during the night, so I should be just fine and you will be able to reach your little one, should the need arise."

I thanked her profusely. We each went to the bathroom to change into nightclothes and then fell asleep. Liam was exemplary, sleeping until the steward woke us with a cup of coffee. We had a breakfast of rolls and jam, then I seated myself at one of the windows in the lounge and let Liam play with the wooden animals he had been given by Cuddles's nanny. I had found a French magazine and attempted to read the articles, hoping to brush up my long-forgotten French. It was fascinating to see pictures of French fashions and Parisian society. A steward brought me more coffee and biscuits. I was beginning to think that I might be in for a pleasant time after all and felt a pang of guilt for poor Daniel, trying to complete his dangerous task while bunking down in someone else's house without the support of his wife.

While I sat there a continuous procession passed by on the deck outside, taking their morning constitutional, enjoying the bright sea air. I let the low hum of French conversation wash over me as they passed, punctuated now and then by a voice raised in exclamation. *"Mon dieu? C'est vrai?"* Or even, *"Ooh la la!"*

I smiled to myself and went back to my magazine. But when I finally heard an American voice saying, "You can't stop me. I'm grown up and know my own mind!" I looked up. A young girl was striding out, as if annoyed, ahead of a sallow woman in an old-fashioned bonnet who had to break into a run to keep up with her.

"Eleanor," she called. "That is no way to behave. You are too headstrong by half and it will lead to your downfall."

Then they passed me and were gone. I continued to stare at their retreating backs, then turned to Miss Pinkerton, who was sitting in another window, writing a letter.

"Did you happen to see that American girl who just went past?" I asked.

She looked up. "I'm afraid I didn't. I was concentrating on what I was writing. Was it someone you knew?"

"Someone I thought I recognized," I said. "It's strange that we were talking about Reynold Bryce last night because that girl looked just like the young girl in his paintings."

She shook her head and smiled. "Oh, no, my dear. That can't be possible," she said. "He painted those portraits years ago. He's been living in Paris for quite a while now. Miss Hetherington will know. She knows everything about the art world. But maybe later you and I could take a stroll on deck and see if we can spot this young woman again. You didn't notice her in the dining salon last night, did you?"

"No, I didn't," I said.

"Then maybe she is in first class. We'll ask the others at luncheon. Let me know if she comes past again." And she went back to her letter while I had to jump up to rescue Liam who was now crawling with determination toward the door. I would have to ask if there was possibly a baby carriage on board that I could use or I'd spend the whole time at sea chasing after him.

When we went into luncheon I looked around carefully but the girl wasn't anywhere to be seen. I asked if any of the women had seen her. They hadn't but Miss Hetherington was, as predicted, a font of information.

"I met Reynold Bryce several times at soirees in Boston back in the eighties," she said. "In those days he was just making a name for himself. It was really the portraits of the young girl that put him on the map. He painted one every year for five years. Then he abandoned his whole career here and went off to Paris. He had become enamored of the Impressionist movement and the more modern style of painting that was being produced over in France, although I can't say I favor it myself. Anyway, he just upped and left one day and hasn't been back to the States since." She looked up from her soup, pleased that we were all paying attention. "Of course one has to admit that he was born with talent. He is now one of the few Americans to have established himself as a leader among Impressionists. He's a friend of Monet and, one hears, a wonderful mentor to young American artists. His salon is the place to be seen, so one is told."

"The friend with whom I'll be staying is an artist and has secured an introduction to him," I said. "She hopes to be included in his upcoming exhibition."

Miss Hetherington sniffed. "Then she must indeed be talented. It is said that he has a poor opinion of women painters. He is of the old school — that women belong in the home, raising children. Such an outdated notion, as I used to tell my students. I used to say 'I am educating you to be more than a beautiful adornment to your husband. I am teaching you to think for yourselves and to believe that the whole world is open to you.' "

"Quite right," Miss Pinkerton said. "I told my students the same thing. But it was usually the same outcome. They left our establishment determined to become doctors and writers and explorers and six months later they were engaged to some vacuous young man and considered themselves happy and blessed."

"If only it were possible to be happily married and have a career," one of the widows said and sighed.

"Of course it's not. How can it ever be possible," the other widow snapped. "Unless one is Madame Curie."

I stayed silent.

"Speaking of the young girl in the Reynold Bryce paintings," the other spinster, a Miss Schmitt, joined in the conversation for the first time, "wasn't there some kind of scandal or rumor about her?"

They turned to Miss Hetherington, the resident expert. She nodded and leaned closer to us, lowering her voice and looking around before speaking. "I gather, although this has not been confirmed, that she is shut away, of unsound mind."

"Shut away? In an institution, you mean?"

Miss Hetherington shook her head. "No, I understand that she is cared for at home. I am told, on good authority by someone who knew the family in Boston, that she was always a little — shall we say — strange — remote, unworldly. The person who told me said that she couldn't put a finger on it but there was something not quite right about her. Well, one saw it in the paintings, didn't one? As if she wasn't quite of this world. Angelic, almost. That's why he called her Angela, of course. I believe her real name was something quite different. However one gathers that she had some kind of brainstorm or mental collapse and now is a pathetic creature of strange fits and fantasies who needs constant care."

"How terribly sad," I said, thinking that the face that had looked out to sea in that painting had been full of hope and interest for what lay over the horizon.

"That must have been the reason that Bryce stopped painting her," one of the widows said. "She was sliding into madness and her face no longer had that luminous angelic quality."

"One gathers he was very generous to the

family," Miss Hetherington said. "Of course he was born to money. That's how he funded his painting for many years until he made a name for himself. The Bryces are an old Bostonian family, you know."

"We must make it our quest during this voyage to find out who this young girl is," Miss Schmitt said with great animation. "Was she with anyone?"

"Yes, an older woman who could have been a companion," I replied.

"Ah, then we must seek her out." The women exchanged a glance and nodded conspiratorially.

NINE

We met at dinner that night and my table companions reported that they had had no success, except to determine that she was not traveling second class. Since a cold wind had been blowing on deck, she would probably have stayed in the first-class lounge. That cold wind was now accompanied by a decided swell.

"Oh, dear," Miss Schmitt exclaimed as the ship crested a wave then fell again. "I do hope I'm not going to be seasick. I don't think I'm a very good sailor and one has heard that the Atlantic can be so rough."

"It's all a question of mind over matter," Miss Pinkerton said. "You simply tell yourself that you are not going to be ill. You eat hearty meals and take plenty of exercise."

"Quite right," one of the widows exclaimed. They were a Mrs. Bush and a Mrs. Cowper but I hadn't worked out which was which. Then she added, "And I always bring

113

ginger pills to suck. Most effective. I'll give you one after dinner, Maude."

I had crossed the Atlantic twice before and hadn't experienced any seasickness so I hoped for the best this time. Liam seemed to think the whole idea of rolling side to side was quite fun. In fact he had been no trouble at all this first day at sea. I fell asleep watching two dressing gowns swing like pendulums on the cabin door.

Next morning we awoke to clouds racing across a pale sky and a noticeable swell to the ocean, making it hard to walk straight along the passageway. We breakfasted, I played with Liam, and after I put him down for a morning nap, I decided to venture out on deck. As I stepped out into the wind, I had the door wrenched out of my hand and slammed shut. It was lucky that I wasn't wearing a hat or it would have gone sailing over the side. There were whitecaps on a slate-colored ocean and no sign of any living thing. It made me realize how small and insignificant even the largest ocean liner really is. I stared out to the north, looking for icebergs. A young officer passed me and smiled. "You are brave to come outside when it blows such a gale," he said in such a charmingly French accent that it could almost belong on a stage. "You must be an

American demoiselle. The French ladies, they do not venture forth when it blows like this. They worry about their coiffure, their hats, and that the wind will make their faces red."

I laughed. "I don't have much of a coiffure to worry about. My hair refuses to be tamed."

"Like its owner, perhaps?" and he gave me a most flirtatious look, which should have outraged me and prompted me to tell him I was a married woman. Actually it raised my spirits.

"I was looking for icebergs," I said. "Do you think we'll see one?"

"I sincerely hope not," he said. "They have been a constant worry this spring, coming further south than is normal. The captain has decided to take a more southerly course than normal. We would have sailed close to Newfoundland, but that puts us in the path of stray icebergs. So we cross the open Atlantic and risk more storms and high seas. But that is surely better than meeting an iceberg during the night."

"Are we in for a stormy crossing, do you think?"

He shrugged in that Gallic way. "The signs are not good. But do not worry. This ship can handle the worst of seas. I have seen waves like mountains . . ."

Somehow I didn't find this comforting. "Will it not make our voyage quicker if we sail directly across the ocean, rather than going so far north?" I asked.

"The opposite," he said. "You see, the Earth is like an orange, no? If we make an arc like this" — and he drew a rainbow shape with his finger in the air — "it is actually a shorter distance than traveling like this. You understand?"

I didn't really but I nodded. "So will we arrive on schedule?"

"Let us hope. I suspect we will be a little late, unless the wind moves to the west and drives us along with the waves. But we will get you there safely, have no doubt." He saluted, gave me another saucy grin, and went on his way. I continued my walk and when I reached the leeward side of the ship out of the worst of the wind I paused to catch my breath. It was then that I noticed I was not alone. The mysterious girl was standing at the railing, staring out to sea, her light hair streaming out in the breeze.

I went to join her at the railing. "I'm glad the wind isn't quite as fierce on this side," I said. "I thought I was going to get blown away."

She turned and looked at me, then she

grinned. "You look as if you almost were blown away."

I put my hand up to my head. "My hair must look a frightful sight. It won't stay pinned up at the best of times."

"I don't put mine up," she said. "I like the feel of it around my shoulders. I don't think one should have to conform, do you?"

"I'm afraid one does have to eventually," I said. "I haven't always conformed. I have never worn a corset, for one thing. But once you are married it's different."

"You mean you have to obey your husband?" and she wrinkled her button of a nose.

"Not 'obey' necessarily, but not do anything that might let him down or damage his position. I've had to learn to temper what I say. I've always been a trifle hotheaded."

"Me too."

"Are you going to Paris? If so you'll find plenty of people who don't like to conform, so I've heard."

She frowned. "I'm joining my fiancé and his family there. They've been in London and sent me a ticket to join them. But they are Bostonians. Everything has to be done properly and with decorum."

"Then I don't think you'll be going to the

Moulin Rouge or Montmartre."

A wicked smile twinkled in her eyes. "They expected me to sail on an American ship out of Boston but I found this one sailing a week earlier. I plan to enjoy my freedom in Paris before they arrive."

"Mercy," I said. "Your family must be very modern if they will let you run around Paris on your own."

The wicked smile spread. "They don't know. They think I'll be meeting Peter straight away." Then a little sigh. "I had to make the most of my one moment of freedom, didn't I? When I marry Peter I'll have to behave like a Boston matron and hold tea parties."

"I know just how you feel," I said. "I only married recently and I certainly had to think hard about giving up my freedom. But surely you're not traveling alone?"

"No, not exactly. Mademoiselle is with me. She was the French teacher at my old seminary and she is returning home to France so she was asked to accompany me to Paris. I just have to make sure she doesn't find out that Peter won't be joining me for a few days. She'd have hysterics and cable Mama and all would be lost."

Finally I dared to pose the question I had been longing to ask. "Has anyone told you that you look remarkably like the girl in the Reynold Bryce —"

"I know," she snapped, cutting me off. "But I assure you I'm no angel."

"Then it's just a coincidence?"

"No. We're related. Her real name is Adelaide and she's my aunt."

"Your aunt?"

She nodded. "My mother was the oldest of five sisters. Adelaide is the youngest."

I wondered how far I dared to pursue this. "Did I understand that your aunt had been ill?"

Her face became stony. "Aunt Adelaide is of a delicate nature. She is afraid of many things and does not like to venture outside the home, that's all."

Again I remembered the eyes of that child in the portrait. They had not seemed fearful. Had Reynold Bryce created her as he wanted her to be and not as she was?

"Are you acquainted with Reynold Bryce too? What does he say about this resemblance?"

"I've never met him," she said. "He went to Paris before I was born and he never comes home these days. But I do plan to call on him when I'm in Paris. It should be rather fun to meet a real artist, don't you think?"

"It should. I have friends who are hoping to be introduced to him. My friend is an artist, or rather wants to be recognized as an artist."

"How lovely to be able to paint, or to do something exciting. I've been to a young ladies academy where all they care about is manners and looking pretty. So boring." She sounded like a typical girl of her age and rolled her eyes, making me smile.

"Do other family members have such a strong resemblance to your aunt?" I asked. "What about your brothers and sisters?"

"I'm an only child," she said. "My father died before I was born so I never knew him. For many years it was just Mama and me, but then she married again."

"Ah, so you have a stepfather?"

"I do, and I hate him." She spat out the words with venom. "He treats me like a child and won't let me do anything. I had a nice sum of money settled on me and he won't let me touch it. He is rude and overbearing and a bully. I can't wait to escape."

Ah, I thought. So that was why she was marrying the very proper Bostonian — to escape the domination of a hated stepfather. I was about to tell her not to rush into marriage with someone she didn't love when a

120

woman came flying down the deck, arms waving. "Ellie, so there you are, you naughty girl," she called as if the girl was five and not a young woman about to be married. "Again you escape from me. Did I not tell you that it is not seemly to walk on the deck alone. One does not know if you will meet a sailor."

"Ooh, I do hope so," Ellie replied with a wink to me. "Besides I have met this charming married lady who is chaperoning me perfectly."

The Frenchwoman looked me up and down and noted the quality of my dress. "*Mille pardons,* madame," she said. "I apologize for my charge. She is headstrong and will come a cropper one day, I think."

"I suspect Miss Ellie was like me. She needed to breathe some fresh sea air, rather than be stuck in the lounge all day. And as you see, no harm has come of her."

The Frenchwoman gave me a nod, then took Ellie's arm. "Come inside now. You will catch a nasty chill in this cold air without your shawl around you."

Ellie looked back in my direction as she was led away. "I hope to see you again soon," she said and I realized I hadn't given her my name. As I went to find the nearest door to the second-class portion of the ship

I heard the chaperone say, "You must learn not to talk to strange women, Eleanor. She had a most wild appearance and she was Irish too. What's more I do not believe I saw her in the first-class dining room."

I decided that I was heartily glad that Ellie was going to have those few days of freedom in Paris.

TEN

Of course I had to relate my findings to the ladies at the dinner table, but I gave just the bare bones of the story — that Angela in the painting was really called Adelaide and was the girl's aunt. Also that Ellie had denied her aunt was mentally defective, merely anxious and timid and did not like to leave the house. I refrained from mentioning that Ellie had planned to spend a week alone in Paris or that she hated her stepfather. The women were impressed with my sleuthing and, having found out the truth, turned their gossip to other passengers, especially a couple whom they suspected of not really being husband and wife.

The dressing gowns on the cabin door swung a little more that night and I awoke in the morning to a gloomy gray day with rain peppering the windows. The promenade deck was deserted, apart from a sailor who was swabbing it down, looking very miserable in the process. There was no question of going outside. I sat reading in the lounge. Liam played, crawling over to other passengers and being fussed over everywhere. There was a concert in the afternoon and a whist drive in which I didn't participate but which was won by our two widows, much to their satisfaction. I could feel myself slipping into a pleasant slow routine in a safe cocoon with the real world and its problems slipping farther and farther away. I had to remind myself from time to time that I had left a husband alone and in danger in New York.

In the middle of the night I was awoken by Liam's cries. I went over to his crib and found that he had been sick all over his bedding. This was strange as he seemed to be enjoying the ship's motion until now and had eaten well that evening. I called the night steward and had new bedding brought for Liam, but he vomited again and again. I fed him boiled sugar water from a spoon but he wasn't able to keep it down. I began to feel frightened. This was more than simple seasickness. I suspected something in the pureed food had upset his delicate digestive system, or, worse still, had poisoned him. Of course all this commotion awoke Miss Pinkerton. I apologized but she was touchingly concerned and asked if there was anything she could do. Really there was nothing, but sleep was impossible with a child screaming and vomiting nearby.

In the morning he fell into exhausted slumber and I sent my own soiled night-clothes to be laundered. When he awoke he was listless as he sucked at the breast, but then promptly vomited again. I had the steward summon the ship's doctor. He came, examined Liam, and said it could be food poisoning or a particularly virulent stomach grippe that sometimes went around confined quarters like ships at sea. Either way there was nothing to be done except to try to keep some liquids down him, and maybe give him a little tincture of opium to help him sleep. I declined the latter and held him in my arms, offering the breast whenever he awoke. He had never been sick before in his life and it terrified me to see my normally lively child lying there, his skin clammy to the touch and barely responsive. Even his cry had become weak, like a kitten's.

I consoled myself with the knowledge that we would be landing in France the next day. But then Miss Pinkerton came down to the cabin to report that there was stormy

weather ahead and we would not make Le
Havre on Friday, as scheduled, but a day
late. My spirits fell at such news. A sick son
and now a storm ahead. I didn't leave the
cabin but I could tell immediately when we
sailed into the storm. The ship creaked and
groaned, and there was even the occasional
deep resounding thump as she slapped
against an extra large wave or fell into the
trough behind it. It was hard to keep my
balance when I stood up with Liam in my
arms. Miss Pinkerton returned to report
that half the passengers were now seasick,
the crew was working busily to secure
anything not bolted down and to swab
floors. Not a pleasant atmosphere, she said
with her typical understatement.

I suppose it was because I had been up all
night and hadn't eaten properly, and also
that the air in the room was stale and tinged
with my child's vomit, but suddenly I too
was overcome with seasickness. I heaved.
The room spun around. I lay on my bunk,
being flung from side to side, wishing I were
dead. The steward brought me a basin, a
wet washcloth, and some tea. It lay on the
table untouched until a particularly violent
wave sent it crashing to the floor. Up above
I could hear the distant sound of objects
falling and breaking. I tried to sit up to

nurse Liam but he would hardly take anything. In my current state I might not have been producing milk anyway.

The next twenty-four hours were like a never ending nightmare. Miss Pinkerton observed my current state and took charge, bringing me down bouillon, ice water, and ginger tea and tempting me to drink. She reported the dining room was less than half full at lunch time, and by dinner there were only twelve people apart from herself and Miss Hetherington. The widows and Miss Schmitt had also succumbed. I spent the night alternately worrying that the ship might go down and then wishing it would so that I could be out of my misery. The night seemed to go on forever and having an inside cabin with no porthole meant that I had no idea when dawn was breaking and whether the day showed any promise of improving conditions.

Miss Pinkerton went up to breakfast and came back to report triumphantly that there were only three people in the dining room and that the waiter had turned positively green when she asked if she might have scrambled eggs and bacon to keep her strength up. She also reported that the upright piano in the second-class lounge had broken loose from its moorings during the night and had careened about the room, demolishing everything in its path as well as itself. All that was left was the keyboard, standing up like a skeleton with the pedals sticking out below it.

When I didn't smile she bent closer to me. "My dear, you must make an effort, for your child's sake. How can you provide him with the nourishment he needs if you just lie there? Come on now, buck up. Try sitting up and sipping a little broth."

"I can't," I wailed. "The room spins around and I feel as if I'm going to faint."

"Nonsense. Remember what we said before? Mind over matter, dear. Mind over matter."

I tried, closing my eyes as the walls lurched around me. I staggered across to the crib and picked up Liam. His eyes fluttered open, then closed again. His cheeks already looked hollow and sunken. I made a supreme effort and spooned a little of that broth into his mouth. He moved his tongue a little as if he liked the taste. I tried a little more, then put him to the breast. He sucked a few times before falling back to sleep. I hoped this was a good sign. God knows I needed some kind of good sign right now.

The ship continued to roll violently all day. We should have been arriving in Le

Havre right now, I thought. I thought of Sid and Gus, awaiting my telegram to say that I was on my way to Paris. What if they worried and cabled Daniel, making him worry too? The thought of seeing them, of knowing I was in safe and capable hands, made me feel a little hope for the first time. By nightfall I tried a little bouillon and a small square of dry toast, then fell asleep.

The next morning I awoke to complete silence and darkness. It was so eerie that I experienced a moment's panic, fearing that I had died and was in a coffin. "I'm alive!" I shouted and tried to stand up, banging my head against the top bunk. That, of course, brought me back to the reality of where I was. I felt my way across the room and turned on the electric light. Miss Pinkerton, still sleeping in the top bunk, groaned and raised her head. "What is going on?" she asked. "Ah, you're standing. That's a good sign. But it's only five o'clock. Too early to get up yet."

"We're not rocking anymore," I said. "And it's so quiet."

"That probably means we have docked in Le Havre," she said. "I will put on my robe and go up on deck, if you like."

She climbed down nimbly, put on her robe, and left the cabin. Liam slept on, which was rather alarming. I stood over his crib, watching him breathe, and finally couldn't stand it any longer and gave him a little shake. He woke up instantly, looking around him with frightened, bewildered eyes. When he saw me he held out his arms and started to cry. Then vertigo overcame me again and I had to sit down, gathering what little strength I had before I could pick him up. I had just about managed to bring him over to my bunk when Miss Pinkerton appeared again.

"Good news. We are in port. They are just making fast the lines now. And it is daylight and not raining. In fact it promises to be a fine day. So how are you feeling?"

"Like a limp rag," I said. "I still can't stand up without the world spinning around."

"Of course you can't," she said. "You've both been very ill. I have been concerned about you. And if you take my advice you will not attempt to travel anywhere today. Take a pension in Le Havre until you are both fit to resume your journey."

"I'm being met by friends in Paris," I said. "I'm sure they'll take good care of me and know what is best."

"But that child should be seen by a competent doctor as soon as possible. I didn't like the look of the one on the ship. Never trust a man with big mustaches."

I had to smile at this, the motion feeling strange and unpracticed after days of worry.

"I'm going to get dressed and then go up to breakfast," she said. "I'll have something sent down for you. What do you fancy?"

"I don't think I could eat anything yet," I said. "Maybe a cup of tea."

"The French have no idea how to make proper tea," she said. "But peppermint or chamomile might be good for you. And a boiled egg. That's what you need. I'll go up and order it. None of this nonsense about bread and jam for breakfast. I told them 'We are Americans. We expect a hearty breakfast not this mamby-pamby nonsense.' "

As soon as she had left I staggered down the hall to the bathroom and attempted to wash. I had to lean against the wall to prevent myself from passing out, and only just made it back to the cabin. I washed and changed Liam and nursed him. He seemed a little more interested but horribly weak, like me. Then I took a clean dress from the closet and was going to change out of my nightclothes when I was overcome with nausea and dizziness again and had to lie down. At that moment there was a tap on

131

the door and the steward entered with a tray containing a pot of tea, a boiled egg, and toast. The tea was weak and slightly scented, made in the French manner, but for now that suited me just fine. I sipped at it, then dipped the toast in the boiled egg. I was going to finish it when I decided to try some for Liam. He sucked away with enthusiasm at this new flavor so I gave the rest of the yolk to him, then ate a few spoonfuls of white myself. This gave me just enough energy to take my clothes from the closet ready for repacking and I was dressed with my hair up when Miss Pinkerton returned.

"Ah, there you are," she said, giving me a nod of satisfaction. "I'm glad to see you're up and about again. So the boiled egg did the trick, did it? I knew it would. My friends also came to breakfast today looking like death warmed over. Miss Hetherington had to force Miss Schmitt to eat an egg. 'It's for your own good,' she told her. We can't have anyone lagging behind on the tour." She looked at the open closet door. "Ah, I see you have your things ready for repacking. I believe the trunks are in the hall outside. I'll bring yours in and help you pack. I don't suppose you're up to that yet."

She did and packed with great efficiency while Liam and I watched. Finally the news came that we could clear immigration in the second-class lounge and then were free to go ashore. Porters arrived to whisk away the luggage. I thanked my patient steward and tipped him as generously as I was able. He wished me and *"le petit"* well and Miss Pinkerton helped us up to the lounge and then, after the minimum of formalities, toward the gangplank. The bright sunlight was so strong after days in my windowless cabin that I stood blinking and almost blinded.

"Come along, my dear." Miss Pinkerton took my arm firmly and led me down the gangway to the dock below. We located the porter with my luggage and followed him through customs before emerging to the street beyond with the station on one side and a line of horse-drawn cabs at the curb. I fought to keep my balance as the ground still rocked under me as if I was at sea.

"I must send a telegram to my friends telling them which train I am taking," I said to Miss Pinkerton, who was still standing beside me. "They promised to meet me at the station."

"Very well. Leave the luggage and your child here with me." She turned to the porter. *"Attendez ici. Elle va à la gare,"* she said in an atrocious French accent.

133

Off I went into the station. A train was standing at the platform, puffing smoke as if impatient to leave. I saw from the board that it would be departing in fifteen minutes. Everywhere there was commotion as porters flung baggage aboard and doors slammed. I decided that I was in no condition to rush and join that hubbub. I'd take the next train in an hour and a half. That would give me enough time to locate a telegraph office and send a telegram. As I made my way back I began to feel worse and worse. The ground still lurched as if I was at sea. My head started spinning. I could see Miss Pinkerton with Liam in her arms. He was wriggling and crying for me and she was looking as if she didn't quite know what to do. I staggered toward them as the singing in my head grew louder and louder until suddenly the world went black.

ELEVEN

I came to, spluttering, as smelling salts were waved under my nose and saw a circle of people around me. Among the faces, I recognized Miss Pinkerton's friends. Then I saw Liam's frightened face in Miss Pinkerton's arms.

"What happened?" For a moment I couldn't remember.

"You fainted. Most dramatic. Went down like a tree," Miss Hetherington said. She was kneeling beside me. It had been her smelling salts that had revived me and she now held her handkerchief to my forehead, where I had apparently struck it as I fell. "Nasty knock on the head too. That will need to be cleaned up."

"There's a train in an hour and a half," I said.

"Sit here." Miss Hetherington dragged me onto the bench and said, "Keep this handkerchief pressed to the cut. I don't think you should be going anywhere in an hour and half. Utter folly."

"Quite right," Miss Pinkerton agreed. "You are in no condition to travel to Paris today. Your son needs to see a doctor. You need to get that cut seen to and we don't want you passing out again. We'll find you a room in a hotel nearby and you can stay there until you are sufficiently recovered."

"But I'll be all right if you can help me onto the train," I protested. "You'll be coming to Paris, won't you?"

"Actually not," Miss Hetherington said. "Since three of us have been so affected by the crossing we decided we should recuperate here before embarking on a long train journey. We'll take you to a pension with us. You can send a telegram to your friends explaining that you have been delayed. Now stay there. I will locate a vehicle for us."

And off she went, striding out toward the waiting line of carriages.

I was too weak to resist because I knew in my heart that she was right. The ground still swayed and my head was now throbbing like billy-o. I thought I might be sick again. Liam whined and wanted to come to me.

"Mommy is resting," Miss Pinkerton said, holding onto him firmly. "She'll be fine in a minute. Just be a good boy."

The women were wonderful. Although they only spoke a few words of French they managed with gestures and sheer determination to have us loaded into a large open carriage and taken to a pension on the waterfront. Miss Hetherington inspected the rooms and pronounced them clean if simple and unadorned. I was half dragged up the stairs. Someone else brought my bags and I was placed in a small room with shutters half closed. Already exhausted by this amount of activity, I lay back gratefully with Liam beside me. They then had the proprietor summon a doctor and gave me pen and paper to draft a telegram to Sid and Gus. I wrote, *Delayed in Le Havre. Unwell. Pension Bellevue. Will travel as soon as able.*

Off went the stalwart Miss Hetherington to have this sent to Paris. Miss Pinkerton stayed with me while the other women went for a stroll along the seafront. A doctor arrived and pronounced Liam on the road to recovery but instructed me to confine his diet to breast milk and boiled sugar water to give his stomach time to heal. Then he patched up my head, and recommended that I get plenty of good nourishing food and fresh air. It would be foolish and dangerous to think of continuing my journey until I was stronger, he said, wagging a finger at me. To do so might put me and my child in danger of a relapse. Then he gave me a prescription for a tonic and bid me adieu.

I lay in my narrow bed, feeling like a limp rag and so glad that I was not facing an almost three-hour train journey. I don't think I could have sat upright for that long. The proprietress came in with a tray of fresh rolls and peppermint tea. I sipped the tea, managed a whole roll, and felt a little stronger. Liam nursed, then fell asleep beside me. I lay back too, feeling the fresh sea air coming in through the shutters.

I awoke to Liam crawling over me in an attempt to escape from the bed. My head still throbbed but my stomach felt less queasy; in fact, I felt a little hungry. I stood up, held onto the wall because the ground still swayed, then made my way across to the window and pushed open the shutters. Below me was a glorious scene. The sun sparkled on blue water. Red-sailed fishing boats were bobbing in the harbor. Fishermen in bright blue smocks were unloading their catch on the dock. The air resounded to the cries of seagulls. Two young children walked past wearing a local costume and wooden shoes. It was all so picturesque and so foreign.

"Look Liam," I said, picking him up. "We're in France."

By lunchtime the tonic had been delivered. It was a dark sludge that tasted disgusting but I dutifully swallowed a tablespoonful. I was served a hearty bowl of soup and sat in a chair by the window, wondering if Sid and Gus would send me a telegram in reply. Actually I was half hoping that they would come to Le Havre themselves to escort me to Paris. It was the sort of thing they would do. But when darkness fell there was no word from them. For dinner I managed a freshly caught sole and buttery potatoes. Liam was also showing interest in food again and was quite annoyed when all he was offered was the breast.

After a good night's sleep I began to feel more like myself and suggested that I might travel on to Paris that day. My head was now clear enough that I was also thinking of the extra cost of another night at a pension. Miss Hetherington wouldn't hear of it. Her sick friends didn't feel up to the long train journey to Venice yet. She said we would all stay one day more and then travel as far as Paris together. They would then continue on to Venice, and I'd be in the capable hands of my friends. Since my legs felt like jelly after coming down the stairs to breakfast I had to agree that traveling with friends would be preferable to traveling alone and trying to manage Liam and my luggage when I felt as weak as a kitten. So I agreed and thanked them for all they had done.

"Nonsense. We unprotected women must stick together," Miss Hetherington said.

So I spent a second delightful day sitting in the lounge overlooking the seafront. First I wrote to Daniel, telling him that I had arrived safely in France but that I was resting in Le Havre due to a bad case of seasickness. I thought it prudent not to mention that Liam had also been very ill. No need to worry him when he had so much to worry about already. I told him I'd send another letter as soon as I reached Sid and Gus.

This small task left me quite tired and I lay back in my chair, watching the busy scene in the harbor outside my window. It was all so foreign and fascinating with peasant ladies in white lace caps and the fishermen in their blue smocks, contrasting with the red sails. No wonder the Impressionist painters were so keen to paint here. After lunch Therese, the landlady's daughter, came to amuse Liam, whose eyes no longer looked sunken. It was a huge relief to hear him laugh loudly when Therese knocked down a tower of blocks. I tried him on a little mashed potato and gravy that night and he ate well. It seemed that our ordeal was finally at an end. By tomorrow night I'd be safely with Sid and Gus.

In the morning we set off, the wagon piled high with ourselves and our luggage, for the station. I noted the departure time of the train then paid a boy to deliver my telegram to the telegraph office. Sid and Gus would probably be waiting anxiously, I thought. They'd be so relieved to know I was all right and finally on my way. Miss Hetherington found an empty compartment for the six of us plus Liam and the train pulled out of the station. Yesterday's good weather had given way to a steady rain as we made our way toward the capital city. The French countryside looked bleak and gray, rainswept scenes of fields divided by lines of poplar trees, just coming into leaf. We passed the massive cathedral at Reims, rising above the sloping roofs of the town.

"Catholics, of course," Miss Pinkerton said when the other women remarked how magnificent it was. "Why can't Protestants build decent cathedrals?"

Liam had just fallen asleep on my lap

when we came into the outer suburbs of Paris. After having lived in New York for four years, the thing that struck me was that this was a city of low buildings. In New York we were used to new skyscrapers and apartment blocks. Even the tenements were five or six floors high. Here church spires and domes rose above rooftops. And to my disappointment these buildings did not resemble my vision of Paris. They were small and mean and dirty, reminding me of the back streets of Belfast or Liverpool. The only difference was that these houses all had shutters, some brightly painted, some peeling. And there were bright advertising signs painted on house walls. Signs advertising Gauloises cigarettes and Dubonnet and other unfamiliar names. Then I spotted something in the distance above the rooftops, an ironwork tower, impossibly high. I pointed excitedly.

"Look," I said. "Over there."

"Goodness me," Miss Pinkerton exclaimed. "I heard it was quite a monstrosity, and it is, isn't it? I wonder they didn't take it down after the exhibition."

"I suppose it's progress," Miss Hetherington said. "We must get used to such things. Skyscrapers and Eiffel Towers. Impressionists and Post-Impressionists who daub on colors willy-nilly and call it painting. That's what the world is coming to."

Personally I thought the Eiffel Tower was spectacular and gazed at it until the train went around a bend and it was lost. The train was slowing, and with a final huff and puff we pulled into Saint-Lazare station. Porters swarmed into the carriage, whisking away bags so rapidly that one never expected to find them again. I stood on the steps of our carriage looking out over the crowd and the smoke, an expectant smile on my face, as I tried to spot Sid and Gus.

"Do you require a taxicab?" the porter who was balancing the mountain of our luggage on a barrow asked.

"We require to be taken to the Gare de Lyon to catch our train to Venice," Miss Hetherington said in efficient French. "This young lady will be met by her friends. You may leave her luggage here and take ours out to the curb."

"Do you see your friends yet?" Miss Pinkerton asked.

I was still looking around, Liam perched on one hip. "No, not yet."

"Why don't you stay here with the bags and we'll go and locate them for you," Miss Hetherington said. "What do they look like?"

I described Sid's cropped black hair and mannish attire and Gus's predilection for peasant clothing and shawls. Miss Hetherington looked aghast. "Sapphists are they? Bohemians? My dear, are you sure you should be staying with them? One hears the most extraordinary things about the way these artists live. I'm not sure that your husband would approve, seeing that he works in government."

I assured her that Daniel knew all about Sid and Gus, who were my neighbors at home, and that they were my dear friends. Miss Hetherington gave me a strange look before she sent her troops out across the station to find Sid and Gus. They returned ten minutes later to say that there was no sign of them.

"Oh, dear," I said. "I wonder if the telegram was never delivered. I thought it was strange when they didn't reply to me or even come to Le Havre to escort me. I suppose I'd better take a cab to their residence."

"They are expecting you?" Miss Pinkerton asked. "These artistic types are known to be flighty."

"They know I'm coming. They responded to my cable."

"Well, then. We'll help you into a cab and all will be well." She motioned to a porter to bring my trunk and carpet bag to a waiting fiacre. Liam and I were loaded in. I shook hands all around and thanked them again for their kindness. Then the driver flicked at the whip and off we went, rattling over the cobbles.

"Is it far?" I called out to the cabby over the noise of the hoofs and wheels.

"No, madame. Not far at all. Ten minutes."

We left the noise and bustle of the station and immediately we were in a street more like the Paris I had dreamed of as a child. The street was lined with plane trees and on either side were light-yellow stone buildings, four and five stories high, decorated with wrought-iron balconies. Some of them had shops at street level, with bright awnings hanging over them, and there was a café on the corner with tables outside on the sidewalk. Nobody was sitting at the tables as it was still drizzling, but a man and woman walked arm in arm under his big umbrella — the woman holding the leash of a small poodle dog. On the corner was a flower seller standing beside her barrow of spring flowers. We turned into a treelined square with a lovely ornate gray stone church on one side. Two priests in flat black hats were standing on the steps and a bell was tolling.

But right after the church we entered a smaller street and clearly a less salubrious area. There were bars and gaudy signs for cabarets mixed in with green-grocers and bookstores. There was even an occasional girl lounging against a wall trailing a feather boa. I'd seen enough of them in New York to recognize what she was, making it clear that this area might be more active when the sun went down.

I also saw that we were coming into the Paris of artists. We passed three of them, walking together, one of them carrying a canvas while his friends were in animated conversation, gesturing with their hands. We emerged into an open area with a fountain in the middle. A street sign announced it to be the Place Pigalle and I vaguely remembered having heard of it. Then I saw a windmill, illuminated with electric lights and knew why. This was the famed Moulin Rouge cabaret where the cancan was born and the girls wore next to nothing. The boulevard that led from Pigalle was wide and treelined but almost immediately we turned into a narrow side street that ascended a hill. There were shops and cafés close to Place Pigalle but as the street went up the hill it became more residential. The cab halted.

"Is this it?" I asked.

"*Oui,* madame. Rue des Martyrs." He climbed down, took Liam from me, and assisted me. "I will bring the baggage," he said, handing Liam back to me as the child started to cry.

I managed to open the heavy wrought-iron and glass front door with my free hand and entered into a dark foyer. There was a faint smell of drains, and someone had been cooking with garlic. On one side of the foyer a flight of stone stairs curved up. The only adornment was a large, sad-looking potted plant on a marble table and a speckled mirror on the wall. As I stood looking around, wondering which apartment might be Sid and Gus's, I noticed that there was an open doorway beside the front door, leading to a dark cubbyhole. As I approached it a large woman emerged. She was dressed in a high-collared black dress. Her dark hair was pulled back severely from her sallow face and she wore a black cap with trailing black ribbons perched on her head.

"*Bonjour,* madame," I said, smiling at her.

"What do you want?" she asked, staring at me as if I was a worm that had just crawled onto her clean floor. "There are no rooms available if you are looking for one."

I recoiled at the unfriendly reception. "I'm

here to visit my friends, Mademoiselle Walcott and Mademoiselle Goldfarb, who reside here," I said, my brain wrestling with long-forgotten French. "I am Madame Sullivan, just arrived from America. Perhaps you can tell me the number of their apartment."

She folded her arms across a large bosom. "They are not here," she said coldly.

TWELVE

"Pardon?" I asked, not sure that I'd understood her correctly.

She repeated it, spitting out the words slowly as if for an idiot.

Of course, I thought, realizing my stupidity. They had gone to the station to meet me as planned and somehow been delayed. I should have waited longer.

"I expect they went out to meet me at the station and somehow we missed each other," I said in my halting French. "Do they keep their door locked, do you know? Or do you have a key so that I can go up and wait until they come back?"

"I told you, madame. They are not here," she repeated. "They have gone."

"Gone? Gone where?" I demanded. I could hear my voice, shrill and echoing in the tall narrow hall.

"How do I know? I have not seen them for one, maybe two days. At least I know they did not return home last night because they were not here when I locked the front door at eleven. This is a respectable household. The door is always locked at night."

"And they didn't tell you where they were going?"

"I am the concierge, not their confidante," she said. "I do not ask questions. They pay their rent and what they do with their time is their own. The rent is paid until the end of the month. It matters not to me whether they are here or not." And she gave a very Gallic shrug.

"But they are awaiting me," I said. "I sent a cable from America. They replied that they were glad I was coming. They told me to send a telegram to inform them which train I was taking from Le Havre and they would come to meet me." I fought to find the words to make this clear to her in French. "Did a telegram not arrive for them this morning?"

"The telegraph boy did come. I told him they were not here. He went again."

By now the cabby had brought my bags into the hall and stood there behind me, waiting to be paid.

"This is mad," I said, not knowing the word for ridiculous. "It doesn't make sense. They are not the type of people who would

150

depart and not tell me."

But a small voice nagged at the back of my brain that they were that type of people. They did lots of crazy things on impulse. The one thing they wouldn't do would be to let down a friend.

She shrugged again. "What can I say? If they are not here, you cannot visit them, can you? I suggest that madame return her bags to the vehicle and go to a hotel until her friends come back. If they decide to come back, that is."

I was tired, I was weak. The floor was beginning to sway again as if I was back on the ship, and now I was angry too. "Absolutely not," I said. I opened my purse and rummaged in it. "Look." I waved a piece of paper at her. "Here is their cable. Do you see? I will translate if you don't read English. It says, 'So excited you are coming to stay. Send telegram with arrival time and will meet train at Saint-Lazare.' You see. They are expecting me. Obviously something has delayed them but they will return shortly. Now please escort me to their room and I will await their return."

My confidence in speaking a foreign tongue grew with my indignation until at the end I was gesturing with my free hand like a true Frenchwoman. She sighed. "Very well. I will take you to their rooms, if you insist. You'll have to wait for the trunk. My husband will bring it up when he returns. Me, I do not intend to carry it up five flights of stairs." She started for the staircase. "Follow me," she said.

I hoisted Liam higher on my hip, and followed her up the stairs, then a second flight, then a third. Our footsteps echoed in the high stairwell. We passed closed doors on each landing, there was no sign of life except for the woman in black and myself. As we started the fourth flight my weakness overcame me and I began to feel dizzy again.

"I must stop and rest," I said, leaning against the bannister. "I have been unwell. That was why I couldn't travel on from Le Havre before this. I should have been here two days ago."

She spun around, glaring at me. "I hope you don't bring a sickness into this house. What was wrong with you?"

"Mal de mer," I said. "The ship came through a bad storm."

"Oh, *mal de mer.*" She shrugged again as if I was making a fuss over nothing. "You are not at sea now, are you?" And on she went again, up the next flight, leaving me to stagger after her with Liam in my arms.

I managed to keep going because I had to

and I was terrified of fainting with Liam in my arms. At the top of the stairwell there was a skylight and rain drummed on it loudly. The concierge stopped outside one of the doors, now breathing heavily herself, and stood, hand on bosom, catching her breath, before she produced a bunch of keys from her belt. She examined them, selected a key, then turned it in the keyhole. "Voilà, madame," she said, and motioned for me to go in. "As you can see. There is nobody here. I leave you to decide what action you wish to take."

"I will stay and await my friends," I said. "And I will need a key if I choose to go out. Do you perhaps have an extra one?"

"In my office, downstairs," she said. "I will want a deposit of five francs."

"Madame is kind," I said, with sarcasm. "I am Madame Sullivan. May I know your name?"

"Hetreau," she said. "Madame Hetreau."

I nodded, not able to bring myself to say I was pleased to make her acquaintance.

"I'll leave you then," she said, and slammed the door shut behind her.

I stood alone in a large, light room; sparsely furnished and with a cold, damp feel to it. The smell of oil paints, linseed oil, and foreign cigarettes lingered in the air.

The high ceiling was molded and an improbably grand chandelier hung in the center of it. On one side long windows opened onto a narrow, wrought-iron balcony. Rain was streaking those long windows.

"Hello?" I called hopefully. No reply.

A look around me revealed a faded velvet sofa and two high-backed armchairs on one side, a dining table on the other, and in the window an easel set up with a canvas on it, a sheet beneath to catch the spatters. A palette of paints rested on a table beside it and brushes stood in a glass jar of some kind of cleaning fluid — was it turpentine? I tried to remember.

As I walked over to examine the painting I spotted Gus's favorite black fringed shawl thrown carelessly over the back of the sofa. A book lay open on a side table. Sid's ebony-and-silver cigarette holder lay across an ashtray. There was a loaf of bread on the table, crumbs on plates, fruit in the fruit bowl, a cheese board with rind lying on it. Everything about the scene indicated that this was a room in which people had been living until very recently. More than that — as if people were in the process of living in it at this moment. I half expected them to come leaping out from that door on the left, laughing at my face. "Surprised you, didn't we, Molly. How did you like our little trick?"

But then I reasoned that they were playful but not cruel. Surely they would not have put me through something as harrowing as this, knowing I had been ill. And anyway, the concierge had said they were not here. Presumably she had checked before she locked the door last night. And the messenger boy had been sent away with the telegram undelivered. Then I noticed that among the correspondence on the mantelpiece there was another telegram — the one I sent from the dock saying that I was unfit to travel on from Le Havre.

Could it be that they went to meet me there after all? And couldn't find me for some reason? Perhaps they mistook the name of the pension in which I was staying, or . . . I broke off this train of thought as I tried to remember . . . did I actually say I was docking in Le Havre? Surely Daniel had done so in his cable to them. But what if neither of us had spelled it out and they had mistakenly gone to Cherbourg instead? I gave a sigh of relief at having come up with a plausible explanation and went to explore the rest of the apartment. There was a small kitchen to one side of the living room. On the other was a hallway with a large but rather primitive bathroom containing an enormous claw-footed tub, a lavatory, and a bidet. Beyond it was a bedroom with a ridiculously ornate bed and a chest that might have come from Versailles, and finally a small box room containing a narrow bed, made up with fresh linens, and beside it a baby's crib. Seeing this brought tears to my eyes. They were expecting me. They did know I was coming. I'd have to show this to the hostile concierge woman to prove that I had a right to be here.

I went back to the main room, put Liam down on a bearskin rug by the fireplace, and wondered about lighting a fire. It felt awfully cold and damp. There were ashes in the grate, quite cold, but there was a half-full scuttle of coal beside it. I found newspaper and started a fire. The chimney was smoky but I began to feel better as the welcome warmth spread across the big room. I sat in the armchair by the fire and nursed Liam. Then as he fell asleep, I put him in the crib and decided that I felt hungry myself. The remains of the meal on the dining table looked inviting until I discovered that the bread was hard as a rock. I cut myself a slice of white soft cheese and then scooped some pâté out of a crock. Suddenly tiredness overcame me and I went to lie down next to Liam. *When I wake up they'll be here,* I told myself.

I awoke to thunderous knocking and leaped up, my heart pounding. For a moment I couldn't remember where I was but then I ran for the front door, hoping for a telegram. *Have been detained. See you tomorrow,* or something that might explain their disappearance. But it was only a thin and bony Frenchman with a drooping mustache bringing up my trunk. He lingered as if he expected a tip, then grunted when I gave him one that was obviously not as big as he expected. I hadn't quite figured out French money yet, although there seemed to be about five francs to the dollar. I was glad to have the trunk; opened it and found a clean diaper for Liam. I would have to ask the procedure for doing laundry. I suspected that grouchy Madame Hetreau would not be pleased. I certainly couldn't hear any other babies in the building. Maybe there was a laundry nearby to which I could send Liam's clothes.

The question of money jumped into my head. If Sid and Gus were gone for a while, how long would the cross concierge let me stay? And I'd have to supply my own food.

"This is ridiculous," I said out loud and my voice echoed from the high-molded ceiling. Something was seriously wrong. Sid and Gus cared about me like a sister. They would never let me worry about where they were and what had happened to them. As I carried Liam across to the bathroom to change him I tried to come up with plausible reasons for their absence. They had gone to the country for a day and been in a vehicle that had met with an accident. Or one of them had suddenly taken ill, as I had, resulting in their need to stay on.

But they could still have sent a telegram, even from the French countryside — unless they were both seriously hurt and lying unconscious in a hospital . . . or dead. I felt a great lurch of fear in the pit of my stomach. I was alone in a strange country. How would I ever find out what had happened to them? What would I do if they had died?

Calm down, I told myself. So they have been away for one day. Maybe they are in a small village with no telegraph office. Maybe they are in an automobile that broke down miles from the nearest town. And at this very minute they are worrying about me arriving and finding nobody home. By tomorrow morning we'll all be sitting around their fire, drinking Sid's disgusting coffee, and laughing about this. Thus reassured I finished changing my son and went into the kitchen to look for something I could prepare for an evening meal. I was reluctant to go out just in case some message came from my friends, and I have to confess that I didn't fancy going down all those stairs, out in the pouring rain, and then up again, with no buggy for Liam and no free hand to hold an umbrella.

There was plenty of butter and cheese in the larder, as well as potatoes, onions, and a few wilted carrots. I cooked the carrots and a potato and mashed them together with butter for Liam, then fried some potatoes and onions and drizzled melted cheese over them for me. After I had finished my meal I realized that I should write to Daniel. I had promised to write again as soon as I reached Paris. He would be worrying about us and want to know that I was safely with Sid and Gus. No need to tell him that I did not feel safe at this moment. I looked around and located Sid's writing desk on a side table. As I opened it the first thing I saw was a postcard, showing a scene by the painter Monet, addressed to Miss Augusta Walcott, and on it were scribbled two words: *Absolutely not!* And it was signed, if I could read correctly, *Reynold Bryce.*

So they had made contact with Reynold Bryce although if this postcard was anything to judge by, it didn't sound as if he had welcomed them in the way that they hoped. But it was posted three days ago, giving me proof that they had been here to receive it when it arrived. I turned it over in my hand, wondering what the "Absolutely not" referred to. Maybe they had been discussing a painting, maybe this was an academic debate they were carrying on by postcard and they were actually the best of friends. Still, one thing I knew now. Gus had met Reynold Bryce. If they didn't turn up by tomorrow, at least I'd have one person I could go to.

Then I reminded myself that Gus had a cousin here too. He was a Walcott with money and influence. He'd know what to do if Sid and Gus were injured or in trouble. It shouldn't be too difficult to locate him. I did have allies in the city after all. Thus comforted I decided to wait until tomorrow to write to Daniel. I got ready for bed, curled up into a ball between those cold sheets, and tried to sleep. But sleep did not come easily. Down below me the city was waking up. I heard singing, raucous laughter, shouts, a police whistle. This latter made my thoughts go to my husband. Was he safe? Would they make another attempt on his life? And how did you stop people who could throw a bomb into a carriage, or take a potshot at him as he walked down the street?

"I wish I were home," I whispered to myself, but then I remembered. I had no home. The tears came then and I cried silently into my pillow.

THIRTEEN

I awoke to the loud cooing of pigeons, right outside my window. Bright stripes of sunlight were coming through the shutters onto my wall. As I opened the shutters pigeons flew off the balcony railing with the loud sound of flapping paper. I blinked in the strong sunlight, then put on my robe, went through to the living room, and opened the French doors onto the balcony. I saw that this was an attic of sorts with those French doors cut into the steep gray tile roof. Down below me the street was coming to life — a store owner unwinding the awning over his shop, a café proprietor putting out chairs on the narrow sidewalk, a boy going past on a bicycle carrying long sticks of bread, the greengrocer putting out a display of cabbages, small boys going off with schoolbags on their backs. The sounds echoed up from the narrow street — horses' hoofs on cobbles as a dray made a delivery of wine barrels, a woman shouting in a harsh voice, the pigeons flapping again as they sought another place to land.

Then I leaned out and saw the view that Sid had been so proud of. In one direction the city sprawled out below us, its butter-yellow stone glowing in early morning sunlight, a morning mist hovering over the Seine River. I could see a large dome and maybe those twin towers were Notre-Dame? And when I looked up between the rooftops I could make out a large white building taking shape on the top of the hill. This was the new church Sid had written about. I must go and have a look for myself, I decided. The view would be spectacular.

I was already feeling better, sure that all would be explained and made right today. Sid and Gus would arrive, panting and laughing. "You'll never guess Molly, Gus got a crazy idea to rent a motor and drive to Le Havre to surprise you only it was an awful old banger and it ran off the road in the middle of nowhere and we had to spend the night in a ditch." Yes. That would be it. A perfectly reasonable explanation.

When I went back into my bedroom Liam was awake and playing happily with his own feet. He beamed when he saw me and tried to turn over and pull himself up, encumbered by his night-robes. I picked him up and took him to the window. The pigeons had resettled on the balcony and he clapped his hands in delight, causing them to flutter off again. I dressed us both then carried him cautiously down all those flights of stairs.

Madame Hetreau stepped out of her cubby immediately when she heard my footsteps. I wondered if she lurked there all day, waiting like a giant spider for her prey.

"They do not return, I think," she said. Did I detect the hint of a gloat?

"No, they haven't returned yet." I gave her my most confident air. "I expect we'll learn today what happened to them."

"Perhaps they have found a wealthy bene-factor and gone to live with him," she said. "Many girls do in this city. It is hard to survive alone."

"My friends have plenty of money and no interest in rich benefactors," I said. "Now perhaps you can tell me where I can buy milk. I see a baker's shop across the street but presumably the milk is delivered daily."

"The American misses have a liter deliv-ered," she said. "You will find it in the wooden box beside the front door."

"Thank you," I said, thinking that she had probably been planning to use it herself if I hadn't asked.

"And if I need to go out, it is difficult to take my baby with me. Do you know of a reliable woman who might watch my child from time to time?"

"Perhaps I could . . ." she began, her brain thinking how much she might charge me, now that she knew my friends were not without funds.

"Preferably a woman with a young child of her own," I added quickly. I was certainly not going to confine Liam to a dark cubby with her.

"The baker's wife has just had a child," she said. "Perhaps she might oblige." She shrugged.

"Thank you," I said. "I'll speak to her when I go to buy bread. And you promised me a key. Five francs deposit, I believe you said."

She disappeared into her dark cubby then returned holding up two keys. "The larger one for the front door, the other for the apartment," she said as I paid her. I knew I had left the apartment unlocked but I certainly wasn't going up all those stairs again.

I pushed open the heavy front door and stepped out into the street. Down here the world was still in deep shadow and it was chilly. I wrapped Liam's blanket more tightly around him, then crossed to the shops on the other side. For now I'd just buy bread. Later I'd need to bring in supplies for lunch and dinner. The small bakery smelled heavenly and the baker made a big fuss over Liam. "My wife has just presented me with a fine son like yours. She is my second wife — a good girl from the country, like me, with no nonsense about her. My first wife died, alas, in childbirth and the child died with her. Such is the way of life, no?"

I took the baguette and a croissant which he wrapped in paper. "Your wife," I said carefully. "I wonder if she might consider watching my child if I have to go out? I have just arrived in Paris and the friends I expected to see are not yet here. So I know nobody. I would pay her, naturally."

"I don't see why not," he said. "I'll ask her."

"Thank you, I'm most grateful," I said.

"You can't be too careful around here," he said. "There are plenty of girls with babies, but they are artists' models or work in another profession at night. Not what you would want for your son, eh? My wife is a good girl. Pure. Simple. And a good cook too. With her you need have no worry."

I went back across the street and had a

good breakfast of fresh bread, creamy butter, and apricot jam while Liam chewed on a crust, clearly anxious to get back to his regime of solid food again. I played with him then put him down for a morning nap. I decided that I would send Daniel a cable simply saying, *Arrived safely in Paris. Love Molly and Liam.* That way he wouldn't worry and I wouldn't have to write to him until I knew what had happened to Gus and Sid.

The morning passed with no communication from my friends. I realized I'd have to go out to buy food and decided this would be a good time to make the acquaintanceship of the baker's wife and see if I felt comfortable leaving Liam with her. Then, if there was still no word from Sid and Gus, I should go and find Reynold Bryce and see if he knew anything or could tell me where I'd find Willie Walcott.

I struggled down the stairs again with Liam and went across to the bakery. It was now shut but I banged on the narrow door beside the shop window and it was answered by a buxom young girl.

As soon as I explained who I was her face lit up. "My husband tells me that you need help," she said. "I am Madeleine. Come upstairs, please."

She led me up to a neat little room. A bassinet stood in the corner. The baby in it had a mass of dark hair and a little old man's face. "He's beautiful, is he not?" she said. I agreed that he was.

She poured me coffee. We chatted although I found it hard to keep up with her rapid French. "I would be happy to watch your child for you," she said. "And if he gets hungry, do you give him the bottle?"

"No, I'm feeding him myself."

"No problem. I have plenty of milk to spare." And she emphasized this by hoisting two impressive breasts.

This was overly generous, I thought. I hadn't anticipated hiring a wet nurse for him. "I will be back in time for when he needs to eat," I said, "but thank you for the offer."

We agreed on a very reasonable price. I kissed Liam and told him I'd be back very soon. I heard him crying as I went. I lingered at the bottom of the stairs, not sure about leaving him, but the crying soon stopped and I went about my errands. I asked where to send a cable and was directed to the telegraph office just beyond Pigalle. Then I returned to the Rue des Martyrs and bought vegetables, eggs, and some ham, returning with my string bag full to find Liam sleeping happily on the baker's bed with pillows around him.

"He is so content. You can leave him longer if you wish," Madeleine said.

"I should return to the apartment now to see if there is any news from my friends," I said. I wouldn't put it past the hostile concierge to turn away a telegram messenger if I wasn't there. So I carried a now grouchy Liam up all the stairs again and made us a boiled egg for lunch. The afternoon dragged on. I tried not to worry but worry consumed me. There had to be something very wrong. Sid would not have gone away without her cigarette holder. If they had been going away for any length of time they would have cleared up the remains of a meal first. And my overriding reason for concern — they knew I was coming. They were expecting me.

I took Liam back to Madeleine across the street. She was cooking, making dumplings to add to a delicious-smelling stewed chicken, but she wiped her hands on her apron and beamed at us. "Look what I have found, *mon petit,*" she said to him, going over to a box on the table. "See?" And she held up a Noah's ark with carved wooden animals. "It was mine when I was a child. My grandfather carved it for me." I left Liam happily playing with this and crept quietly away. I had no idea how I was going to locate Reynold Bryce but Paris was a city of artists and he was supposed to be the mentor of American artists here. Someone would know where to find him.

I walked down the street, back to Place Pigalle. There was a café at the intersection of two of the streets leading off Pigalle — a narrow building with glass windows and the sign *Café de la Nouvelle Athènes* painted above the door. There were tables outside but the day was fresh and they were unoccupied. However inside I could see a group of young men clustered around a table. I moved closer to the window. Their attire, ranging from workers' overalls to shabby jackets to well-cut dark suits, and the way they gesticulated with their hands in animated discussion, indicated that they might well be artists of some kind. Then I spotted a sketchbook that one of them had open and charcoal in his hand. I was about to go in when I also noticed that there were no women among them. I couldn't think that women were barred from a café, as they were from taverns in New York. The men were only drinking coffee, by the look of it. A perfectly respectable establishment. So I took a deep breath and went in.

Conversation stopped at the table. The

man behind the marble counter looked up from the glass he was drying. "Are you looking for someone, mademoiselle?" he asked.

"Luckily he is not here, or there would be hell to pay, no doubt," one of the young men said.

"I need help," I began but the young men laughed. "Then you are in the wrong place. None of us has a sou, *chérie*. That is why we come here. Bernarde is tolerant of us. He lets us sit here all day for the price of a cup of coffee."

"No, forgive me," I said. "Perhaps you can tell me how to locate some American painters."

"There are no American painters in Paris," one of the men said quickly, then noting my surprise added, "only copiers and dabblers." At the murmur from his companions he turned to the man beside him. "What? You disagree? I confess that some of them have facility with the brushstroke. La Cassatt is not at all bad."

"That's decent of you, Pablo." The man beside him dug him in the ribs. "She sells her paintings for more money than you, you must confess."

"But when has an American ever created a new movement, a new school of art?" He waved his hands in dramatic gesture. He was small and dark with black hair flopping boyishly across his forehead and he spoke with a strong accent that clearly wasn't French. "I hear they still think Impressionism is avant-garde in America."

And the others grinned and chuckled.

"So you believe that the role of the painter is to constantly come up with something new, do you, Pablo?" one of them asked. "Not to paint with honesty the world as one sees it?"

"Are the two not one and the same?" Pablo demanded.

Before this turned into a philosophical discussion I interrupted. "Messieurs. A minute please. I have to find these American painters. So there are no American artists in your circle here?"

"Americans have money," one of them said. "They would not choose to live and work in Le Bateau-Lavoir as we do."

Bateau? That was a boat, surely, and *Lavoir* had something to do with laundry? "A laundry boat?" I asked. "But we are far from the river, are we not?"

This set them laughing. "We live and work on the slope of Montmartre, above us here," a portly young man, rather better dressed than the rest, said to me. "We call our building Le Bateau-Lavoir because it reminds us of the flimsy way the laundry boats on the Seine are built with gaps between the floor boards. But to answer your question, there are no Americans among us, I regret."

"Americans keep to themselves," the small dark one called Pablo said. "They never seem to learn the language properly."

The one in the well-cut suit roared with laughter at this. "That's a good one coming from you, *mon vieux*." He dug the small dark one in the side. "Your French is still atrocious."

"I think I have learned it rather well," the other replied haughtily, but they all laughed.

"You speak it with a lisp, like a girlish Spaniard," a man across the table said.

The small one called Pablo rose to his feet. "You insult me and my nation. I will challenge you to a duel."

"Sit down, Pablo, do," the man nearest him dragged him down again. "You are alarming the young woman and there are few enough of us already without killing us off one by one."

The dark man turned to me. "I'm sorry, mademoiselle," he said. "I'm afraid I have the hot temper of my race. You wished to know something?"

"I wondered if you might have met two young American women? One of them wears her hair cut short, like a man, and the other is a painter?"

"There are plenty such in Paris," one of them said. "Go down to Montparnasse and see."

"I remember meeting two such Americans," Pablo said.

"When? Where?" I asked.

He shrugged. "Some weeks ago. At a salon. Possibly *chez* La Stein? One of them had brought a painting with her. I did not think much of it, so I don't bother to remember."

This was getting nowhere. I was beginning to feel more and more desperate, as if I was racing against time. "And if I wish to find out the address of the American painter, Reynold Bryce? Do any of you know where I might find him?"

"Reynold Bryce," one of them said, leaning back in his chair to study me as if I might be the object of his next painting. "Why would you wish to find him? He is passé, boring, not of this century."

"Perhaps she wants to model for him?" Pablo said, giving me a roguish look.

"I heard he does not paint people anymore. Only boring landscapes with lots of pretty flowers in them like his friend Monet."

"I hear he likes his girls young and innocent," the roguish one continued. "And one can see that she is not innocent, are you, *chérie*?" His flashing dark eyes challenged me with a most flirtatious smile.

"You insult the lady," the well-dressed man beside him said. "Now her husband will challenge you to a duel."

"This I should enjoy. I have been dying for a duel. I haven't shot my pistol for days."

"Behave yourself, Pablo," another said. "This is France, not Spain. You are simply too hot-blooded."

"Not at all. I am a man who knows what he likes. She can always model for me. She has interesting bones and that red hair — exciting."

"You'd probably paint it blue," one of them remarked.

"No-no. That is all behind me now. No more blue for Picasso," he said. "I see the future and it is exciting."

The man who was the best dressed among them, wearing a three-piece suit, touched my hand. "Do not worry, *chérie,*" he said. "You should have no concern about posing for Picasso. If he paints you, you will wind up with three heads, one breast, and one eye. And possibly blue hair. Completely unrecognizable."

"I paint her as I see her," the little Spaniard said.

"I clearly see two breasts," the well-dressed one commented, eyeing me a little too closely. "Anyway, *mon cher* Picasso," he went on, "you know very well that Fernande would kill you or maybe her if you dared to paint another woman. You know how jealous she is."

I felt this banter had gone on long enough. They clearly had all the time in the world. I was racing against the clock. "So nobody knows where I can find Monsieur Bryce?"

"La Stein would know, don't you think?" one of them suggested.

"Possibly she knows, but she wouldn't tell. They hate each other. He is an anti-Dreyfusard of the worst order."

"That's true." They nodded agreement.

The word, "anti-Dreyfusard" meant nothing to me. "What's that?" I asked.

"You have not heard of the Dreyfus Affair? The army officer who was sent to Devil's Island, falsely accused because he was Jewish?"

A vague memory of something Sid had written came back to me. "Oh, yes, I think I was told about this."

"The affair has divided Paris. There are those for Dreyfus who think that he should be reinstated and restitution should be made, and those who are against him — the anti-Semites. And there are plenty of them."

"Speaking of which, there goes our friend Degas," one of them muttered. "In a hurry again."

A lean man with a black beard strode out on the other side of the road.

"I don't know why he can so hate Jews, when he himself is of mixed race," someone muttered.

The well-dressed one turned back to me. "So naturally Bryce hates La Stein as she is Jewish and she hates him with equal passion because he is so intolerant. No, she would be no help to you."

"So you don't know where I might find Reynold Bryce?" I repeated. "It is very important that I locate him quickly." It was like trying to herd cats to keep them from branching out on tangents, and my head was beginning to spin from having to speak and understand so much French.

"Somewhere more expensive and civilized than this place, I am sure," someone answered. The others chuckled.

"Try the cafés on the Champs-Élysées. Try the other bank of the Seine. I hear the Americans are fond of Saint-Germain-des-Prés."

"No, no," another insisted. "She should try one of the hotels where rich Americans stay. They will surely know there. They come to buy his paintings."

"Where are these hotels?" I asked, desperation now showing in my voice.

"Have you just fallen from the moon, mademoiselle?" one of them asked. "How do you know so little about Paris that you have not seen the Ritz, the Meurice, the Regina?"

"Because I just came into the Saint-Lazare station and all I have seen of Paris is this one little quarter," I said sharply. "I have my small son with me too, which makes moving around difficult."

"Now we've upset her," Pablo Picasso said. He reached out and took my hand. "Please forgive us. You can take the Métro, change at Étoile, and Line 1 takes you to the first arrondissement where all the rich people stay in the fancy hotels."

"Thank you." I smiled at him and again my smile was returned with a sexy wink. "*Bon chance, chérie.* Good luck," he said. "But if you don't find him, come back. We always welcome a pretty face in Montmartre."

I swallowed back my frustration, thanked them, and left.

Fourteen

I crossed the boulevard to the area with the fountain and found steps going down to a station of the Métropolitain railway. When I saw that long flight of steps going down into darkness I was extremely glad that I hadn't tried to bring a squirming and heavy baby with me. It also occurred to me that these steps would be impossible to negotiate with a buggy, should I acquire one. I bought a ticket, went through a turnstile, and down more steps to an underground platform. A great blast of air signaled the arrival of a train and I held onto my hat as it came thundering into the station. I was about to board when I noticed that the carriage in front of me had the words *Première Classe* on them. *Holy Mother.* How was I to know there were two classes on subway trains? No wonder this part of the platform had been so empty. I had to sprint back along the platform to the second-class carriages.

There was now a subway line in New York and I had ridden it a couple of times, but I still couldn't quite put aside the feeling of terror as we were swallowed into a dark tunnel, moving impossibly fast, leather straps swaying above our heads, windows rattling, everything creaking. I was glad when we finally reached the Étoile station and I could walk on terra firma again, following tiled passages to another platform where I'd take Line 1 to the Tuileries.

I came up into fresh air again at the Tuileries station. As my eyes adjusted to bright light I just stood there, rooted to the spot, while other passengers jostled past me. I had never seen anything so magnificent in my life. Apart from New York the only city I had seen was Dublin, which was fair enough in its way, with its squares of elegant Georgian buildings. But this was glorious. On the other side of a broad boulevard a long colonnade of buttery stone buildings, perfectly proportioned, stretched as far as the eye could see. On my side were wrought-iron railings and behind them some fine-looking gardens and what appeared to be a palace beyond. This was finally the Paris I had dreamed of when the Hartleys' governess told us about her travels and showed me postcards she had brought home with her.

I decided to start my inquiries at the Ritz, since that was a hotel everyone, including myself, had heard of. I stopped a police-man, looking very smart in his uniform with its high-crowned blue cap, and asked direc-tions. I realized then the benefits of wearing Dodo's clothes. The policeman addressed me as if I was a person who would naturally want to know where the Ritz hotel was. "Only a little way, madame. Follow this street, take the next turning to the right and you will come to the Place Vendôme. You will see the column and behind it the Ritz hotel itself. Only a short stroll on such a fine spring day."

Then he saluted and I thanked him, walk-ing along the boulevard, admiring the shops beneath the colonnade and the carousels in the park to my left. It was the sort of place I'd have liked to linger, but I pressed on around the corner and saw the column he had spoken about ahead of me. It was tall and green and looked like something that might have come from ancient Egypt. And behind it that glorious curved creamy stone building with the flags flying outside had to be the Ritz.

I had to pluck up courage before I went in through those impressive doors. I half expected the doorman to stop me but he opened the door for me and said *"Bonjour, madame,"* in a way that made me realize he also thought I might belong there. So there really was something to that old adage "clothes make the man." I looked around, wondering whom to ask, when a most superior young man in a black suit and high collar approached me.

"May I assist you, madame?" he asked in English.

"I hope so," I replied, relieved that I didn't have to explain in French. "I wondered if you could tell me the address of the American painter Reynold Bryce. I have been asked to visit him, but I have mislaid his address."

"I'm sorry, madame, but I do not know," he said. "Monsieur Bryce is a resident in our city. At the Ritz we only entertain visitors and tourists. Maybe one of my superiors might be able to assist you, but I think not."

I was trying to keep calm although my frustration was mounting by the minute. "Then could you perhaps suggest where I might find out about him? Is there a place where Americans living in Paris meet?"

"There is the new American Club, madame," he said. "I understand that all Americans of means and position are members there. Surely your Mr. Bryce would qualify."

"The American Club? Of course." I let out a sigh of relief. "And where is this club?"

"It's in Passy, close to the Trocadéro."

"I'm afraid that means nothing to me," I said. "I'm newly arrived in the city."

"I understand the club is actually situated on the Quai de Billy, beside the Seine."

"Is it very far from here?" I was horribly conscious of a clock ticking away inside my head.

"Not too far, I think. You can go on foot. It is a pleasant walk. All you have to do is proceed to the Place de la Concorde, go down to the Seine, and then follow the quai until you come close to the Eiffel Tower. Maybe fifteen minutes. No more."

Just then I heard a voice behind me speaking English and saying in imperious tones, "Where the devil have you been, Henrietta? You've kept us all waiting for hours. It's just not on, you know."

I turned around cautiously and went cold all over. Because I knew that voice. It belonged to Justin Hartley, the landowner's son from Ireland, the man I thought I had killed when he was trying to rape me. He was standing at the foot of the marble staircase and looking up as Miss Henrietta, my former classmate at the big house, came down toward him.

"Pardon me, but I am feeling unwell," I stammered and made for the nearest chair with its back to that staircase.

The young man was most solicitous. "Madame, is there something I can get you? A glass of water perhaps?"

"No, thank you. I'll be all right in a minute." I took out my handkerchief and held it up to my face.

If he came this way I was lost. I was sure he knew there was now a price on my head in Ireland, and nothing would please him more than turning me in. He had never forgiven me for the brain damage he suffered when he hit his head on our stove, and that his injuries had forced him to leave the army. He would like nothing better than to see me hanged.

"Stop being so impatient, Justin," Henrietta's voice carried across the wide foyer.

"But I hate to be kept waiting, you know that."

"We're on holiday, aren't we? And doesn't Mama want to join us?"

"She decided to rest. Now come on. Get a move on, for God's sake. We need to be back in good time to change if we're to dine at Maxim's."

I heard the voices come closer, then pass

right behind me. I kept the handkerchief pressed to my face and hoped that my hat was concealing most of that tell-tale red hair. I waited like that for a good minute after they must have gone, trying to control my panic. I was safe in France, surely. Justin Hartley could do nothing to me here. And I was now married to an American. But I couldn't shake off the fear that somehow the English authorities might catch up with me and drag me back to Ireland to stand trial. I had been an unwilling participant in that failed jail break in Dublin, but a participant nonetheless. And the English didn't care too much about details when they convicted would-be republicans.

I removed my handkerchief to see the young man still looking down at me with concern. "Are you feeling better, madame? It would be no trouble to fetch you a glass of water."

"No, thank you." I stood up, now horribly conscious that Mrs. Hartley, Justin's mother who had taken such an interest in me, was also now in the hotel. I had to get away from here as quickly as possible. "I must be on my way. Turn down to the river at the Place de la Concorde, you say?"

"That's right, madame. The Quai de Billy. Close to the Trocadéro gardens. You can't miss it."

I thanked him, came out of the Ritz, and crossed the Place Vendôme. I was still in such a state of panic that I almost didn't see a motor car, driven fast, until its klaxon sounded, making me leap backward, my heart now pounding. I would never get used to the speed of automobiles and the way they came up on me. I made my way back to the gardens and that lovely colonnade and turned right as instructed. I wondered if it really would only take me fifteen minutes to walk to the American Club, and wondered how long it would then take to reach Mr. Bryce's house. I couldn't leave Liam with Madeleine for too long, especially not past his next feeding. It wouldn't be right, even though I trusted her to take good care of him. I started walking even faster in the shade of the colonnade, not daring even to glance at those enticing boutiques and little cafés. The colonnade ended at a vast open area with what looked like an Egyptian obelisk in the middle and traffic circulating at great speed around it. Vague memories stirred of those long-ago French lessons. "Place de la Concorde," I muttered, and waited until the policeman who was directing traffic from a platform in the middle of the street blew his whistle for us to cross.

As I made my way down to the river I felt the fresh breeze in my face, tinged with that smell of water and rotting things that seems to come from rivers.

The scene along the riverbank was quite delightful with more gardens and what looked like a palace beside me, more impressive buildings on the far bank and a procession of little steamers, tugboats, and barges making their way up and downstream. And there ahead of me that improbable edifice, Mr. Eiffel's tower, soaring over the rest of the city. How could those women not have been impressed by it? To me it was a marvel and I would have liked to have had time to go up it.

I should have been excited to finally be living my geography and history lessons but I was too engulfed in worry to really appreciate what I was seeing. Now it wasn't only a question of finding what had happened to Sid and Gus. It was also the additional fear of being found by Justin Hartley. And I had to complete my task and get back to Liam. It was a greater distance than the man at the Ritz had suggested. My feet were beginning to hurt and I was feeling hot and thirsty by the time I came to the sign saying Quai de Billy and saw the club with its stars and stripes hanging over the front entrance. I hoped that there might be cold drinks or maybe even an ice-cream soda to be had at the club as I went up to the front door and knocked. The elderly porter who opened it stepped back in surprise at seeing me.

"Yes, ma'am. May I help you?" I was glad to hear an American accent and not to have to speak French any longer.

"You may. I'm trying to find Mr. Reynold Bryce. Is he a member here?"

"Mr. Bryce is indeed a member," he said. "But he's not here at the moment, I'm afraid. In fact . . ." then he paused.

"Perhaps you'd be good enough to find me his address."

"I'm sorry, ma'am but it is against club rules to give out the address of a member."

"Look," I said. "It's very important that I speak to him soon. I've come over from America —" I decided to stretch the truth a little, "— with a message from his family. But I omitted to bring his address with me."

He stood, effectively barring the door to me.

"May I come in and speak to the club secretary?" I stepped forward, wondering if I could force my way past him. "I'm sure he'd be able to assist me."

"Come in?" He bristled. "Madame,

women may not enter the club except on special ladies' nights."

My frustration was now threatening to boil over. "I had no idea that people in Paris could be so unhelpful and that a fellow American would be so rudely received at the American Club. I thought it was a city of good manners."

"You could go to the Prefecture of Police," he suggested. "All foreigners must register with them when they move here. Perhaps they will be able to tell you more."

"And how far is it to this prefecture?" I snapped.

"On the Île de la Cité. If you walk up to the Champs-Élysées you can find the Métro and it will take you. Or if you cross the Seine you will find an omnibus that takes you along that bank, but the Métro would undoubtedly be quicker —"

"Jesus, Mary, and Joseph," I muttered. "I don't have all the time in the world, you know. I have left my baby and have to get back to him. And I'll certainly let Mr. Bryce know how unhelpful you were to a visitor from New York."

"What's going on, Harry?" A man in unmistakably American tweeds came to the front door. He gave me a friendly smile. "Is old Harry here being as stuffy and difficult as usual?"

"I'm trying to find the address of one of your members," I said. "I have an important message to deliver to him. But apparently Harry is not allowed to give out information about members and I, as a woman, am not allowed in."

The man laughed. "Quite right. If they relaxed those rules we'd have every wife in Paris hunting down her husband when he needs to escape for a bit of peace and quiet."

"This is no joking matter," I said coldly. "I have an important message for one of your members and it needs to be delivered to him immediately."

"I'm sorry," he said. "Don't get upset. Look, if you'd care to write it down, I'll make sure he gets it when he next shows up."

"It's Mr. Reynold Bryce," I said. "Does he come in often?"

"Reynold Bryce?" The expression on his face changed. "Oh, I see." He exchanged a glance with the doorman that I didn't quite understand.

"Is something wrong?" I asked.

"Are you a family member?" he asked.

"No, just a friend of the family."

"Look here," he said. "We think there might be something strange going on. Mr.

McBride, the newspaperman from New York, went around to see Bryce a couple of days ago. But when he got there he found policemen stationed outside the house. They wouldn't let him in and they wouldn't tell him anything. We've checked the newspapers since and no mention of Reynold Bryce, so we can't think what might have happened."

"All the more reason for me to go there myself," I said. "I have to find out what's happening, for his family's sake."

"Of course you do," he said. "I'd escort you there myself, but I'm due at a meeting with my bank manager. And one does not keep one's bank manager waiting, especially if one wants to eat next month."

"So you know Mr. Bryce's address?"

"It's on Rue François Premier," he said. "I don't know the number, but I presume you'll deduce which one it is if it still has policemen outside. If not, the neighbors will know. They are a nosy lot, the French. They like to keep an eye on what's going on around them."

"And the Rue François? Is it far from here? I have to get back to my child and . . ."

"No, not too far, is it, Harry?"

Harry was looking most displeased that the young man was betraying a club confidence in this way. He simply shrugged. "Not for me to say, sir," he said.

The young man grinned. "Go back along the quay until you get to the bridge. I believe it's called the Pont de l'Alma. It's the first proper bridge you'll come to. Then take the Avenue Montaigne away from the river until you come to Rue François Premier. Not far at all."

"Thank you, you've been most kind," I said.

"Not at all." He tipped his homburg to me. "Always delighted to assist a damsel in distress. Are you alone in the city or is your husband with you?"

"No, unfortunately. His business keeps him in New York," I said.

"If you need a gentleman to escort you, I'd be happy to show you some of the best night spots." He held out a hand. "Frank Lahm at your service."

"Mrs. Molly Sullivan," I said. "I'm delighted to make your acquaintance, but I don't think I'll be wanting to visit any night spots in the near future. I'm staying with friends."

"Ah, I see." His face fell. "Well, you can always find me here if you need anything." He touched his hat again and set off. I gave the porter a barely civil nod and turned on my heel. By now my heart was really thumping and it wasn't just from tiredness after walking so far at such a great clip. The nagging worry that I had tried to keep at bay had risen to the surface again. Something was wrong at Reynold Bryce's house. Police were standing outside. Had Reynold Bryce committed a crime or had something bad happened to him?

FIFTEEN

The late afternoon sun was now blazing down on my back, and I was glad when I could move into the dappled shade of trees. Paris was a wonderful city for trees, I thought. Hardly any streets in New York were treelined, but this city appeared to be all parks and boulevards. No wonder Sid and Gus were so — I broke off this thought as a sob hiccupped into my throat. Something had gone wrong at Reynold Bryce's house. And only a few days ago he had sent Gus a postcard with the words "Absolutely not" scrawled across it. That showed they had been in recent communication and that he didn't need to explain what those words meant. Had he been threatened in some way? Had she begged him to go to the police, or escape from the city? And he had emphatically refused. In which case were she and Sid also in danger from this threat?

I walked faster and faster, my shoes pinching horribly. They were a pair I had accepted from Dodo and in truth a little tight for me. But I had taken them as the pair I had been wearing at the time of the fire were fit for nothing but housework and shopping. Finally I came to the bridge and found the Avenue Montaigne. More lovely buildings in good repair. Clearly an affluent neighborhood — an automobile with a chauffeur was idling outside one of the houses. I remembered that Reynold Bryce came from a monied family and wondered how much of his wealth came from his paintings. He really was a world away from those threadbare young men in the café. No wonder they knew so little about him and despised him as old fashioned and out of touch.

I saw the sign for the Rue François Premier and turned left, finding it hard to breathe now. Was I about to find out what had happened to Sid and Gus? I walked the length of the street and found nothing. In frustration I turned and realized that the Rue François Premier went in both directions across Avenue Montaigne. So I retraced my steps, crossed the avenue, and came at last to an attractive circle with a fountain in the middle. The houses around the circle had shrubs and trees in front of them, enclosed in wrought-iron fences, and

outside one of these an enclosed black carriage was stationed as well as an automobile.
As I approached I spotted a blue-uniformed
policeman standing just inside the front
entrance. So it appeared that I had finally
found the right house. I walked boldly up
the three steps and the young policeman
stepped out to intercept me.

"What do you wish, madame?" he asked.

"Is this not the residence of Mr. Reynold
Bryce?" I asked.

"It is."

"Then I should like to enter. I have come
from America and wish to speak with Mr.
Bryce."

"I am afraid that is not possible," he said.

"Why? What has happened? Is something
wrong?"

"I'm sorry, madame, but Mr. Bryce may
not receive visitors," he said, looking extremely uncomfortable now.

"Do you have a superior officer present?"
I demanded, not about to be shoved aside
for a third time. "I should like to speak with
him. I have come all this way. It is most
important that I see Mr. Bryce."

"Wait here, please," he said. "I will see if
anything can be done."

I stood alone in the cool shadow of a
foyer. It was not one private home but

another apartment building with an elevator in an attractive wrought-iron cage ascending through the middle of the foyer while a red-carpeted staircase snaked up around it. Beside the front door were four bells, the bottom one with the name *Bryce* beside it. I was tempted to press it and see if I could summon Mr. Bryce for myself, but at that moment a door opened and my policeman returned, this time followed by a thin, middle-aged man dressed in a dark suit. He had a long lugubrious face with bags under his eyes that made him look like a bloodhound.

"Madame?" he said. "I understand that you come from the family of Monsieur Bryce in America?"

I decided that this little lie would be the only way of getting information. I pushed the word perjury to the back of my mind. "That is correct. I was asked to deliver a message to him from his family."

"May I ask what that message was?"

"Certainly not," I said. "It is a private message, meant for Mr. Bryce's ears alone, and I am growing rather tired of being thwarted like this. I'm sure Mr. Bryce would not be happy if he found I'd been kept waiting in the front hall."

He stared at me, looked around, then said,

"You had better come in."

He led me through to the ground-floor apartment. Once inside there was a grander foyer than the communal one — furnished with two gilt chairs with a small bronze sculpture of a ballerina between them, potted palms, and gilt-framed paintings lining the walls.

"We will sit here, if you don't mind," he said, indicating the two chairs. "My men are still working in the other rooms."

A door was open on my left and I saw the back of a policeman who appeared to be dusting the back of a chair with a feather duster. I had seen this done before. "You're looking for fingerprints," I said. At least I tried to say it, but the word was outside the scope of my vocabulary. I tried saying, *"impressions de doigts"* meaning "impression of fingers." He looked confused. I mimed the making of a fingerprint and he nodded, understanding.

"Ah. *Les empreintes digitales* — this is new science for us. How in the name of God do you know of such things?" he demanded.

I was about to say that my husband was a police captain in New York, but didn't want word of this getting back to Daniel. "I am acquainted with the methods of the police," I said. "We know all about fingerprints in

America." I didn't add that they had never been allowed as admissible evidence in court, in spite of the police insisting they were the only infallible tool the detective had. Then the import of that police work struck me. "But that must mean that a crime was committed here."

He nodded. "This must remain confidential for now, but I am afraid to report to you that Monsieur Bryce is dead."

"Dead? You mean murdered?"

"It would appear so. I am sorry to be the reporter of bad news."

I nodded. I neither knew nor cared about Reynold Bryce, but my immediate thought was that if someone had killed him, his death might have had something to do with Sid and Gus's disappearance. Were they now in danger, or . . . I hardly dared to frame the thought . . . were they also dead? I swallowed hard. "When was he killed?"

"Two days ago now. We have kept this knowledge to ourselves hoping to identify the killer before the press might learn of it, and we had the American ambassador breathing down our necks."

I tried to keep my face calm and composed. "And do you have any idea who might be responsible?"

He looked at me strangely. I suppose I had

become so used to questioning people that I had forgotten it was neither normal nor ladylike. Most women would have had the smelling salts out by now, swooning at the mention of a dead body.

"Suppose I start asking the questions," he said. "I am Inspector Henri of the Sûreté."

In spite of the gravity of the situation I had a ridiculous urge to grin, because his name, pronounced in French was *on-ree,* and the words *"on ri"* mean "one laughs." I'd never seen anyone who looked less like laughing.

"And you are?" he continued, taking a small black notebook from his jacket pocket.

"Madame Sullivan."

"And you come from?"

"New York."

"But Monsieur Bryce he was from Boston, no? So how are you connected to him? You are a family member?"

"No, not a family member." I decided not to stretch the truth too far. It always had a way of coming back and biting me. "I am acquainted with several Bostonian families." This was true. Gus came from Boston.

"And you came to Paris specifically to deliver a message to Mr. Bryce?" he went on.

"No. I came to Paris to stay with friends.

A family member asked me visit Mr. Bryce."

"I understood he had no family." He stared at me, long and hard.

"No immediate family," I said. "The people I know are cousins."

"And the message?"

"Is no longer relevant, now that he is dead."

He frowned. "It might well be very relevant."

"Why?" I asked. "How could a message from America affect a murder in Paris?"

"We are trying to find out who might have a reason to kill Reynold Bryce," he said. "We can fill in details of his life in Paris but we have no knowledge of his life in America. For all we know he had enemies over there."

"Mr. Bryce has not lived in America for many years," I said.

He shrugged. "Maybe he had swindled someone, or he stood to inherit money, or was leaving his fortune to the wrong person. There are many reasons that might make a person choose to kill. Old hatreds can simmer on for years." He paused. Apart from the ticking of a clock in a nearby room and the sound of a chair being moved, there was silence in that foyer.

"I'm sorry, I can't help you with any of this," I said, now desperately racking my brains for a message that would not implicate me in any way. "My message was simply from a young cousin, thanking Cousin Reynold for the picture that he painted for her tenth birthday."

"I'll need the names of these cousins," he said. "And you say you've just arrived in Paris. Are you sure you haven't attempted to see Mr. Bryce before?"

"Of course not. I've only just arrived in Paris."

He was continuing to stare hard at me. "The housekeeper reported an American woman visitor on the day he was killed. Where were you two days ago?"

"That is easy to answer. I was at a pension in Le Havre with a group of American women. I was recovering from a very bad case of seasickness and too weak to travel."

"I see."

"I only arrived in Paris yesterday."

"And your first task in a strange city, after you had been sick and too weak to travel, was to come straight to Reynold Bryce, whom you apparently don't know, to deliver a message from a child about a painting." He paused and stroked his mustache. "Interesting, don't you think? If it was my first day in Paris I'd be enjoying the sights, sitting in a café, going to the Louvre, and I'd wait for a convenient moment to visit a man I didn't know. Unless, of course, the message wasn't quite so innocent — a warning maybe? A threat? You did say it was no longer relevant."

"No. Absolutely not." And as I said the words I felt a chill run down my spine. They were Reynold Bryce's words to Gus, scrawled across the postcard. "And I don't know why you seek motives from America when surely it is most likely that the murder was committed for the simplest of reasons."

"Such as?"

I looked around me. "It appears that Mr. Bryce was a rich man. He could have surprised a thief." I didn't know the French word for burglar.

"There are no signs of a break-in."

"You spoke of his housekeeper. Was she not here?"

"Unfortunately she went to the market and when she came back . . ." He stopped in mid-sentence. "None of this concerns you, madame," he said. "The French police will do their work and find the murderer, trust me. That will be all for now, but I shall probably wish to speak with you again, regarding Bryce's family connections in America. Please write down for me your name and address in Paris and do not think of leaving the city without my permission."

"I have no intention of leaving the city, Inspector. As I said, I have only just arrived, and wish to make the most of my stay here."

One of the doors opened and a policeman popped his head around it. "Inspector?" he said, "Oh, I'm sorry, I didn't realize you were busy."

"What is it, Clement?"

"There's something I'd like you to see in the study."

"Very well." He tore a sheet of paper from his book. "Please write your name and address for me, madame, and I shall return."

As soon as he had gone I went over to the door, listening as closely as I dared, to hear what the young policeman might have found, but I could hear nothing. So I sat down and wrote my address on the paper. Then I got up and paced around, wondering how I could ask about Sid and Gus. The light in the foyer was poor so I went closer to look at the paintings. There was a lovely landscape with a row of poplar trees, and another with a bridge over a lake with water lilies. I wondered if they were Bryce's own work until I read the signature on the latter picture. *Monet.* So he collected the works of other painters. If he had these paintings in a front hall, he must have a more impressive collection inside. Would there be a picture that was worth stealing among them?

On the wall tucked away to one side of the front door was another painting, smaller than the rest. It was in deep shadow. I went over to it and saw that it was one of the Angela studies. Not a completed painting, but a rough sketch. She was older than in the picture on Dodo's nursery wall — already turning into a young woman. This time she was holding a bunch of wildflowers. She was looking at the painter with a mischievous grin. Again I was struck by the resemblance to Ellie, the girl on the ship. And as I studied her expression I saw the humor and liveliness in those eyes. This was not the face of a half-wit.

"Sorry to keep you, Mrs. Sullivan." I spun around as the inspector returned. "Admiring the paintings, are you? These are more my kind of style. Not like that modern rubbish they're turning out now. Fauves, this latest lot call themselves. Wild ones. I think it's just an excuse for not being able to paint properly." He went over to the Monet. "Now take this, for example. Here's someone who knew how to paint. Old Monet. They were good friends, you know. He and Bryce. He'll be upset to learn of Bryce's death. Almost all the old Impressionists have died off now. Only that Renoir man and Degas . . ."

"May one ask how Mr. Bryce was killed?" I interrupted him. "Did his death indicate a violent struggle? Did it appear that he knew his attacker and was caught by surprise?"

He came closer to me, staring hard at my face. "You ask a lot of questions for someone who apparently has no interest in this case," he said. "Are you sure you're not a lady journalist, hoping to get a scoop?"

"I am not. But before my marriage I used to be a private investigator in New York City. I'm afraid I can't stop being fascinated by crime."

"*Mon dieu.* A lady investigator. What is the world coming to?" He shook his head.

"Perhaps you could satisfy my curiosity on just one thing then," I went on cautiously. "Was Mr. Bryce all alone when he was killed? There were no other bodies or signs of other people being killed at the same time?"

"What are you suggesting?"

I decided to take the plunge. Surely I had nothing to lose at this stage and the worst that could happen was that the inspector would think I was a crackpot. "I'm afraid I haven't been quite honest with you, Inspector," I said.

"Ah, so now we're getting to it." He gave me a triumphant smile as if he'd suspected me all along. "Come on, then. Out with it. What was the real message?"

"No, this has nothing to do with any message. You see I came to visit Mr. Bryce because two friends of mine are missing. At least they may just have gone away, and nothing might have happened to them, but they are not at their address in Paris and Reynold Bryce may have been one of the last people with whom they communicated."

"How long have they been missing?"

"At least two days, maybe longer. The concierge was not sure."

"And these friends of yours are Americans?"

"Two American ladies. One is a painter. That was why they had been communicating with Mr. Bryce."

"Age?"

"Late twenties."

"And these two ladies were good friends of Mr. Bryce, were they?"

"No. They had only just been introduced to him."

"Then what makes you think their disappearance had anything to do with Mr. Bryce's death?"

"He sent a postcard to one of them two

days before he died."

"And this postcard had some kind of warning written on it? Something that made you uneasy?"

I considered this. "Well, no. Not exactly."

He took my hand and patted it. "Then I think you have no cause for concern, *chère* madame. There were no extra bodies found. No signs of a struggle elsewhere in the apartment. And American ladies are known for flitting across the Continent on a whim. They'll turn up again, I'm quite sure."

"Thank you."

The inspector opened the front door for me. "I wish you a pleasant stay in Paris, madame. However, if you can think of anything to do with Bryce's family in America that might have a bearing on this case, you can always leave a message for me at the Sûreté."

The policeman at the door nodded to me as I passed him and walked down the steps, out to the street. I gave a sigh of relief. Sid and Gus's disappearance seemed to have nothing to do with the death of Reynold Bryce. Perhaps they had already returned home and be waiting for me. I hurried to the nearest Métro station.

SIXTEEN

When I reached the bakery I found Liam had already been fed and was sleeping peacefully. I apologized but Madeleine laughed. "I am here at home with one baby, madame. What difference does another one make? And your son, he is delightful. He has so much joie de vivre."

"Yes," I said. "He is a lot like his father." And a great longing for Daniel came over me. When could I hope for a letter? Was he still safe? I wanted nothing more than to feel his arms around me.

When I entered the front hallway of Sid and Gus's building the concierge popped out like a spider springing from its lair on passing prey. "So you're still here. And no, your friends have not returned. Me, I think they have found a place they like better. In a more chic neightborhood."

"But they were expecting me here," I said. "And why would they leave their possessions behind?"

"Americans have money. They buy new possessions and toss out the old," she said. "Or they plan to collect their things before the end of the month."

I trudged wearily up those flights of stairs and let myself in to the silent apartment. Dust motes danced in slanted evening sunlight. Gus's shawl still lay over the back of the chair, her painting still half finished, the paint dried out on her palette. I went into their bedroom and opened the wardrobe. There was Sid's favorite velvet smoking jacket. There was Gus's fur-lined opera cape. All their clothing was here. They had not gone anywhere intentionally. I realized I should have to go back to Inspector Henri and give him a description of them, and. . . . I hardly dared to form the thought . . . have him check against bodies of females that had recently come to the morgue. But surely that wasn't possible, I said to myself. I was being overly dramatic. Sid and Gus were brave and healthy women. A woman alone might be lured into a dark alley and murdered, but there is safety in numbers. Any miscreant would find them formidable foes.

But that didn't rule out the possibility of an automobile or carriage accident outside the city. I closed the wardrobe door and paced to the window and back. The sun's last rays were making the white stone of that half-built dome at the top of the hill glow pink, as if it was on fire. Such a beautiful, inspiring scene. No wonder Gus had wanted to paint it. I turned away again. It was the not knowing that was so hard. I couldn't just sit here and wait for news. And I certainly didn't feel like doing the things one should in Paris — enjoying myself at the cafés or the Louvre — while my friends were missing, and also never knowing when I might run into the Hartleys.

"Who else might have any idea where they went, Liam?" I asked my son who was crawling across the wood floor to me with a look of determination on his face. I tried to think whom they might have mentioned in their letters. Gus's cousin Willie Walcott for a start. I had no idea where I might find him but he was an artist who knew Reynold Bryce. American artists obviously met at the same establishments. One of those would be the American Club but I would only go back there to face the rude porter again as a last resort. And it wasn't likely that Willie Walcott was a member. It didn't look like the sort of place that accepted young art students. The Walcotts were a wealthy family, but surely a young artist would find the formality horribly stuffy. There must be places where he would congregate with other art students. Hadn't they mentioned something about the other bank of the Seine? Perhaps my new artist friends from the café in Pigalle would know. I didn't think I should go to seek them out this evening. From the little I had seen, the Place Pigalle was not a suitable environment for a woman alone after dark.

I bent to pick up Liam before he knocked over a table with a plant on it. "Time to feed you, my love," I said. I made him some bread and milk then attempted to nurse him, but he was quickly bored with both, indicating that my friend in the bakery had indeed shared her own milk with him. Ah, well, rich children had wet nurses, didn't they? I bet the Hartleys had a wet nurse. I shivered as this amusing thought rapidly became serious. To know that Justin Hartley was in the same town compounded the worry that already threatened to engulf me. Surely I was worrying for nothing over that, I told myself. Paris was a big city. It wasn't as if I was likely to bump into them dining at Maxim's. They probably weren't staying long and I'd be too busy with my own matters to want to make the round of the tourist sites at this moment.

I washed Liam and dressed him for bed. He no longer wanted to go down but to play, so we stacked blocks and played peekaboo for a while until I began to feel really hungry myself. My body was now ready to catch up after all those days without food. I went into the kitchen and looked at the remains of the ham, the bread, the eggs. None of them had much appeal and the bread was already too hard. I decided that I would put Liam down for the night and then treat myself to a meal out. The little brasserie at the bottom of the Rue des Martyrs had seemed wholesome enough. I put Liam into his crib, sang to him, and then when he fell asleep I tiptoed out. I didn't like to leave him but no harm could come to him in a crib he couldn't climb out of and Madame Hetreau was just downstairs.

Madame Hetreau must have been preparing her own meal because she didn't leap out on me when I went past. Outside the street was bathed in deep twilight. The brasserie was still almost deserted at this hour. I scanned the menu for something inexpensive. The owner recommended his onion soup. I wasn't sure that a soup would fill me up but when it came it was encrusted with bubbling cheese and crispy bread —

hearty enough for a meal.

"Some wine, madame?" he asked, and not being too confident about the water in this part of the city, I allowed him to bring me an eighth of a liter. Then, already having been daring I ordered a coffee. "But you must have my baba au rhum," the owner said. He had already plied me with questions as he served and discovered I was newly arrived from America and here alone. I couldn't quite tell if he was being friendly or had something else in mind, but he brought the dessert and did not let me refuse. It was delicious and laced with rum too. I hadn't quite counted on the alcohol in that dessert and was feeling pleasantly squiffy when I paid my bill and got up to leave. At that moment the door opened and a couple came in.

"Ah, there she is again, my little redhead," said the man and I saw that it was the Spaniard, Pablo Picasso. With him was an olive-skinned girl, half a head taller than he was, with a scarf wound around her head gypsy-style and black flashing eyes. "You see, Fernande," he said to her. "Now you see why I should like to paint her — such unusual coloring and a good strong jawline."

The tall one glared at me in unfriendly

fashion. "Only if you let Max paint me," she said, and played with her scarf.

"You know what I have said to that," he snapped. "Nobody else sees you naked. Don't mention it again."

"And yet you think you can paint other women and I won't mind?"

"It is the head that interests me, you silly goose," he said. "You can sit beside me, if you wish. And she is an American. A visitor. No threat to you."

"She is no better than she should be." Fernande was still glaring at me. "No respectable woman sits alone in the evening."

"I assure you I do not want to sit alone," I said. "I was supposed to stay with friends here, but something must have happened to them. They have vanished. Nobody has seen them."

"Did you find your Mr. Reynold Bryce? Did he not know where they are?" Picasso asked.

"I —" I stopped, remembering the inspector's desire to keep the murder hushed up for now. "I went to his residence but I was not able to speak to him."

"If these friends are American, she should go to La Stein," Fernande said. "That place is always full of Americans. So boring."

I remembered he had mentioned something about La Stein that morning. " 'La Stein' — what is that?"

"You mean *who* is that," he said. "She is an American lady. A rich American lady. She buys paintings. She bought one of mine so she must have good taste for an American. And there are always gatherings at her house."

"Where is this house?" I asked.

"On the Left Bank, by the Jardin du Luxembourg," he said. "Rue de Fleurus. What is the number, Fernande?"

She shrugged. "Why should I remember? I only went there once with you and it was boring. Nobody spoke French and they ignored me. Me, I do not like being ignored, especially by you."

"As if I ever ignore you, my darling. You know I cannot bear to be parted from you for an instant." He gazed at her with such intensity that I felt distinctly embarrassed.

"Rue de Fleurus," I repeated, before they could fall into a passionate embrace, right there in the restaurant.

"Ask anybody. They will know the number. Her parties are loud and go on all night."

"Thank you," I said. My wine and the rum in the dessert suddenly made the room swing around. "I must go back to my son," I said.

"If you decide you would like to model for me, you can usually find me at the café, if I am not working," Picasso called after me. "And if I work, I'm at Le Bateau-Lavoir."

I thought that any woman who went to model for Picasso would be taking her life in her hands. And I smiled until those words echoed in my head. Had Sid and Gus taken their life in their hands doing something foolish? These people in Paris were not like New Yorkers. They were passionate and wild and jealous. They spoke of duels and pistols. And one of them had killed Mr. Reynold Bryce, a respectable American, in his own home.

I pulled my shawl around me, bid everyone a hasty good-night and hurried home. The Rue des Martyrs, where it met the boulevard near Pigalle, was now coming to life. A girl wearing a short skirt and showing black fishnet stockings almost up to her knee was leaning against a lamppost on the corner. A couple walked past, arms entwined about each other. A group of young men came toward me, singing lustily — something about *"Auprès de ma blonde, qu'il fait bon dormir,"* meaning "It would be good

217

to sleep next to my blonde"? Such things would never be heard in New York.

They called out to me as they passed on the other side of the street. "Hello, *ma belle*. Come with us. We go to the Moulin Rouge. Come and dance and drink."

I ignored them, suddenly feeling alone and vulnerable. I heard ribald comments as I fled toward my front door and went inside. Madame was back on alert this time. "You've been walking the streets, I see."

"I had no food for my evening meal. I needed to eat."

"It is not wise to wander the streets alone in this part of the city," she said. "People will get the wrong idea about you."

"I'll remember that. Thank you." I gave her a civil nod. As I went to walk past her up the stairs she called after me, "How long do you think you'll remain here to see if your friends will return?"

"Until I find out what has happened to them," I said. "You told me that the rent had been paid until the end of the month so it doesn't really concern you whether anyone stays in their apartment or not, does it? Good night, madame."

Then I stomped up the stairs. I had had a long, frustrating, and frightening day and I was not prepared to tolerate Madame Hetreau's attempts to intimidate me.

SEVENTEEN

I awoke to wind rattling the shutters. Outside clouds were racing across the sky bringing the promise of rain. Not an auspicious start to a day when I would be roaming the streets once more. Liam was awake and full of energy, babbling noisily and wanting to get up and going. I took him with me down the five flights to buy our breakfast. The baker made a big fuss of Liam and put a sweet roll into my bag for him. "You have cheered up Madeleine marvelously," he said. "She had not recovered her full strength after the birth of the baby and had lost her joie de vivre. Last night all she could talk about was your son and how funny and clever he was."

"I was delighted to find her," I said. "It would have been a huge problem to carry my son around with me all day."

I told him I'd be bringing Liam over later, then went to buy food for my evening meal.

Meat was horribly expensive so I settled on a piece of fish and some more cheese. I gazed with awe at the selection of cold meats, cheeses, and pâtés. Since I didn't know the names of any of them I could only point, feeling like an idiot. Then up the stairs again for a good breakfast. The fact that there was still no telegram, no communication at all from Sid and Gus only reinforced my fear that something terrible had happened to them. Even someone lying in a hospital bed can arrange to have a telegram sent. This had to be more than a simple accident or missed train or even a sudden sickness. Were they prisoners or no longer alive?

It was almost a physical pain to let this thought enter my head. Sid and Gus had become the sisters I never had. I couldn't bear it if anything had happened to them. But there was also fear for myself. What was I supposed to do alone in a strange city? Would Daniel rather that I returned to New York or that I stayed on here alone? Then there was the question of money. I had a little to keep me going, but not enough to pay rent for months to come. Ah, well, I thought with a grim smile. I could always become an artist's model. It appeared my face and coloring might be in demand. This ridiculous notion cheered me up a little. I fed Liam some mashed carrots, dressed him for the day, left his dirty diapers soaking in a pale of borax, then carried him over to Madeleine. She did indeed seem pleased to see me and I lingered longer than I really wanted to, chatting to her, answering her questions about New York and my life there. She was intrigued to know that my husband was a policeman.

"But that is so dangerous, no?" she asked. "I would be in fear every time he left me. You must be a brave woman."

"No," I said. "I am also in fear, but it is his job. Right now I worry about him all the time. I hate to be so far away from him."

"Then why did you abandon him and come here?"

"I had to leave the city because bad men were making threats on the life of me and my child. They blew up our house and killed my sweet servant girl."

"*Mon dieu,* you poor little one," she said. "How tragic for you to be alone like this. You and I will be friends, no?"

And she held out her hand to me. I took it, feeling the warmth of that chubby, work-worn hand in mind. "Thank you," I said and blinked back tears.

Liam was already delighted to return to

his Noah's ark so I tiptoed away and off I went. My mention of Aggie had me thinking of her again. My present worries had pushed her loss from my mind, but now I pictured her in stark contrast to the round and healthy-looking Madeleine. Poor little Aggie who never had a chance to know joy in her life. And the guilt flooded over me again.

I thought I caught a glimpse of the group of young artists sitting in the Nouvelle Athènes. I wondered when they got any painting done. I asked the man in the ticket booth at the Métro station for directions to the Jardin du Luxembourg. He told me to change to Line 1 as I had done the day before, to get out at Châtelet station, cross the Seine, traverse the Île de la Cité, cross the second bridge until I came to the Boulevard St. Michel. If I followed that I should come to the Jardin. It seemed like an awfully long way. I just hoped I located this rich American called Stein quickly and that she hadn't also decided to vanish. I tried to remember whether Sid or Gus had mentioned her in any of their letters. An American art collector and a female one at that was just the kind of person whose acquaintance they would have sought, surely?

I came out of the Métro at the Châtelet station to find it was already raining. I opened my brolly and headed for the bridge across the Seine. Holding it tilted down against the wind and rain I almost didn't notice the magnificent fortress on the other side of the bridge and had to stop — wind-swept and rain blown, midway over the Seine — to admire it. There were mutterings of annoyance while the crowd had to part around me but I didn't care. As I continued I passed between imposing yellow stone buildings, one with an arched gateway and sentry boxes beside it, the other with columns and a gilded portico. I took them for palaces until I read that the one with the arch was the Prefecture of Police. This then was where Inspector Henri said he could be found. And the one opposite was the Palais de Justice. I was glad I wasn't a criminal. The French clearly took their justice seriously.

I had forgotten that this was an island, or not quite understood the Métro man's directions because I was surprised to come to another bridge over another branch of the river. There were houseboats lining the bank, children playing in the rain on one deck, a line of laundry hanging limp and sorrowful on another. Bateau-Lavoir, "laundry boats," I said to myself remembering the name of the building where the artists lived in Montmartre. Then I was on the Left Bank and the feel of the city became quite different from the elegance of the Right Bank I had encountered the day before. This area was full of students, lively young men gesticulating as they walked and talked, smoking little brown cigarettes, with books tucked into their jackets to keep them from getting wet. And on kiosks and walls there were placards advertising cabarets, or with cartoons containing political messages on them. Then there was one that had *Justice for Dreyfus* written across it in bold black letters while over it someone had painted in bright red paint *All Jews Out of Paris.* I remembered the young artists talking about the anti-Drefusards and saw that it was indeed a topic that was dividing the city. I passed several more such posters as I went down the Boulevard St. Michel, most of them with a message of hate painted over them. I wondered how many people could possibly agree with this foul sentiment. Enough to deface every placard, I thought.

I stopped to ask about the Rue de Fleurus and learned it was on the other side of the park. On a sunny day I would have welcomed a stroll across such delightful gardens but walking beneath chestnut trees that dripped rain onto me was not quite as desirable. The park was deserted apart from a couple that huddled together under his rain cape and a nursemaid who was stoicly determined to give her young charge his daily fresh air, no matter what the weather was like. There were miniature waves on the boating lake. The carousel stood idle. I was feeling thoroughly damp and bad tempered by the time I finally reached the other side of the gardens and located the Rue de Fleurus.

This was also deserted. I had hoped to find a neighbor and ask where Madame Stein might live, but nobody was venturing out. It was another typical Parisian street of uniform stone buildings and ironwork balconies, as if one giant hand had designed a whole city in one fell swoop. Of course I found out later that this was true. In the mid-nineteenth century the emperor Napoleon III had decided to tear down the unsanitary and crowded medieval city and asked Baron Haussmann to modernize it. Haussmann created the wide, treelined boulevards and uniform style of buildings that make the city so unique and attractive.

Not knowing what to do next I started peering at the plates beside front doors, hoping to find one of them that said *Stein*. Luckily she did not live too far from the park and I found her quite soon. I rang her doorbell then walked up to her apartment on the second floor. As I tapped on the door a strong female voice yelled, "Come in!"

I opened the door and stepped into a narrow hallway.

"If it's the butcher take the meat through to the kitchen," the voice went on in English. "And it better be a nice plump *poussin* this time, not some scrawny old hen that has died of old age."

The voice came closer and a big-boned woman with a towel around her head came out into the hall. She stopped in surprise when she saw me.

"You're not the butcher," she said.

"No, I'm not."

"Then what the deuce are you doing in my front hall?"

"My name is Sullivan and I came to see you. I've just arrived from New York and . . ."

"Came to see me? My dear girl, you should know that I never see anybody before luncheon. I've only just woken up. It's simply not civilized." She turned back to where the hall disappeared into darkness. "Leo!" she yelled. "Make sure you don't come out in your underwear. There's a young lady standing in our foyer." Then she turned back to me. "If you want to pay a call on me, then come to one of my salons like everybody else. You'll usually find people here most evenings although Saturday night is when we have our big weekly shindig. A painter, are you? Or a buyer? Because I should warn you that you won't get me to part with any of my paintings."

It was as hard to stop her as a train thundering down the track at full speed. "Mrs. Stein," I began.

She held up her hand. "Hold it right there. It's Miss Stein or Gertrude if you like. I'm not big on formality. I'm not married either. Never intend to be."

"But you spoke to someone called Leo," I stammered, wondering if I had committed a faux pas and Leo was perhaps her lover.

"My brother. We're sharing the place at the moment, and sharing our passion for collecting art too. I suppose you'd better come in. We can't stand talking here."

She led me through to a light and airy drawing room. It was elegantly but sparsely furnished. I couldn't tell what the wallpaper looked like because every inch of the walls was covered in paintings — some of them quite lovely — portraits of young women with flowing hair, ballerinas on stage, picnics in a park, and some quite incomprehensible — wild daubs of bright color with cats hanging in midair and women with two faces. I wrenched my gaze away as she said, "Well, sit down then. What was it you wanted?"

I perched on the edge of a brocade sofa. "I wondered if you had come across two friends of mine. American women — Miss Walcott and Miss Goldfarb."

"Yes, I met them when they first got here," she said brusquely. "Why, have they sent you with the olive branch? Are you supposed to mediate a peace between us?"

"A peace between you? Had you quarreled?"

"Let's just say there was a parting of the ways. They came to one of my Saturday night salons. I rather liked Goldfarb — got a good brain, one could tell. Didn't think so much of the other one. A bit wishy-washy. She brought a couple of her paintings to show me. I thought she might have a smidgeon of talent and told her so, but she needed to take some lessons in the handling of color. Hadn't got a clue about mixing shades. I said I could recommend someone to tutor her. I guess she didn't care for that too much because the next time I met them she said she had been promised an introduction to Bryce. I pointed out that if she went to Bryce she would no longer be welcome at my place. 'You have to choose carefully,' I said. She replied that she didn't wish to offend me but was hopeful he would include her in his upcoming exhibition."

Miss Stein paused, leaning forward toward me in her chair as she continued rubbing her hair inside the towel. "Personally I didn't think she had much of a chance with him. 'He's stuck in the depths of Impressionism,' I said, 'and he thinks women only belong in the kitchen or the bedroom.' Besides, what about Miss Goldfarb? We know what his opinion was about Jews. Exactly why I broke off all contact with him. Still, he got his just desserts in the end, didn't he, although I shouldn't speak ill of the dead, I suppose."

"You know about Reynold Bryce's death?" I asked cautiously.

"Of course. It was in the *International Herald* this morning. Stabbed by a hotheaded young Jew, so they surmise."

"They know who killed him?"

"A young Jewish man was seen running away down the street about the time he was killed," she said. "I'm not surprised, frankly, after his outspoken tirades against Jews. I'd have willingly done it myself, odious man. He liked to think of himself as the doyen of American artists here, but all he wanted really were sycophants around him, people who painted the way he did, no innovators, nobody with creative genius."

I was trying to process what I had just learned. If a young, zealous Jew killed Reynold Bryce then his death might have nothing at all to do with Sid and Gus's disappearance.

"So do you remember when was the last time you saw my friends?"

She stared out of the window. "Some time ago. Not recently, that's for sure. You have to understand that I see a lot of people."

"Not recently," I repeated.

"Why are you so keen to know when I saw your friends?" she demanded.

"Because they've disappeared. I don't know where they've gone and I'm worried about them."

"Perhaps they got tired of Paris and went to seek the sun on the Mediterranean. Lots of people do."

"No," I shook my head firmly. "They haven't gone away, not deliberately anyway. All their things are still in their apartment. And they invited me to stay with them. They knew I was coming."

231

"Well, that's a rum do." She rubbed her head vigorously with the towel. "What do you suppose might have happened to them?"

"I don't know, that's the problem," I said. "I don't know where to start. I know they were in contact with Reynold Bryce because there was a postcard from him posted just a day or two before they vanished."

"So where are you staying?"

"At their apartment at the moment," I said, "although the landlady keeps suggesting that I move on. I suspect she'd like to relet their room, although I don't think she can throw me out until the end of the month."

"Well I suppose we could always put you up here, if it came to that," she said.

"That's very kind, but no thank you," I replied. "I have a small baby, for one thing. And I want to stay on at my friends' place just in case some mail or any kind of message comes that might give me a clue as to where they've gone."

"Quite right." She nodded. "So there's no hint at all as to what might have happened to them?"

"None at all. It's as if they vanished in the middle of a normal day. There was food still on the table, Miss Goldfarb's cigarette holder, Miss Walcott's shawl. I was really worried when I heard that Reynold Bryce had been murdered, because I thought that perhaps . . ." I paused, and then said, "But if the killer was a young Jewish man, then surely a fellow Jew would not have been one of his targets."

"I wouldn't have thought so. Unless he was deranged. Some of these young artists do go off their rockers, you know. Or aren't quite stable to begin with and then they drink enough absinthe and go off the deep end. Have you spoken with any of their friends?"

"I don't know who their friends are. I know that Augusta Walcott has a cousin here. He arranged the introduction to Mr. Bryce."

"Oh, yes. Willie Walcott. Another of Bryce's golden boys, following him around and hanging on his every word. Of course young Willie is a very pretty boy, in fact I shouldn't be at all surprised if . . ." She broke off, but then added, "Well, none of that matters now."

"Do you have any idea where I'd find Willie Walcott?"

"He lives somewhere in Montparnasse," she said. "Most of the American painters favor that area over Montmartre. Americans like their creature comforts, don't they? And Montmartre does tend to be a trifle primitive — and wild."

"Do the Americans have a gathering place where he might be found?"

"I'd try the Closerie des Lilas on the Boulevard Montparnasse," she said. "Not too far from here, although I doubt anyone would be there at this hour. Far too early for people to want to socialize."

I had to smile. "I'm sorry I disturbed you," I said. "I have a young child and I'm used to rising at dawn these days. I'd forgotten that life is more leisurely for other people."

"Do you have a husband somewhere or have you dumped him?" she demanded frankly.

"He's back in New York. He's a policeman and there was a spot of trouble so he wanted me safely far away from the city."

"I see." She frowned. "You don't think your spot of trouble could have anything to do with your friends' disappearance?"

This had never occurred to me before and I felt myself going cold all over. Could the Italian gang have such a long reach that they were able to harm my friends this far away? Were they at this minute enjoying watching my feeble attempts to find Sid and Gus before they swooped to attack me? In which case — my heart did a terrifying lurch — Liam wasn't safe with the baker's wife.

I stood up. "I have to go," I said. "I'm sorry to have troubled you."

"Not at all. I quite enjoy a little drama. Write down your name and address, and I'll let you know if I hear anything. You're welcome to come on Saturday night and ask people yourself. You never know. It's a small community here. We enjoy minding each other's business."

I wrote on the back of my American calling-card and handed it to her.

"We may see you on Saturday then," she said.

"I'm not sure about that. I can't leave my son in the evening."

"Bring him with you. We'll find a closet to put him in." Then she laughed at my shocked face. "Other parents have done it before now. In my experience, which isn't great, I confess, babies can survive almost anywhere."

"Unfortunately mine has already learned to crawl and is turning into an escape artist," I said. "But thank you all the same. I'll see when it comes to Saturday."

She held out her hand to me and pumped mine heartily. "Best of luck to you. I'm sure it will all turn out all right. Things usually do."

Not for Reynold Bryce, I thought as I walked down the stairs.

EIGHTEEN

I was in the right part of the city to go immediately to seek out Willie Walcott, but Miss Stein had created a new fear for me — that Sid and Gus's disappearance might have something to do with my "spot of trouble" in New York. Surely an Italian gang couldn't have found out about my trip to Paris and sent someone to harm my friends? And even if they'd heard that I was to be sent to Paris, how could they have discovered Sid and Gus's address? Then I realized that an Italian gang in New York might well have affiliates back in Europe. If they were resourceful and powerful enough they might have infiltrated the New York police, or bribed someone there to report on the doings of Captain Sullivan and his family. Someone could have seen the cable, addressed to my friends. It was entirely possible that they now knew where I was and were watching me, waiting to strike.

So my first thought was to rush back to Liam to make sure he was all right. But then it struck me: Where could I take him to be out of harm's way? With a heavy child in my arms I'd be an easy target. It would be simple to push me in front of a subway train if I had a baby in my arms — or in front of an approaching carriage or automobile. Or even to grab Liam from a passing vehicle. I stood by the gilt railings that surround the Jardin du Luxembourg in an absolute agony of indecision. Was Liam safer with the baker's wife? Didn't Italians love their babies? Surely no gang could be black-hearted enough to murder a baby to punish his father. I decided I'd seek out Willie Walcott before I returned home. It would be one less time I'd have to leave Liam.

Fortunately a policeman, with rain dripping from the brim of his cap, was patrolling the gardens, or I would have walked unnecessary yards in the wrong direction. He pointed me to the Boulevard du Montparnasse at the far end of the park. Accordingly I trudged along, my brolly about to give up the unequal task of battling the wind and rain, feeling miserable and scared and horribly alone. I knew Miss Stein now, I tried to tell myself. She was someone I could turn to if I really needed help. I knew the baker's wife. I wasn't quite alone. It just felt that way.

I came at last to the Boulevard du Montparnasse and again I was in luck. The Closerie des Lilas was actually on the corner where it joined the Boulevard Saint-Michel. It had an awning over outside tables and chairs, looking damp and abandoned at this moment. There were lights on inside and I could see heads, including womens' hats, indicating that this café might be an acceptable place for me to venture alone. I felt a pleasant draft of warmth as I went inside along with the enticing aroma of brewing coffee. A bell jangled above the door and a young man in an apron came over to me. "*Bonjour,* madame," he said, wiping his hands on the apron. "Are you here to join someone?"

I was about to ask my questions and then leave again but the coffee smell was too good to refuse. "I'm alone, monsieur. Maybe some friends will be coming in later. I'd just like a coffee."

"You are from England?" he asked in English.

"From America. Originally from Ireland."

"Ah. From America. We have many American visitors who come to this café. Poets, playwrights, artists. Which are you?"

"I'm not . . ." I began then changed my mind. "I write a little poetry," I said, remembering that Sid had been asked to join a group of poets. "I'm newly arrived here."

"Ah, then you should meet Monsieur Tarkington." He turned his attention to a table by the far window at which a group of men were sitting. "He considers himself a fine poet — don't you, monsieur?"

"Don't I what?"

"Albert thinks you consider yourself a fine poet," a young man with red hair said. The person who was being addressed, the Monsieur Tarkington, was an older, more sober-looking individual than the rest of his companions, in his dark three-piece suit with a watch chain draped across his vest. He had a sad-looking, not very handsome face.

"The very finest," he said. "Although the world likes to think of me only as a novelist. Novels make money, so I write them, but poetry is the true stuff of art. You're a poetess yourself, madame?"

"I write a little," I said, stretching the truth.

He stood up. "Booth Tarkington. Come on over and join us. We're deep in discussion on whether poetry per se needs form."

I went over and took the chair he had pulled out for me. Coffee was brought and I drank gratefully. The damp coldness had combined with my fear to chill me to the bone. I noticed that some of the men at the table were drinking something bright green in small glasses. It was a fascinating color but I didn't like to ask them what it was, not wanting to appear a neophyte.

"So you've just arrived in Paris, have you?" the young redhead asked, eyeing me with interest.

"I have and I'm trying to locate a couple of friends. One is also a poet, a Miss Elena Goldfarb from New York, and the other is the painter Willie Walcott."

"I met the Goldfarb woman once at a reading," another of them said. "A week or so ago. She read a poem. Not at all bad."

"But you haven't seen her since?"

"Can't say that I have."

"What about Willie Walcott then?"

"Oh, him. He's in here all the time," the red-haired one said. "Stay put and he'll show up. Especially if it's around mealtime and someone might treat him to food. Willie is a great cadger, in spite of the fact that he must be dripping with family money."

"I heard his father had cut off his allowance because he dropped out of Harvard," the dark one at the end of the table said. "So he has to rely on selling his paintings or the charity of his friends."

"Rather the latter than the former, I suspect," Booth Tarkington said. "From what I saw the boy didn't have too much talent. More a copier than an innovator — still stuck in Impressionism. At any rate he hasn't managed to impress any of the top name dealers. Vollard won't touch him."

"Reynold Bryce seemed to take a shine to him," someone suggested.

Two of the others looked at each other and laughed. "Well, he would, wouldn't he?"

"You mean because his painting style is in imitation of Bryce's?"

The man was still smiling. "Of course. That's exactly what I mean."

Booth Tarkington put a hand over mine. "Sorry, we shouldn't be making fun of a guy if he's a friend of yours. That's not quite kosher, is it."

More laughter. "Booth, you can hardly use the words 'kosher' and 'Bryce' in the same sentence, old man."

"Did you know that Reynold Bryce is dead?" I asked.

They nodded, their faces growing somber. "We just read about it in the paper this morning. We've been talking about it. We're not entirely surprised."

"Why is that? I've never actually met Mr. Bryce myself."

"Let me put it this way — he wasn't shy about expressing his opinions. Not just about Jews, but about art and literature too. If he didn't like something he'd not only trash it, he'd try to get everyone else to do the same."

"The paper said that a young Jewish man was seen running from his house."

"That's the most likely," the redhead said. "A hotheaded young guy fresh from Russia, I'll wager. They do things like that. Rush in and stab someone. Thank God we live in America where we behave in a civilized fashion."

"And dispatch people neatly with guns," Tarkington said. We all laughed.

At that moment we were hit with a blast of cold air and someone said, "Talk of the devil."

I saw the resemblance to Gus immediately but Willie was decidedly the more handsome of the two. Actually Miss Stein's description of him as a golden boy was not wrong. He had that same angelic air to him that I'd seen in Bryce's paintings and in Ellie, whom I'd met on the boat. His face was framed with light blond curls. He had clear blue eyes and an overall look of surprise. He also looked very pale.

"Hail and well met, fellows," he called, waving a hand to them as he came over to our table.

"It must be almost lunchtime. Willie's here," one of them called.

"I had to get out of the house today," Willie said. "I just heard about poor old Reynold. I'm completely in shock. I can't believe it. Who would kill him? How could anyone just walk into his apartment in that neighborhood and stab him? It doesn't make sense."

He looked around the group. "It had to be someone he knew, don't you think? I mean, he had servants there and probably a coachman standing outside. Did they steal anything, do you know?"

"The papers seemed to indicate it was a Jew, taking revenge," one of the group said.

Willie sighed. "That's probably the most likely. Reynold was becoming more rabidly anti-Semitic by the minute. He said if they reinstated Dreyfus to his former rank he'd leave Paris and go home and if you knew what Reynold felt about home, that was indeed a rash statement. But what a stroke of bad luck for me. He had promised to put two of my paintings in his next exhibition."

He came over to the table and gave me an inquiring look.

"A friend of yours, Willie," Booth Tarkington said. "Asking after you. Came all the way from America to catch up with you. Did you leave a broken heart behind?"

Willie frowned as he stared at me. "I've never seen her before in my life."

"No, you haven't, Mr. Walcott," I said hastily because I could feel all those eyes on me, "But I am a good friend of your cousin Augusta. In fact I came over to stay with them — at their invitation — only to find that they are not here. So I wondered if perhaps Gus had told you anything that might shed light on where they've gone."

"Oh, so you're the Irish girl." He smiled at me now, such a devastating smile. "Yes Augusta did mention that they were expecting an Irish friend from New York. But you say they are not at their apartment?"

"No. I've been there two days and no sign of them, and no note."

"That's certainly strange." He pulled up a chair and sat beside me. "Maybe they got fed up with the primitive conditions of Montmartre. That is where they moved to, isn't it? 'Wanting to be in the heart of the art world,' so they said. As if Montmartre is any more the heart than Montparnasse is. I

245

told them that but Augusta's companion seemed to be rather opinionated and apparently some relative of hers is a painter there and she seemed to think he was the cat's whisker when it came to the art world."

"That's right," I said. "She discovered a long-lost cousin. Maxim Noah, wasn't that his name?"

Willie Walcott shrugged. "Doesn't ring a bell with me. Anyhow they wanted to be closer to what he called the Navel of Creativity."

"They haven't moved again," I said. "They've left all their things."

"Sorry, but I can't help you," he said. "The last time I saw them was a couple of weeks ago when I told them I'd set up a meeting with Reynold Bryce for them. They were very thrilled. I never did hear how it turned out because Reynold told me he was busy on a new painting and didn't want to be disturbed." And he made a strange face, looking for a moment like a petulant child.

There was no point in staying any longer. I rose to my feet. "I have to go," I said. "Maybe I could have your address, Mr. Walcott, and give you mine, just in case you hear anything about your cousin."

Willie Walcott and I exchanged addresses. "Do come up and visit me if you feel like it.

Don't be put off by the girls who live on the first floor," he said. "They are dancers, not what you might think they are." He promised to get in touch with me if he heard anything about Sid and Gus. I got up and tried to pay for my coffee. Protests came from all around the table. "But we haven't even started discussing your poetry yet. You simply can't go."

"I'm sorry," I said. "I'll come back another time."

"Come to the poetry circle on Monday. It's a lively group," the redheaded one said. "We meet here, but it tends to be something stronger than coffee."

I left them and found that the rain had eased to a fine misty drizzle. I followed the Boulevard Saint-Michel in the direction of the Seine, anxious now to get back to Liam and frankly at a loss of what to do next. At least Willie Walcott had suggested someone else I might contact — the Jewish relative that Sid had met, who had clearly impressed her, much to the annoyance of Willie Walcott. And my Montmartre painter friends would surely be able to help me locate him. But it seemed like one of those childhood games in which one stumbles around blindfolded and everyone yells out "warmer" and "colder" as one seeks for something. I was getting nowhere and time was ticking on.

On the Boulevard Saint-Michel students were now pouring out of buildings on my right, making for the small cafés and bistros along the street. They laughed and shouted to one another, apparently without a care in the world except for a small group that stood up on a fountain, shouting through a bull horn. "Justice for Drefus now!" they chanted. "Reinstate him. Punish the true guilty one."

Their words were answered with some cheers and some catcalls. I hurried past, not wanting to get caught up in a brawl.

As I approached the Île de la Cité a great bell tolled, ringing the Angelus for midday. I suspected it must come from Notre-Dame and longed to see that church for myself. But I had no time to play sightseer and besides, I needed to steer clear of any sights that might attract tourists like Justin Hartley and his family. As if in answer to the great bell of the cathedral other bells took up the midday chime across the city until the air reverberated with their sound. It was a while now since I had lived in a Catholic country and the sound of the Angelus stirred something in me — a memory of the safer, simpler days of my childhood when the church played a big part in my life.

I crossed the river to the island and hesitated as I approached the Prefecture of Police. Should I perhaps seek out Inspector Henri and file an official missing persons report? Or . . . and here I hesitated, not wanting to consider the thought that lurked at the back of my mind . . . ask if any bodies brought into local morgues might match the description of my friends. I approached the guard on duty then turned away again. One more day, I told myself. I'll give it one more day. At least I now knew where to come.

The great cacophony of bells had died away, leaving the sound lingering in the air — except for one small bell that continued to ring somewhere close by on my left. It seemed to be coming from inside the court-yard of the Palais de Justice. Suddenly I was filled with a deep desire to be in a church again. My past experiences hadn't been positive, but that had nothing to do with God — more with bad priests. I followed the sound until I came to what was obviously a thin, tall church attached to the stout walls of the palace. I found an entrance, went in, and stood, mouth agape. The walls were entirely composed of tall stained-glass windows rising as if to heaven. At the far end was an exquisite rose window and as I stood there the sun must have peeped between clouds because stripes of colored light illuminated the floor. At the high altar a priest was saying mass while a few devout souls knelt in the front pews.

I stood there, gazing in awe, and found myself praying. "Let them be safe, oh God. Holy Mother, keep them safe. Keep my husband safe. Keep my son safe." It didn't seem right to pray for myself, but I hoped that God and the Holy Mother might take that prayer for granted. As I turned to leave I noticed I wasn't alone. Someone was standing at a side altar, gazing up at the window above. For a second I almost believed I was seeing an angel — and then I realized that the vision in blue and white with long white-blonde hair curling around her shoulders was none other than Ellie, the girl I had met on the ship.

Nineteen

She was staring, lost in thought or contemplation as a shaft of light fell on her, completely oblivious to my presence or that of anyone else. I went over to her and she started in alarm as she perceived someone beside her.

"Hello," I said. "I'm sorry. I didn't mean to startle you."

For a second she looked as if she might shy away, like a nervous colt, then her face broke into a smile of recognition. "Why, it's you. We met on the ship, didn't we?" she whispered. "How lovely to see you again. Isn't this glorious? I've been coming every day since I arrived and I still can't get over the beauty of it."

"It is glorious," I agreed.

An old woman in black turned to glare at us. We grinned to each other and made our exit. The rain had indeed stopped and a watery sun had appeared between dark clouds.

"So have you been enjoying your freedom in Paris?" I asked, realizing I didn't know her last name. "I'm afraid I only know you as Ellie, and that wouldn't be quite proper, would it?"

"Who cares about being proper." She laughed. "We're in Paris where nothing is supposed to be proper. Do call me Ellie. My given name is Eleanor May, which I hate. And yours is?"

"Molly Sullivan," I said. "Please do call me Molly since we're not required to be formal here."

She nodded. "In answer to your question I've been having an absolutely glorious time, Molly. Enjoying every single moment of it." She looked around. "Look, I'm going to get some lunch. Will you join me? It's a lovely city but it's rather sad to always eat alone."

"I really shouldn't," I said looking around me as the midday crowd crossed to the Right Bank of the river. "I've left a woman looking after my baby son."

I saw her face fall and realized how young she still was. "Do you not have to eat with your chaperone? Or have you managed to escape from her?"

"Oh, she's already gone." A mischievous

smile lit up her face. "I'm all alone until Peter gets here at the end of the week. Isn't it thrilling?"

"How did you manage that?" I asked, having observed the most attentive chaperone on the ship.

"It was rather simple really. Everyone at home thought I was going to meet Peter and his family at the Ritz as soon as I arrived. The dreadful mademoiselle thought that too. So her job was only to escort me to Paris and deliver me to the Ritz — which she did. Peter thinks I'm arriving at the end of the week, at the same moment he gets here, so I've fooled all of them."

She looked and sounded like a naughty ten year old.

"How did you manage to pull that off?" I asked.

"Simple. You just tell people what they want to hear. I've become rather good at it."

"But won't there be trouble when Peter finds out you've been staying at the Ritz for a week without him?"

She laughed. "How will he find out? I'm not staying at the Ritz, silly. I couldn't afford that kind of money. I'm actually staying at a dear little hotel on the Left Bank . . . on the Boulevard Saint-Germain. It's called the Hôtel d'Alsace and it's quite dinky but famous because Oscar Wilde actually died there. You know about him, don't you?"

"I most certainly do, but I'm surprised that you do."

The wicked grin again. "I know a lot of things I'm not supposed to. I say, do be a sport and come and eat with me. I know a great little bistro and it won't take long. They serve students who have to hurry back to class. They all try to flirt with me, which is fun in a way, but makes me a little uneasy, being alone. I have to keep telling them my stern and strict papa has gone for a walk and will be back shortly." She paused and there was an expression on her face I couldn't quite read. Something had definitely troubled her. Then she smiled again. "Come on. It's just back across the bridge. My treat. I'm spending my stepfather's money and enjoying every moment of it."

She slipped her arm through mine. "I really can't," I said, hunger and a desire to be with a friend in a strange city wrestling with my maternal instincts. "Liam has to be fed soon. I'm still nursing him."

"Then we'll go back to your place first," she said. "Where are you staying?"

"In Montmartre," I said. "At a friend's apartment."

Her face lit up. "Montmartre. *Ooh,* I've been wanting to go there, but not quite daring to alone. Come on, let's go together. You can show me around."

She almost dragged me off toward the Right Bank. I saw no reason not to let her come with me. Frankly I was in sore need of some good company.

"Is Montmartre really as wicked and sinful as they make out?" she asked. "Naked girls and opium?"

I had to laugh. "I haven't encountered any naked girls or opium yet, but it does seem to be quite primitive. And lots of artists."

"Oh, yes. Artists. I met some artists who wanted to paint me when I was walking in the Jardin du Luxembourg. I was sorely tempted to say yes, but then I thought if Peter happened upon a naked portrait of me, there would be trouble."

"There certainly would." The talk about artists had reminded me of her connection. "I don't suppose you had a chance to visit Reynold Bryce, did you?"

"Before he died, you mean? Wasn't that awful?"

"Ah, so you heard about it?"

She nodded, biting her lip like a small child. "It was an awful shock. It really upset me. I kept thinking that I'd seen him alive

255

only a day before. I went to see him the day I arrived. I thought he might take me out to dinner, actually."

We had reached the Métro station. "Oh, the underground railway. I've been dying to take a ride on a subway train. How exciting." And she ran ahead of me down the steps. A train came thundering in and this time I knew where to stand for the second-class coach.

"So you were telling me about Mr. Bryce," I said as we took seats on a wooden bench and the train began to move. "You saw him the day before he died. Was he surprised to see you?"

"Surprised, yes. Pleased, no." She paused, bumping against me as the train went around a bend in the track. "He looked as if he was seeing a ghost to start with. Then I told him who I was and he said, 'Of course you are.' Then he told me he was in the middle of painting and didn't have time to see me that day and I should come back when he'd finished.

"I said that my fiancé would be arriving in a few days and I didn't know what his plans were for us.

" 'Fiancé? Good God, has it been that long?' he said. Then a voice called out from another room and if my French was correct it told him to hurry up because she was getting cold. He looked quite embarrassed. 'You see. Now is not a good time,' he said, and led me back to the front door." She turned to me with a bleak face. "And then he was dead."

"Yes, it's sad, isn't it? They say it was a young Jew, angry about Bryce's outspoken anti-Semitism."

"Do they?" She paused. "Well, I suppose that was a good reason for killing him."

"I don't know about that," I said. "You can't go around killing people who insult you or disagree with you or society would be a highly dangerous place."

"Have they caught this young Jewish man yet?"

"Not yet as far as I know. I expect they will, unless he flees to Spain or somewhere."

"Good," she said. "I hope they do catch him."

We changed trains and then came up into daylight again at Pigalle. Ellie suggested that she wander around and look at things while I fed the baby. I was relieved to find Liam playing happily. He had already had some good soup, Madeleine told me. I went into her bedroom and nursed him, but he didn't seem too interested, making me wonder if she had done this too before I arrived. But the good thing was that he was safe and he was happy. Ellie was bubbling over with enthusiasm when I met her again on the corner of the Rue des Martyrs. "Do you know that they have a market for artist's models in the square every Monday? It's too bad that Peter arrives next Monday or I'd be tempted to try my luck. Although I suspect I look too pure for most of their paintings. And I've found somewhere good to eat. Come on. I'm starving."

She led me to a little bistro on the far side of Pigalle. The place was redolent with the scent of herbs and garlic and several tables were full of young men who might have been artists or poets. Some of them looked up as we passed, and one or two called out to Ellie. We sat in a corner and Ellie ordered us two bowls of the rabbit fricassee. "I was told it's their specialty" she said. "I've only been eating things that I know would appall them at home. I've tried frog legs and snails too. I'm going the whole hog since this is my one chance of freedom."

"Ellie," I said hesitantly. "Are you sure you're doing the right thing by getting married right away? You clearly want to experience life first."

She gave me a bleak stare. "What choice do I have? I simply can't live at home any longer. My mother is completely under the dreaded stepfather's thumb now and I'm ordered around like a little girl. And I can't touch my trust fund until I turn twenty-five or I marry . . . so it's the only option really."

"But do you love Peter?"

"Of course not. I hardly know him. But he's good-looking and he treats me as if I was made of porcelain and might break, so I'm sure he'll take good care of me."

"Do you want to be taken care of?"

"Not really."

"Then don't do something you'll regret."

"You mean stay on in Paris and make my living as an artist's model?"

"Not quite as extreme as that." I had to laugh. "I don't think artists' models make enough money to keep them in the style you're accustomed to. And it seems to me as if most of them become the mistress of the artist who paints them, which I certainly wouldn't want for you. But you could put off marriage and go to a ladies' college for more education. My friends went to Vassar and loved every moment of it."

"I'm afraid I'm not the best student," she said. "I'd feel stupid in a college of brilliant bluestockings."

"Then what would you like to do?"

"Live life. Be free. Travel. Make friends.

Go dancing."

The waiter put down two bowls of rabbit fricassee and a basket of bread. "You like to dance?" he asked in broken English. "In Montmartre are many dancing places. You must come to the Moulin de la Galette on Sunday. Dancing *en plein air* — how you say?"

"Outside?" she asked.

He nodded. "*Oui.* Very nice. Beside the old windmill. I go there with my friends. You have good time with us. You will come?"

"I don't know . . ." she turned to me for approval. "Should I go? Will you come with me?"

"Ellie, I'm a married woman with a baby. I can't go out dancing."

"You will be quite safe with us," he said. "Many many people at the Moulin. All dancing and having good time."

"It does sound lovely," she smiled wistfully. "But I don't know about coming up here alone at night. Is it safe?"

He laughed then. "Mademoiselle, the dancing begins in the afternoon. Of course it continues under the stars but you can depart when you wish. Many families bring picnic. You will have good time, I think."

She looked at me again. "In the afternoon, Molly. You could bring your baby. It would be fun."

"Yes, it does sound like fun," I said. "But I have a lot of things on my mind at the moment. I'll join you if I can."

She beamed at him again. "I'll try to come, even if Molly is an old stick-in-the-mud."

"I will await you, mademoiselle. My name is Jean. My friends and I we study at the École des Beaux-Arts to be painters." He paused then added, "And pay for our existence by being waiters."

Ellie held out her hand to him. "I'm Ellie," she said and gave him a radiant smile.

TWENTY

After lunch we walked together up the crooked cobbled streets of Montmartre. Actually I was glad to have company as a woman walking alone always feels a little vulnerable, especially in an area of narrow alleys like this — wild, bohemian, untamed. I wanted to seek out Maxim Noah, Sid's cousin, just in case he had any information about what might have happened to them. I had no idea where he lived and worked but I did now know that a group of artists could be found at the building they called Le Bateau-Lavoir — the laundry boat — and I suspected that Montmartre was small enough that artists knew each other. Narrow cobbled streets led to flights of steps. Respectable stone houses now gave way to shacks as we went higher. There were goats tethered on a plot of grass and someone was growing what looked like beans and asparagus in a small garden behind a shed. It was a strange transformation to be in this primitive and rural environment and yet only steps from a civilized city. Ellie, of course, found it enchanting, especially when we came up the final twisty street to the summit and the great half-built dome of the church reared above us dazzling white, while below us the whole city was spread at our feet.

"Isn't it magnificent?" she said, spreading wide her arms as if to embrace it. "Being up here with you makes one forget all of one's troubles, doesn't it? The rest of the world simply doesn't matter. I am all-powerful."

I looked at her fondly. "You are too young to have troubles," I said. "Inconveniences, to be sure, but . . ."

"You don't know the half of it," she said. "And I can't tell you. It's something I have to figure out and get through on my own." She turned away from me, staring out to where the city melted into distance and the great shape of the Eiffel Tower dominated all else. Then suddenly she swung around, all smiles again. "I'm so glad I met you, Molly. It's good to have a friend in a strange city, isn't it?"

I agreed that it was.

"Molly, would you do me a favor? Would

you say that we've been together all the time I've been here? That we've seen the sights together?"

"Why should I say that?"

She hesitated, looking down at her neat little shoes, now rather mud-splattered. "Just in case anyone finds out about my being here alone and wants to know."

I took it that by "anyone" she meant Peter. "How could anyone find out, unless you tell them?"

She sighed. "I don't know. I think I'm safe, but . . ." She looked around, then exclaimed. "Look. There is the windmill that Jean told us about. The one with the dancing."

"I don't think I'd want you to come up here on your own," I said. "It is very remote, isn't it? And the people we have passed were not altogether savory."

"Oh, come now, Molly. Don't tell me you never did anything rash and exciting in your youth?"

I smiled at the fact that she saw me as an old woman, even though I was not quite twenty-seven. "Yes, I've done plenty of rash and exciting things," I said, "but they haven't always been fun and I've put my life in danger several times."

"Have you?" she asked. "Do tell me."

"I have been a detective," I said. "And now I'm married to a police captain."

"Really?" Her look became wary suddenly. "You aren't over here to help the police, are you?"

"Not at all," I said. "I'm supposed to be enjoying myself with dear friends, only they've upped and vanished, so I'm trying to find out what happened to them."

"Oh. I see." She gave the great edifice one last look. "Come on, let's go on down. It's quite chilly up here and it might rain again."

"I need to find a relative of my friend who lives somewhere up here," I said. "I'm hoping he knows what might have happened to them." As we passed the Moulin de la Galette, with its gay posters advertising the Sunday *bal,* I saw an old gentleman with a beard sitting at an easel, painting. I asked if he knew Maxim Noah and he shook his head, not taking his eyes from the trees he was filling in on an enormous canvas. I then asked for the Bateau-Lavoir and was given directions to that, easily enough.

"They call themselves painters," he muttered as we turned away. "Painters? Don't know much and don't want to learn."

We went down a flight of steps and came out to where a sprawling building of tacked-together timbers looked as if it was in danger of sliding off the side of the hill. As we approached the entrance I saw that this was the top floor while the rest of the building clung below to the steep hillside. It looked fragile and highly dangerous.

"Do you really think we should go in here?" Ellie asked. "It looks absolutely awful. Like a den of thieves."

"I expect we'll be all right," I said, sounding braver than I felt.

She stepped back suddenly. "I don't think we should go inside, Molly. It looks too dirty and horrid. In fact I think I've seen enough of Montmartre. It's too primitive, isn't it? How funny that some artists should live like this while others have lovely apartments in the best part of the city. It doesn't seem fair, does it?"

"You mean Mr. Bryce? He's the only one I know of who lived in the best part of the city. And he's dead, poor man. That doesn't seem fair either, does it?"

"I suppose not." She twisted a strand of hair around a finger, staring at the open door of the Bateau-Lavoir hanging crookedly. "Look, why don't we go back to the city. I know a heavenly little tearoom on the Rue de Rivoli. They make cakes to die for. Won't you come with me?"

"I can't," I said. "I have to find my friend's

266

cousin and see what he can tell me. But you don't have to come with me. I understand."

"If you're really sure." She stared at me, then at that half-open door. "I have to go now," she said. "You'll be all right on your own, won't you?"

"I'm sure I will."

I watched her go down the hill with her dainty little steps. There was something I didn't quite understand about Ellie — and I realized I didn't even know her last name.

The front door opened with a creak and groan. I went in and looked around, not knowing which door to knock on. Then I heard the sound of male voices and laughter from down below. I descended a narrow staircase with care, as there were broken boards and little light. The building didn't smell too savory, as if there were no drains and someone had burned their cooking. And in the background that ever-present odor of oil paints, linseed oil, and dark cigarettes.

Down one flight I went, then a next. Then on the very bottom floor a door was open and I heard voices coming from inside.

"What do you think?" a voice asked. "Is it good?"

"Not bad, Guillaume. Not your best."

"It needs more work, doesn't it?"

I approached the door and tapped on it. "Pardon me," I said.

They looked up at me, startled as if they were naughty schoolboys who had been caught out doing something wrong.

"Madame? You look for someone?"

"I do," I said. "I am looking for the painter Maxim Noah? Do you know where I might find him?"

"Maxim? Is he awake? Go and bang on his door. Tell him a foreign lady is here."

"He lives here?" This was a stroke of luck.

One of them got up and I heard the stairs creak as he went up one flight. The fat one nodded to me with recognition. "I remember you. You came to the Nouvelle Athènes the other day. Did you find your friends?"

"I'm still looking. Maxim Noah is a cousin of one of them so I thought that maybe . . ."

"Oh, so she is the American lady he was talking about. Quite excited to have met her. I suppose these Jews feel rather vulnerable at the moment, all alone here at a time when . . ."

He broke off as heavy workman's boots clomped down the stairs.

"Someone to see me?" he asked. "Is it my newfound American relative?" He came into the room, a handsome black-eyed boy with tousled hair and a jacket patched at the elbows.

"Mr. Noah?" I held out my hand. "I am a friend of your cousin Elena."

"Enchanted." He didn't sound particularly enchanted and the hand that took mine was wary.

"I'm sorry to disturb your work," I began.

This produced a chuckle all around. "Work? He was in bed with Jojo, no doubt."

"How is Jojo, by the way?" the fat one asked. "We haven't seen her for days. Have you grown so jealous that you hide her away from us?"

"She hadn't been well. A mere cold but she stays in bed." He looked at me again. "How can I help you, madame? Has my cousin sent you to look at my paintings, perhaps? You wish to buy one? I have many for sale."

"Enough to paper the walls," one of them said and they laughed again.

Maxim's eyes flashed dangerously. "You insult my art because you do not understand it. Ask Picasso. He understands. He knows that art must move away from representation and the artist must have freedom to express his inner soul."

"Then your inner soul must be quite murky," one of them said. "Your paintings are terribly dark and gloomy. If this lady put them on her wall she would want to commit suicide instantly."

"Do not listen to them, madame," Maxim said. "You come to see for yourself. I go first to make sure that Jojo is dressed properly for your visit."

He ran up the stairs. I looked around at the group. "I take it that Jojo is his mistress?"

"And very possessive he is about her too," the fat one replied. "Won't let a man near her. Won't let her out alone. Of course, she's very young and beautiful. A dangerous combination with so many wolves like us around."

I thanked them for their help then followed Maxim up the stairs back to the top floor. I waited in the hallway, looking across at another door on which was scrawled, in blue chalk *Au rendezvous des poètes* ("The meeting place of poets") and realized I could see how Sid and Gus had been excited to come to a city like this, where art and poetry and the bohemian lifestyle were not frowned upon.

"Please enter, madame." Maxim opened a door behind me and I went into one of the sorriest rooms I'd ever seen. I had grown up in an Irish peasant's cottage. Our life had been simple in the extreme but we had a good stove, the pots were polished sparkling clean, our battered furniture was also polished and decorated with pillows made from scraps. In short it was a friendly, homey sort of place. This room was barely furnished, with no adornments. The floor was bare, with uneven boards, and in the far corner was an unmade iron bedstead. The only saving grace was a window that looked out across the city, letting light stream in. Under the window was a table with half a loaf of dark bread, next to a palette of paints, a brush still lying across it. A canvas on an easel still glistened with wet paint. There was no sign of the mysterious Jojo. Maxim had spirited her away.

"Madame. Please sit." He motioned to a wobbly cane chair. "I would offer you some tea, but alas I have no spirit for my little stove. As you can see our life here is . . . how you say . . . simple?"

I nodded.

"But if I sell a painting soon, all will be well. Your friend, Mademoiselle Goldfarb, she promises to take some of my paintings back to New York when she departs. She is very kind and very rich, no?"

I was about to say she wasn't very rich, just comfortably situated, then I realized that to Maxim she would appear to be so. As he spoke I was studying the paintings tacked to the walls. The man downstairs was right — they were gloomy in the extreme. Great gashes of dark colors, mouths open in screams, burning houses, strange flying figures. They were the stuff of nightmare.

"It was a lucky day that we met at the poetry reading, don't you think? Imagine — Miss Goldfarb searches the whole of Paris for her cousins and doesn't find them, and then we meet by chance."

I was still examining the bleakness of the studio. "What about the rest of your family?" I asked. "Are they not still in Paris?"

"All dead." He sighed. "My parents died when I was a child. I ended up in the orphanage. Not a pleasant place."

"I'm so sorry. That's why you paint such sad scenes."

"I have seen much sadness. Family is important, don't you think? Family is the most important thing in the world."

"I suppose it is. I too have no family but my husband and child, so I know how it feels."

He nodded. "I am so happy to find a cousin. Mademoiselle Goldfarb tells me that my family in New York has done well. I am glad for them."

"Yes, I believe they have prospered. Sid doesn't talk about them much. They don't approve of her lifestyle."

"Ah." He nodded. "She too has her problems, then. Life always makes problems, no?"

"So how exactly are you related to her?" I asked.

"My mother, she was also from the family Goldfarb. She told me two brothers left Poland. One went to America, one to Paris."

"So your grandfathers were brothers?"

"So it seems. So tell me — what do you think of my art?"

"It's striking," I said tactfully. "Different."

"Picasso says it shows genius, and Picasso he is a genius himself. He says the world is not ready for us yet. And that is true. Most people want pretty pictures on their walls. I too can paint pretty pictures if I have to. But I must paint where my soul is." And he thumped his chest. A most dramatic young man.

"You should paint the occasional pretty picture to pay the rent," I said. "Every artist has to compromise."

"I try this. Believe me, I do try this, but it leads only to destruction. So you will buy a painting?"

I gave an embarrassed smile. "I'm afraid

I'm not rich like my friends. I'm the wife of a poor policeman."

"No? A policeman? In America?"

"In New York."

"Ah, I see." He nodded. "So you do not come to Paris to buy paintings."

"No. Actually I came to find you because I'm worried about Miss Goldfarb and Miss Walcott."

"Worried, why?"

"They've vanished. I arrived in Paris, expecting to stay with them and they are not at their apartment. Nobody knows where they have gone. Have you seen them recently? Have they said anything to you about leaving the city?"

Those sorrowful dark eyes turned to me. "No. I know nothing that explains this. Last time I saw them they were happy. The artist lady hopes for one of her paintings to be in the big exhibition. She was working to complete a new canvas. Why should they leave Paris at such a moment? Unless they have been taken ill, do you think?"

"Surely even from a hospital bed they could write to me, or get someone to write to me. And their landlady would know. And is it likely that they are both taken ill at the same time?"

"They could both have eaten bad food

and been poisoned. There are bad oysters in the city, so I am told. Many people are sick. Some die."

My stomach lurched. Food poisoning. Why hadn't I thought of that? But surely if one has food poisoning it usually strikes at home, several hours after the meal. Wouldn't the landlady have been consulted about which hospital or doctor they should go to? Still, it was a possibility I hadn't considered and it gave me a new area to search.

I stood up from the rickety chair. "Thank you for your time, Mr. Noah. I must go. I have left my child with a local woman. I wish you luck with your painting."

"Thank you." He took my hand. "And I wish you good fortune in your search for your friends. I pray that nothing happens to them. I could not bear to lose my newly found cousin. I too will ask and search for them everywhere most diligently."

As I left Le Bateau-Lavoir I sensed, rather than saw, a small dark figure slip in through the front door. So Jojo, the mistress, had been hiding outside until I left. Obviously he didn't want to give a bad impression to a potential buyer from America.

TWENTY-ONE

An attractive boy, I thought as I picked my way down the flights of steps back to the Rue des Martyrs. Dashing and magnetic, if a little on the tragic side. I could see why Sid was excited to have discovered this long-lost cousin. Perhaps she'd take him back to New York with her and introduce him to her family, if . . . And I broke off the thought at that *if.* If she was still in Paris and was all right. I knew I'd have to visit the hospitals and the morgue and I dreaded the thought of it.

I retrieved Liam, clearly not anxious to leave Madeleine, who had now introduced him to the delights of French pastries, and stopped to pick up supplies for our evening meal before I carried him back across the street. As I opened the front door Madame Hetreau darted out of her hiding place — the spider once more catching the fly.

"Ah. So you return," she said. "You have

been enjoying yourself, I suppose. They tell me you leave your child with the baker's wife and you're off on your own chatting with men in cafés."

I bristled at this suggestion that I was ignoring my child because I was off having a good time, but I controlled my voice before I said, "Because I've been searching for Miss Goldfarb and Miss Walcott, naturally, and I couldn't take a child with me all over Paris." Luckily my rusty French had improved during two days of speaking it constantly so that I no longer had to search for words and the sentence came out with the right amount of force.

She recoiled a little at this. "And you still haven't found them, I take it."

"Unfortunately no. Miss Goldfarb's cousin suggested that they might have taken ill after eating bad food — oysters, maybe."

"I wouldn't know," she shrugged, giving me the impression that she wouldn't be concerned if they had died of bubonic plague as long as it didn't in any way affect her.

"I can't think of any other reason that they would have vanished leaving no word for me," I said. "So I'm afraid my next task will be to visit the hospitals and morgues in the city. Perhaps you can suggest where I should start if my friends were taken ill in this place."

"I think I would have heard if your friends came down with poisoning," she said. "And I heard nothing. One minute they were here and the next they were gone. Me, I still think they decided to take a jaunt and left the city. Perhaps they decided to return to New York."

"Not leaving all their clothing behind."

Liam squirmed and I attempted to hang onto the bag of groceries. "I must take him upstairs. He's getting heavy."

As I turned away she called after me. "One minute, madame. I believe a postcard might have come for you." She reached into Sid and Gus's mail slot and held it out to me. "I can think of no one else to whom this might apply."

I put down the bag of groceries and took it from her. The front was a painting of a woman drinking tea. I turned it over. It was addressed in an elegant hand I didn't recognize. I was able to translate that it was addressed "To the Lady from New York staying at 35 Rue des Martyrs. . . ."

The message area was left blank.

I looked up, puzzled, to see Madame Hetreau staring at me. "Is it from the American ladies?"

"No," I said. "I've no idea who it is from. I don't recognize the writing. And there's no message. What can it mean? Did it arrive today?"

"This morning. Right after you went out."

I held it out to her. "You've seen it — why would someone send me a blank postcard?"

"I have no idea, madame."

Liam made a grab for it, and I had to hang onto him lest he tumble from my arms. "I have to take him upstairs," I said. "Thank you for alerting me to the postcard."

She almost hadn't, I thought as I trudged up the stairs. She'd only handed it to me as an afterthought. Was she going to leave it hidden in the mail slot and her conscience finally got the better of her, or had she genuinely forgotten about it? As soon as I entered the apartment I put Liam in his crib, protesting loudly, and sat on the bed, turning the postcard over in my hands. Who could have known I was here and sent me a postcard? And if someone had bothered to do so, why was there no message on it?

I looked at the picture on the front again. An attractive painting in the Impressionist style of a woman drinking tea. That was all. I carried it over to the window and stared at both sides in the light, wondering if there might be some kind of hidden message. But there was none. "To the Lady from New York" . . . the person who had written this didn't even know my name. Unless "the Lady from New York" wasn't intended for me at all, but for either Sid or Gus. Perhaps I was hoping for too much from this postcard, thinking it might be some kind of message for me. Perhaps the simple explanation was that Gus had admired a painting. Someone she had been chatting with had seen a postcard with a rendition of this painting on it and sent it to her as a kindly gesture.

I sighed, put it down on the bed, and went into the kitchen to prepare an evening meal for us. I tried to put it from my mind, but it was the first communication of any sort I had received, even if it made no sense to me. A woman drinking tea from an elegant little cup. Were Sid and Gus in some kind of danger? Did they want me to meet them at a tea salon? Might they have left a message for me there?

I remembered the worrying thought that had occurred to me earlier — that the Cosa Nostra gang in New York had somehow managed to find out I was coming to Paris and had harmed or kidnapped my friends. But then why leave me unharmed, walking around the city for three days? Nothing had made sense since I arrived in Paris. Nobody in the artistic community seemed to have seen Sid and Gus recently. Their cousins were happily going about their business. And yet someone had murdered a fellow artist and I had come to not believe in coincidence. Tomorrow I would make a list of tearooms in Paris and see if that produced any result.

Liam had a bad night. I suspect his stomach could not handle the amount of food that Madeleine had tried to put into him. I took him into bed with me, lying him on my own stomach and feeling the comforting warmth of his body against mine. I longed for Daniel and his arms around me. How soon could I hope for a letter from him, I wondered. I lay there, listening to the noises of the street below — laughter, shouts, singing. It sounded as if the rest of the world was having a good time in Paris. Eventually I drifted off to sleep and dreamed of the woman in the painting. "Really it's quite obvious, isn't it?" she said to me and put down her teacup with a bang.

I awoke, realizing that the bang that had woken me had been a shot fired in the street. I laid the sleeping Liam beside me and went over to the window. I opened the shutter but heard nothing more. I remembered all the talk of duels and Picasso saying that he hadn't shot his pistol for days. This was a violent city. Lots of things could go wrong here. I tried to fall back to sleep, wondering what the woman in my dream had meant when she said it was quite obvious.

The next morning I awoke with a headache that thundery weather and lack of sleep would always bring on in me. Liam seemed quite recovered from his fretful night and was raring to go. I nursed him, fed him farina for his breakfast, and then made myself a boiled egg with yesterday's stale bread. I wasn't going down all those stairs just to get a fresh loaf. Then when we were both washed and dressed I took Liam back to the bakery.

"If I am imposing on you too much, please tell me," I said.

Madeleine looked amused. "Too much? Madame Sullivan, I grew up looking after seven younger brothers and sisters and helping out on the farm. Two small children and one small apartment seems like a holiday for me. Besides, I like to play with your son. My own baby is still too small. All he wants to do is eat and sleep. Your boy makes me laugh."

So I left him with a clear conscience,

knowing that Madame Hetreau would probably be gossiping again with the neighbors about the flighty woman from America who was off gallivanting and leaving her baby to strangers. I had asked the baker whether there might be any tearooms in the neighborhood. He mentioned a couple of cafés that served tea. "But not exactly tea salons, Madame. For those you must go to the better arondissements — the first and the sixth. That is where people do not have to work hard all day and have time to take tea with their friends," he said.

I thanked him and took the Métro back to the city center. I remembered Ellie mentioning a teahouse on the Rue de Rivoli, so that seemed like a good place to start. I walked the length of the colonnade glancing into all the little shops and cafés until I finally found an attractive establishment called Angelina. It did look very inviting with its display of exquisite pastries and little marble tables. I stood hesitating in the doorway, wondering what to say that would not sound completely mad, when I heard voices echoing from the arched ceiling of the colonnade.

"Really, Mother. You can't want tea at this hour. I promised Porky that we'd meet him at the Louvre." And Justin Hartley and his family were coming toward me, only a few steps away. I couldn't think what to do. If I ran on ahead I would surely be noticed. If I went into the tea shop their mother might well prevail and follow me inside.

"Madame wishes a table?" A chubby little man with an impressive mustache appeared at my shoulder and literally escorted me inside. Out of the corner of my eye I watched Justin and his family go past. So he had gotten his way again. For once I was grateful. I took the chair the patron had pulled up for me and sat. This was clearly going to be an extravagance, especially for one who has no idea how long her money has to last, but I really couldn't back out without looking an awful fool, and risk another encounter with the Hartleys. I ordered a pot of tea and the smallest pastry I could find. The café owner joked, "Ah, madame wishes to preserve her excellent figure," and I didn't contradict him. When he brought the tea I asked, "I understand that two friends of mine, American ladies, like to frequent this tea salon. I had hoped to run into them here. One of them wears her hair cut short like this. Dark hair. Very striking. You'd remember her."

He frowned. "No, madame. You must have confused us with another establishment. I do not recall these ladies coming in here."

"Oh, dear. I am sorry. I wonder which other tearoom they might have meant?"

"Perhaps you are thinking of Ladurée on the Rue Royale," he said. "Or maybe Maison Cador on the other bank of the river in Saint Germain. They are both fine places, in their way." He shrugged as if it was almost an insult to compare them to this queen of establishments.

I sat, enjoying every sip of the tea. Being raised in Ireland tea was as familiar to me as mother's milk and I still hadn't learned to fully appreciate the coffee that Daniel and Sid and Gus preferred. The little pastry melted in my mouth. Quite heavenly, as Ellie had said. But when I received the bill I realized that I must not be trapped into taking tea at the other establishments. I thanked the proprietor and made my way first to Ladurée and then across the Seine to the Left Bank where I found the Maison Cador. Neither of these teahouses remembered seeing Sid and Gus. I stood for a long while outside each of them, looking around for any kind of clue. The trouble was that I didn't know what I was looking for.

By the end of the day I had covered every notable tea salon in the city and was none the wiser. If Sid and Gus wanted to convey a message to me from a blank postcard and a picture of a woman drinking tea, they had not succeeded. I had to conclude that the postcard was meant for one of them and had no hidden meaning. I retrieved Liam, bought some vegetables and a neck bone to make soup and went back to number 35. I braced myself for Madame Hetreau's caustic comments as I came into the front hallway and steeled myself to tackle the stairs. I had already gone up the first three or four before a voice behind me called, "Madame. One moment. I believe I have something else that might be for you." And she held out another postcard.

TWENTY-TWO

I almost slipped in my hurry to come down.

"I found this today," she said. "It had been put by mistake in the slot of Monsieur Du-Pont who is away at the moment and I only noticed it when I was dusting. But it seems to be from the same person as your postcard yesterday, no?"

I took it from her. It was another reproduction of a painting — this time it was of a mother and child. The child was about the age of Liam, dark-haired like him, and naked in his mother's arms. Again it was addressed to *La Dame Américaine qui visite* . . . in a hand I didn't recognize. Again there was no message.

I held it out to Madame Hetreau. "Does this mean anything to you?"

"The child resembles your son a little perhaps."

He did resemble Liam. So I had to take it that the postcard was meant for me. But apart from that I was completely in the dark.

I felt my feet dragging as we went up the stairs. It had been another day of foot-slogging and frustration. And all I had to encourage me were two postcards. I realized I hadn't studied the postmarks and how stupid this had been. If they had both been mailed from a community outside Paris then I'd know that my friends were there and trying to contact me. I couldn't think why they'd need to contact me in this fashion, but it gave me enough hope to take the last two flights of stairs more quickly. Liam was a bit clingy this evening, finally resenting the fact that his mother wasn't with him enough. He didn't want to be put down, so I held him on my hip while I put the postcards down side by side on the table.

They were both posted in Paris. I let out a sigh of disappointment. And this latest one had been mailed the day I arrived. So that was one day before the postcard of the tea-drinking woman. Someone was sending me one postcard per day. Surely that was significant? Then I turned them over and examined the paintings. Both in the Impressionist style, most attractive. I wondered for a moment whether they had been painted by Reynold Bryce, since I knew he had specialized in painting children once upon a time. But his angelic child had been more idealized and sentimental than this — a true painting of the Victorian era. This painting of mother and child was real and alive. Were they both by the same person? I studied the signature but it was too small to read.

Tomorrow I would show the postcards to the artists I had met, both at the Nouvelle Athènes and across the Seine in Montparnasse. One of them must surely recognize the painter. *And if they did, then what?* I asked myself. What would that tell me? All I could say was that someone was sending me pretty pictures. They were nothing like Gus's paintings, so I couldn't take it as a sign that they were from her. And they were sent from someone who didn't even know my name.

I played with Liam, trying to be the bright and cheerful mother he deserved, but it was hard when my head was so full of worry. I'd have to go to the police. To Inspector Henri. Then to the hospitals and morgues as planned. And if nothing turned up, I'd have to do the inevitable and write to Daniel asking him to book me a passage home before my money ran out even if that meant putting myself and my child back in danger. We ate, bathed, and fell asleep. I hoped for some kind of instructive dream, but I was so tired that I don't remember dreaming at all. Next morning I awoke early, fed Liam, dressed, and waited impatiently to resume my quest. It wasn't that I was looking forward to possible visits to a hospital or a morgue, or to the police, but I wasn't good at sitting and doing nothing, and there was no point in visiting the cafés too early in the day. Artists did not seem to be early risers. And if I wanted to enlist the help of Miss Stein, then I knew she didn't receive guests before luncheon.

Liam was in a particularly affectionate mood, wrapping his little arms around my neck when I picked him up and covering my cheek with sticky kisses. So I sat him on my knee and bounced him to his favorite song, "Horsey, horsey don't you stop. Just let your feet go clippety clop." Watching him laugh gleefully as he flew up and down made me forget my anxiety for a few moments and did us both good. But then, of course he was not as anxious to be left with Madeleine and I felt guilty when I crept away while he was engaged with his Noah's ark. It wasn't right to keep leaving my son like this. But then I reminded myself that rich children were raised entirely by nannies and only saw their mothers on special occasions. I knew he was safe and warm and

290

well-fed and I simply couldn't carry him around with me all day.

I set off down Rue des Martyrs and made first for the Nouvelle Athènes. I could see the usual group of young men around their table as I walked in. The enticing aroma of coffee enveloped me and I thought how lovely it would be to be free enough to spend every morning sitting with friends, with all the time in the world. Then I reminded myself that as well as having no set schedule and no responsibilities, these young men lived in a tumbledown shack without heat or running water and had to sell a painting in order to eat. Not such an enviable life after all!

Some of them looked up as I came in and I noticed that Maxim Noah was among them today.

"It's the good lady from America," he said. "You have had second thoughts? You come to buy a painting today?"

"As if she'd buy one from you when she could have one of mine at a good price," the young Spaniard Picasso said. "One can see that the lady has good taste."

I had to smile. "I'm afraid I can't afford to buy from either of you, even at a good price," I said. "I came back because I need your help. I am still looking for my missing

291

friends — for your cousin, Maxim. I have heard nothing from them since I arrived here and I am very concerned. But in the past two days I have received two postcards and I wondered what you could tell me about the paintings on them."

I placed the two postcards in front of them.

"Old style Impressionism of the last century," one of them muttered. But Picasso said, "Surely, they are Cassatt? I recognize the brushstrokes."

"Cassatt?" I tried to remember if this was a word I had heard before.

"Mary Cassatt," Picasso said. "Not a bad painter for an Impressionist."

"Do you know where I would find her? Does she live in Paris?"

"She used to live just around the corner but I hear she has moved away."

"To a better neighborhood," someone else commented. "Her paintings actually sell for real money."

"Do you know where this neighborhood might be?" I asked impatiently.

They shrugged, having little interest in a woman painter. Then one of them looked out of the window. "Monsieur Degas would know," he said. "Surely he and La Cassatt were good friends?"

"And where would I find this Monsieur Degas?"

"He usually stops in here for an absinthe." They looked at each other for confirmation.

"I haven't seen him since he heard of the death of Reynold Bryce. Those two were great friends, were they not?"

"They were both anti-Dreyfusards. I don't know about friends. I thought it was with Monet that Bryce was so friendly. Not that one sees Monet anymore, now that he has gone into hibernation outside the city."

Really they were most annoying in the way they went off on tangents.

"So does anyone know where M. Degas lives?" I asked.

"Around here somewhere. One often sees him."

My frustration was about to boil over when one of them said, "You are in luck, madame. Here he comes now." And the thin, dark man with the glowering face was striding toward the café door.

"That must be my signal to leave," Maxim said. "I know what he thinks about me and it's not pretty."

"Sit down, Maxim." Picasso yanked on his arm. "He won't want to join us. You know what he thinks of our painting. He despairs of all of us equally."

The tall man pushed open the door, looked across at the group at the table, glanced at me with a glimmer of interest, then nodded to the waiter. "The usual, Bernarde." Then he sat himself down with his back to the rest of the company and took out the newspaper to read.

"Monsieur Degas," the well-dressed member of our table whose name I had not yet learned called across to him. "Will you not join us?" The speaker grinned to his friends and I suspected he had only said this to annoy.

"Thank you, but no. I am mourning the loss of a good friend and have no wish for companionship or light banter," Degas replied.

"Then perhaps you can assist this lady who visits from America. She wishes to know the address of Mary Cassatt. She has recently moved, no?"

Degas turned to look at me. "Mary Cassatt?" he said. "Yes, she moved away. She now lives in the civilized and rarefied air of the first arrondissement. On the Rue de Marignan, madame. Just off the Champs-Élysées. I believe, if my memory does not fail me, that it is number ten. In any case there is a small café directly opposite with a striped awning and her house has an impressive green front door."

"Thank you, monsieur." I could have hugged him.

"You come from America to visit Miss Cassatt?" he asked, nodding as the waiter put the glass of green liquid in front of him.

"Oh, she's American?" I blurted out and saw him looking at me curiously.

"But naturally. Now that Reynold Bryce is no more, we must count her as the premier Impressionist from your country. A fine painter, for a woman."

I chose to ignore that last line. I had encountered it often enough when I had been told that I was not a bad detective, for a woman.

"If you wish to buy one of her paintings, I think you must be prepared to spend a good amount," he went on. "Her work has become popular, both here and in her homeland. She paints sentimental subjects, you see — babies, families, all suitable for any drawing room. Not like the subjects that some of us choose." And he gave a wry smile. "And now that Bryce is dead, no doubt his paintings will command a higher price." The smile faded. "Such a loss. Such a waste. And they still haven't found out who did this vile deed. Curse the damned Jews. If I ever find the man that did this, I will happily strangle him personally."

"You are quite sure it was a Jew who killed Bryce, are you?" one of the men at the table called across to Degas.

"But naturally. Did they not say that a young Jewish man was seen running from Bryce's house?"

"Propaganda!" a raised voice shouted. I think it was that of Maxim Noah. "Blame everything on the Jews, no? So convenient."

I had no wish to get into a political debate. I thanked Mr. Degas hastily, nodded to the group of artists, and left. *Mary Cassatt,* I said to myself. *An American painter. Had she sent me the postcards, and if so, why?*

As I crossed Pigalle to the Métro station I felt a tiny spark of optimism for the first time. I didn't remember Sid and Gus mentioning Mary Cassatt, but she was an unmarried American woman painter, so it was quite likely that Sid and Gus might have made her acquaintance. *But so what?* I asked myself. They had written about Willie Walcott and Maxim Noah and neither of them had any idea where Sid and Gus might have gone. But one of the cards was mailed on the day after they vanished. And there was the likeness to Liam. Surely all those were significant. But why not address the postcard with my real name? Unless, of course, they did not want anyone to know I was staying with them. Again my thoughts went back to the Italian gang and the fact that I too might be in danger.

I didn't care that it was still midmorning. I would find this Miss Cassatt and then if the interview led to nothing helpful, I'd make the rounds of hospitals and go to the police. With resolute step I descended into the darkness of the Métro and was soon on my way to the Champs-Élysées. It was a long street, I knew, and I had no idea where the Rue de Marignan might be found along its length. So I decided to start at one end, at the Place de la Concorde and work my way up to the Arc de Triomphe. As I came up the steps into the noise and traffic of that great oval space the sky was heavy with the promise of more rain. In fact it felt as if it might also thunder. Not a pleasing prospect. I started to walk up the avenue, first passing between gardens with buildings that looked like palaces set back among the trees. On a sunny day it would have been a delightful stroll, but the first drops of rain pattered onto me within a few minutes and I was forced to put up my brolly. After the gardens I came to a traffic circle with the Rue Montaigne leading off to the left. This was a name I recognized. I had taken that road to the Rue François Premier, where Reynold Bryce had lived and died. Miss Cassatt had indeed moved to a good area of the city. Either she was independently wealthy like Mr. Bryce, or her paintings sold well, or . . . I considered a third possibility . . . she had a rich lover. Such things were accepted in Paris, so I was told.

I hadn't gone much further up the Champs-Élysées before the heavens opened and rain came down in a great deluge. The gravel path turned to mud beneath my feet, then to puddles, then small lakes. Wind whipped the rain to drench my skirt as I struggled to control the umbrella and then, to crown it all, there was a flash followed by a crash of thunder almost overhead. I was horribly aware that I was walking under trees. I put my head down and stomped on resolutely. I was so intent on battling the storm that I almost walked past the Rue de Marignan. It was a narrow, treeless side street, and thank God it wasn't very long, as another clap of thunder rumbled overhead. But it appeared that number 10 was at the far end. I sloshed miserably forward, telling myself I was a fool for undertaking this in such weather. Miss Cassatt would not be pleased to see a drowned rat on her doorstep and I'd probably come away having learned nothing new.

At last I found it — an impressive white stone building with the obligatory wrought-iron balconies and, as M. Degas had remembered, a solid green front door. I knocked on this with some trepidation. It was opened cautiously by a maid, unmistakably French in a black dress and frilled white apron.

"*Oui,* Madame?" she asked.

"I have come to see Miss Cassatt," I said. "My name is Sullivan. Madame Sullivan. I have just arrived in Paris and think she might know two friends of mine."

"Please come in." She opened the door wider so that I could step into a foyer. It had a white marble floor onto which I was now dripping. "You are American?"

"I am from Ireland, but I live in New York, where my friends also live. I am sorry to disturb Miss Cassatt so early in the day, but it is a matter of importance." At least I hope that is what I was saying. I was feeling too cold, miserable, and depressed to be able to think clearly in a foreign tongue.

"Please wait here," the maid said. "I will tell Mademoiselle Cassatt that you have arrived. And may I take your umbrella? The weather, it is most inclement, no?"

I agreed that it was. She went up a flight

299

of stairs while I attempted to make myself look more respectable in the gilt-framed mirror. I looked up as the maid returned down the stairs. "Miss Cassatt will be happy to receive you," she said. "Please follow me."

We went up the flight of marble stairs and the maid pushed open double doors into a large room, decorated very much in the French style with brocade drapes at the windows and more brocade on curly white and gold chairs. A pleasant-looking woman who appeared to be in her forties rose from one of these chairs. "Mrs. Sullivan," she said, holding out her hands to me. "Dear me, you really have been weathering the storm, in more ways than one, haven't you."

"I'm so sorry to disturb you, Miss Cassatt," I said. "And I have no idea why I am here, but I received two postcards with copies of your paintings on them, and I wondered if they might have anything to do with the disappearance of my two friends, Miss Goldfarb and Miss Walcott. Are you acquainted with them? Can you tell me anything about what has happened to them?"

"I believe I can," she said. "Won't you sit down and take some coffee? I'll ask Celeste to bring us some."

"I'm afraid I'll make your sofa rather wet," I said.

She smiled. "No matter. Please sit."

I perched on the edge of the sofa while Miss Cassatt went out of the room and I heard her calling in French for the maid. Then the double doors at the far end of the room started to open. A face peered around the door. I jumped up, giving a little cry. Then they were running toward me, arms open.

"Molly, you have found us at last," Gus said. "Thank God."

TWENTY-THREE

It was all too much for me. I turned on them — the anger, fear, and frustration all boiling over at once. "Just what did you think you were doing, leaving me all alone and not telling me where you had gone?" I demanded. "Was that your idea of a game, because it wasn't mine. I've been worried sick. I've been traipsing all over Paris looking for you. I thought something terrible might have happened to you." And to my intense shame and embarrassment I burst into tears.

They sat me down, one of them on either side, and tried to comfort me while I sobbed.

"Molly, dearest," Gus said. "Listen, do. We were so sorry to put you through such torment. We knew you'd be worried, but we couldn't think how else to contact you. The postcards were Mary's idea. I'm so glad you were smart enough to figure them out. We thought the child looked like Liam."

"What do you mean — how to contact me? Why not leave a note for me if you were planning to be staying somewhere else? You had told me you'd meet me at the station — what was I to think?"

"I know, dear Molly," Sid said. "We have agonized about what to do about you, but you see it is no game. It's all too real and too horrible. No one can know where I am. The police are certainly looking for me. I am wanted for murder."

I gulped back tears and looked up at her white and strained face. "For murder? You?"

She nodded.

"Reynold Bryce?" I stammered out the words. "Did you kill Reynold Bryce?"

"Of course she didn't," Gus said, "But she must be the prime suspect in the eyes of the police."

"Why?" I asked.

We broke off as the maid came in with a tray of coffee and little cakes on it. I glanced at Gus.

"It's all right. Celeste is completely loyal to Miss Cassatt, and she has been absolutely wonderful," Gus said as Celeste poured coffee for us. "And she speaks no English, which is useful."

All the same I waited until Celeste had

disappeared again before I repeated my question. "Why do the police think you killed Reynold Bryce?"

"Because I was discovered standing over him as he bled to death," Sid said. "Here, have some coffee to warm you up and I'll explain." She handed me a cup and I sipped, gratefully, although I could feel my hand still trembling.

"It was like this, Molly," she continued. "Remember I wrote to tell you about Reynold Bryce and how Gus hoped to secure an introduction to him through her cousin and to be included in his upcoming exhibition of paintings."

I nodded.

"The introduction took place. We attended a soirée at his house. Gus corresponded with Reynold Bryce. He seemed friendly and encouraging at first and she had high hopes that he'd include one of her paintings in the showing. She went to visit him a week ago taking several of her paintings with her. Then the next day we got a rude letter saying there was no way he'd consider any painting by her in one of his exhibitions. Poor Gus was devastated. She wrote back, begging him to reconsider, and received a curt rejection. Then on Sunday we were having tea here with Miss Cassatt and told her about Mr. Bryce's sudden change of heart. Mary suggested it might be because he'd seen me with Gus and realized I was Jewish. She said he was rabidly anti-Semitic, a leader among the anti-Dreyfusards and went out of his way to make sure that Jewish artists and writers were not included in anything that might publicize their work."

"How mean-spirited," I said and took another welcome gulp of coffee.

"I was furious, naturally," Sid continued, glancing across at Gus. "That poor Gus's chances should be dashed because of me was absolutely unfair. I decided to go and confront him and tell him he was not to punish Gus because of her connection to me. Gus and Mary tried to dissuade me from going but I was adamant. I stalked off to his home. I rang the bell. No one answered. I tapped on the front door and it swung open. I called out. Again nobody answered, so I went in and made my way through to his studio. I thought he might be too absorbed in his painting to have heard my knocking. He was there all right. He was sitting on a chair, looking at the painting he was working on. I went right up to him. 'Now look here, Mr. Bryce,' I said. He looked up at me and there was terror in his eyes. For a moment I thought that he had red paint splattered across his front. Then I saw he was clutching at a knife that had been plunged into his chest. Blood was seeping across his white shirt, Molly. It was awful. I've never seen anything so ghastly in my life."

I nodded. I had seen several dead bodies in my time and one never really gets over the shock of them.

She turned to look at Gus again, and swallowed hard. "I didn't quite know what to do. He was trying to pull out the knife but I knew if he did that, the blood would come gushing out of the wound and he'd quickly bleed to death. I put my hand out to stop him. 'No, don't do that,' I said.

"At that very moment I heard someone behind me. Footsteps coming into the room. I spun around, afraid that it might be Bryce's attacker. But it was his housekeeper. She was standing in the doorway, staring at us in horror. Bryce opened his mouth, looked at her, tried to speak. An awful gurgling moan came out, and then he died. She backed away and ran screaming for help. 'Murder! Assassins!' she was shouting."

Gus reached out and took Sid's hand. "Sid realized right away how bad it would look for her," Gus said. "She was sure the housekeeper must have recognized her as we had both been to the soirée. He had just written me a rude letter then a postcard, saying that there was no way he'd ever consider my amateurish and substandard paintings. Also she was Jewish and his feelings on Jews were well-known. A perfect double motive."

"So what did you do?" I asked.

"I didn't know what to do," Sid said. "I was sure they'd come and arrest me and that would be the end. But then I saw that the window was open. It overlooked the street and outside there was a little garden of shrubs and a small tree."

"I remember it," I said. "I went to his house and found out he had died."

"Luckily I have renounced skirts," Sid went on, her voice sounding calmer and more confident now. "I eased myself out of the window and into that tree. I heard the screams and running feet. I waited until the street appeared to be empty then I lowered myself to the ground and ran off as fast as I could. I made it back to Miss Cassatt's house without anyone seeing me, or so I thought."

"We thought we should get a cab back to our place immediately," Gus said, "but Miss

Cassatt said we should stay put until we were sure we were safe. We just prayed that the housekeeper had been so shocked that she hadn't had time to recognize Sid. But then we learned from asking in the neighborhood that a young Jewish man was seen running away from the house. Obviously they thought Sid was a young man, on account of the trousers and her short hair."

"I see," I said. "So what happens now?"

"I suppose we remain hidden until they catch the real killer, or we try to make it to the coast and take the next steamer bound for America." Sid sank her face into her hands. "We hate to compromise Miss Cassatt in this way. She insisted we stay here, even though she hardly knows us, saying that we women needed to stick together. She's been so wonderful to us. Such a pillar of strength, but we'd certainly not want her to be accused of harboring a fugitive from the law."

"But you can't go back to your place in Montmartre," I said. "Madame Hetreau would sell her own grandmother for tuppence."

This made them laugh. "Yes, she is rather frightful, isn't she? And so nosy," Gus said. "You see now why we had to contact you through the postcards. We were sure the police had been to our house and the housekeeper had identified Sid. Mary volunteered to go herself but we couldn't let her, in case she was followed back here. In fact we couldn't give any hint of where we were, sure that the dreadful Hetreau would relay any scrap of information to the police, in the hope of getting a reward."

"She almost didn't want to let me use your apartment when you were not there," I said. "And now she takes great glee in asking me if I've found you every time I come back."

"You didn't leave Liam with her, did you?" Gus asked.

"Of course not. He's with the baker's wife, across the street. She's an absolute dear, although she's been stuffing him too full of food."

The attempt to brighten up the atmosphere failed like a slowly deflating balloon. "So you'll have to stay put for now, won't you?" I asked.

Sid sighed. "It all seems so hopeless, Molly. I'm so glad you are here. You're a real detective. You'll know what to do."

"I don't really see what I can do to help in a strange city," I said hesitantly. "It seems to me that your only hope is to find the real killer."

"Exactly what I said," Gus exclaimed with enthusiasm.

"But wait a minute," I said. "When I was at the house they were dusting everything for fingerprints. Surely that will exonerate you, Sid."

She shook her head. "No, it won't. When he was trying to remove the knife and I tried to stop him I know I must have touched it as well as his hand. I had blood on my hands afterward. My fingerprints will be on that knife."

"Oh, dear. That's not good," I said. "Now the fact that strikes me is that he wasn't dead when you arrived and the front door was open. That indicates to me that he had just been stabbed before you got there and that maybe the killer slipped out as you went into the studio."

"You mean he was in the house at the same time?" Sid shuddered. "How awful. I might have been his next victim."

"He probably only had one knife," I said. "I suspect he did what he came to do and then all he wanted was to get away. You are absolutely sure that there was nobody else in the room? Was there anywhere one could hide?"

Sid frowned. "There was a red velvet curtain hanging as a backdrop for the painting he was working on. I suppose someone could have hidden behind that," she shuddered.

"Now think, Sid. Sometimes we take in more details than we realize. Was there anything about that room that struck you as different, odd, unusual? No bulge behind the drapes? No sixth sense that somebody else was breathing?"

Sid closed her eyes, then shook her head. "It all happened so fast, Molly. I came in, went straight up to him, and saw he was dying. I didn't have time to look at my surroundings. When I did, afterward, it was only to look for an escape route. I saw the open window and made for it."

"Never mind," I said. "Perhaps by now the police have identified a fingerprint on that knife that matches a known criminal. And even if they have your fingerprints, they wouldn't know how to start looking for you, especially if they think you are a young man."

Sid clutched at my hand. "Molly, you are so calm and wonderful and efficient," she said. "I know you'll be able to help me prove my innocence."

"I'll do my best," I said. "It seems to me we have to establish who would want to see Mr. Bryce dead. Either it was an unplanned murder — he surprised a burglar who thought the house was empty — or someone came with the intention of killing Mr. Bryce."

I felt Sid shudder. "He was a horrible, rude, and prejudiced man," she said. "But nobody deserves to die in that manner."

My brain was working rapidly, trying to think how a good detective would tackle this, what Daniel might do in these circumstances, and whether Inspector Henri, whom I had met at the scene, would know how to carry out a thorough investigation. My gaze moved around the elegant room, taking in the heavy swags of drapery, the paintings on the walls, the little cakes on the silver salver. It was the height of cultured living and it seemed so strange to be sitting here and discussing murder. "I think the fact that he was sitting in his chair is important," I began slowly. "That indicates he probably knew the person who was in the room and was comfortable with him, or her. Perhaps he had been sitting chatting before he was stabbed. If it had been a burglar or someone had surprised him he would have jumped to his feet, turned to confront them, and then fallen to the floor. There would have been some signs of a struggle and the inspector said there weren't."

"Unless he did stand up but slumped back into his chair after he was stabbed," Sid pointed out.

"I don't know how you two can discuss this so calmly," Gus said. "Murder is so terrible, and the fact that your life might be in danger, Sid . . ."

"We'll get through this somehow," Sid said. "Not the welcome we planned to give poor Molly, is it? And after what she had just been through in New York, and the awful rough crossing too. We had so many exciting things planned for you, Molly. If only you hadn't become ill on the ship and had arrived on time none of this would have happened."

"You can't say that," Gus said. "Don't go blaming poor Molly."

"Of course I'm not blaming her. I'm just saying the timing would have been different. We wouldn't have gone to tea with Mary, would we?"

"It's strange on what small coincidences our fate hangs," Gus said.

On that profound note Mary Cassatt came back into the room.

TWENTY-FOUR

"I thought I'd stay out of it and give you time to explain everything to your guest," Mary Cassatt said. She came over to us and pulled up one of the curly-backed gilt chairs beside me. "A horrible business, is it not, Mrs. Sullivan?"

"The worst," I said.

"They tell me that you are a real and proper detective," Miss Cassatt said, giving me an encouraging smile. "We're all hoping that you'll be able to help them."

"Neither real nor very proper, I'm afraid," I said. "I gave up my business when I married . . ."

"See, Sid, what we were talking about earlier today," Mary Cassatt turned to Sid, wagging a finger at her. "Marriage is the biggest restrictor of women's freedom and progress and creativity. Look at Berthe Morisot. She was producing the most exciting paintings, then she married Manet's brother and then what?" She turned back to me. "Sorry, Mrs. Sullivan. As you can see we were discussing this very subject earlier today. Please do continue. Even if you've given up your profession, you still possess the skills, don't you?"

"I don't really see what I can do," I said. "I won't be allowed access to anything they found in that room and the police certainly won't share with me what line their investigation has been taking, if in fact they are pursuing a line of investigation."

"Molly thinks he must have known the killer," Sid said. "He was sitting in his chair and he would have been standing if taken by surprise by an intruder."

"The inspector said there were no signs of a break-in and no signs of a struggle," I said, "which probably means that Bryce let in the murderer himself through the front door, given that his housekeeper had gone out. They came back to his studio. Bryce sat while they talked and then was caught completely by surprise and stabbed."

"There was an open window," Sid said. "Someone could have entered and left that way as I did with relative ease."

That was true.

"I'll go and have a chat with the housekeeper if she's still there and the police have gone," I said. "Maybe I can get her to tell me something. And then there are Bryce's fellow artists." I turned to Miss Cassatt. "I know that there was a lot of ill feeling between the Impressionists and those coming after them. I've met several of the new generation — a young man called Picasso from Spain who seems quite a violent type."

"Ah, yes. Strange little man. He has some talent if only he'd paint some real pictures." Mary Cassatt laughed.

"And I met your cousin, Sid."

"You have a cousin here too?" Mary Cassatt asked, looking inquiringly at Sid.

"I just discovered him. He's also a painter. His name is Maxim Noah."

"I don't think I know of him," Mary said. "Another of the new breed?"

"He showed me his paintings," I said, without further comment.

Sid's face lit up. "Isn't he wonderful? So full of passion and his paintings are so expressive. Gus and I were talking about bringing him back to New York for an exhibition. He has no family here any longer, you know. My mother would be thrilled."

"Maybe we could ask him to help us," Gus suggested. "He is obviously right at the heart of the artistic community, and perhaps

316

he also mixes with fellow Jews."

"Reynold Bryce had certainly made himself unpopular with both communities," Miss Cassatt said. "Artists and Jews. As you know he ran the most influential exhibition in the city every summer, the one all the foreign buyers come to. And he had virtually shut out all those young painters who call themselves Fauves or Modernists. To him art had to be representational. I can't say I disagree with him. But unlike him I admit that we are in a new century, a century of automobiles and electricity and telephones. There must always be progress."

"So do you think it's possible that a young painter who was thwarted by Bryce would come to kill him?" Gus asked.

"You were thwarted by him, my dear," Mary Cassatt said. "Did your thoughts turn to murder?"

Gus laughed. "Of course not, although Sid was so angry that . . ." And she turned to look at Sid.

"I went to give him a piece of my mind, not a piece of steel in his gut. There is a difference," Sid said.

"But some of those young artists are not so controlled," I pointed out. "Picasso was itching to fight a duel and complained he hadn't shot his pistol for several days."

"Ah, duels. They are different," Mary Cassatt said. "Among the young men of Paris they are a major form of sport. They will fight duels on the least little excuse. Usually over a woman, but an insult to a painting might do as well."

"So if a painter challenged Reynold Bryce to a duel but he laughed and refused, might the challenger feel affronted and come to stab him?" I asked.

"Unlikely. The heat of the moment would have passed. The challenger would shrug and go his merry way. None of them takes anything too seriously for too long."

"Miss Cassatt, do you know of any particular painters who have crossed swords with Reynold Bryce recently?" I asked.

"I am afraid I am a trifle out of touch these days." Miss Cassatt gave an apologetic smile then reached to pour herself a cup of coffee from the tray. "An aging has-been. I was never allowed into the cafés with them, of course."

"Why ever not?" I asked.

"Women are not part of café society in Paris. At least, not respectable women. Artists' models are sometimes permitted."

"I've been into several cafés," I said. "There was never any indication that I was about to be flung out."

"Ah, but you're a novelty. A visitor from abroad. Should you want to join them on a regular basis I can assure you it would be different."

"Perhaps I could go and ask more questions. You have not heard any gossip about anyone else with whom Reynold Bryce might have fallen out? Outside the art fraternity, I mean."

Mary Cassatt shrugged. "Again that is the problem with being a woman. Bryce's life revolved around the American Club where they don't admit women. He was quite chummy with the American ambassador and went to diplomatic functions — he was the poster boy of American art, of course; unlike me, hardly recognized in my own country. So I really can't tell you too much about his private life. All I can say is I was never invited to dinner with him."

"What about women?" Sid asked suddenly. "Don't they say *cherchez la femme*?"

"I haven't heard of a mistress," Mary said. "His wife is still back in America — amicably separated all these years, so one understands, but not divorced. But I was once at a gathering in which someone said, 'If Bryce is coming, lock up your daughters.' "

"So he had a bit of a roving eye," I said.

"What one might call a roué," Mary said,

"Which of course is quite acceptable in Paris. Their sexual mores are certainly not ours. Any man who doesn't have a mistress is considered odd, even a pansy."

"His housekeeper will know about that," I said. "If I can get her to talk. Is there anyone else who might be conversant with his personal life?"

Mary Cassatt shook her head, then said, "Of course there was his good friend Monet, but he has now forsaken Paris for his home in Normandy. I understand that Bryce often used to spend his weekends out there. It really is a delightful spot, so I'm told. I've never been invited personally."

"I'll write to Monsieur Monet and ask if I might visit him," I said. "Old friends confide secrets to each other, don't they?"

"I also understand that they had fallen out recently over Reynold Bryce's anti-Semitic rants. He was always prejudiced, of course, but recently he had become so extreme and outspoken against the attempts to reinstate Dreyfus. It's as if these attempts to give him back his old rank in the army have lit a flame under anyone with anti-Semitic leanings. All that fraternity feel that Jews are gaining too much power in banking and commerce in Europe and must be stopped. Ridiculous really when you realize that most Jews in the city are poor immigrants who have arrived from Russia or Poland with nothing and only want a safe place to feed their families."

"If it was a Jewish rabble-rouser who had come to confront Bryce, he would certainly not have let him in," Gus said. "He'd have had to climb in through a window and somebody might have seen that."

"I don't think there would be much point in my asking questions among the Jewish communities here," I said. "If there are certain places where Jewish immigrants gather regularly. You'd know that, Sid."

"I went to several synagogues but it would be no use, Molly. They'd never confide anything to an outsider. They didn't even want to talk to me, a fellow Jew." She got up from the sofa and walked across the room, pulling back the drape to peer out. "But I could have given it another try. I wish there was something I could do. I hate being cooped up here."

"I trust I am not making your stay too unpleasant," Mary said dryly.

We laughed. "You are being wonderful to us, Mary," Gus said. "We can never thank you enough for taking us in and we only hope you are not compromising yourself by having us here."

"Speaking of which," Mary said. "The first order of business would be to send for Mrs. Sullivan's things and have her move in with us."

"Oh, no, I couldn't impose on you, Miss Cassatt. I have a young child for one thing."

"Sid and Gus already told me about your baby," she said. "And it seems to me that you have two ready-made child minders who are dying to amuse him, since they are not able to leave the premises. As for me, my family has gone home to America for a while, leaving me alone here, so I gladly welcome your company."

"But is that the wisest thing for me to do?" I said while at the same time thinking there was nothing I'd like better than to be safely here with Miss Cassatt and my dear friends. "What do I tell Madame Hetreau? If I say I've given up the search and am going home, she'll feel free to help herself to your things and I'm sure you wouldn't want that. And if I tell her I've located you and am going to join you, she can pass that information on to the police."

"That is a bit of a tricky problem." Sid returned to perch on the arm of the sofa, beside Gus. "Molly is right. What can we tell her and not put ourselves in jeopardy?"

I thought for a moment then said, "I did

suggest to her that you might have been taken ill with food poisoning as I'd been told that bad oysters had brought several people to the hospital. If I told her that this was indeed true, that you had gone out of town to visit friends and had been caught in an epidemic there — typhoid maybe — placed under quarantine, and not allowed to travel . . . that might satisfy her and also give you a good alibi."

"You see, the girl is brilliant." Sid clapped her hands.

"I can say that I'm now permitted to join you and am taking you your possessions," I said.

They nodded, looking at each other with satisfaction.

"And the witch Hetreau will be delighted she can relet our rooms," Sid chuckled.

"But that would be an awful task for you, Molly, packing up all our things," Gus, ever the thoughtful one, said.

"How many of the items in the apartment are yours, apart from the clothes and Gus's paintings?" I asked. "Does the furniture belong to you?"

"The place was furnished in a basic sort of way," Gus said. "We did buy a few items, but given the circumstances, we'd be happy to donate them to Madame Hetreau, as

Miss Cassatt certainly wouldn't want them."

"I'm not sure how I would manage to bring everything down the stairs by myself," I said. "Madame's husband might help if I paid him enough, but then would it all fit in a cab?"

"There is a carter I've hired on occasion when we've moved to the country for the summer," Mary said. "A solid, reliable sort. I could send him to help you with the packing and to carry down the trunks."

She stood up and clapped her hands. "Well, that's settled then. I'll send a message to him right away. And now if word gets out that I've got company, it is a delightful woman from New York and her baby that I'm entertaining. Nobody that might arouse any suspicion." And she gave us a triumphant smile then strode from the room, leaving Sid and Gus looking at each other hopefully.

TWENTY-FIVE

The carter agreed to send over a wagon to Montmartre that evening. I refused Mary Cassatt's offer to join them for luncheon, not wanting to leave Liam a moment longer and realizing the amount of work that lay ahead of me. The morning's storm had passed, leaving a blue sky and steaming sidewalks. I went straight back to the Rue des Martyrs. When I told Madeleine that I would not be needing her services anymore she looked genuinely so crestfallen that I paid her double the amount we had agreed upon and promised to bring Liam to visit as often as possible. On my way out the baker shook my hand and thanked me for bringing his wife out of the depression that had engulfed her after the baby was born. Then I felt even worse about leaving her and realized I really would have to make an effort to visit, if and when I could solve Reynold Bryce's murder.

Madame Hetreau was nowhere to be seen as I let myself into the front hall. I was tempted to tiptoe upstairs and get on with the job, but knowing the sort of person madame was, I realized she might accuse me of trying to smuggle out objects belonging to her when she caught me leaving. So I tapped on her door and she opened it, her hands white with flour.

"Oh, it's you," she said.

"I've come to say good-bye, madame," I said.

"You've given up looking for your friends, have you? And you are returning to America?" She looked pleased.

"On the contrary," I said. "After much searching I have managed to locate my friends. It is as I suspected. They went to visit acquaintances in a small village in Normandy not knowing that typhoid had broken out there and were immediately placed under quarantine . . ."

"*Mon dieu* — I hope they will not think of returning here, bringing a dreadful disease with them," she said.

"They will not. They have decided to stay in the village, and now that the quarantine has been lifted, they want me to join them. A man will be coming for their belongings. They have asked me to pack their trunks for them."

"So they will not be returning to this house?"

"No, madame. Feel free to let the rooms again," I said.

"They will just be taking their personal effects, no?" she asked. "I know that they purchased some items of furniture, but they will not need this out in the country . . ." She spread her arms expressively.

"They only want their personal effects," I said. "Anything else they donate to you."

"Ah," she said, really looking pleased now. "Please give the ladies my best compliments when you see them and tell them I hope they will have fond memories of their stay in Paris."

"I will do that," I said.

"If you need help with the heavy trunks, my husband will be home later," she said.

"Thank you, but I understand the carter will be bringing a boy to help him."

As I started up the stairs she called after me, "So how did they finally contact you? They sent no letter here."

"They were not allowed to send a letter, owing to the quarantine and the possibility of contamination on the envelope," I said. "Those postcards led me to an acquaintance who knew where they had gone."

"Ah," she repeated and I couldn't tell whether she believed this story or not. It didn't really matter. I hadn't identified the village or given her any name she could pursue. I carried Liam up the stairs, set him down with his toys, and started work. The weather had improved and the sun shining through those French windows had made the apartment warm and muggy. I opened the windows and stood on the balcony for a moment, taking in the scene one last time. As I dragged trunks from a closet, I could see that my task was going to be a daunting one. Packing up my own clothes only took minutes. Dismantling Liam's crib was not hard. But Sid and Gus had a multitude of clothes, books, Gus's paintings and art supplies, as well as paintings they had bought from other artists and other souvenirs they had acquired. There were some good pieces of Limoges china plus a delightful small sculpture of a ballerina, several mirrors, a camera, and a coffee set, all of which required careful wrapping and packing. I found tissue paper in one of the drawers and set to work.

I was interested to see that the paintings they had bought were all rather more modern than my taste — blue faces, flying cats. There was one of a young girl with enormous dark eyes, peering into a dark empty room that I thought was well-done, but strangely disturbing and was glad it wouldn't hang on my wall. I stacked them one by one, then finally packed the painting Gus had been working on. Luckily the paint had now dried. It really wasn't great art, I thought as it went into a crate. I could see why Reynold Bryce hadn't wanted to include her work and it had nothing to do with her companion being Jewish. I picked up the postcard that Reynold Bryce had written two days before he died. "Absolutely not," it said. The definitive answer when Gus had begged him to reconsider his rejection of her work. I dropped the postcard on top of the paintings and shut the crate.

I was hot and perspiring and ready for a cup of tea when the carter came at five. I held Liam safely out of the way as trunks and cases were carried downstairs. Madame Hetreau appeared to have a good snoop and made sure that I hadn't packed anything belonging to her. I noticed her nod of satisfaction when she saw that an armchair and a lot of cooking equipment were being left behind.

"You will give the ladies my regards," she reiterated as the carter helped me up to the seat on the wagon. I said I would and thanked her for letting us stay, which was ridiculous, but at least it meant we parted on good terms. "*Bonne chance,* good luck," she called after me.

I saw Madeleine waving from her upstairs window, her baby in her arms. The Nouvelle Athènes was crowded with people as we passed. I wondered if my artist friends were still there and when they ever did any work. I wondered if the morose Monsieur Degas was sitting alone, sipping his absinthe. I realized I'd be sad to leave this lively neighborhood and go to a more sedate part of town. Perhaps there would be a time when Sid's name had been cleared that we could move back here again. I toyed with those words. So easy to say and yet I had no idea how I would ever manage to save her. If it was indeed a young Jew who had killed Bryce, then the police might be able to find the culprit through interrogation and intimidation at the local synagogues. If it was someone else, then I didn't see how I could possibly find out who that might be. It seemed I had no way of infiltrating Bryce's inner circle, since I was not admitted to the American Club and could hardly call upon the ambassador. Tomorrow I'd try to talk to the housekeeper and see if she'd let me take a look at Mr. Bryce's rooms, but I didn't even know if the housekeeper would still be in residence or if the police would still be stationed outside. I let out a big sigh. I had been through days of sickness and worry. I was tired. I wanted a rest, not a mammoth task.

Paris was at its liveliest as we moved away from Montmartre. Streets were full of evening commerce. A church bell was tolling for a six o'clock service while people stopped for a glass of wine at the outdoor cafés. I heard snatches of song from inside bars and cabarets. It seemed that everyone was having a good time, glad to be alive on a warm June evening. We passed the Saint-Lazare station where I had first arrived, so full of excitement and hope, then crossed the wide Boulevard Haussmann with its fine stores and elegant women. I looked longingly at those enticing shop windows. What fun it would be to have the money and leisure to go shopping here, like two young American women we passed, their arms full of packages.

"We can't go back to the hotel before we visit Worth," they called to two older women ahead of them.

Then we crossed the Champs-Élyseés with its fine carriages and dangerously fast automobiles and came at last to the Rue de

Marignan. Celeste opened the door to me with such a strange, disapproving look on her face that I wondered whether she had been against her mistress inviting me to stay. "Ah, you have returned with all your belongings," she said loudly. "You do not travel lightly, madame."

"But these are not . . ." I had been about to say "not all mine" when she cut me off. "Not too much baggage for a lady from America. I understand." Then she held up a hand for me to be quiet. "Madame is in the drawing room with a guest," she said. "An inspector from the Sûreté."

"Ah." I understood now. "Should we go straight up to our rooms then? We have no wish to disturb."

But at that moment Mary called out, "Molly, have you returned? Come and let me say hello to little Liam. I've been dying to see him again."

I went through into the salon and saw that Inspector Henri was now seated on the brocade sofa. He stood as I came in and then his expression changed as he recognized me. "I know you," he said. "You're the woman who showed up at Bryce's house the other day. You said you were a relative of his with a message. And now this lady tells me you are a relative of hers. Are you related to the entire American art fraternity here in Paris?"

"Good evening, Inspector," I said, nodding gravely as Liam, sensing my tension, clung to my neck. "I did not say I was related to Monsieur Bryce, if you remember. I said I brought a message from his relatives. And it is quite usual in any country that well-known artists have connections with each other."

Mary came and put a hand on my shoulder. "I did not realize you had met our dear Molly, Inspector," she said. "Please, do sit, both of you. I'll have Celeste bring us all a glass of wine. And dear little Liam. How he has grown."

She went to ring for Celeste, while I adjusted my thoughts to realize that I was to be either related or a dear friend of Mary Cassatt.

"Was Miss Cassatt the friend you were looking for when you asked me those questions?" Inspector Henri asked as I sat with a squirming Liam on my lap.

"No, those two ladies were unfortunately taken ill, away from Paris," I said. "Typhoid, so I understand."

"So of course Molly came to me and I insisted that she come to stay immediately," Mary added, coming back to join us.

I had no idea what the inspector might have discovered that made him come to question Miss Cassatt, but she was clearly rattled by it. Had he been tipped off that the fleeing Jewish man had come to her door? I decided that attack was the best form of defense. "So how is your investigation proceeding, Inspector? Are you making good progress? Do you have a suspect yet?"

"Not yet, madame. I came to see Miss Cassatt because I know her to be a leading member among the American artists. I thought maybe she could tell me more about Monsieur Bryce —"

"But I just pointed out to the inspector that the fraternity of artists here is just that — they do not include women in their intimate chats. My only meetings with Reynold Bryce were at such formal occasions as the ambassador's garden parties. Of his personal life I knew nothing." She turned to the inspector. "I am a very private person, Inspector. I do not frequent the cafés or dance halls. I do not listen to gossip. I am sorry that I cannot help you. I wish very much for the truth of Monsieur Bryce's murder to be revealed. It is a terrible thing that such a respected member of our community should die a violent and senseless death."

The inspector looked as if he might have been ready to give up and leave when Celeste appeared with a carafe of wine and three glasses.

"It's very good. I bought several cases last time I was in Bordeaux," Mary said. "One thing I have learned during my long stay in France is to appreciate good wine."

The inspector sat down again rapidly and accepted the glass she held out to him. I decided I had to make the most of this opportunity. "So tell me, Inspector. When I was at Monsieur Bryce's house your men were looking for fingerprints. Did that search not produce any . . ." I didn't know the word for clues. It was frustrating that my French was limited to the vocabulary of a schoolgirl. "Clues, Mary?" I turned to her for help.

He smiled. "Ah, yes. The lady detective. I had forgotten that. There were fingerprints on the knife, madame, but as yet we have not identified them. But we will. Rest assured we will."

"Only one set of fingerprints?" I asked.

He gave me a suspicious look, his head tilted a little. "You believe there was more than one killer?"

"No. I wondered . . . if someone is stabbed he does not always die instantly. He would

335

try to grasp the knife and remove it. His own prints would be on it."

He nodded approval. "*Bien sûr,* madame. You are right. His own fingerprints were on the knife, as well as those of several other persons."

"Several?" I said.

"It was a common kitchen knife as found in any good kitchen or restaurant in Paris."

"From his own kitchen, perhaps?"

"His housekeeper says certainly not. None of her knives is missing. But she does not seem to me like a particularly neat and tidy person, and she was rather hostile when we tried to question her."

"Interesting," I said. I was actually wondering why the housekeeper mistrusted the police, but I knew little of police interrogation tactics in Paris. Maybe she did not enjoy being bullied or threatened.

He looked up sharply. "What do you imply by that, madame?"

"Only that the sort of men who were Mr. Bryce's social equals had probably never been in a kitchen in their lives and wouldn't know where to find the knives," I replied, moving away from my thoughts on the housekeeper.

"That is true, if the killer was indeed Mr. Bryce's social equal," he said. "He was a patron of many poor artists, was he not? And the killer was not necessarily a man. The knife was good and sharp. A healthy woman could have plunged it in."

"Mercy me," Mary Cassatt said in English, and took a hasty sip of her wine.

"And if the killer was not a person Mr. Bryce knew but perhaps a Jewish man, angry at his anti-Jewish sentiments, as has been suggested?"

"He was alone in the house, madame. He was hard at work, painting, and did not like to be disturbed. I do not think he would have admitted such a person, if he even bothered to answer the front door himself while his housekeeper was away."

"The person could have forced his way in," Mary suggested.

"Then Mr. Bryce would not have been sitting down," I said before the inspector could answer. "The intruder would have stabbed him in his foyer, not been brought through all the way to his studio."

"Alas, there was the window," the inspector said. "Mr. Bryce always kept a window open because of the smell of paint and turpentine. The window was high enough above the street to make entry difficult, but an agile person could have managed it, entered when Mr. Bryce left the room, and waited for the right moment to strike."

Mary shuddered again. "Too horrible to contemplate," she said.

The inspector smiled. "You do not seem to have the strong stomach of your relative here," he said. "But then she was once a detective, was she not?"

I could tell from his tone that he hadn't quite accepted my story. He was not sure who I was and was suspicious about why I was here and whether I had anything to do with Mr. Bryce's death. I realized I had to tread carefully or I might find myself cast in the role of prime suspect.

"But surely anyone attempting to climb in would have been seen," I said. "The Rue François Premier is quite busy."

"You forget those houses have small gardens facing the street. One could hide among the shrubs for the right moment."

"Dangerous, surely," I said. "Anyone going over to the window would spot the person immediately."

"Criminals often enjoy risks, madame, as you, being a detective, should know. So tell me, where was this detective agency of yours?"

"In New York," I said. "I closed it when I married. Now I am only a wife and mother and enjoy the leisure to visit family and friends."

"Your husband is generous to allow you to travel without him."

"He is busy at work, like most men. He thought it would be a perfect chance for me to travel when I had friends in Paris."

"Your husband, what profession does he have?"

Oh, dear. I suspected this might be coming and didn't really see a way to avoid it. "He is a police captain in New York," I said. At least that might allay suspicions about me, but I now ran the risk that he would contact New York for verification. And the last thing I wanted was for Daniel to hear that I was somehow mixed up in a murder investigation.

TWENTY-SIX

"Thank heavens he has gone," Mary said as she returned to the salon, having escorted the inspector to the door. "Such a lot of questions. I began to think he had been tipped off that our friends were hiding out here."

"I know. It was most uncomfortable, knowing that they were upstairs, within his reach. And he is obviously suspicious of me."

"You met him before, I understand?"

"I went to Mr. Bryce's house, knowing that he had been in recent contact with Sid and Gus and hoping he might know where they had gone. I arrived to find the police stationed outside and Bryce dead. In order to gain entrance I said I was a friend of his family with a message for him. I got the feeling he thought the message I had come to deliver was in some way significant and that I was hiding the truth from him."

"Ah, so no wonder he was interested when I claimed you were also a dear friend of my family at home," she laughed. "What a mess, Molly." She broke off and extended a hand to me. "I may call you Molly, may I not? Since we are now almost related?"

"Please do," I said. "And I can't thank you enough for taking us in."

"The little one looks as if he's ready to sleep," she said, looking fondly at Liam who was snuggled against me, sucking his thumb. "I can finally have Celeste show you to the room I have prepared for you. Or do you want to let him meet his anxious aunts first?"

I glanced down at Liam. "I think we should make the most of a sleepy child and put him down," I said. "Sid and Gus will have ample time to spoil him later."

Mary smiled and rang the bell. Celeste appeared and escorted me up two flights of stairs. It was an attic room like the one in Montmartre, with French doors opening onto a balcony, but much more cozily and elegantly furnished with blue and white wallpaper and a blue and white chenille bedspread and curtains. The crib had been assembled in the far corner, and looked most inviting with lace pillows. I put Liam down. His thumb came into his mouth and he was asleep straight away. I went over and opened the French windows, stepping out onto the narrow balcony. The street below was quiet, apart from the distant sound of a horse's hoofs moving at a fast trot as it pulled a light carriage or a cab. The sky beyond the rooftops held the last lingering glow of red and etched in black against that sky the Eiffel Tower rose. Seen close like this it was an awe-inspiring sight. It reminded me that whatever was happening, whatever difficulties we might be facing, we were, after all, in Paris.

If they could see me now in Ireland, I thought, and then I remembered that other disturbing fact. One person who knew me from Ireland, who wanted my destruction, was also here in this city. Thus sobered I sat at the little writing desk and wrote to Daniel, telling him that I would be staying for a while at the charming residence of the painter Mary Cassatt and that all was well with Liam and me. I had already enjoyed meeting interesting artists and poets and could see the Eiffel Tower from my window. When I read it through it sounded quite jolly. I just hoped that he was safe and well and the message would cheer him up. I sealed the envelope then went down to join the others.

In spite of everything we spent a pleasant evening together. Mary was careful to make sure that the drapes were closed before Sid and Gus came into the salon at the front of the house. "I think that policeman just wanted to question other American painters for details of Bryce's life," Mary said, "but one can't be too sure. He may have come here on a tip and wanted to observe my reaction."

"We were scared stiff when he stayed so long, weren't we, Sid?" Gus said. "I suggested we hide in the wardrobe, just in case he decided to come looking for us."

"But I said there wasn't much point. Our belongings were all over the room, which might have given away our presence if he decided to come up and look."

"Thank heavens he didn't," Mary said. "I should have been so flustered if he'd wanted to go upstairs I couldn't have invented a good reason for a bedroom that was clearly occupied. But we will have to be careful. Maybe we shouldn't use this room unless the drapes are drawn. I'm going to ask Celeste to check whether anyone is watching this house."

"In which case I wonder if I'll be followed when I go out," I said.

"Surely not. Now that he knows your

husband is a fellow policeman," Mary said. "He must think that your behavior is beyond reproach."

Silently I thought that she didn't know much about the police. I'd encountered several whose behavior left a lot to be desired.

Dinner was delicious. Mary might have retained her Pennsylvania accent but the cooking was pure French with even the vegetables covered in sauces delicate enough to make one weep. We drank wine and even managed to laugh a little.

"Tomorrow is Saturday," Gus said. "Will you be going to Gertrude Stein's, Mary?"

"Oh, I don't think I'll bother," she replied. "I find these new young artists too tedious in their pretentious desire to be modern."

"But you could take Molly with you," Gus said. "You never know, she might learn something about Reynold Bryce."

"That is a name never to be mentioned in the Stein household," Mary said.

"Don't be so sure." I looked up from my coffee cup. "They may well enjoy discussing him now that he is dead. Carcasses often attract vultures, you know."

The others laughed.

"That might be true," Mary said. "I'm quite willing to go if you'd like to, Molly.

The Steins' salon is something to be experienced, at least once if you want to feel the pulse of the Parisian art world."

"We certainly enjoyed it when we went," Sid said. "I must say I'm beginning to develop cabin fever, however pleasant our surroundings are."

"It's not that," Gus said. "It's this terrible thing hanging over your head. We're all waiting for doom to fall."

There was an uncomfortable silence.

"I'll go straight to work in the morning," I said, trying to sound more confident than I felt. "The first thing to do is to see if I can interview the housekeeper, and maybe find a way to get in and see the studio for myself."

"But what do you hope to find there?" Gus asked.

"I'm not sure, and it's possible that the police have already carried away any incriminating evidence, but it's always good to start with the scene of the crime. At least, that was what Paddy Riley, my old mentor, used to say."

"From what Inspector Henri said the housekeeper didn't sound like a pleasant person," Mary said.

"Maybe she just had an aversion to the police," I suggested. "Some people do.

Besides, I'll be using all of my Irish gift of the blarney. I'll have her eating out of my hand."

"Isn't Molly wonderful?" Gus said. "You should see all the clever cases she has solved back in New York."

I wished they weren't quite so confident in my abilities. For one thing I was not at all sure that I could charm a hostile French-woman when my French vocabulary was sadly lacking. Still, I had promised to do my best. Liam was sleeping soundly when I went up to bed. I stood looking down at him, thinking how easy life was for babies and how quickly they adapt. He had come across an ocean, then from a seaside pen-sion to a noisy Montmartre attic, and now to this tranquil street and had slept peace-fully in each of them. I bent to kiss his forehead.

"I wish your daddy was here," I whispered. "He'd know what to do."

And he'd make sure that I stayed well away from a murder case, I reminded myself. So maybe it was a good thing that he was thousands of miles away in New York. I climbed into bed and lay listening to distant sounds. I was safe. I was among friends. I should have been able to sleep, but sleep wouldn't come. How could I possibly find out who killed Reynold Bryce? I was not the police, able to compare finger-prints or examine the details of Bryce's life, and I didn't have the ability to question large numbers of people. I'd be floundering in the dark as usual.

Start with what you know: that was another of Paddy Riley's favorite sayings. What did I know about Reynold Bryce? He had inherited wealth and had established a reputation for himself in the States as a painter of rather sentimental Victorian pictures. Then he had abandoned America and his wife and gone to live in Paris. He had never returned to the States. Why was that? Had it been a hasty departure? Could he have perhaps run off to Paris with another woman? But then it would have been the subject of general gossip. Why had he left his wife behind, or had she refused to accompany him?

What else did I know? He was bigoted, prejudiced, and opinionated. Such people make enemies. I also got a hint that he had an eye for the ladies. Was there one lady in particular at the moment? The housekeeper would know about that, surely.

Apart from that he frequented the American Club, where I was denied entry. I knew that he was a leader among the anti-Dreyfusards, a friend of Degas and of Monet. One of my first tasks should be to find out when and where his funeral would be held. Surely his old friend Monet would come to Paris for the funeral. Perhaps other friends would be there to chat and reminisce about him. With some sort of plan now in my head, I finally fell asleep.

I was awoken by a tap on my door and Celeste came in, bearing a cup of tea on a tray. "A fine summer day, madame," she said. "Your friends say you prefer tea in the morning to coffee." She set down the tray. "If you have laundry to be done, this is the time to give it to me."

"I'm afraid my baby's clothes get extremely dirty," I said, but she waved this aside. "No problem, madame. I will take them when I come back for your tray."

It seemed odd to have someone waiting on me again, and I couldn't help thinking about little Aggie and her willingness to do the laundry. I pictured her scrawny form bent over the washboard as she scrubbed away. Poor young thing. She never had a chance to enjoy life.

Liam awoke and finding himself in a strange room, cried for me. I took him into bed with me and nursed him, bringing a feeling of peace to both of us. When I took him down to breakfast he was delighted to find his aunts from across the street waiting to play with him and didn't complain at all when I slipped out. It was indeed a lovely day. The yellow stone glowed against a blue sky. It was the sort of day for picnics by the river, strolls though the gardens, shopping on the Boulevard Haussmann. But instead I turned onto the Rue François Premier and made for Reynold Bryce's ground-floor apartment on the circle at the far end of the street, close to the river. I was relieved to find no policeman standing outside, but then wondered if that meant that the place was now locked up and the housekeeper would not be there either. *What would happen to her?* I wondered. Had Reynold Bryce left a provision for her in his will? Ah, that would be another avenue to pursue, if I could find out who his lawyer was. He was a wealthy man. To whom had that wealth been left?

I stood on the front steps of the building, staring at the little garden behind the railings. Sid had indeed been agile to have climbed into the tree and then have dropped down onto the street. To me, wearing a long, tight skirt, it looked almost impossible. But then terror gives people skills they didn't know they possessed. Had the murderer really entered and left by that route? If so he must also be strong and agile. I looked at the windows. They now appeared to be shut — or was that one on the end not quite closed? But climbing up would be even harder than climbing down. There was a gate in the railings. I wondered if it was unlocked. I came back down the steps and walked around to it. I had just reached in to jiggle the lock open when someone called, "What are you doing, madame?"

I withdrew my hand rapidly and turned to see a gaunt, hard-faced, elderly woman in black, wearing an old-fashioned black bonnet, coming toward me at a rapid rate.

I glanced hastily around the little garden and my eye fell on the lilac bush. "Very well. I confess," I said. "I love the smell of lilac and I wanted to pick a small sprig to take with me. Are these not public gardens?"

"No, madame, they are not. They are the private property of this building."

"I am sorry. I am a visitor to Paris. Do you live here?"

"Yes, madame. Until now, that is. I was the housekeeper of the American, Reynold Bryce. You heard of his tragic demise, I expect."

"I did. My condolences, madame. It must

have been a great shock for you. And a great loss."

"Indeed," she said. "I had taken care of Monsieur Bryce since he came to Paris nearly twenty years ago. He was like a son to me."

"He was a good employer, then?"

"Of course. I would not have stayed with an inferior employer. He was the best, madame. Generous. Liked my cooking. Of course I learned to cook the sort of food that Americans like, and he learned to appreciate the finer ways of French cooking." She glanced up at the windows, now with shades drawn. "I won't say he was the easiest man, especially if he was working. He did not like to be disturbed. And he liked to get his own way. One could not cross him. But that is how the great men are, isn't it? Great art means great temperament."

"And he lived here alone, all this time?" I asked.

"I was in residence, madame."

"But I meant that he never remarried."

"He had a wife at home in America, madame." She sounded shocked.

"I knew this," I said. "But she never came to visit him — never once in all these years?"

"No, madame. There was a falling out, but she was a good Catholic. She did not believe in divorce."

"And he never found anyone else?"

She looked at me suspiciously. "You show great interest in this. Who sent you here? You are from a newspaper in America?"

"No. Nothing like that," I said. "I show interest because I came here with a message from Mr. Bryce's family."

"He had no family," she said sharply.

"No immediate family, that is true. But his second cousin Louisa. Did he not mention her? He was always fond of her when she was a child."

"I don't recall . . ." she said. "Maybe. I never detected him expressing any sentiment for a family member."

"Anyway, she still has fond memories of him." I had rehearsed this speech and made sure I could deliver it smoothly in French. "She was very young before he went to Paris, of course. However now she has married well and has now moved into a fine big house in Boston. She dearly wanted to have one of her cousin's paintings on her walls so she asked me to call on him and see if there were any pictures he had recently painted and hadn't sold."

"He has not been painting much recently," she said. "And she should understand that his paintings now command high prices —

higher still now that he is no more, I should think."

"Money is not a problem for her," I said. "She was prepared to pay the correct price, you understand, but she wanted something fresh and new, not a painting that someone else had owned before." I was rather pleased with this approach. It was something I thought up during my shower this morning, something simple that would arouse no suspicions and make no difficult claims for me. It appeared to have worked.

"Ah," the old woman nodded. "She wishes to buy a painting."

"The lady in Boston knew I was coming to Paris. 'Please select a painting for me, my dear,' she said to me. 'I give you carte blanche to buy one. Tell Cousin Rennie it is for me and he will help you select a good one.' "

The housekeeper shifted her feet uneasily. "As I said, I don't think you will find new paintings that remain unsold. He has hardly touched a canvas in a year or more. In fact I thought that maybe he had given it up all together. But then recently he found the urge to paint again. Not the charming landscapes he had been painting like his friend M. Monet, but a very different subject, you understand. Not one I approved of at all." She glanced up at the windows with a frown, then looked back at me, shaking her head.

"This new painting, is it finished?"

"He only just started it."

"And there are no other paintings in his possession that would now come up for sale? His cousin in America will be so sad to learn he has died."

"Indeed she will, madame. We are all sad. M. Bryce is a great loss."

"So I really hope his cousin Louisa will have a painting to remember him by. I wonder if it might be possible to see around his home and inside his studio for myself, so that I can write to her and describe which paintings his cousin might wish to purchase."

"No, madame. That would not be possible," she snapped. "The apartment is shut. Nobody is allowed to go in by order of the police. I myself have not been allowed to sleep in my room or to clean anything. I have been staying with my sister, which is most inconvenient as she has no room for me. I only came today to retrieve certain personal items, before the police decide to throw them out. And there is food in the pantry that will be spoiled soon, if it isn't spoiled already. I had pies and cakes . . .

Monsieur Bryce loved his pies, madame. I expect they have spoiled already, but I thought I would just see what could be saved."

From the way she said this and her defensive posture I sensed there was more to her visit than looking for spoiled pies. She was uneasy, knowing that she shouldn't be here. She had expected to slip in unnoticed and now here I was asking questions. I wondered if she only intended to help herself to a bottle or two of good wine or if she had her eye on something more valuable, like the silver, or maybe even a painting.

"Of course, it would be a shame to let good food spoil," I said, nodding agreement and watching the hint of a smile twitch at her lips.

"It is too bad," she said. "After all these years to be told that my services were no longer needed and I should find employment elsewhere. The inspector told me to come on Monday morning to give the place a thorough cleaning and then I'm finished. No more. I must find a new situation and I am no longer young. If I ever found the swine that took Mr. Bryce's life, I would run him through with a knife myself."

"The knife that killed him — I understand from the inspector that it was an ordinary kitchen knife."

She shrugged. "He asked me if it came from my kitchen. I told him it was an inferior knife to the ones he would find in this establishment. Mr. Bryce only liked the best. Stainless steel, you know. Very modern. And now . . ." She turned away from me.

I put a gentle hand on her shoulder. "I understand how hard it must be for you, madame."

She nodded, putting her hand up to her mouth. "Mr. Bryce would never have wanted me to be cast aside in this manner. He appreciated all that I did for him."

"Perhaps I could help you to go through the pantry to pack up the food," I suggested but that clearly went too far.

"Certainly not, madame. That would be quite wrong," she said. "I do not plan to stay long and I would be in much trouble if the police knew I had admitted a stranger. If you want to gain admission to this apartment to look at Mr. Bryce's paintings, you must first ask permission from the police. *Bonjour.*" She gave a curt nod and then went up the steps, putting a key into the lock.

So much for my Irish powers of persuasion, I thought. I didn't think Inspector Henri would be too willing to accept yet another story from me.

TWENTY-SEVEN

I felt frustrated as I walked back to Miss Cassatt's residence. Surely I should have been able to find out more from the housekeeper. Unfortunately she was clearly anxious to get in there, help herself to what she had come for, and then escape. I was in her way and there was no point in putting myself on her bad side. Had I learned anything from her, I wondered? Well, for one thing I knew that nobody would be at Mr. Bryce's apartment on Sunday, if I could find a way in. Also I learned that he had not been painting much recently and his paintings now commanded a high price. So perhaps we had this all wrong — it might have been a simple art theft gone wrong. I wondered if the housekeeper knew which paintings had been hanging in the studio and whether one might be missing.

I arrived back to find Sid and Gus kneeling beside one of the crates of paintings I had retrieved from Rue des Martyrs. They were holding them up to show to Mary Cassatt, sitting across from them on the sofa.

"Honestly, you two," came Mary's voice from the sofa. "A more eclectic mix I have never seen, and most of it, I'm sad to say, is junk. These Fauvists, they'll never last. Fauvism, Cubism, they are fads. They'll vanish in a puff of smoke, hopefully giving way to good art again."

"What about this one?" Sid held up another painting.

Mary leaned back to examine it. "That's not bad. The artist can at least handle a brush well. Rather melancholy, but most of them are. It seems that to be modern means you can find no joy in life."

They looked up as I came into the room, and Gus held out a hand to me. "Molly, you're back. Any luck?"

"I met the housekeeper," I said. "I tried my best with the Irish charm but I can't say I achieved much. She is furious at being thrown out by the police and was hoping to slip back in unnoticed. I don't think she was at all pleased that I found her there. She said she was just rescuing some food before it spoiled and that may be true, but I sensed she wanted to get her hands on more than cakes and pies."

"Steal from her dead employer, you mean?" Gus looked shocked.

"I don't know about that. It could be just taking things she felt she was entitled to. But either way she was not going to let me in, and she didn't disclose much about Mr. Bryce, except what we already know: he and his wife had a falling out, but she's Catholic and wouldn't divorce him. They haven't seen each other since he came to France but there was no mention of another woman in his life."

"Was there any mention of another man?" Sid asked.

We all reacted with surprise. "Holy Mother of God, I never thought of that. Have there been any rumors of that ilk, Mary?" I asked.

Mary shook her head. "I can't say I've heard any rumors about his private life recently. Of course everyone in Paris is expected to have a mistress, so that would hardly have been worth mentioning. But a male companion? I'm sure I would have heard about that."

"The one thing I did ascertain is that nobody will be at the apartment tomorrow. The housekeeper is coming back on Monday to give the place a thorough clean so I really must try to get a look at it before everything is moved and packed away."

"How do you propose to get a look at it, dare one ask?" Sid said.

I grinned. "I was hoping to borrow a pair of your trousers and climb up the tree. It seemed as if the end window wasn't quite shut tight, so I thought . . ."

"Molly, you'll be arrested for breaking and entering," Mary said. "You'll also make Inspector Henri even more suspicious about you than he already is."

"Molly, don't take any stupid risks for me," Sid said. "I'm sure it will all sort itself out, and if it doesn't, we'll just find a way to slip out of the country and catch a boat home."

"I've been thinking about that," I said. "If I am caught I'll confess to being a newspaper reporter, hoping to write a scoop on Reynold Bryce for the Boston papers. They can be annoyed with me, but they wouldn't charge me with anything. Newspaper reporters can get away with murder —" I broke off at that choice of words. "I didn't mean that literally," I said.

"What will you think of next?" Gus shook her head.

I looked around the room, now bathed in midday sunlight. "Where's Liam?"

"Sleeping like a baby," Gus said. "We played with him and then put him down for his morning nap. He's such fun now. We love his laugh. Sid kept balancing a matchbox on her nose and then letting it fall."

Sid laughed. "It didn't fail to amuse him for a good half hour."

"Babies are wonderful, aren't they?" I said. "I was thinking last night about how uncomplicated life is for them. As long as they are warm and fed and have someone they trust near them then nothing else matters." I fought back an unwelcome surge of emotion. After what we had just gone through tears were liable to resurface too often. Having prided myself on being such a strong woman I couldn't abide this show of weakness. Instead I turned my attention to the paintings. The one that now lay on the sofa was of the young girl with haunted dark eyes.

"I particularly noticed this one when I packed them up," I said. "It's quite good, isn't it? Sad, but well-done."

"It's one of Maxim's," Sid said.

"Who?" Mary asked.

"My cousin. Maxim Noah."

"Ah yes, you spoke of him, I remember now," Mary said. "You say you just discovered him living in Paris?"

"It was rather fortuitous," Sid said. "Right before I left, my mother wrote to tell me we had relatives in Paris and asked me to look them up. I went around several synagogues but I couldn't find any Goldfarbs who could have been related. Then I was at a poetry reading and was chatting to this most attractive young Jewish man. We started talking about families and when he said that his mother was a Goldfarb and her father had come from Eastern Europe when she was a small child I started asking questions. And it turned out that his grandfather had had a falling out with his brother. One had gone to New York, one stayed in Paris. And the brother's name was Nathan, which was my grandfather's name. Wasn't that an amazing coincidence? So we concluded we were long-lost cousins. He lives in a shack on Montmartre. Horribly primitive, but I think he'll make his name as a painter very soon. I plan to take some of his pictures to New York and maybe bring him over some time and hold a showing for him."

"How interesting," Mary said. She bent over the painting, then sat back on the sofa again. "Yes, I think his work does show some promise. When all is well again I'd like to meet him."

Gus touched Sid's arm. "And do you

think he'd be able to help us? He could go anywhere within the Jewish community without arousing suspicion. He could attend meetings at synagogues and of the pro-Dreyfusard brigade. They might have an idea who carried out this murder."

Sid hesitated, then shook her head. "I don't think I want to get anyone else involved, especially not Maxim. If he knows we're in hiding he may be questioned by police and have to reveal our hiding place. Or appear to be a suspect himself. For the same reason you can't contact Willie Walcott, Gus. We can't put family members in danger."

"I could go and talk to Willie Walcott," I said. "I got the feeling he knew Mr. Bryce quite well." And as I said the words I felt a sudden chill. Gertrude Stein had described Willie Walcott as a very pretty boy. And I remembered the petulant look on his face when he had said that Bryce was painting again and didn't want to be disturbed. Could there be something to Sid's suggestion after all?

"He will probably be at the Steins' tonight," Mary said. "Willie likes to see and be seen, if you know what I mean. I believe he likes the social aspects of art more than the actual painting."

"What do you think of him as a painter, Mary?" Gus asked.

"Technique's all right, I suppose, but I'd call him another of the copiers. He can give you a good, lifelike rendition of the Seine, but it is entirely in the style of Monet or Reynold Bryce. I'm sure such pictures sell well at home, but I don't think any of you Walcotts are lacking for money, are you?"

"I heard that his father had cut off his allowance when he dropped out of Harvard," I said.

"When did you hear that?" Gus demanded sharply.

"When I met him at the café in Montparnasse. The other fellows said that he was good at sponging off his friends for meals."

"How strange," Gus turned to Sid. "We never got that impression, did we? He let us think he was doing awfully well, that he was chummy with Reynold Bryce, and moved in the right circles."

I'm sure he was chummy with Reynold Bryce, I thought. Out loud I said, "I'll cross-question him tonight, if he comes to Miss Stein's salon."

Celeste appeared at the doorway. "Madame Sullivan, your son is awake and crying."

I jumped up. "Excuse me," I said. "Duty calls."

Duty calls, I repeated to myself as I went up the stairs. It seemed as if life these days was one long round of duty: to my husband, my child, and now to my friends. I tried to remember if ever there was a time when I was carefree. Not for many years, if ever. How I had envied Sid and Gus their freedom to do exactly what they chose on a whim. Well, at this moment I didn't envy them, and it was my duty to help them.

After I had fed Liam and we had taken our own midday meal Mary contacted some friends about borrowing a baby carriage. I went to pick it up and then Mary and I took Liam for a stroll along the Seine. Liam was enthralled by the traffic on the river and Mary and I enjoyed the lively Saturday afternoon scene — families picnicking on the grass, lovers walking arm in arm, a brightly decorated pleasure craft going past.

"How I love Paris," Mary said. "It's always so full of life and people know how to enjoy themselves. In America work always comes first. Never in France." She turned to look at me. "Now your friends have the right idea. They have learned how to live for the moment."

"They have money. It helps," I said.

"Without it I imagine they'd have very different lives."

Mary paused, looking out across the Seine to the Eiffel Tower. "Do you think you'll be able to help them?" she asked. "I can't bear the thought of Sid shut in a French jail. She'd go mad."

"I'll do what I can," I said. "But I can't possibly do as good a job as the police. I have no access to any evidence they took from Mr. Bryce's house. What if someone had been blackmailing him? Or he had just broken up with an unsuitable woman? I have no way of finding out those things. In fact I'm beginning to think that their best hope is to leave the country. If Sid dresses properly as a woman again, who would think of stopping them?"

"Unless the police have their names by now. A woman who goes around dressed in male garb does attract attention, you know. I think they are quite safe for the moment in my house."

"It's very good of you to take this risk," I said.

She smiled. "We women have to stick together," she said.

TWENTY-EIGHT

That evening we dined early and then Mary and I set off for the Steins' apartment on Rue de Fleurus. I was prepared to take the Métro and then walk but Mary insisted on hiring a cab. "The Métro on Saturday night is full of undesirables," she said, "and later on, when we return, it will be full of drunks."

I must say it was pleasant to be *clip-clopping* across the Seine, past the imposing shape of Les Invalides and then down several attractive boulevards lined with bars and restaurants just coming to life until we reached the Rue de Fleurus. Other cabs were disgorging their passengers outside the Steins' building while younger, impoverished artists were approaching on foot, some carrying paintings under their arms.

We could hear the buzz of conversation and a burst of laughter long before we came to the Steins' front door, which was now wide open. Other people were going in so we followed them.

"Gertrude and Leo don't stand on ceremony," Mary said. "The only criteria for being admitted are passion for art, good conversation, and the ability to hold liquor. "Ah, there she is, now. Gertrude!" And she forced her way through the crowd.

Miss Stein turned from the group she was standing with. "Why, if it isn't Mary Cassatt. It's a long time since you graced us with your presence." And she held out her hand to Mary. "What brings you here?"

"Not trying to sell you a painting, that's for sure," Mary said with a laugh. "I know your taste is for the avant-garde and I am hopelessly mired in tea parties and domesticity. Actually I have found myself a new model — Master Liam Sullivan, aged eight months. And I have brought his mother with me. Molly Sullivan. I believe you two have met."

Miss Stein's sharp eyes focused on me. "Ah. So you've come back at the proper time," she said. "Welcome. Did you find your friends yet?"

I decided that I had to lie to her although she wasn't the kind of person one should lie to. "I did, and you were quite right. They got held up out of the city with no way of communicating."

"So all's well that ends well? That's good. Help yourself to a drink. I know it's France but some of my guests prefer a good strong bourbon." She indicated a table in the corner around which several young men were hovering. "Move aside, fellows, and let the ladies in!" she bellowed. "They are dying of thirst and you're hogging it all."

Mary grinned at me as they stood aside for us. I noticed that one of them was the young Spaniard, Pablo Picasso. "Ah, the lady with the red hair," he said. He turned to the men beside him. "One day I will paint her."

"If Fernande allows you," his companion said.

"Miss Stein is going to buy one of my paintings," Picasso said. "We may move to an apartment with running water then Fernande will love me and be happy."

"And still not let you paint other women," the man said and they laughed.

I took the glass of wine that Mary offered and we moved away. My gaze was drawn to a group in the middle of the room, clustered around a large, heavyset man. He had dark skin, large jowls, and a face that looked like a cross between a shrunken head and a gorilla. I nudged Mary. "Who is that exceptionally ugly man over there?"

"Oh, him? That's Vollard — he's the most important art dealer in Paris. If he likes your work, you are in. He and Reynold Bryce had a long-standing mutual loathing. Reynold said it was because he only liked beautiful objects around him and Vollard's face distressed him, but it was really because Vollard had called his paintings trite and meaningless."

Even as she was speaking Vollard looked up and saw Mary. "Ah, *la belle* Cassatt comes to grace us with her presence," he said and held out his hand to her. "What are you doing here? Not trying to sell Gertrude a picture."

"I came to be sociable, Monsieur Vollard," Mary said, "And to introduce my young friend, Mrs. Sullivan, visiting from America."

"If she wants to buy paintings she had better come to me," Vollard said. "I only deal in the best."

"She is not buying. She is reporting on the art scene for her newspaper back home," Mary said, catching me off guard. We had never discussed this. "Everyone at home wants to know about Reynold Bryce."

"He insulted the Jews once too often," Vollard said.

"Is that what everyone thinks?" I asked.

Vollard looked around the group. "What else could it be? A robbery and nothing is taken? I don't think so. He has not helped himself to someone else's wife lately that I have heard — or even someone's mistress, or volatile young people like our dear Picasso over there might have stabbed him."

"Did he ever help himself to someone's wife?" I asked.

Several heads were shaken. "Or mistress?" I continued. "He was still officially married, wasn't he? Did he have mistresses?"

"Not since Pauline," one of the group said. "And that was some time ago now."

"Pauline?" I realized instantly how helpful Mary's ploy had been. I was a reporter, therefore not personally involved. They were quite willing to share gossip with me.

"Pauline Hubert. She was a model, but she never modeled for him. He stuck to his landscapes."

"Did she leave him or the other way around?" I asked.

"She got too old," one of them said and there was a general chuckle.

"Someone told me he was painting again," another of the men said to his companions, seemingly unaware now that I was part of the group.

"Really? That explains it then. He had quite a twinkle in his eye when I met him at the American Club last week. I said to him, 'You sly old dog. I think you're on the prowl again.' "

"And what did he say?"

The first man smirked. "He said, 'You're never too old for that sort of thing, are you?' "

They realized I was standing with them and the speaker gave an embarrassed cough. "My apologies, ma'am. Poor form."

There was an uncomfortable silence.

"Has anyone heard when his funeral will be?" I asked.

"I heard he wanted his body shipped home and a grand state funeral in Boston."

"That sounds like Reynold. Never slow about coming forward, was he?"

"I wonder if they will release his body if they don't apprehend his murderer," I said and saw their reaction. Ladies, even reporters, do not speak about bodies and murderers. I excused myself and moved away. Pauline Hubert had been cast aside because she was too old. That sounded like a good motive for murder. And then there was the invisible wife in America. The good Catholic who didn't believe in divorce. Might she want to marry again or to get her hands on his money and have paid someone to come over and finish off her husband?

I wished I could ask Daniel to check into Mrs. Reynold Bryce, but I couldn't. He had enough on his plate and wouldn't be pleased to hear his wife was showing interest in a Parisian murder.

The evening went on. More people arrived until the salon was crowded to the point of not being able to move. The air was heavy with that strange scented smoke of French cigarettes and I felt hot and clammy. The noise level had risen until it was almost unbearable, with everyone around me shouting to be heard. I had put down my drink as I was in constant danger of someone jogging my elbow. Mary was swallowed up somewhere in the crowd. I looked around, feeling like a wallflower, as one does at a gathering where one knows nobody, and saw Maxim Noah, standing at the fringe of the crowd looking as awkward as I felt. His face lit up as he noticed me. "Madame Sullivan, the friend of my cousin. I did not expect to see you here? What news of Elena — did she return to Paris?"

"No, and they are going to stay away for the present," I said. "They have been ill."

"I am so sorry. Will you be going to visit them?"

"Possibly soon."

"Please give them my very best wishes for their recovery."

"I will," I said. I noticed that he appeared to be alone. So was Picasso. So the artists didn't bring their mistresses with them to social events. "Do you come to Miss Stein's salon often?" I asked.

He smiled. He had a most disarming smile. "I get one good meal a week this way. And I hope that one day she may buy one of my paintings."

"Everyone is talking about Reynold Bryce," I said. "You heard about his murder, I'm sure."

"I am not interested in passé American painters," he said. "I am sorry he died, but it was no great loss to the world of art."

"They are saying that he was killed for insulting Jews. Have you heard any rumors about that? Do you attend the synagogue?"

He shrugged. "I don't practice my religion. What did Karl Marx say: 'Religion is the opium of the people?' We Jews have followed the same god for thousands of years and look where it's got us — persecution and no place to call home. Art and beauty — those are my religions. At least they mean

375

something. But I'm stuck with my race. If a Jew killed this Bryce fellow, then I expect he deserved it. Me, I never met the man, so I can't really pass an opinion." Then his face lit up. "Ah, good. They're putting out the hot canapés." And he was gone.

I stood close to the door until I spotted Willie Walcott's blond curls. He too had closed in on the food table. I wondered how many of the impoverished artists here only came for the food. No, that was doing them an injustice. With people like the frightening Monsieur Vollard here as well as the Steins there was always some hope of selling a painting. I forced my way through the crowd, making for Willie. He moved away from the food table at that moment so that we came upon each other more rapidly than I had anticipated.

"Oh, hello there," he said. "You're Gussie's Irishwoman, aren't you?"

"You make me sound like the lady who comes to scrub the floors or iron the sheets."

He blushed at this, his fair skin turning bright red. "Oh, jeepers, sorry. I didn't mean it like that."

"No offense taken." I smiled.

"So did you finally discover where Cousin Gussie and her friend had popped off to?"

"Yes, I did, thank you."

"Oh, that's good." He didn't ask any more questions and I gathered that he wasn't really interested in what had happened to his cousin. I was tempted to add that she had fallen down a mine shaft or been abducted by white slavers. He probably would have responded, "That's good." So a rather self-absorbed young man.

"I think we're in danger of being trampled if we stand here," I said. I noticed he was carrying a plate piled with vol-au-vents, oysters, cheeses in one hand, and a glass of champagne in the other. "Here, let me take your glass before you find the contents of your plate plastered to your front."

He grinned, handed me the glass, then followed me to a less crowded corner. "It is extra full tonight, isn't it?" he said. "Word got around that Vollard was coming and everyone wants to get into his good books."

"Why is that?"

"His exhibition is the one that counts."

"More than Reynold Bryce's?" I asked.

A spasm of pain or annoyance, I couldn't really tell which, crossed his face. "Well, Reynold won't be holding an exhibition this year, will he? Vollard will be the only show in town this summer."

"Will you have any paintings in it?"

"No. I'm not, shall we say, in fashion, so

it seems. One is expected to hurl paint at a canvas and paint a rhinoceros with a baby sitting on it if one wants to be noticed. I simply can't do that. That's why Reynold's death was such a shock. At least I could usually count on being part of his shows."

"I'm glad to see you here," I said.

"You are? Why?"

"I got the impression the other day that his death had really upset you. So it's good to see you're out and about in company and not moping at home."

"It was a bit of a shock, that's all." His face colored again. "I mean, who would have expected old Reynold . . ."

"I don't think he expected it either," I said. "Do you have any idea who might have killed him? What is the general opinion among your crowd at the cafés?"

"We heard it was a Jewish fanatic. Why, did you hear something different?"

"I'm a newcomer here," I said. "I don't know anybody. But obviously one is intrigued when a prominent member of an expatriate community is murdered. I wondered if there was more to it."

"I think a Jewish fanatic is the most likely," he said carefully. "He did say some absolutely damning things about Jews and what should happen to them. Tact was never

Reynold's stong point. If he didn't like something, he said so, and loudly. Someone once commented that he really thought that God created him and then He rested."

"You were a close friend of his, weren't you?"

Again the pink cheeks. "Not really," he said. "When I first arrived he was kind to me. Took me under his wing, you know. And he was decent about including my paintings when he had a showing. But he was like a little boy, really — easily bored. If he found a new toy, he dropped the old one and forgot about it."

"Like Pauline?" I asked.

He looked startled. "Pauline? How did you hear about her?"

"Some of the people here mentioned her. They said Reynold Bryce had broken with her because she was too old."

He looked amused now. "Is that what they said? How funny. Anyway that was ages ago."

"So had he found a new toy more recently?" I asked.

"So one heard."

"A who or a what?"

"Both, I think I can safely say. But I'd prefer not to discuss this subject any further, if you don't mind. I find it highly distasteful, especially with one who didn't even know him. And I would like to eat my food before it gets cold." He looked around. "What happened to my glass?"

"I put it down on that table," I said. "One of the waiters must have cleared it away."

"Damn. I'd better go and get another one. I need a steady supply of alcohol to keep me going."

With that he turned his back on me. *Interesting,* I thought. Willie Walcott had been that new toy once. Had he been angry at being cast aside? Or had there been more new toys since him? And Willie was impoverished, so I had heard. Had he been relying on some kind of financial help from Reynold Bryce? And if Reynold had cut off that help . . . I paused, trying to picture the innocent-looking Mr. Walcott plunging a kitchen knife into Bryce's chest. It didn't seem likely, and yet I had learned by now that murderers are often the most unlikely of people.

I wondered who might know about the details of Reynold Bryce's private life and be willing to talk about it. I tried moving about the room, invisible, and listening in with the hope of overhearing gossip, but I didn't hear his name mentioned once. This was the Parisian art world of today, I gathered. Reynold Bryce belonged to yesterday and as such he had become irrelevant. But one thing I could surmise — they didn't think that one of their own might be responsible or they'd have been discussing it.

I tried infiltrating groups and asking questions but at any gathering where people know each other intimately they showed no interest in an outsider. I was looking for Mary, hoping that we could make an early exit when I felt someone take my hand. It was that rather frightening Creole man, Vollard.

"You are looking for something, madame," he said. "And you do not find it. A lost lover, maybe? A new lover?"

I laughed. "I am happily married, monsieur."

"So is everyone in this room. That does not preclude the taking of lovers. It is an amusing sport and less exhausting than tennis. Everyone does it."

I wondered for one awful moment whether he was suggesting that he might fill that role for me. But then he went on. "You are a fish out of water here. Why did you come?"

"I'm newly arrived in Paris. I'm staying with my friend Mary Cassatt. She thought I should experience the Steins' salon at least once."

"Ah, La Cassatt. Is she painting these days? Tell her to work harder. She is one whose work I can sell at the drop of a hat. And the best prices too."

"And Reynold Bryce?" I asked. "Can you sell his paintings at the drop of a hat?"

"He never brought his paintings to me. Perhaps he feared I might reject them, or perhaps he thought he could do better without the middle man. And maybe that was true. He always sold well with Americans who like pretty landscapes on their walls. Personally I always felt he was a good journeyman, a good craftsman but lacking in brilliance. You compare his paintings of the Seine to Monet's and you'll see the difference. Monet's light glows on the water, the trees are alive in the wind. To view his painting is an experience of the heart, while Bryce's are merely for the eyes."

"They are saying the price of his paintings will rise now that he is dead," I said and he laughed.

"What a mercenary thought from such charming lips. Possibly true. It will rise because there are few paintings available for sale. Supply and demand, you know. He had money. He didn't need to paint. Again proving he was only a journeyman. The others — Renoir, Degas — they would die if they were not allowed to paint."

"Who do you think might have killed him?" I asked.

"Bryce?" He shrugged, making his whole large body shake like a half-inflated balloon. "Any number of people. He said exactly what he thought and didn't care whose toes he trod on."

"But surely you don't kill someone because he insults you?"

"I do not personally, madame, but there are many in Paris who might. We are a passionate mob, madame. A mongrel mob from all over the world. We fight duels over women and over perceived insults. But one hears he was stabbed with a kitchen knife. This was not a spur of the moment act of passion. Someone came prepared to kill him. And a common kitchen knife too. So it all points to the Jewish immigrant they suggest — poor and fanatic. A dangerous combination."

Mary appeared at my side then. "Are you about ready to leave? They'll go on all night and I'm getting too old for such things."

"Oh, no, Mademoiselle Cassatt. You will be forever young. When are you going to bring me more paintings? My little gallery is bare without them," Vollard said.

"You are a flatterer, Monsieur Vollard,"

she replied, "but I am going to start work on a new piece. This lady's charming son is absolutely made to be a model, if I can ever get him to sit still."

We took our leave and were assisted into a cab.

"Well?" Mary asked as we set off. "Did you discover anything?"

"Not much. Most of them weren't at all interested in Reynold Bryce or his death. The consensus is that it was indeed the Jewish fanatic. But I did have a long chat with Willie Walcott and he had definitely been a close friend of Bryce's, shall we say, and was peeved that Bryce had found a 'new toy,' as he put it. So I'm rather curious to know who or what that new toy was. I can see I'll have to have another chat with the housekeeper when she comes to clean the place on Monday. But I really want to take a look for myself tomorrow, if Sid will lend me her trousers."

Mary shook her head. "And to think I had a quiet life until you ladies descended on me." But she was smiling.

As we came down the steps and out into the night air I opened my purse. "I did manage to pull off one thing," I said. And I held up a champagne glass.

"You stole a glass from the Steins? Why?"

"It was Willie Walcott's glass. I offered to hold it for him, but I hid it behind a curtain until he went for another one. Then I tipped out the remainder of the champagne and stuffed it into my purse. So if the police want to match fingerprints, we now have a set of Willie Walcott's."

A worried frown came over her face. "You really suspect Willie of doing this horrible deed?"

"He had a lot to lose. If I can just find out from the housekeeper when she saw him last at Bryce's apartment and what she overheard between them. I imagine she would be the type that listens at keyholes. Whether she'll confide in me is another matter. I may have to suggest that the police suspect her. . . ."

"I'm glad I only paint pictures for a living," Mary said as she hailed a cab. "Such a peaceful occupation compared to yours."

Twenty-Nine

I was awoken to the sound of bells, ringing out all over the city. I lay, watching stripes of early sunlight on my wall, listening first to the sweet chime of a nearby bell, then the deep reverberating hum of more important bells until the whole city seemed to be enveloped in sound. Liam stirred, turned over, and pulled himself up on the side of his crib.

"Ma!" he said. *"Ma ma ma ma."*

"Liam, you're standing," I exclaimed. And almost talking too, I realized. I felt guilty that I was spending so much time apart from him and had missed his acquiring of two new skills. I picked him up.

"Can you say, 'Mama'?" I asked.

He looked pleased with himself. *"Ma ma ma ma ma,"* he repeated.

"How about 'Dada'?"

He looked concerned. Obviously the word stirred a memory of a man he hadn't seen recently. "Dada will be so proud when he sees Liam can stand and talk and maybe even walk soon." As I said the words I felt a terrible tug at my heart. How long before we saw Daniel again? Was he safe? When would I hear from him?

After I had taken care of Liam's needs and had a quick breakfast of croissant and apricot jam I changed into a pair of Sid's trousers, tucked my unruly hair into a beret that Sid had bought as a souvenir, and set off, carrying a stepladder that Celeste used to dust the picture rails. I didn't think the outfit would convince anybody that I was a young male gardener, but in fact I didn't pass anyone as I walked down the Rue François Premier. Mary had surmised that Parisians were either at mass or sleeping in late on Sunday mornings and this seemed to be the case. I reached the circle with the fountain at its center and made my way to the little garden outside Reynold Bryce's window, unlatched the gate, and slipped inside. Still nobody was in sight, unless someone was observing me from an upstairs window. That thought had never occurred to me before — had the police checked who lived in Reynold Bryce's building? Did he get on well with his neighbors? Did he get on too well with a neighbor's wife?

I set up the stepladder behind the lilac bush so that I would be unseen by all but the most prying eyes. I was glad that the shutters on the downstairs windows were hooked open. One less step to gain entry. I was about to go up the stepladder to the most likely of the windows when I heard the light click of footsteps approaching. Immediately I turned my back away from the street and pretended to be pruning the lilac bush. The footsteps stopped.

"Shame on you," a scratchy voice said in French. I half-turned to see a shrunken old woman in that fearsome black favored by French widows. She clutched a missal and wore a lace mantilla, proving she had just been to mass. She wagged a finger at me. "It is wrong to work on the Lord's day, young man. If your master makes you do it, then shame on him."

Then she set off again, light feet tapping on the deserted sidewalk.

I let out a huge sigh of relief then quickly went up the ladder and out of sight into the lilac branches. Twigs and leaves got into my way, but I pushed through them until I was level with the base of the window. It was a push-up sash and it appeared that either the wood of the frame had buckled or the paint had blistered, not allowing it to close completely. The blinds were drawn so I couldn't see into the room beyond. I removed the kitchen knife I had purloined from Celeste's kitchen and eased it under the frame. Then I levered as hard as I could. I felt the window judder but didn't move. I jiggled as I levered, felt the catch give and the window begin to move upward. A little more effort and it was wide enough open for me to crawl inside.

I pushed the blind aside, closed the window after me, and stepped into the darkened room. With all the blinds closed it was like stepping into the depths of the ocean. The room had that closed-up, musty smell, tinged with the odors of oil paint, linseed oil, and turpentine, with which I had now become familiar. I moved cautiously to the door, which was closed, opened it and listened. Complete silence. I ventured forth and moved through a dining room, a library, a parlor before I found myself in the front foyer where I had spoken with Inspector Henri. I was about to open one of the doors leading from the foyer when I realized that I had failed the most basic test of breaking and entering — I was not wearing gloves. Hastily I felt for a pocket handkerchief, but I realized that these were not my clothes and thus I had no handkerchief with me. So

I used the fabric of my shirt to hold the door handle. This door led to a hallway with two bedrooms leading from it. I looked around them, opened a top drawer, and extracted a handkerchief monogrammed *RB* and used it to wipe the drawer pull clean. I didn't think anyone would have counted the handkerchiefs at this point and Reynold Bryce no longer needed it.

Thus armed with the handkerchief to prevent fingerprints, I now looked around the room. It was a typical man's room — silver-backed brushes on the dresser, various jars of pomade and even hair dye, showing that he was more than a little vain, but no other adornments. No photographs, no letters; nothing to give a clue as to who lived there, or what kind of person he was — except there were good paintings on the walls. After going through a few rooms I realized that Reynold Bryce had a fine collection of Impressionist art. Worth a pretty penny, I decided. Enough to make his wife decide to kill him off? Had the police checked whether she might be in France herself? Then I decided that she would not have stabbed her husband if she'd come over to kill him. Stabbing is always too risky. Unless you strike at exactly the right spot the victim may well live. The knife could hit against one of the ribs and not penetrate far enough. Or a strong person could wrestle the knife away before one has time to deliver the blow. It takes skill or luck to kill with a knife. Which did Bryce's murderer have?

I prowled the other rooms, even pulled out drawers in his desk, but I didn't know what I was looking for. Surely important papers would have been removed? Last of all I located the kitchen, now looking neat but forlorn with its bare scrubbed pine table and pans hanging above the stove. An unpleasant smell of stuffiness and rotting vegetables lingered in the air. It appeared that the housekeeper had only taken the good stuff yesterday. I opened a door that led to a pantry with well-stocked shelves, and beyond it a dark square of hallway leading to a pitifully small room that must have been occupied by the housekeeper. All that remained now was an unmade bed, a thin upright chest, and a wardrobe with the door hanging open to reveal no clothes inside. She had definitely taken all her things yesterday. I wondered whether the police would mind. Then I made my way back through the dining room to the room into which I had entered, Reynold Bryce's studio. I didn't want to betray my presence by pulling up any of the blinds so I groped about on the wall until I discovered an electric light switch. Thank heavens he was a modern man and I didn't need to light the gas.

Harsh light now bathed the room. I saw that it was barely furnished. There was a long unpolished wooden table on which painting equipment still stood. Beside it a captain's chair, in which presumably Reynold Bryce died. At the far end a blue velvet drape was hung as a backdrop, cascading like a waterfall over steps of various height. And beside this was the painting he must have been working on when he died. I stopped short, staring in surprise. This was no landscape. The painting was of a young girl with huge dark eyes, staring out with a half-frightened, half-curious expression. She was naked with the neat little breasts of an adolescent. The painting was by no means finished with a large area below the breasts only vaguely sketched in.

As I stood there examining it I realized that I had seen her before. She was the same girl from Gus's painting — the one painted by Sid's cousin Maxim Noah. What's more the paint on the canvas wasn't even completely dry where he had daubed it on thickly. There were blobs of paint on his palette and brushes standing in turpentine or lying on the table. One was now hard and stiff with paint. He hadn't cleaned his brush. That must mean that he had been in the middle of painting when he was killed.

Why had nobody mentioned the model? Had the police now questioned her? Surely she must have been here, in this room, when his assailant came in. I looked around. There was a narrow space behind the velvet hangings. Had she hidden herself there when there was a ring of the doorbell . . . and . . . I took this one stage further. . . . Had she witnessed the whole thing from behind this drape? Or, the other possibility . . . had she been the one who had stabbed the painter?

I was examining the room, inch by inch, when I heard a sound. It was the clatter of something being dropped nearby. In an instant I crossed the room and flicked down the light switch, leaving me blundering in darkness. I opened the door an inch or two and listened. Somebody was definitely moving about the apartment. I knew I should make for the window as quickly as possible, but curiosity made me hesitate. I eased the door open and started to tiptoe across the dining room. There was another *clunk,* this time sounding dangerously close, probably inside the kitchen. The kitchen door was now closed and I didn't dare to open it.

Much as I wanted to see who was in there, common sense won out. If it was the police I had no way to explain my presence. If it was the murderer returned to retrieve something incriminating, I'd be the next victim and if it was the housekeeper, making another raid on her master's belongings, then there was no way I could pump her for information in the future if she encountered me here. I felt my way back across the studio, eased myself out of the window onto the stepladder, then folded it up, and let myself out of the garden as silently as possible. The street was still deserted. I crossed the circle and went to stand behind the fountain that graced the middle. After what seemed like hours of standing and holding a stepladder, I saw a figure emerge from Reynold Bryce's building. It was the housekeeper again and this time she was carrying two bulging canvas bags.

I smiled to myself as I watched her scurry off. She'd cleared out her room of her own possessions yesterday, so today she was clearly stealing. It might be a good piece of knowledge to hold over her when I went back tomorrow to find out more about that model. I walked back to Mary's house, returned the stepladder, and changed into more normal garb.

"We're glad to see you in one piece," Sid said as I appeared in the salon where they were drinking coffee. "We half expected to hear you'd been dragged away in chains."

"It was touch and go for a while," I said. "The housekeeper returned while I was there. Luckily she was so intent on helping herself to Mr. Bryce's things that I was able to slip away again."

"Mercy me," Mary said. "And did you learn anything important from this risky endeavor?"

"Yes, I did, actually. Reynold Bryce was painting a portrait of a young girl when he died. The paint was still slightly wet. And it was the same girl that Maxim Noah painted in your picture, Gus."

"Really? You think she was in the house when he died?" Gus asked. "Or — you don't think she killed him, do you?"

"That's what we have to find out. I thought I'd go and seek out Maxim Noah and get the name of the young woman from him. I wish I'd known this last night because I could have asked him at the Steins' party."

"He was there?" Sid's expression brightened.

"He was, and he sent you his best regards."

"You didn't tell him where we were?"

"Of course not. I stuck to our story that you had been taken ill while visiting the countryside and were still there, recuperating."

"That's good," Sid smiled again.

"And I also tried to ask him what the Jewish community was saying about the death of Reynold Bryce."

"That was smart of you, Molly," Sid said. "And what did he say?"

"He said he never attended a synagogue and wanted nothing to do with his religion. He said he was stuck with his race, but his real religion was art."

"That's a lot of help," Gus said. "Still we now have a real lead to follow, don't we? If Molly can track down the model we might be getting close to the truth."

"Isn't that a little dangerous?" Mary asked. "I mean, if she did kill Reynold, or she was in cahoots with who did it, you're running an awful risk, Molly. Some of these models — well, they aren't the best sort of girls. They can also work as prostitutes by night, you know. She could be involved with a criminal type who came there to rob Reynold, or blackmail him. . . ."

"She's right, Molly."

"Don't worry. I said I was going to ask Maxim Noah about her. He'll know what sort of girl she is. And I expect the police must have checked her out by now. If she has criminal connections they'll have taken her in." I took the cup of coffee that Gus had poured for me. "I wish I could find an excuse to go and talk to Inspector Henri. I'm dying to find out how far along they are with their investigation."

"The French police don't take kindly to interference," Mary said.

"Neither do the New York police," I said. "My husband will never share details of any crime he's working on with me."

"That's because you'd run straight out and try to solve it before him," Sid said, with a grin.

"Contrary to popular belief I do not go around looking for trouble," I said. "Trouble just seems to come and find me."

"Do be careful, Molly," Gus said. "Maybe it would be a good idea to ask the police how they are getting along, and if they are making good progress, then you can stop taking these risks."

"Don't worry, I've several things planned that won't involve risk," I said. "If I go and find Maxim this afternoon and get the model's name from him, I can find out more about her. And then I'm going to talk to the housekeeper in the morning, when she's cleaning up Mr. Bryce's apartment. I want to hear what she's got to say about the model, and whether she was in the studio when the housekeeper left to go shopping. I'd also like her opinion on your cousin, Gus."

"On Willie? What's he got to do with this?"

"Nothing, I hope. But he fell out of favor with Mr. Bryce recently and I just wondered . . . well, what sort of relationship he had had with him, and whether . . ." I stumbled, not knowing how to put this without offending.

"We asked ourselves the same thing," Sid said. "But we didn't know about his lack of money at the time. You want to know whether Mr. Bryce was supporting him financially and thus —"

"Hold on a minute," Gus said. "You're not suggesting that my cousin might have anything to do with Reynold Bryce's death, are you? I've known Willie all my life. We used to play together at their summer cottage in Maine. He's a good bit younger than I, but a sweet and funny kid. I'd say there was no malicious bone in him."

"I'm sure he had nothing to do with the

murder, Gus," I said hastily, although I wasn't so sure. I suspected that Willie Walcott did have a few malicious bones in him, given the right circumstances. Maybe tomorrow I'd learn whether he had been to visit Reynold Bryce recently and what had transpired between them.

THIRTY

That afternoon, after I had put Liam down for his nap, I took the Métro back to my old neighborhood in Montmartre. The cafés were full but I saw no sign of Maxim or any of his artist friends. So I trudged up the many steep alleyways and steps until I reached the very summit of the hill and found Le Bateau-Lavoir building. The front door, as usual, was half-open. I stepped inside and heard no sound of voices.

"Hello?" I called. *"Bonjour?"*

Nobody answered me. The place was as still as a morgue. I came out again. An old man was sitting on the fence opposite, smoking a long, old-fashioned pipe. He looked up at me and grinned, revealing a toothless mouth. "You won't find them there on a Sunday afternoon," he said. "They'll be at the Moulin, with everyone else."

Of course. The afternoon dance at the

Moulin de la Galette. I followed the lane around, past gardens where people were working or just enjoying the fresh air, until I came to the windmill. It was in a garden, surrounded by a high wall. I heard the thump of lively music long before I reached the entrance. The place was packed. I could hardly squeeze up the steps and in through the narrow opening in the wall.

"Two francs, mademoiselle," a voice to my right said in my ear and I saw that there was a gatekeeper.

"I'm sorry," I said. "I'm not staying. I'm just looking for someone who might be here."

He gave me a patronizing smirk. "You are not the only person who tries that, mademoiselle. If you wish to enter, you must pay the same as everyone and that is two francs."

Grudgingly I fished two coins from my purse. "Enjoy yourself," he said. "But beware of pickpockets. Guard your wallet, eh?"

I clutched the purse to me as I forced my way into the crowd. All over the grounds tables were spread with picnics and wine, and families sat around them, laughing, talking, eating. They seemed to be mainly working-class people, dressed in their Sunday best: women in big hats, children in white lace, men in straw boaters. But among them were also young men and women dressed in the latest fashion who had chosen to escape to this environment where class didn't matter. Those not lucky enough to secure a table stood together with glasses of wine or beer in their hands. And in the middle was the dance floor, also packed with couples dancing a suggestive dance I had never seen before. I started to thread my way between groups, looking carefully for any sign of Maxim. I remembered also the young waiter at the café who had invited Ellie to join him. I wondered if she'd be daring enough to come to something like this alone or whether her fiancé had arrived in Paris yet. But as I made painfully slow progress I saw nobody that I recognized.

"Hello, *ma belle.* Come and dance." A hand came around my waist and I was propelled to the dance floor.

I turned to see a young student, his breath already reeking of wine, giving me a cheeky smile.

"No, monsieur. I do not wish to dance," I said.

"Of course you do. A pretty demoiselle like you should not be alone. Especially one with dangerous red hair."

"But I'm married, monsieur," I said. "My husband would not approve."

He laughed. "If you come here alone, that is his fault, no?" The hand on my waist pressed more forcefully.

"I am here with friends," I said. "I'm looking for them. Have you perhaps seen an inspector from the Sùreté?"

"An inspector? Here? My god, I hope not. That would really spoil our fun. You are friends with an inspector?"

"I am. And I'm married to one."

"My apologies, madame. It was only a jest." He let me go, hastily.

I decided not to push my luck again. I had done my best and it appeared that Maxim and his friends were not here. I would have to wait until they returned to their weekday routine at the Nouvelle Athènes.

When Celeste let me in to Mary's house I detected a faint odor of paint and turpentine. Mary appeared at the top of the stairs.

"Oh, you are painting?" I asked her.

"Not me, Augusta," she said. "She decided to try and capture the rooftops and chimney pots from my attic window. So how was your quest?"

"Impossible," I said. "There was nobody in Le Bateau-Lavoir and someone suggested they were all at the ball at the Moulin de la

Galette."

"Of course. That's where they'd be on a fine Sunday afternoon. I used to go there myself when I lived in the neighborhood."

"I went but I didn't see them," I said. "And I had to fight off a forceful young man who wanted me to dance with him."

Mary laughed. "Yes, you always find a few of those. Well, never mind, you'll find him when he's back at work, I'm sure."

"I can't really make any progress until I know the name of that model," I said.

"You can always ask at the model market in the morning," Mary said so casually that I thought she was joking.

"Model market?" I saw she wasn't smiling. "There really is a market for models?"

"Absolutely. Every Monday morning. In the Place Pigalle. Artists come from all over Paris to find the right model for the subject they want to paint."

"The models just stand there, like cattle in the market at home in Ireland?"

Mary laughed at my indignation. "Well, some of them sit. And they chat together and share stories on which artists can be trusted and which can't."

"Fascinating," I said. "I'll go there tomorrow then. Now that Reynold Bryce is dead this girl may be looking for new work."

Mary nodded. "Of course the girl might not want to talk to you. They are highly suspicious of anything to do with the police."

"I can pretend to be newly arrived and looking for work. That Spaniard Picasso already said that he wants to paint me."

Mary snorted. "I'd stay well clear of him, my dear. He has a mistress with a temper, so we hear. You might wind up with a knife stuck into you."

I laughed too. "I observed that for myself. Don't worry, I've no intention of actually serving as a model. I don't think Daniel would approve."

"Well, there's nothing more you can do today," Mary said. "And it's a lovely Sunday afternoon. Would you like to take that son of yours for a walk in his buggy? I'm dying to get out of the house myself. We could walk down to the Trocadéro gardens and maybe even across the Seine to the Eiffel Tower. I know a little ice-cream shop and there's a merry-go-round that you could take Liam on."

"It sounds wonderful," I said. "I'll go and get him ready. It's only too bad that Sid and Gus can't join us. I hate to think of them trapped inside on a day like this."

"I know. It must be hard for them, but

with your astute detective skills I'm sure it will all be solved satisfactorily soon and they can start enjoying Paris again."

My "astute detective skills"! I just hoped I was getting somewhere. To me it felt as if I was one of those little mice in a cage, running around and around in circles. Maybe tomorrow would be a turning point, I tried to tell myself optimistically.

I tried to put aside my concerns as we pushed the buggy through the gardens and Liam delighted in watching sparrows and dogs and children playing. Celeste served a delicious dinner but I found it hard to eat. Only the meringue with chestnut stuffing slipped down easily, and I was glad when it was finally time for bed.

I awoke at first light, my nerves taut and my brain telling me to get up as there was work to be done. A mist from the river hung at the end of the street and hid the rising sun, but it promised to be another fine day. I looked down at Liam, still sleeping peacefully in his crib. *No cares in the world,* I thought. He probably won't even remember that he nearly died in a bomb blast, that his nursemaid covered him with her own body as the roof came down. He doesn't know that his father's life is constantly in danger or that his mother has to try to find a murderer. I went to the bathroom to complete my toilet before he awoke, then nursed him and carried him down for the boiled egg that had become his new favorite food.

When he was finally settled on a rug in the salon with Sid and Gus I slipped away, joining the morning crowds on the Métro back to Place Pigalle. I came up to see that the area around the fountain in the middle of the Place was now full of young women, some of them skimpily clad, one actually wearing a bustier and fishnet stockings, others dressed more demurely. One or two were smoking. Others were drinking coffee or something stronger as they sat chatting with artists. I walked among them, looking for the girl in Reynold Bryce's painting, but didn't see her.

"Are you new?" one girl called to me. "Yes, you. You must be new or you wouldn't be stupid enough to stand on my pitch."

"I'm sorry," I said. "I'm not a model. I'm looking for one myself."

"Oh, you're a painter, are you?" Her demeanor toward me changed and she took a provocative pose. "My rates are reasonable and they say I have the best legs in Paris."

"I'm looking for a particular type," I said. "Young-looking. Big dark eyes. Lots of dark hair. I saw a picture of her and now I have to paint her too."

The woman looked around, then shrugged. "I don't know who you mean," she said.

"So a model who resembles that description doesn't come to the market?"

She shrugged. "I've never seen her and I'm here regularly."

Another brilliant thought struck me. "What about a model called Pauline? Used to pose for Reynold Bryce?"

"Pauline?" She looked amused. "Pose for him? That's an interesting way of putting it." She leaned toward me blowing stale cigarette breath in my face. "You don't want to paint her, my dear. Too much temperament. Besides, she's already chatting with Monsieur Degas over there."

"She's here?" I looked around until I spotted Degas's tall, lean form. Then I saw the girl he was talking to. "That's Pauline?"

"That's right. Pauline Hubert. Used to be Bryce's mistress."

I couldn't believe it. I stood there, staring at her. She was beautiful, with ash-blonde hair piled high on her head, perfect bone structure, and an air of patrician purity about her. And she was young. In her early twenties at the most. So what sort of joke had been shared when that man at the Steins' declared she was too old?

I hesitated then made my way toward her. I wasn't at all sure what I was going to say. Degas saw me first. "Ah, it's the young lady from America. *Bonjour,* madame. What brings you to our model market? Curiosity? Don't be embarrassed. There are many tourists who are curious about us. They think this must be a den of vice, but it is simply a way for artists to find the body they wish to paint. I'm trying to persuade Pauline here that I would like to paint her in her bathtub. So far she resists." And he gave me a wicked smile.

"Pauline?" I pretended to be surprised. "Were you not painted by Reynold Bryce once?"

"He painted me, yes." The eyes that observed me were cold and I could tell she was trying to work out who I was. "Several times. But he was satisfied with none of them. He was not a man who was easily satisfied."

"You must be sad to learn of his passing," I said.

She shrugged. "It means nothing to me. That is all ancient history now. Frankly I was glad to walk away from him. Old and boring, and too possessive."

"Do you have any idea who might have wanted to kill him?" I asked.

Her eyes narrowed. "What are you, a reporter?"

"Possibly," I said, holding her gaze.

She looked at Degas then shrugged. "I can tell you nothing. Frankly I don't think he was worth killing. One only kills a person who stirs up deep and violent emotions. Love, hate, jealousy. They might drive someone to kill. But Reynold — he was of your generation, Monsieur Degas."

"Thank you for the compliment, mademoiselle," Degas said, looked at me, and grinned. "This old man of the past still manages to sell his paintings for a nice amount. If you pose for me, *chérie,* your face will be seen around the world. And that nice little body too."

"Make it worth it for me while I am still living," Pauline said. "I have no interest in being famous after my death."

He looked at me and smiled again. "She drives a hard bargain, this one, but look at the face. Look at the bone structure. The face of an angel."

"And the temper of a devil, monsieur. Beware," Pauline answered, giving him a challenging gaze.

"Perhaps you can help me," I said. "I am

looking for a particular model. Young, luxuriant dark hair; big dark eyes like a waif. An innocent child."

Pauline and Degas looked at each other and shrugged. "One does not see too many innocent children around Place Pigalle," Pauline said. "If they come here, they do not stay innocent for long. I do not recall seeing the one you describe."

THIRTY-ONE

I wandered around the market once more, then abandoned this particular search and tried the Nouvelle Athènes. but it must have been too early for the painters. Their usual table was empty. I would have to come back later, after I had tackled the housekeeper. I couldn't risk missing her at Reynold Bryce's. And as I descended into the gloom of the Métro I thought about Pauline. From what she said her affair with Reynold Bryce had ended some time ago and was as much her decision as his. She had the temperament to stab someone, but had made it clear that he wasn't worth stabbing. And the interesting fact was that she didn't know the little dark waif whom Reynold Bryce had been most recently painting. Nobody did. So who was she and where did he find her?

I stepped into the Métro car and we rattled off into darkness. I have to confess that I felt a knot of apprehension in my throat as I walked down from the Champs-Élysées to the Rue François Premier. I had to approach this conversation with the housekeeper in the correct manner. I'd only have one chance and if she shut the door on me, then that would be that. There was an added complication that the police might be guarding the place or even sitting inside with the housekeeper to make sure she didn't take anything. I had no idea what I might say to them to gain admittance.

As I approached the Rue I saw that there was indeed a young policeman standing in the street. *Oh, dear. Now what?* I wondered if there was any way into the building from the rear. There was often a janitor in residence in such buildings, wasn't there? And trash would not be carried through that fancy front entrance. I prowled the outside of the building and halfway down the block, where the Rue Bayard approached the Seine, I found a small wooden door, propped open by a garbage can. I went through a cobbled archway and found myself in that central area between buildings. In contrast to the attractive façades that faced the street, these walls were unadorned. There was even laundry hanging from one window on the far side, and it didn't smell too good either. I crept along, hugging the wall, until I came to what had to be Reynold Bryce's building. And I was right. Behind an iron railing a narrow flight of steps went down to a door. I stepped down gingerly, tried the door. It resisted at first but in response to a good shove from my shoulder it creaked open. I was in a basement, in complete darkness apart from the light that came in through the open door. I heard the roar of what must have been a furnace and smelled the odor of laundry and garbage. At least if it was in darkness I was not in danger of bumping into a custodian down here. I felt my way forward until I found a flight of stone stairs going up. I followed them until my hands touched another door. A crack of light was coming under it. I turned the knob and opened it a few inches. I was staring at the back of the elevator. I came out and inched my way around until I was in the foyer. No sign of any police presence and the front door to Reynold Bryce's suite was ajar. I tiptoed past the elevator, across the marble floor, and in through that door.

Still no sign of a policeman. I still hadn't come up with anything credible to say if I encountered one, but spurred on by success so far I listened for noises indicating where the housekeeper might be working. Hearing nothing I peeked into the salon, then went through to the dining room and the studio. There was no sign that she had been in any of them. Everything lay as I saw it last with a film of dust over the long mahogany table. I returned and pushed open the swing door to the kitchen. Pots and pans had been stacked in boxes and the shelves had been cleared. So at least I knew she had been working here. I returned to the foyer and went down the hall leading to the bedrooms. I froze as I heard a muttered exclamation coming from Bryce's bedroom, then I tiptoed toward the sound. The housekeeper was in there, taking items out of the chest of drawers. For a moment I wondered if she had counted the handkerchiefs and noticed that one was now missing. She went on removing shirts and underclothing and placing them in a trunk that now lay on the feather mattress of the stripped bed.

Now I had to think how to attract her attention without startling her and making her cry out. I retreated a few paces then called, "Madame, are you here? A message for you from the inspector."

She came out, her eyes darting nervously, wiping down her hands on her apron. "The inspector? What does he want now?"

Then she stopped when she saw me. "You? What do you want? You are not from the police. You should not be here. Get out immediately or I will summon the constable outside."

"Ah, but he let me in, madame," I said. "The inspector understands that as a representative of the Bryce family in America I would want to ask you some questions and be here when you pack up his things."

"What kind of questions?" she snapped. "I don't need to answer any questions. There is nothing I can tell you."

"You could begin by telling me what was in those large bags I saw you carrying away yesterday." I held her gaze and noticed the eyes darting nervously again. She ran her tongue over her thin lips.

"I don't know what you mean," she said at last.

"Of course you do. You went in and helped yourself to Mr. Bryce's things. As a representative of Mr. Bryce's cousin — who may well inherit all of this, I should report this criminal act to the police. I have not done so, but I will if you do not help me now."

"Help you to do what?"

"Find out who killed him, of course. Maybe the police will discover the truth, maybe not. I intend to, and I am sure you

416

want to find out who killed your employer."
She gave a suspicious half nod. "Now — let
us start with the model he was painting."

She pursed her lips. "Shosette," she said.
At least that was what it sounded like. Not
a name I recognized. "Shosette Petit."

"Where did he find her?"

"I believe an artist brought her to meet
Monsieur Bryce."

"Do you know where she lives? Where I
can find her?"

"I do not. I know nothing about her. He
had only started painting her a few days
previously. He brought her in and said to
me, 'This is Shosette. I'm going to be painting her. Make sure you cook enough luncheon for two.' "

"What did you think of her?" I asked.

She shrugged. "She didn't appear to be a
bad little thing. Not like some models who
are no better than they should be. Very
quiet, never said a word to me. But then
her French wasn't very good."

"It wasn't? Where did she come from?"

"I'm not sure. Eastern Europe, or Italy?
I've no idea. All I know is that she spoke
with a strong accent and didn't always have
the words to express herself. But no matter.
He was very taken with her. He never
painted portraits these days, but he had to

paint her." She paused, wiped her hands again, then said, "He was that kind of man. He liked to have the young and beautiful around him."

"Like Willie Walcott?"

She looked surprised. "Walcott? Yes, Monsieur Bryce enjoyed his company for a while. He tried to paint Monsieur Walcott, but he was not satisfied with the result. Nothing came of it."

I tried to phrase the next question. "You say 'enjoyed his company.' Did he stay here for a while, as his special companion?"

"He sometimes slept . . ." she paused, then glared at me. "What is it that you suggest? Absolutely no, madame. Monsieur Walcott might have sometimes stayed in the guest bedroom, but then Monsieur Bryce was hospitable. He had guests to visit frequently." I thought privately that she would not have known if someone had tiptoed down that hallway at night.

"But Monsieur Walcott hadn't been a guest here for a while?"

"Not for a month or more."

"So you hadn't seen him for a month?"

"Except for the brief visit last week."

"Last week? You mean right before Mr. Bryce died?"

She nodded. "I believe it was the day

before Monsieur Bryce was killed. It's all rather a blur to me now, madame. The shock, you know."

"Of course, it was a tremendous shock to you. But can you remember anything about the visit of Monsieur Walcott? Was it just a pleasant social call? Do you know why he had come?"

"He was upset, madame, I can tell you that much. He stormed in, waving something at the master."

"Something?"

"A piece of paper, madame. Maybe a letter?" She frowned, trying to remember. "And Monsieur Bryce told me to get on with my work. I asked if Monsieur Walcott would be staying for lunch and Monsieur Bryce said a firm 'No.' So I went but I overheard the young man saying 'You've let me down. You're a liar.' " She looked up at me now.

"Did he say why?"

"They spoke English, madame. After eighteen years of the master shouting at me in his native tongue I can understand a lot, but not when American people speak quickly together. Anyway shortly afterward the young man went."

"And did not return again? You never saw him after that moment?"

"I did not. But I told you, after that is all a blur. One horrible nightmare. I can't bear to think about it. Seeing my poor master there, and that fiend standing over him. I might have been killed too if I hadn't run out, screaming for help."

"Did you describe the man you saw standing over him to the police?"

"That's just the problem. All I saw was the knife in Mr. Bryce's chest and all that blood and his poor face, his eyes imploring for help. A slim young man, rather dandified. That's all I could say."

She looked around the room. "I should be getting on with my work."

"I'll help you," I said. I opened the wardrobe and began to hand her down his jackets and suits. "Do you want them with tissue paper between them?"

She hesitated, not wanting me to get involved but glad to have someone helping her. "Yes, that would be a good idea."

"So to return to that terrible day, madame," I said, looking up as I lay a black smoking jacket into the trunk. "Was this model Shosette not there when he was killed? Wasn't he working on the painting of her at that very moment?"

"She had walked out that morning," the housekeeper replied. "They had some kind of altercation. I heard raised voices. I heard the front door slam. When I came to the studio to see what was wrong Monsieur Bryce was standing there alone at his easel. He said to me, 'Silly girl. She'll be back if she knows what's good for her.' "

"And did she come back?"

"Not as far as I know. He ate lunch alone and then I had to go to the market to get the meat for his dinner. He was alone when I left him. That's all I can tell you."

"Presumably the police have questioned this girl?"

"They tell me nothing, madame. All I know is she was not the one who plunged the knife into him. That's all that matters."

"So she was definitely not in the apartment when he was killed?"

She looked around. "I cannot say 'definitely.' She could have hidden but I do not see how she could have slipped out past us. I was at the front steps, you understand."

"There is a way out through the basement, is there not?"

"Yes, but usually it is kept locked and not easy to find for those who do not know the building well."

I found it, I thought. *Others could too.*

"And anyway," she said, looking up as she placed a pile of white shirts into the trunk.

"Why would she want to kill Monsieur Bryce? He was giving her employment."

"You said yourself they had an argument that morning and she went out and slammed the door."

"Monsieur was a temperamental man. He often fought with people. Perhaps she was temperamental too. That sort often are. But what cause would she have to kill him?"

"That is the main question, isn't it," I said. "What cause would anyone have to kill him?"

"I can't answer that. Perhaps the answer lies across the ocean. One thing I ask myself is why all these people suddenly arrive on my doorstep from America — after all these years?"

I was suddenly alert. "All which people?"

"You, for one," she said, pointing an accusatory finger in my direction. "You arrive, saying you bring a message from his family. That is what the other young woman said too."

"Which other?"

"The one who resembles the painting in the foyer, with the blonde hair."

"Ah," I nodded. "I know the person of whom you speak. She came to visit him the day before he died, no?"

"She did, madame. But he was occupied

and told her to go away. He was annoyed that she was here. He said to me, 'It's never over, is it, Claudette? Now it starts again. It's going to haunt me for the rest of my life.' I asked him, 'What is, monsieur?' And he said, 'That specter.' "

" 'Specter'? He meant the young blonde girl?"

"He said no more. But she returned the next day."

"The day he was killed?" I could hear my voice, shrill and louder than I intended. I hoped it had not carried to the policeman outside.

"That very day, madame. She arrived when he had just finished his lunch and gone back to his studio. She looked very . . . flustered. Her cheeks pink. She said she had to see him. It was important. So I took her through to him. He said, 'Leave us, Claudette.' And I did. I went through to clean up the dining table —"

"But did you get a chance to hear what was said?"

"Madame, I am not the sort who listens at keyholes," she said defensively. "But I did overhear the young lady say, 'I don't want your money. I don't need your money.' "

"That's interesting," I said. "And what happened after that?"

"I do not know. When I came back to the studio to tell him I was about to go out and was there anything special he wanted she had gone. I tried to ask him about her but he shouted at me. He said, 'Isn't it time you went to the market? Do you think I want the leftover meat that has been visited by flies?' So I went. And when I returned with the shopping he was sitting there, dying."

She looked up at me with hopelessness in her eyes. "If only I had stayed, he might still be alive."

"You might also be dead, Claudette," I said. "Someone came, intent on committing murder."

"You may be right. At night I lie there, asking myself over and over what I could have done to prevent this."

"You were fond of him."

She nodded and wiped away a tear. "He was my life, madame. For eighteen years he was my life. Now I have nothing. Nowhere to go. All alone."

"I'm very sorry," I said. "I should go and let you get on with your work."

She looked up at me. "You will tell his relatives at home that I did my best. And if they inherit his fortune and care to send a small gift to me . . ."

"I'll tell them," I said, feeling awful that as

far as I knew there was no relative at home. I resolved to speak to the inspector and Reynold Bryce's lawyer to see if some provision could be made for Claudette.

THIRTY-TWO

I left by way of the front door. The policeman had no way of knowing I was not a resident of one of the other flats, I reasoned. I nodded as I passed him and said, *"Bonjour"* in a sprightly manner. He didn't attempt to stop me. I heard a distant clock chiming eleven as I hurried along the Rue François Premier. I was in two minds of what to do next. I would have to be back at Mary Cassatt's house to nurse Liam at lunchtime, but should I go to seek out Willie Walcott or Ellie before I went in search of Shosette Petit? Which one of them was more important? All three had been upset with Reynold Bryce, all three had had words with him. But Willie had apparently seen him the day before he died and there was no reason to believe he had returned. Shosette and Ellie had definitely been with him on the day he died. I couldn't think what either of them might have to do with his death, but I was particularly concerned about Miss Ellie. There were enough discrepancies between the truth and what Ellie had told me to raise some red flags.

For example she had told me she had visited him the day before he died but he hadn't had time to see her. That much was true. What she hadn't said was that she had returned the next day — shortly before he was killed. Why had she kept quiet about that? And then I remembered one more thing — she had asked me to lie and say that we had been together all the time she had been in Paris. At the time I had thought that was in case her fiancé worried she had gone around unchaperoned. Now it seemed she might have wanted me as her alibi.

I decided I had to see her right away. Liam would be well-fed by Celeste and his aunts if I didn't return on time. So I set off to cross the river to the Left Bank and the Hôtel d'Alsace. I hoped she was still staying there and hadn't moved to the more elevated world of the Ritz. I had no wish to seek her out there, with her most proper fiancé and his family. It would be rather awkward to have to question her about a possible involvement in a murder.

I crossed the Seine at the Pont des Invalides, then followed the quay until I came to the Boulevard Saint Germain. The fine day that had seemed so perfect this morning was now a little too warm for comfort and I could feel the fabric of my dress sticking to my back. One of the disadvantages of acquiring clothes from a rich acquaintance was that they weren't as comfortable as the muslins and shirtwaists I was used to wearing before my marriage. At this moment I'd have given anything for a white cotton shirtwaist. And a pair of comfortable shoes. The road stretched on and on. I watched fishermen along the river, a tug pulling a string of barges. It all looked very cool and inviting. I tried to concentrate on the task at hand. Ellie had chosen to lie to me. She told me only about her meeting with Reynold Bryce the day before he died. Why was that? And why had she wanted me to be her alibi?

It didn't make sense. He was a friend of her family. He had once painted her aunt, long before she was born. She had never met him. I had assumed the visit had been a courtesy call. So why had she returned on the day he died, and why, in heaven's name, had the housekeeper heard her say, "I don't want your money." It sounded almost like a threat or a case of blackmail. I had come to suspect that Ellie was not the angelic being she appeared. She had shown herself to be a devious little miss. She had misled both her family and her fiancé about her journey to Paris. Was it possible she had uncovered some kind of scandal about Reynold Bryce and had confronted him with it? And he was trying to pay her off? So why then didn't she want his money?

I stopped to watch some children playing by the river. They were dancing around barefoot, in ragged clothing, squealing in delight as a bigger boy tried to splash them. And slowly an idea took shape in my head. Why had Reynold Bryce suddenly forsaken a country where he enjoyed considerable success and fled to Paris and never once returned home? Why had his wife not come with him? "Eighteen years" ago, the housekeeper had said. *Eighteen years.* And what had one of the men at the Steins' party said about Reynold Bryce? He had thrown Pauline over because she was too old. And hadn't one of the men at the Nouvelle Athènes said, "lock up your daughters"?

Reynold Bryce liked to have the young and the beautiful around him. The housekeeper had acknowledged that. But what if it went further? I stopped, frowning into the distance at the sturdy buildings on the Île de la Cité, because I hardly dared to form

429

the thought, let alone say it out loud. *What if the Angela in the paintings wasn't Ellie's aunt at all?*

I turned away from the river at the impressive Orsay train station and found the hotel on the Boulevard Saint-Germain nearby. It seemed to be a pleasant and not too pretentious hotel, one that I would have enjoyed staying in myself. I realized as I approached the front desk that I still did not know Ellie's last name.

"You have a young lady from America staying here," I began slowly. "Her first name is Ellie and she has beautiful blonde hair, but I'm afraid she never told me her last name."

The clerk had obviously been impressed by Ellie and her hair. His face lit up. "You mean Mademoiselle Hatcher. Eleanor Hatcher."

"That's right. Is she available at the moment?"

The face clouded again. "Oh, no, madame. She has left us, only this morning. She is to join her family members at the Ritz."

"I see," I sighed. "Thank you."

I was now hot, tired, and frustrated and the last place I wanted to go was the Ritz. I was sorely tempted to go back to Miss

Cassatt's and then go to see Inspector Henri at the Sûreté and tell him what I knew about Ellie and what I suspected. But I couldn't do it. In spite of the way she had tried to use me I was still rather fond of her, and I wanted to give her the benefit of the doubt. I suspected she'd lie to me again but I had become quite good at recognizing a lie. If she didn't want to tell me the truth, I'd have to go to the police. I'd tell her that too.

Wearily I trudged back across the Seine at the Pont de la Concorde and then along the Rue de Rivoli, grateful for the colonnade and its deep shade, until I stood eventually in the Place Vendôme, admiring the column and the graceful sweep of buildings beyond it. I took several deep breaths before I dared to enter the Ritz. I was conscious that I now looked sweaty and red-faced and my hat was probably askew. Indeed the doorman, not the same one as on the occasion of my last visit, did eye me with suspicion and ask, "May I assist you, mademoiselle?"

I told him curtly that it was "madame" and I had come to visit my friend Miss Hatcher who was currently a guest. He gave a perfunctory nod and admitted me. I looked around carefully before I entered the lobby. The last thing I wanted at the moment was to bump into Justin Hartley. But the lobby was deserted apart from an elderly couple who were studying a map at one of the glass-topped tables and a fashionably dressed woman who was standing at the front counter. "But I don't see how you have the nerve to charge me for that!" Her voice carried across the hotel lobby.

I went up to the front desk and asked for Miss Hatcher.

"I will call her room, madame," he said. "Whom shall I say wishes to see her?"

"Mrs. Sullivan from New York. It's a matter of great urgency."

He tried an internal telephone then shook his head. "She does not appear to be in her room, madame."

"Is she perhaps in the suite of the family with whom she is staying?"

"The Sloane family, no? I will try for you." He did, then shook his head once more. "Maybe they are in the restaurant. It is almost time for luncheon and Americans like to eat very early."

He indicated the direction of the restaurant. I made my way through to it with some trepidation, pausing to straighten my hat and blot my face when I came to a gilt-framed mirror in the corridor. The restaurant was breathtakingly opulent, with light pouring in from high windows, reflecting from mirrors and sparkling from chandeliers. The white-clothed tables had upholstered curved seats around them and were separated by tall potted palms. At this hour most of the booths were empty with a low buzz of conversation coming from a few tables. The maître d' pounced on me before I had a chance to look around.

"You require a table, madame?"

"I'm looking for friends. Monsieur and Madame Sloane and their party?"

"This way, madame. Will you be joining them?"

Oh, Lord. I hadn't wanted a formal presentation. "I can find them myself. No problem," I said.

"It is no trouble, madame." He strode out ahead of me to a table in the far corner. Seated at it were a large florid man, his bad-tempered looking wife, a pink and chubby younger man, a similarly chubby young woman, and amid them, like the peacock in the henhouse, was Ellie. She was smiling shyly at something they had said to her.

They looked up as we approached. "A visitor for you, monsieur," the maître d' said.

They stared up at me, except for Ellie who was blushing bright pink.

"I'm sorry to trouble you, Mr. Sloane," I

said. "But I am a friend of Miss Ellie's and I wonder if you could spare her for a moment."

"We're just about to eat, young lady," he said. "If you're a friend of my son's fiancée you're welcome to join us." He turned to look at Ellie.

"Not really a friend," Ellie said, waving a hand dismissively. "Just an acquaintance, and I'm sure I wouldn't want to spoil my first meal in Paris with my new family for a spot of female chitchat."

"It's really rather important," I said. "I was just speaking with the housekeeper, Claudette, and it seems that you forgot certain items . . ." I gave her what I hoped was a meaningful stare.

Ellie's face was now bright red. She licked her lips nervously. "Perhaps I'd better . . ." she began. "If you could possibly excuse me for a moment."

"Really, Ellie, I don't see what can be so dashed important that you have to interrupt a pleasant meal," Peter said. "Especially for a near stranger."

"I wouldn't dream of interrupting a family reunion but this matter can't wait," I said. "If I can just have Ellie to myself for a few minutes, I'll be gone. I have friends waiting for me elsewhere."

Peter stood, ungraciously, allowing Ellie to slide out of her place. I let her go ahead of me out of the restaurant. The moment we were out of earshot she turned on me. "What do you think you're doing, embarrassing me in front of my in-laws? I felt like a complete fool. I don't know what on earth you want with me. We only shared a couple of casual conversations in our whole life."

"Oh, but I think you do know, Miss Hatcher," I said. "And it's up to you. You can have the conversation with me, or with the inspector from the Sûreté."

Those blue eyes opened wide. "I don't know what you're talking about."

"Yes, you do. I'm talking about Reynold Bryce's murder. I was curious as to why you didn't mention that you had seen Mr. Bryce on the day he died."

"It didn't come up in casual conversation. Why should I tell you anything?" she glared defiantly. "I hardly know you."

"And yet you wanted me to lie that we had been together during all of your stay in Paris. At the time I thought you merely wanted to give your in-laws the impression that you were chaperoned during your stay here if they discovered you had been in Paris longer than you had told them. But later I realized it was quite different. You wanted an alibi, didn't you?"

"For what?"

"For killing Reynold Bryce."

"But I didn't kill him." She looked around in case anybody was within earshot, then took my arm, dragged me into an alcove, and sank onto the bench there like a deflated balloon. "I swear I didn't kill him."

"That's not what the police think," I said. "They know you came to visit him right before he died. The housekeeper has testified that you looked flustered and uneasy and insisted on seeing him. And she heard you say, 'I don't want your money.' " I decided to risk pushing this one step further. "And the Hôtel d'Alsace is missing one knife from their kitchen — a knife that has fingerprints on it."

She gave a sob and buried her face in her hands. "Then it's all over, isn't it? The truth will come out and Peter will never want to marry me now."

"I believe they still use the guillotine in France," I said matter-of-factly.

She dropped her hands with a look of pure terror on her face. "But I didn't kill him," she whispered.

"The police won't believe you. After all, you had the best motive, didn't you?"

She looked utterly hopeless and a tear

436

trickled down her cheek. "How did you find out?"

"That Reynold Bryce was your father? I didn't, until now. But I started putting two and two together and making four. The fact that he left America suddenly eighteen years ago, and that must be around your age. And his wife refused to come with him — broke off all contact with him actually. And I learned that he had a predilection for young girls and he was actually painting another one when he died. Is that why you came to Paris early — to see him and to kill him?"

"I didn't know," she whispered. "I swear I didn't know. The first visit really was a courtesy call. I'd heard about Reynold Bryce, of course, and that he had helped our family financially, and was extremely wealthy so I thought at least he'd treat me to a good meal — maybe ask me to stay with him until Peter arrived. But he didn't want to see me. He was most unwelcoming — rather rude actually. He told me to go away; he was busy. You were right. He was painting a young girl — younger than me, I think. And the way he spoke to her and looked at her made me feel strange. And the way he looked at me too. There was something I couldn't quite explain . . . he seemed angry but at the same time almost triumphant, amused, pleased with himself."

She was looking directly at me now, willing me to understand. I suspected she was desperate to share her secret with someone. She waited until a party of four Americans had walked past us, heading for the restaurant, then she continued.

"So I came away feeling annoyed and upset. I couldn't understand his attitude to me. Wouldn't he have been glad to see someone from home, a member of a family he used to know well? And then it hit me. Certain things I'd overheard at home and not understood. Conversations that were broken off when I came into the room. Something my stepfather had said: 'How long are you going to let this charade continue?' and 'Thank God she'll soon be married off and no longer be your responsibility.' " She paused, staring out blankly past me into the hallway. "I thought he was just being his usual horrible self. But there was that painting in Mr. Bryce's hallway and I couldn't get it out of my mind. You know, one of the Angela paintings. It must have been one of the last ones because my aunt Adelaide looks quite grown up. But the problem was it looked so exactly like me that it was frightening. And then I realized the truth about what had happened and why he'd fled to Paris. Aunt Adelaide was really my mother. He must have seduced her and when she found out she was going to have a baby it was too much for her delicate nature. She'd always been naïve and led a very sheltered life. She must have been so overwhelmed that she had a nervous breakdown. And my adoptive mother was the only sister who was married at the time and wanted to have a baby of her own, so I was handed over to her. And everybody who knew kept quiet. But silly Mama must have spilled the beans to my stepfather."

"I see," I said. "Yes, that is how it must have been. How very tragic. So you decided to kill your father. To make him pay for what he had done."

"Yes," she said. "That's what I decided to do. If he had welcomed me, told me the truth, wanted me in his life, I might have forgiven him. But that complete and utter rejection — it was too much. There he was, enjoying a good life — rich, famous — when my poor little mother's life had been ruined forever. I decided that such a man does not deserve to live. I slipped into the hotel kitchen and took a sharp knife and carried it in my purse to my father's house."

"And the housekeeper admitted you?

Weren't you scared that she'd be a witness to his murder?"

"I didn't think about that. I didn't care about anything anymore. I did worry about the young girl being there. I thought I'd somehow have to lure him away or find an excuse to get rid of her. But when I went into his studio he was alone. And the housekeeper left us alone too. I told him I'd figured out the truth and he looked amused and said, 'Good for you. Obviously smarter than your mother, then.'

"Then he asked me why I had come. What I wanted from him. Was it money? I said I'd come to kill him. I got out the knife. I told him how he'd ruined my mother's life and my life and he didn't care about us at all. As I came toward him he didn't look afraid — amused rather. He got up, grabbed my wrist, and twisted it until I had to drop the knife.

" 'Now stop being a fool. Go home and forget all about me,' he said. 'And we'll say no more about this absurd incident. If you come back, I'll have you locked up as insane — do you understand?' I turned and ran out of the house."

"Leaving the knife on the table."

She nodded. "Yes. That's the problem, isn't it? My fingerprints will be on that knife. I keep waiting for the police to come and find me."

"Since they don't have your fingerprints on file and since the housekeeper has given a description of the assailant being a slim, dark young man I don't think that will happen," I said.

I saw a glimmer of hope in those eyes. "You mean I'm safe?"

"I think you're safe," I said. "Of course, you'll be carrying this secret with you for the rest of your life, if you're smart. It's not the sort of thing you should share with your fiancé."

She nodded. "Good Lord, no, I couldn't share it with Peter." She reached out a slim white hand and put it over mine. "I'm sorry I was rude to you earlier. I'd been so frightened."

"I understand." I smiled at her.

"Thank you," she whispered.

"Would you like one last piece of advice from me?" I said. She nodded. "Don't marry him. He seems like a spoiled and unpleasant young man. Marriage is for a terribly long time with someone you don't love."

She nodded again. "You may be right. But I can't stay at home any longer, not now that I know the truth."

"If I were you," I said slowly, "I'd have a talk with your adoptive mother. Tell her you know the truth and you want the money that was settled on you now. Then I'd go to New York and start a life of your own."

"That sounds a little like blackmail."

"Not blackmail. Just coming from a position of strength for the first time. And showing them that you can't be pushed around."

"But it does sound like fun. I thought maybe I'd stay in Paris. It's lovely, isn't it?"

"Yes, it is."

"And romantic," she added. "Maybe I'll find myself a dashing Frenchman."

She got up, smoothed down her skirt, then held out her hand to me. "Thank you again. I'd better go back now. They'll be missing me."

And she walked off down the hallway, past the mirrors, and into the restaurant, her little head held defiantly high.

THIRTY-THREE

I was feeling quite satisfied with myself as I walked back down the hallway and into the main lobby of the Ritz. I had figured out Ellie's connection to Reynold Bryce. I hadn't found his killer but I had eliminated one suspect. At least I hoped I had eliminated her. A tiny sliver of doubt crept into my head. She had lied most expertly before now. She had shown herself to be devious, ruthless, and self-serving. But her account of what happened at Reynold Bryce's house rang true, and beneath that façade of bravado she was still a young and frightened girl.

So that now left two people I should go and see: Willie Walcott and the young model Shosette. Of course it still could turn out to be a stranger, a Jewish activist angry at Mr. Bryce's tirades against Jews, but then the question arose as to how he could have gained entrance. The housekeeper was out and had presumably locked the front door behind her. If the doorbell had rung Mr. Bryce would have answered it himself. That meant he wouldn't have been sitting in his chair when he was killed. There was the open window but it would have taken a good deal of gall to enter the garden and climb in that way, knowing that Mr. Bryce was in the house. In the room, actually. If he'd heard someone scrabbling at the window ledge he'd have gone to look. He'd have shouted. People would have heard. So a stranger was unlikely.

I was deep in thought and not at all alert for danger when suddenly a hand grabbed me by the wrist. It was all I could do not to scream. I looked down and saw Mrs. Hartley, Justin's mother, sitting in one of the high-backed chairs.

"It is you! I thought it was when I saw you going into the restaurant. Little Molly Murphy. What on earth are you doing here?"

She looked much older than when I saw her last and she sounded friendly enough, but I was well aware that I had almost killed her son, and surely no mother forgives that.

"I'm visiting friends in Paris, Mrs. Hartley," I said. "I'm a married woman now, with a young son."

"Well, isn't that grand." She beamed at

me. "We wondered where you'd gone, when you left home. Of course I always knew you'd make something of yourself. You were too good for that cottage. I saw it then. And you have made something of yourself. Isn't that grand?"

There was something about the innocence of her smile, the lack of that patrician edge to her voice that made me realize this wasn't the same woman I used to know. Something had happened to her. Something in her mind had gone.

"I must be going, I'm afraid," I said. "I have friends expecting me for lunch."

"Well, isn't that grand," she said, now stroking the hand she held. "But what a pity you can't stay and meet my children. Justin is here, you know. And Henrietta. They're out shopping, but they will be returning soon. Can't you stay?"

"I really can't," I said.

"Then I'll give them your best wishes, shall I? I know they both remember you fondly. You remember Justin, don't you? Such a handsome boy. Such a pity he had that terrible riding accident. He had to leave the army, you know. Still, he always would take awful risks when he rode. Just like his father. My husband is dead now, you know. Justin is now lord of the manor. Isn't that grand? He takes good care of me. And the girls come to visit. And my grandchildren. I wish you'd come back to Ireland and visit me too. You always were such a bright little thing."

I wondered how I could make her let go of me without causing a fuss. "I really must go, Mrs. Hartley. So lovely to see you again."

"And you too, my dear." She patted my hand and I took the opportunity to pull it away. Then she looked up, smiled, and said, "Oh, here they come now!"

I moved away quickly, ducking into a group of people heading for the restaurant. As I left I heard her say, "You'll never guess who I have been talking to? Little Molly Murphy."

And I heard Henrietta's reply. "Have you, Mother. How lovely. See, we've brought you your favorite chocolates."

They didn't believe her, I thought jubilantly as I moved out of the group and let them pass, eyeing me with strange stares. Justin and Henrietta thought I was a figment of their mother's fantasy. I stood, watching and waiting, until they went up the stairs, then I slipped out. Thank goodness I'd not have to go to the Ritz again. That had been too close for comfort.

I was glad when I finally saw the Rue de

Marignan ahead of me and knocked on Mary's front door. Celeste opened it, giving me a strange and wary glance. "Ah, you have returned at last, madame. There is a gentleman waiting to see you. He has been waiting for some time."

"A gentleman?"

"From the Sûreté, madame. In the front salon."

"And my son? I ought to attend to him first."

"All is well with him, madame. I have just made him a puree of vegetables, so he is well-fed."

"Thank you, Celeste. I'd better see the inspector right away then. I wonder what he wants now?"

She gave a wonderfully Gallic shrug. I took off my hat, left it on the hat stand in the hall, then went through to the front salon. Inspector Henri had been sitting on one of the gilt armchairs. He got up as I came in. "Ah, Madame Sullivan. You return at last. Have you had an interesting stroll this morning? Or perhaps it was shopping in the Boulevard Haussmann? Or meeting a friend for coffee?" He motioned to a chair opposite him. I sat. He resumed his former place.

"I did meet a young friend at the Ritz," I

said. "But what brings you back here, Inspector? Have you been kind enough to come to tell me that the murder of Monsieur Bryce is solved and you have caught the murderer?"

"Alas no, madame. But I think we may be getting closer. I have come because I am interested to know what you were doing at Monsieur Bryce's apartment this morning."

"Jesus, Mary, and Joseph," I muttered. That dratted housekeeper spilled the beans after all. But he went on. "My man recognized you when you left, but he is puzzled because he did not see you enter."

"He wouldn't have," I said, weighing whether the truth would be preferable to a lie at this juncture. "I came in through the courtyard and up the janitor's stair."

"And may one ask why?"

I was still fishing desperately for a good explanation for this behavior. "The primary reason being that one of your men was standing outside and would not have let me enter."

"But why should you want to enter in the first place?"

"Ah. It is as I told you — a member of Mr. Bryce's family was interested in buying one of his paintings. She asked me to select one for her and I had promised to do so. I

met the housekeeper who said that everything was to be packed into crates today, so
I realized that I would have to take a look at
his paintings myself so that the family was
not cheated out of his best work. This family member was prepared to pay fair market
value, although it is quite possible that the
family member may inherit the estate anyway, so it was only fair . . ."

He held up his hand to silence me. "We
have received cables from the police in
Boston. Mr. Bryce has no family to speak
of."

"Second and third cousins, Inspector. Also
he has a wife," I said. "They were never
divorced, so I presume she has a good claim
on his estate."

His eyes narrowed. "Madame, we are well
aware of this wife. Our colleagues in Boston
are checking on her with a great deal of
interest. As you say, she stands to inherit a
considerable fortune. And if you have been
sent here by her, my supposition should be
that she sent you here to arrange for his
murder."

"You know that can't be true," I said, trying not to sound flustered because I realized
I had put my foot in my mouth royally this
time. "I only arrived here the day after his
murder. I have witnesses to attest to my be-

ing in Le Havre until that date."

"So you were not sent here by his wife, then?"

"Of course not. I don't know the woman. Never met her."

"So why this unhealthy interest in the murder of Reynold Bryce? If a remote cousin wanted to see one of his paintings, I do not think you'd risk sneaking into a crime scene to catch a glimpse of it. Not even if this person was your dearest friend. I know I wouldn't take such chances."

"Maybe it is the detective in me that wants to see justice done?" I suggested.

"You wish to solve this case yourself and prove the police to be idiots?"

"Of course not. I'm just interested. For example, Inspector, it was not made clear that he had a young model in the room and that she left in anger that morning. She would have been the first person on my list of suspects. What do you know about her?"

"Naturally she was brought in for questioning instantly. She's a young Russian immigrant. Came here with her brother about three years ago. Her real name is Hodel Klein. She calls herself Josette Petit to sound more French and less Jewish. She lives with other young refugee girls in a shack on Montmartre. Her French is extremely limited but I understood that much."

This time I understood the pronunciation of her first name. Josette, not Shosette. The housekeeper's accent had been strange.

"And is she a suspect in your mind?"

"No, madame, she is not."

"Why not? The housekeeper said she walked out that morning, upset."

The inspector was now giving me a patronizing smile that annoyed me. "She left because her employer sent her home. He said he didn't feel like painting anymore that day and told her to go away and enjoy herself. She was upset because she was only going to be paid for a half day and she had counted on a full day's pay. Other than that she said he paid well, she was glad to get the work, and she'd only been sitting for him for a few days so she knew very little about him."

"And you don't think she might have returned that afternoon when the housekeeper was out — to kill him?"

"For what reason?" he asked. "He was employing her. She was getting good money. And nothing was taken from the house." He leaned toward me. "Furthermore there is one good reason that I believe she was not responsible for his murder." He paused.

"Her fingerprints are not on the knife."

"You were able to take fingerprints from the knife?"

"Several sets. One of them smaller, probably from a woman. Of course if the knife was used in a restaurant kitchen it is possible that it was touched by several hands there. But the little Jewish girl. No. She was not among them. Neither were her fingerprints on the windowsill and we are sure the killer must have made his exit that way, because the housekeeper was never far from the front door and would have seen anyone trying to escape through the foyer."

"So you have not yet managed to identify any of the fingerprints on the knife?" I asked.

"If I had, I should not share that information with you."

"I just wondered whether the gossip is correct and it really was a young Jewish man who killed him. I expect you've collected fingerprints at various synagogues and Jewish meeting places?"

"We have rounded up several of the leading Dreyfusards. They all have perfect alibis and what's more they know nothing of this murder. If it was committed by a young Jew then he was acting as a lone wolf and our chances of bagging him are small unless he is arrested again on another crime. If I were he, I would have fled to a Jewish community in another country — Austria, Hungary, Germany, even England."

"So it sounds as if you're giving up," I said bluntly.

"Of course we are not giving up. Someone always knows. Someone will talk. You'll see."

I got up. "I might have something that is of help," I said. "Excuse me for a moment." I went up to my room and returned with the wine glass. I set it on the table before the inspector. "This is a wine glass I took from Mademoiselle Stein's Saturday party. Willie Walcott had been drinking from it. His fingerprints will be on it."

"And what has this Mr. Walcott to do with the crime, in your opinion?"

"Probably nothing, but he and Mr. Bryce used to be good friends. There was a falling out, and they saw nothing of each other for several months. Then Mr. Walcott appeared at Mr. Bryce's apartment the day before he died. He was angry, shouting, waving a piece of paper, and saying, 'You've let me down. You're a liar,' or similar words."

"And how did you find out about this?" he asked, his eyes focused on the glass.

"The housekeeper told me," I said. "I asked her who might have been to visit Mr.

Bryce before he died and she mentioned Mr. Walcott's name. So I acquired the glass."

"To test for Mr. Walcott's fingerprints? Presumably yours are also on the glass now?"

"Absolutely not. I picked it up with my handkerchief, taking care not to touch the places where he had been holding it."

He was looking at me with a modicum of respect now. "That was a smart thing to do, if you were actually involved with this case, which you are not. I am sure you are a fine detective in your way, but I am telling you this: a murder investigation belongs to the Sûreté. It is no place for amateurs and you may well do more harm than good. You may alert a suspect that we have been watching him. Or, you may find that you are his next victim. So leave the detecting work to the professionals, madame, and enjoy your stay here in Paris."

He got up, took out his handkerchief, and carefully wrapped the glass in it, then gave me a curt bow. "You say your husband is a policeman?" he asked as he walked toward the door. "Does he let you assist him in his criminal cases?"

"Of course not," I said and he laughed.

"Wise man," he said and walked out.

Thirty-Four

"Well?" Sid's head came around the door the moment Inspector Henri had gone. "Have they arrested anyone yet?"

"Far from it," I said as Sid came over to sit beside me. "I think they are completely in the dark."

"But still looking for this supposed young Jewish man?" She frowned. "I hate being cooped up here, never knowing when the ax will fall."

"I really think you're worrying for nothing," I said. "If anyone had seen you running to this address, the inspector would have questioned Mary. Had the place searched. But he hasn't. If you want to know the truth, I believe he suspects me."

"You? Why on earth would he do that?"

"Well, for one thing I was seen coming out of Mr. Bryce's place this morning. And I've been showing too much interest in how he's getting on toward solving the case."

"But that's plain silly," Sid said. "The man is a simpleton. If you don't solve it soon, Molly, we'll just have to go home. We can't stay cooped up like this."

I felt a lurch of fear. If they went home, I'd have nowhere to stay. I couldn't impose upon Miss Cassatt's hospitality after Sid and Gus were gone. And Daniel wouldn't want me to return home yet. I wished I had had a letter from him. Maybe there was one at this moment at the Montmartre address.

"Do you have any ideas at all?" Sid touched my arm, making me start. I'd obviously been staring out, lost in worry. She leaned closer. "You don't really think that Gus's cousin might be responsible?"

"It's possible," I said. "Although he came to see Reynold Bryce the day before he was killed. I've heard nothing to indicate he returned on the actual day."

"Gus would be devastated," Sid said. "They were close as children. She's fond of him."

Then I felt guilty that I had handed over Willie's fingerprints and suggested to the inspector that he might have a motive.

"I did worm out of the inspector that they've questioned likely Jewish organizations and come up empty-handed," I said.

"So is there anything more you can do?"

"There is one thing," I began. "Reynold Bryce was painting a young immigrant girl. I believe she lied to the police about what happened that morning. I thought I'd go up to Montmartre and see if I can find her."

"Do you think she'd tell you the truth if she lied to the police?" Sid asked.

"I don't know. She'd have no objection to chatting with me if she wasn't involved in his murder, would she?"

"Do you really think you should speak to her? Would the police approve?"

"I'm afraid not," I said.

"Then, Molly, please don't go." Sid touched my arm. "I don't want you to risk getting into trouble. Really I don't."

"The inspector never need know," I said. "I can pose as Mr. Bryce's relative from America again. Ask innocent questions."

"But don't you think you might be putting yourself in danger?"

"I don't think so," I said. "If she shares a house with a lot of refugee girls I wouldn't be out of earshot of help. It's broad daylight, Sid. And Montmartre is a busy place. And if she invites me alone to the cellar I won't go."

Sid laughed. I got up. "I'd better go and feed that child. I've been neglecting him horribly lately."

"Frankly I don't think he's noticed," Sid said. "Gus and I have been amusing him nonstop and Celeste has been feeding him all kinds of delicacies. He's becoming thoroughly spoiled. Oh, and do you know what he did this morning?" She went on as I reached the door. "He stood by himself. If he wasn't wearing all those annoying skirts he'd be walking."

My child had stood by himself and I wasn't there to see it, I thought as I went upstairs. What kind of mother was I? Was it really more important to solve this case and to clear Sid, or to be there for Liam? I considered this and decided that Liam was being fed and amused and quite safe. He'd survive without his mother around him for a few days.

When I tried to nurse him I noticed he was not as interested as he used to be. So that chapter of our lives was drawing to a close. I felt a sadness but also, it must be confessed, some relief too. I changed him, put him down for his afternoon nap, then joined the others for lunch before I set out again.

"You'll be needing new soles on those shoes before the week is up," Mary said as I bid them adieu. "You must have covered every inch of Paris by now."

"My feet certainly feel that way."

"Then take a rest this afternoon. Put your feet up. Read a book," she suggested. "I'm sure what you're about to do can wait until tomorrow. And remember the inspector has forbidden you to interview any more suspects."

Sid and I looked at each other. "I'm going to check in with Sid and Gus's old landlady," I said. "I hope a letter from Daniel might have arrived by now."

I didn't look at her as I left the room. The inspector couldn't stop me having a pleasant chat with a young girl, I decided as I pinned on my hat and left the house. Montmartre was in siesta mode as I came up the steps to Place Pigalle. The busy evening scene had not yet started. The ingredients for the evening meal had already been purchased. The shops were still shut for their long lunch hour. I stopped first of all at the Rue des Martyrs. Madame Hetreau looked surprised to see me. "I thought you'd be off in the country by now," she said.

"I am visiting Paris to do some shopping," I replied, "and wondered if any letters had arrived here for me. Letters from America, I mean."

She shrugged. "Nothing that I've seen."

My spirits fell. "If a letter does come from New York for me it will be from my husband," I said. "Please keep it for me. I have written to give him my new address, but he won't have received it yet."

"I suppose I can do that," she said ungraciously. I suspected she was wanting a fee for holding my mail.

"I'd be most grateful," I forced myself to say.

"Old cow," I muttered as I walked out again. For all I knew a letter had come from Daniel and she had destroyed it. Well, there was nothing I could do about it. He'd get my letter with my new address soon and all would be well. I started up the street, then turned to my right following the narrow road as it curved up to the summit of the hill. I was out of breath by the time I came out to the gardens and open areas at the top and Paris lay before me, the Seine sparkling today in bright afternoon sunlight. The sound of stonemasons working on the nearby church echoed in the still air. It would have been pleasant to have sat for a while on a convenient wall and just enjoyed the sunshine and the view, but I forced myself to get down to business.

A man was walking past with a laden donkey. I asked him if he knew where some

Russian refugee girls might be living. He shook his head and if my limited French was correct he muttered that refugees should stay where they were, with several cuss words thrown in. The *clip-clop* of his donkey's hoofs on the cobblestones died away and there was nobody else around to ask. I decided that the logical place to go would be Le Bateau-Lavoir. Maxim Noah had painted Josette, after all. He or one of his fellow artists would know where she might be found. I followed the street around until I came to the rickety old building, perched precariously on the steep hillside. The door was open and I let myself in. This building too lay in afternoon slumber. Not a single sound anywhere. I tapped cautiously on Maxim's door. There was no answer. I tapped again. "Hello," I called. "Is anybody home? It's Mrs. Sullivan from America. The friend of your cousin, Maxim."

The door opened slowly and I found myself staring not at Maxim Noah but at a face I recognized as Josette herself. In the flesh she looked even younger and more vulnerable, bleary eyed as if just woken from sleep. "Maxim not here," she said in hesitant French.

"Oh, that's a pity," I replied. "Are you Josette?"

461

She looked wary. "Who told you?"

I gave her what I hoped was a reassuring smile. "I saw your painting when I was visiting Reynold Bryce," I said and noted her startled reaction. "I had a message to give him from a relative in America. This relative wanted to buy one of his paintings. He showed me the painting he was working on. The lovely painting of you, *ma petite.*"

"Reynold Bryce is dead," she said flatly.

"I heard. I'm so sorry. And before he could finish your portrait too. May I come in?" I didn't wait for an invitation but barged past her and she didn't try to stop me. "Still, I am sure you will find plenty of work as a model," I went on. "You are so beautiful."

She smiled shyly. "Thank you."

"I also saw a picture of you that Monsieur Noah painted. Are there any more for sale?"

"He does not like to paint me," she said. "He does not like me to be a model either."

Then of course I wondered why I had been so dense. This was surely Jojo, the mistress of whom he'd been so protective.

"I understand." I nodded. "He does not like other men to see you. But he allowed Monsieur Bryce to paint you with no clothes on."

She was looking away now, one hand playing with her hair like an embarrassed child. "He did not know," she whispered. "The money was good. I thought there would be no harm."

"But there was harm, wasn't there?" I said sharply. She looked up with frightened eyes. "That's why you were upset and ran away that morning."

"Who are you?" she asked. "Why do you come here?"

"A friend," I said. "A friend who knows about the history and nature of Reynold Bryce. I know that he liked young girls. And he couldn't keep his hands off them."

"There were others?" she asked.

I nodded. "I know of another girl, about your age. He forced her to do bad things."

"He tried to force me," she said. "He said nobody need know and he'd pay me even more. Such a thing had never happened to me. I was terrified. I fought him, madame. I grabbed my clothes and fled. I went down the back stairs, the way I always had to come and go. Then I dressed myself rapidly and ran home. I was afraid he would come after me, but thank God he did not."

I could understand her indignation but her naïveté was rather surprising. She did, after all, live in sin with a painter. "Did you tell Maxim when you came home?" I asked.

She nodded. "He saw how upset I was. So I told him what Mr. Bryce had tried to do. He was furious. I've never seen him so angry. He stormed out and was gone for hours."

"Where is he now?"

"He has gone, madame. Gone to England."

"To England? But I saw him on Saturday evening, at a party."

She shook her head. "That is not possible, madame. He has been gone for several days now. He has friends over there who wrote to him and said he should join them. They will help him find somewhere to live, and then he will send for me. He said that Paris is not the right place for us. That the people here have no morals and it was not the right place for a young girl like me."

"And yet you live with him? You're his mistress?"

"His mistress? Who told you that?" she demanded, those dark eyes blazing suddenly. "I am his sister, madame. His little sister. The only family he has. He takes care of me."

"Maxim Noah is your brother?" I asked.

She nodded. "My brother Jakob. A wonderful brother too. He brought me safely out of Russia when they burned our village.

He promised to look after me the way our father would have done. We will have a good new life in England."

"I hope you will, Josette," I said. I looked at those big, wistful eyes and my heart bled for her.

As I left Le Bateau-Lavoir I tried to control my racing thoughts. If Maxim Noah was Josette's brother, newly arrived from Russia, then he was definitely not Sid's long-lost relative who had been in Paris for generations. So why had he tried to pretend he was her cousin? And why had he lied to his sister about going to England when he was still in Paris? One thing was sure — Maxim Noah was not to be trusted. It began to dawn on me that *he,* not Sid, was the young Jewish man seen running away from Reynold Bryce's house. I had to go to the Sûreté immediately and tell them what I suspected. Inspector Henri would be angry with me, but he wouldn't ignore what I had to say.

I started down the steep little lane, stepping carefully on the uneven cobbles. There were more people around now: children playing — singing as they turned the jump rope in high little nasal voices — women with shopping baskets hurrying to buy something they had forgotten for dinner. And then ahead of me I caught a glimpse of someone I thought I recognized. The Russian-style peasant's cap, the shock of dark curls. It had to be Maxim Noah himself!

THIRTY-FIVE

Maxim Noah moved swiftly down the hill. I quickened my pace. If he wasn't staying any longer with Josette at Le Bateau-Lavoir I should try to follow him and see where he was hiding out. It was precarious walking in my dainty pointed shoes over the cobbles as the road dropped steeply. He turned to the left, taking a narrow alley between buildings. I followed and came out to see him crossing the road and entering what seemed to be a cemetery. Perhaps he had found a good spot to hide out among the dead, I thought.

I crossed the street after him and went through the gate into the cemetery. It was not like our graveyards in Ireland, with their low granite tombs and Celtic crosses, but full of impressive monuments, angels, cherubs, statues, and mausoleums — veritable houses of the dead for whole families, all piled close together. I looked around but could no longer see him. I took a step or two forward then stopped. Even in daylight I didn't fancy poking around in a cemetery on my own, especially on the trail of a dangerous man. I turned to leave and suddenly there he was, blocking my path.

"Madame Sullivan," he said. "What a pleasure to find you here. You enjoy visiting the dead, do you?"

"As much as you do, obviously, Monsieur Noah," I said. "You find inspiration for your painting here, do you?"

"Sometimes. But today I have other reasons for being here."

"Yes?"

He nodded. "Such as luring you to a place where nobody can see us. I have been keeping an eye on my sister, you see. Such a rickety old building, it's easy to listen to what is being said. I realized that you have discovered the truth."

"The truth that you are Jakob Klein and in no way related to my friend Elena Goldfarb. Why did you claim to be her cousin?"

He looked at me scornfully, as if I was particularly dense. "She's a rich American. I overheard her talking about looking for her family in Paris and I decided she'd be helpful to a poor struggling cousin." He shrugged. "It was easy to convince her. She

468

herself had supplied all the details."

"You deceived her," I said angrily.

"One does what one must to survive. They burned our village. They killed our parents. We came here with nothing. I had my sister to protect."

"And yet you let her model for Reynold Bryce? Was that protecting her?"

I saw anger flash in his eyes. "I had no idea that he would behave in that way. He saw her with me at a showing *Chez Vollard.* He said he'd like to paint her, and if I agreed he would include some of my work in his exhibition. The money was good, and the chance to be in his exhibition — well, it would mean everything. We could not turn it down. But I did not know that he would paint her in the nude. And when she came to me, sobbing hysterically and saying he tried to rape her, I was beside myself with rage."

"So you went to see him."

"And do you know what he said? He laughed and said, 'Do you really think I was going to include a painting in my exhibition by a filthy Jew? I only wanted a way to your little sister.' And I said, 'But she's a Jew too. You didn't mind touching her.' And he laughed and said, 'Sometimes even Jews are enticing enough that one makes exceptions.

There is no logic in the desires of the flesh.' "

"So you killed him."

"The knife was lying there on the table. I was in a red rage. So angry I could not control myself. I grabbed it and plunged it into his chest."

All the time we talked I was horribly aware that he stood between me and the gateway from the cemetery. I knew I had to play for time. Sooner or later someone would come past and I could escape.

"Your sister believes you have gone to England — or was she lying to me as well?"

"I told her I had gone. She is young and innocent. I do not want her implicated in this. And I do plan to go, as soon as I can get enough money together and find a way to ship my paintings."

"Aren't you worried about getting caught if you linger here too long? If I've worked it out, I am sure that others have too. And what about your sister if you get caught? Who will protect her if you face the guillotine?"

He shrugged again. "There will be no guillotine, madame. I was defending the honor of my sister. Any court in France will understand this. They make exceptions for the crime *passionel.* I shall be considered a hero."

"Then I wish you good luck. *Bonne chance,*" I said. I had noticed a couple approaching the gateway to the cemetery. Soon they would be close enough to hear if I shouted for help. I gave him a curt bow and tried to move past him. He put an arm around my shoulder as the couple came closer. "But *ma chérie,* you did not think I'd let you go, did you?" he said and pulled me close to him.

"Don't be foolish," I replied. "I am not your *chérie.*" I tried to shrug him off and instead felt a sharp prick of pain at my side.

"I am efficient with a blade," he whispered into my ear. "One wrong move and it will be your last. We will take a walk, you and I, among the graves."

"Why should I walk with you?" I demanded, my voice sharp with fear. "You'll only kill me anyway, and without the risk of anyone looking on."

"You will walk because you have no choice," he said, and I felt the pressure of that knife digging into me. "And maybe all I want is your money to help me get to England. We shall see how I feel."

And he propelled me forward, one arm draped around my shoulder like a lover, while the other one held the knife firmly at my side. I tried to think how to struggle, to throw him off guard without allowing him to stab me first. He half pushed, half carried me between two mausoleums. Then I heard the crunch of footsteps on the gravel path. Someone was coming. Someone really tall. I could see his head over the top of the roof of the mausoleum. And I recognized him.

"Monsieur Degas!" I called. "It's Madame Sullivan." And I jerked my head back into Maxim Noah's face, hearing a grunt of pain as I connected with his nose. I followed this with my elbow into his stomach and took that brief moment of surprise to wrench myself free. I ran over to Degas. "What a pleasure to meet you again," I said, going up to him and taking his arm.

"I have been visiting the family tomb," he said. "It is the anniversary of the death of my mother. I always take flowers."

"What a fine sentiment," I said. "I have been examining the graves with Maxim Noah."

I tried not to look back, to see if Maxim was still behind me. If Monsieur Degas thought it was odd that I was behaving in this familiar fashion, he was too much of a gentleman to say anything. We walked a few yards up the path when he said, "Madame, is something wrong? What is that I see? *Mon dieu.* Can it be that you are bleeding?"

I looked down at the ground and saw bright splashes of red on the yellow gravel. I put my hand to my side. It came away warm and sticky. "Maxim Noah. He . . ." And I realized I didn't know the French word for "stab." "He wished to kill me," I said and everything started to go black.

I must have sunk onto a tombstone. From a vast distance I could hear Degas's voice booming out, "Help! Murder! Police!" Then a whistle blowing, then strong arms lifting me. The next moments were a haze. I was being carried, seated. Given cognac to sip. Then hands were examining me.

"You are fortunate, madame," a voice said. "It is merely a flesh wound."

A woman hovered over me. Warm water sponged my side. Then a policeman arrived, asked questions. I tried to answer when all I wanted was to be safe at home. Finally I said, "Find Inspector Henri. Maxim Noah must not escape to England. And I want to go home now."

The policeman ran off to find a telephone.

The woman stood beside me, looking worried. "You do not think you should be taken to the hospital, madame?"

"I'll be fine," I said. "Just call a cab for me."

A cab was summoned. The initial wound had not hurt at all, but now the bumping along the street made every breath painful. I was still bleeding and held whatever I had been given as a pad pressed to my side. It seemed like an eternity until we pulled up outside Miss Cassatt's house. Celeste appeared at the door, took one look at me, and started wailing as she helped me upstairs. "Mademoiselle, come immediately. Madame Sullivan is dying!" she called. They were in the salon together, Sid and Gus on the floor with my son, building him a tower of blocks. Mary had been watching from the sofa. Now they all jumped up. My one thought was that I shouldn't frighten Liam.

"I'm fine," I said. "Just get me up to my room and help me out of this dress."

I could see their expressions as they looked at the blood-soaked pad on my side.

"Celeste, summon a doctor immediately," Mary said. She came over and took my arm, helping me up the stairs.

"What happened?" she asked.

"I met Reynold Bryce's killer. He tried to stab me."

"It looks as if he succeeded," she said. "Now no more talking. Let's get this dress off you and we'll see how bad it is."

She worked efficiently and her calmness calmed me too. Although I must admit I got a shock when I saw the slash along the side of the dress and the great red stain spoiling the light silk. At that moment I believe I was more upset by the loss of the expensive dress than the size of my wound. When Mary had me undressed and washed the wound we could see that it was a gash, about three inches long, but mercifully not too deep. The doctor arrived, examined the wound, and pronounced me fortunate. "A little deeper and the knife would have struck your kidney," he said. He produced a salve then applied sticking plaster liberally. "You are not to move until this is healed. No stairs. No walking," he said, wagging a finger at me. "Bandages to be changed every twelve hours and the wound to be kept clean or it may turn septic. It should heal well but you'll probably be left with a scar. That can't be helped. I shall return to examine you tomorrow."

I lay back on my bed, feeling suddenly exhausted and close to tears. The memory of that knife in my side was suddenly all too vivid. He had been planning to kill me. That was clear to me now. And what would Daniel say when he saw my scar? I had tried to do the right thing and taken foolish risks again. I looked up as there was a light tap at the door. Sid and Gus stood in the doorway, not daring to come in. Gus was holding Liam.

"See, there is mama. She is taking a rest right now," she said. "She'll be ready to play with you soon. But let's go and build another castle, shall we?"

Sid tiptoed in and sat beside me. "Molly, I'm so sorry," she said. "You took all these risks for me, and it nearly cost you your life."

"At least we now know who killed Reynold Bryce," I said. "It was Maxim Noah."

"My cousin?" She looked shocked.

"Not your cousin, I'm afraid. Not in any way related to you. He tricked you, Sid. He overheard you telling someone about your quest to locate your family and decided that a rich American relative was just what he needed."

"Oh, dear," she said. "I've been a fool, haven't I? So naïve of me. Now that I think about it, he played me beautifully. He got me to say the name of my relatives, to give their history. I fed him all the information he needed to make his claim. How stupid of me." She shook her head angrily.

"He was a very appealing young man," I said. "And Gus had a handsome cousin here. Perhaps you wanted one too."

This made her laugh. But then she said, "So he was the young Jewish man they saw running away from Reynold Bryce's house, and all this time I thought it was me."

I nodded.

"Why did he kill Mr. Bryce? Because he insulted Jews?"

"That was only part of the reason. The young refugee girl I told you about is his sister. Reynold Bryce had a predilection for young girls. He was painting her and then he couldn't keep his hands off her. When Maxim went to confront him Bryce was most insulting — not only about Jews but also about his painting. In fact he told Maxim that he'd only promised to include his paintings in the exhibition because he wanted Maxim's sister. The knife was lying there on the table. Maxim was in a blind rage."

"So he didn't mean to kill Reynold Bryce," Sid said. "He wasn't a natural killer."

"He meant to kill me," I said. "He had a knife pressed into my side and was trying to drag me into the middle of the cemetery, but Monsieur Degas came by. I shouted out to him and managed to escape. I got a little cut as I wrenched myself away."

"A little cut? It looks awful." Sid took my

hand. "Molly, you're so brave. And you've saved my life. I thought I was headed for the guillotine. I'm not allowed to hug you, I suppose."

"Probably not." I looked down at the strapping at my waist then squeezed her hand.

"What can I do to make it up to you?" Sid asked.

I looked at her fondly. "You and Gus have done plenty for me over the years. You don't need to make it up to me. But just don't disappear and scare me again!"

POSTSCRIPT

Maxim Noah, or rather Jakob Klein, was apprehended by police as he attempted to board a train from Paris. Inspector Henri came later that afternoon to give me the news.

"You should have heeded my warning, madame, and left police work to the police," he said, looking at my white face. "You nearly paid for your curiosity with your life. This Jakob Klein, he fought like a tiger. A dangerous man."

"I'm sorry," I said. "I wanted justice. And I did not think I was putting myself in danger. My husband tells me I am too reckless."

"He is right. But it is a pity you are a married woman, Madame Sullivan. You are a good detective. You took the pieces of the puzzle and put them together."

"Only with luck," I said, diplomatically.

"Do not count on luck to aid you every

time," he wagged a finger at me, but he managed the ghost of a smile as he left me.

I spent a week in bed, being horribly spoiled by my friends, and then finally I was able to enjoy doing all the things a tourist does in Paris. I went to visit Madeleine and we spent some pleasant afternoons together. After I recovered Sid and Gus found a new apartment, this time on the Left Bank near Saint-Germain-des-Prés. Gus went back to her painting, but it seemed her heart was no longer in it. She confided that she realized she wasn't as talented as she had thought and she missed New York. I wrote regularly to Daniel and received regular, if brief, replies. Rebuilding on our house had begun. In the meantime he had taken an apartment in Chelsea, but was waiting for me to choose most of the furnishings. He regretted not being there to see Liam take his first steps or say his first words.

Then a week or so after all this excitement I was wheeling Liam through the Jardin du Luxembourg when I heard my name being called. I looked up to see Miss Pinkerton and the other ladies bearing down on me.

"What a lovely coincidence meeting you here, Mrs. Sullivan," Miss Pinkerton said, beaming at me. "Miss Hetherington and I

480

wondered whether you were still in Paris. We've just arrived from Vienna. Isn't it magnificent? By far the most beautiful city we've seen although I did develop a fondness for Venice. How have you been enjoying your stay here and have you had a good relaxing time? You looked rather peaky when we last saw you."

"A good relaxing time"? I managed a smile. "It's been most interesting," I replied and watched them scurry on their way to Les Invalides.

Days passed. We settled into a routine while Sid and Gus discussed going home or going on to Vienna to meet Professor Freud whose work Gus much admired. Then, one hot day in July, a letter came from Daniel saying that the commissioner had been forced to release the leader of the Cosa Nostra, since nobody could be found to testify against him. He believed that this relieved the threat against us and the most sensible course was to come to terms with the Italian gang. He was booking our passage home and suggested we spend the rest of the summer with his mother, who had returned from her adventure out West saying she'd had a taste of travel, and there was no place like Westchester County.

I smiled as I read the letter. I was going

home, back to my husband. Back to my life.

As to whether I'd even tell him about the murder of Reynold Bryce and my role in the investigation — well, I'd have five long days at sea to decide how much I wanted him to know.

FW 1/15

2/5

Plott

2/19.